LISA JACKSON

PROOF OF INNOCENCE

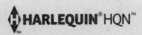 HARLEQUIN® HQN™

ISBN-13: 978-0-373-77877-5

PROOF OF INNOCENCE

Copyright © 2014 by Harlequin Books S.A.

The publisher acknowledges the copyright holder of the individual works as follows:

YESTERDAY'S LIES
Copyright © 1986 by Lisa Jackson

DEVIL'S GAMBIT
Copyright © 1985 by Lisa Jackson

Recycling programs for this product may not exist in your area.

This edition published by arrangement with Harlequin Books S.A.

For questions and comments about the quality of this book, please contact us at CustomerService@Harlequin.com.

® and TM are trademarks of Harlequin Enterprises Limited or its corporate affiliates. Trademarks indicated with ® are registered in the United States Patent and Trademark Office, the Canadian Trade Marks Office and in other countries.

Printed in U.S.A.

CONTENTS

YESTERDAY'S LIES

CHAPTER ONE

THE SWEATING HORSE snorted as if in premonition and his dark ears pricked forward before flattening to his head. Tory, who was examining the bay's swollen hoof, felt his weight shift suddenly. "Steady boy," she whispered. "I know it hurts...."

The sound of boots crunching on the gravel near the paddock forced Tory's eyes away from the tender hoof and toward the noise. Keith was striding purposefully toward her, his lanky rawboned frame tense, the line of his mouth set.

"Trask McFadden is back."

The words seemed to thunder across the windswept high plateau and echo in Tory's ears. Her back stiffened at her brother's statement, and she felt as if her entire world was about to dissolve, but she tried to act as if she was unaffected. Her fingers continued their gentle probing of the bay stallion's foreleg and her eyes searched inside the swollen hoof for any sign of infection.

"Tory, for God's sake," Keith called a little more loudly as he leaned over the top rail of the fence around the enclosed paddock, "did you hear what I said?"

Tory stood, patted the nervous stallion affectionately and took in a steadying breath before opening the gate. It groaned on its ancient hinges. She slipped through the dusty rails and faced her younger brother. His anxious expression said it all.

So Trask was back. After all these years. Just as he said he would be. She suddenly felt cold inside. Shifting her gaze from the nervous bay stallion limping within the enclosed paddock to the worried contours of Keith's young face, Tory frowned and shook her head. The late-afternoon sun caught in her auburn hair, streaking it with fiery highlights of red and gold.

"I guess we should have expected this, sooner or later," she said evenly, though her heart was pounding a sharp double time. Nervously wiping her hands on her jeans, she tried to turn her thoughts back to the injured Quarter Horse, but the craggy slopes of the distant Cascade Mountains caught her attention. Snow-covered peaks jutted brazenly upward against the clear June sky. Tory had always considered the mountains a symbolic barrier between herself and Trask. The Willamette Valley and most of the population of the state of Oregon resided on the western side—the other side—of the Cascade Mountains. The voting public were much more accessible in the cities and towns of the valley. The unconventional Senator McFadden rarely had to cross the mountains when he returned to his native state. Everything he needed was on the other side of the Cascades.

Now he was back. Just as he had promised. Tory's stomach knotted painfully at the thought. *Damn him and his black betraying heart.*

Keith studied his older sister intently. Her shoulders slumped slightly and she brushed a loose strand of hair away from her face and back into the ponytail she always wore while working on the Lazy W. She leaned over the split rail, her fists balled beneath her jutted chin and her jaw tense. Keith witnessed the whitening of the skin over her cheekbones and thought for a moment that she might faint; but when her gray-green eyes turned back to him they seemed calm, hiding any emotions that might be raging within her heart.

Trask. Back. After all these years and all the lies. Tory shook her head as if to deny any feelings she might still harbor for him.

"You act as if you don't care," Keith prodded, though he had noticed the hardening of her elegant features. He leaned backward, his broad shoulders supported by the rails of the fence. His arms were crossed over his chest, his dusty straw Stetson was pushed back on his head and dark sweat-dampened hair protruded unevenly from beneath the brim as he surveyed his temperamental sister.

"I can't let it bother me one way or the other," she said with a dismissive shrug. "Now, about the stallion…" She pointed to the bay. "His near foreleg— I think it's laminitis. He's probably been putting too much weight on the leg because of his injury to the other foreleg." When Keith didn't respond, she clarified. "Governor's foot is swollen with founder, acute laminitis. His temperature's up, he's sweating and blowing and he won't bear any weight on the leg. We're lucky so far, there's no sign of infection—"

Keith made a disgusted sound and held up his palm in frustration with his older sister. *What the hell was the matter with her? Hadn't she heard him? Didn't she care?* "Tory, for Christ's sake, listen to me and forget about the horse for a minute! McFadden always said he'd come back; *for you.*"

Tory winced slightly. Her gray-green eyes narrowed against a slew of painful memories that made goose bumps rise on her bare arms. "That was a long time ago," she whispered, once again facing her brother.

"Before the trial."

Closing her eyes against the agony of the past, Tory leaned heavily against the split cedar rails and forced her thoughts to the present. Though her heart was thudding wildly within her chest, she managed to remain outwardly calm. "I don't think McFadden will bother us," she said.

"I'm not so sure…."

She forced a half smile she didn't feel. "Come on, Keith, buck up. Let's not borrow trouble. We've got enough as it is, don't you think?" Once again she cast a glance at the bay stallion. He was still sweating and blowing. She had examined him carefully and was thankful that there was no evidence of infection in the swollen tissues of his foot.

Keith managed to return his sister's encouraging grin, but it was short-lived. "Yeah, I suppose we don't need any more trouble. Not now," he acknowledged before his ruddy complexion darkened and his gray eyes lost their sparkle. "We've had our share and we know who to thank for it," he said, removing his hat and pushing his sweaty hair off his brow. Dusty streaks lined his forehead. "All the problems began with McFadden, you know."

Tory couldn't deny the truth in her younger brother's words. "Maybe—"

"No maybe about it, Tory. If it hadn't been for McFadden, Dad might still be alive." Keith's gray eyes clouded with hatred and he forced his hat onto his head with renewed vengeance.

"You can't be sure of that," Tory replied, wondering why she was defending a man she had sworn to hate.

"Oh no?" he threw back at her. "Well, I can be sure of one thing! Dad wouldn't have spent the last couple of years of his life rotting in some stinking jail cell if McFadden's testimony hadn't put him there."

Tory's heart twisted with a painful spasm of guilt. "That was my fault," she whispered quietly.

"The hell it was," Keith exploded. "McFadden was the guy who sent Dad up the river on a bum rap."

"You don't have to remind me of that."

"I guess not," he allowed. "The bastard used you, too." Keith adjusted his Stetson and rammed his fists into his pockets. "Whatever you do, Sis," he warned, "don't stick up for him. At least not to me. The bottom line is that Dad is dead."

Tory smiled bitterly at the irony of it all and smoothed a wisp of hair out of her face. She had made the mistake of defending Trask McFadden once. It would never happen again. "I won't."

She lifted her shoulders and let out a tortured breath of air. *How many times had she thought about the day that Trask would return? How many times had she fantasized about him? In one scenario she was throwing him off her property, telling him just what kind of a bastard he was; in another she was making passionate love with him near the pond....* She cleared her throat and said, "Just because he's back in town doesn't mean that Trask is going to stir up any trouble."

Keith wasn't convinced. "Trouble follows him around."

"Well, it won't follow him here."

"How can you be so sure?"

"Because he's not welcome." Determination was evident in her eyes and the thrust of her small proud chin. She avoided Keith's narrowed eyes by watching a small whirlwind kick up the dust and dry pine needles in the corral. Governor snorted impatiently and his tail switched at the ever-present flies.

Keith studied his sister dubiously. Though Tory was six years his senior, sometimes she seemed like a little kid to him. Especially when it came to Trask McFadden. "Does *he* know that you don't want him here?"

Tory propped her boot on the bottom rail. "I think I made it pretty clear the last time I saw him."

"But that was over five years ago."

Tory turned her serious gray-green eyes on her brother. "Nothing's changed since then."

"Except that he's back and he's making noise about seeing you again."

Tory's head snapped upward and she leveled her gaze at her brother. "What kind of noise?"

"The kind that runs through the town gossip mill like fire."

"I don't believe it. The man's not stupid, Keith. He knows how I—we feel about him. He's probably back in town visiting Neva. He has before."

"And all those times he never once mentioned that he'd come for you. Until now. He means business. The only reason he came back here was for you!"

"I don't think—"

"Damn it, Tory," Keith interjected. "For once in your life, just listen to me. I was in town last night, at the Branding Iron."

Tory cast Keith a concerned glance. He scowled and continued, "Neva's spread it around town. She said Trask was back. For you!"

Tory's heart nearly stopped beating. Neva McFadden was Trask's sister-in-law, the widow of his brother, Jason. It had been Jason's mysterious death that had started all the trouble with her father. Tory still ached for the grief that Neva McFadden and her small son had borne, but she knew in her heart that her father had had no part in Jason McFadden's death. Calvin Wilson had been sent to prison an innocent victim of an elaborate conspiracy, all because of Trask McFadden's testimony and the way Tory had let him use her. Silent white-hot rage surged through Tory's blood.

Keith was still trying desperately to convince her of Trask's intentions. "Neva wouldn't lie about something like this, Tory. McFadden will come looking for you."

"Great," she muttered, before slapping the fence. "Look, I want you to tell Rex and any of the other hands that Trask McFadden has no business on this property. If he shows up, we'll throw him off."

"Just like that?"

"Just like that." She snapped her fingers and her carefully disguised anger flickered in her eyes.

Keith rubbed his jaw. "How do you propose to do that? Threaten him with a rifle aimed at his head?"

"If that's what it takes."

Keith raised a skeptical brow. "You're serious?"

Tory laughed nervously. "Of course not. We'll just explain that if he doesn't remove himself, we'll call the sheriff."

"A lot of good that will do. We call the sheriff's office and what do you suppose will happen? Nothing!

Paul Barnett's hands are tied. He owes his career—and maybe his whole political future—to McFadden. Who do you think backed Paul in the last election? McFadden." Keith spit out Trask's name as if it were a bitter poison. "Even if he wanted to, how in the hell would Paul throw a United States senator out on his ear?" Keith added with disgust in his voice, "Paul Barnett is in McFadden's back pocket."

"You make it sound as if Trask owns the whole town."

"Near enough; everyone in Sinclair thinks he's a god, y'know. Except for you—and sometimes I'm not so sure about that."

Tory couldn't help but laugh at the bleak scene Keith was painting. "Lighten up," she advised, her white teeth flashing against her tanned skin. "This isn't a bad western movie where the sheriff and the townspeople are all against a poor defenseless woman trying to save her ranch—"

"Sometimes I wonder."

"Give me a break, Keith. If Trask McFadden trespasses—"

"We're all in big trouble. Especially you."

Tory's fingers drummed nervously on the fence. She tried to change the course of the conversation. "Like I said, I think you're borrowing trouble," she muttered. "What Trask McFadden says and what he does are two different things. He's a politician. Remember?"

Keith's mouth twisted into a bitter grin and his eyes narrowed at the irony. "Yeah, I remember; and I know that the only reason that bastard got elected was because of his testimony against Dad and the others. He put innocent men in jail and ended up with a cushy job in Washington. What a great guy."

Tory's teeth clenched together and a headache began to throb in her temples. "I'm sure that central Oregon will soon bore our prestigious senator," she said, her uncertainty carefully veiled. "He'll get tired of rubbing elbows with the constituents in Sinclair and return to D.C. where he belongs, and that's the last we'll hear of him."

Keith laughed bitterly. "You don't believe that any more than I do. If Trask McFadden's back it's for a reason and one reason only: you, Tory." He slouched against the fence, propped up by one elbow. "So, what are you going to do about it?"

"Nothing."

"Nothing?"

Her gray-green eyes glittered dangerously. "Let's just wait and see. If Trask has the guts to show up, I'll deal with him then."

Keith's lower lip protruded and he squinted against the glare of the lowering sun. "I think you should leave...."

"What!"

"Take a vacation, get out of this place. You deserve one, anyway; you've been working your tail off for the past five years. And, if McFadden comes here and finds out that you're gone for a few weeks, he'll get the idea and shove off."

"That's running, Keith," Tory snapped. "This is my home. I'm not running off like a frightened rabbit, for crying out loud. Not for Trask McFadden, not for any man." Determination underscored her words. Pride, fierce and painful, blazed in her eyes and was evident in the strong set of her jaw.

"He's a powerful man," Keith warned.

"And I'm not afraid of him."

"He hurt you once before."

Tory squared her shoulders. "That was a long time ago." She managed a tight smile and slapped her brother affectionately on his shoulder. "I'm not the same woman I used to be. I've grown up a lot since then."

"I don't know," Keith muttered, remembering his once carefree sister and the grin she used to wear so easily. "History has a way of repeating itself."

Tory shook her head and forced a smile, hoping to disarm her younger brother. She couldn't spend the rest of her life worrying about Trask and what he would or wouldn't do. She had already spent more hours than she would admit thinking about him and the shambles he'd attempted to make of her life. Just because he was back in Sinclair... "Let's forget about McFadden for a while, okay? Tell Rex I want to try ice-cold poultices on our friend here." She nodded in the direction of the bay stallion. "And I don't want him ridden until we determine if he needs a special shoe." She paused and her eyes rested on the sweating bay. "But he should be walked at least twice a day. More if possible."

"As if I have the time—"

Tory cut him off. "Someone around here *must* have the time," she snapped, thinking about the payroll of the ranch and how difficult it was to write the checks each month. The Lazy W was drowning in red ink. It had been since Calvin Wilson had been sent to prison five years before. *By Trask McFadden.* "Have someone, maybe Eldon, if you don't have the time, walk Governor," she said, her full lips pursing.

Keith knew that he was being dismissed. He frowned, cast his sister one final searching look, pushed his hat lower on his head and started ambling off toward the barn on the other side of the dusty paddock. He had delivered his message about Trask McFadden. The rest was up to Tory.

TRASK PACED IN the small living room feeling like a caged animal. His long strides took him to the window where he would pause, study the distant snow-laden mountains through the paned glass and then return to the other side of the room to stop before the stone fireplace where Neva was sitting in a worn rocking chair. The rooms in the house were as neat and tidy as the woman who owned them and just being in the house—Jason's house—made Trask restless. His business in Sinclair wasn't pleasant and he had been putting it off for more than twelve hours. Now it was time to act.

"What good will come of this?" Neva asked, shaking her head with concern. Her small beautiful face was set in a frown and her full lips were pursed together in frustration.

"It's something I've got to do." Trask leaned against the mantel, ran his fingers under the collar of his shirt and pressed his thumb thoughtfully to his lips as he resumed pacing.

"Sit down, will you?" Neva demanded, her voice uncharacteristically sharp. He stopped midstride and she smiled, feeling suddenly foolish. "I'm sorry," she whispered, "I just hate to see you like this, all screwed up inside."

"I've always been this way."

"Hmph." She didn't believe it for a minute and she suspected that Trask didn't either. Trask McFadden was one of the few men she had met in her twenty-five years who knew his own mind and usually acted accordingly. Recently, just the opposite had been true and Neva would have had to have been a blind woman not to see that Trask's discomfiture was because of Tory Wilson. "And you think seeing Tory again will change all that?" She didn't bother to hide her skepticism.

"I don't know."

"But you're willing to gamble and find out?"

He nodded, the lines near the corners of his blue eyes crinkling.

"No matter what the price?"

"What's that supposed to mean?"

Neva stared at the only man she cared for. Trask had helped her, been at her side in those dark lonely nights after Jason's death. He had single-handedly instigated an investigation into the "accident," which had turned out to be the premeditated murder of her husband. Though Trask had been Jason's brother, his concern for Neva had gone beyond the usual bounds and she knew she would never forget his kindness or stop loving him.

Neva owed Trask plenty, but she couldn't seem to get through to him. A shiver of dread raced down her spine. Trask looked tired, she thought with concern, incredibly tired, as if he were on some new crusade. His hair had darkened from the winter in Washington, D.C., and the laugh lines near his mouth and eyes seemed to have grown into grooves of disenchantment. His whole attitude seemed jaded these days, she mused.

Maybe that's what happened when an honest man became a senator....

At that moment, Nicholas raced into the room and
breathlessly made a beeline for his mother. "Mom?"
He slid to a stop, dusty tennis shoes catching on the
polished wood floor.

"What, honey?" Neva stopped rocking and rumpled Nicholas's dark hair as he scrambled into her lap.

"Can I go over to Tim's? We're going to build a tree
house out in the back by the barn. His mom says it's
okay with her...."

Neva lifted her eyes and smiled at the taller boy
scurrying after Nick. He was red-haired and gangly,
with a gaping hole where his two front teeth should
have been. "If you're sure it's all right with Betty."

"Yeah, sure," Tim said. "Mom likes it when Nick
comes over. She says it keeps me out of her hair."

"Does she?" Neva laughed and turned her eyes back
to Nicholas. At six, he was the spitting image of his father. Wavy brown hair, intense blue eyes glimmering
with hope—so much like Jason. "Only a little while,
okay? Dinner will be ready in less than an hour."

"Great!" Nicholas jumped off her lap and hurried
out of the living room. The two boys left as quickly as
they had appeared. Scurrying footsteps echoed down
the short entry hall.

"Remember to shut the door," Neva called, but she
heard the front door squeak open and bang against
the wall.

"I'll get it." Trask, glad for the slightest opportunity to escape the confining room, followed the boys,
shut the door and returned. Facing Neva was more difficult than he had imagined and he wondered for the

hundredth time if he were doing the right thing. Neva didn't seem to think so.

She turned her brown eyes up to Trask's clouded gaze when he reentered the room. "That," she said, pointing in the direction that Nicholas had exited, "is the price you'll pay."

"Nick?"

"His innocence. Right now, Nicholas doesn't remember what happened five years ago," Neva said with a frown. "But if you go searching out Tory Wilson, all that will change. The gossip will start all over again; questions will be asked. Nick will have to come to terms with the fact that his father was murdered by a group of men whose relatives still live around Sinclair."

"He will someday anyway."

Neva's eyes pleaded with Trask as she rose from the chair. "But not yet, Trask. He's too young. Kids can be cruel.... I just want to give him a few more years of innocence. He's only six...."

"This has nothing to do with Nick."

"*The hell it doesn't!* It has everything to do with him. His father was killed because he knew too much about that Quarter Horse swindle." Neva wrapped her arms around her waist as if warding off a sudden chill, walked to one of the windows and stared outside. She stared at the Hamiltons' place across the street, where Nicholas was busily creating a tree house, blissfully unaware of the brutal circumstances surrounding his father's death. She trembled. "I don't want to go through it all again," Neva whispered, turning away from the window.

Trask shifted from one foot to the other as his conscience twinged. His thick brows drew together into a pensive scowl and he pushed impatient fingers through the coarse strands of his brown hair. "What if I told you that one of Jason's murderers might have escaped justice?"

Neva had been approaching him. She stopped dead in her tracks. "What do you mean?"

"Maybe there were four people involved in the conspiracy—not just three."

"I—I don't understand."

Trask tossed his head back and stared up at the exposed beams of the cedar ceiling. The last thing he wanted to do was hurt Neva. She and the boy had been through too much already, he thought. "What I'm saying is that I have reason to believe that one of the conspirators might never have been named. In fact, it's a good guess that he got away scot-free."

Neva turned narrowed eyes up to her husband's brother. "Who?"

"I don't know."

"This isn't some kind of a morbid joke—"

"Neva," he reproached, and she had only to look into his serious blue eyes to realize that he would never joke about anything as painful and vile as Jason's unnecessary death.

"You thought there were only three men involved. So what happened to change your mind?"

Knowing that he was probably making the biggest blunder of his short career in politics, Trask reached into his back pocket and withdrew the slightly wrinkled photocopy of the anonymous letter he had received in Washington just a week earlier. The letter had been his reason for returning—or so he had tried to convince himself for the past six days.

Neva took the grayish document and read the few sentences before shaking her head and letting her short blond curls fall around her face in neglected disarray. "This is a lie," she said aloud. The letter quivered in her small hand. "All the men connected with Jason's death were tried and convicted. Judge Linn Benton and George Henderson are in the pen serving time and Calvin Wilson is dead."

"So who does that leave?" he demanded.

"No one."

"That's what I thought."

"But now you're not so sure?"

"Not until I talk to Victoria Wilson." *Tory.* Just the thought of seeing her again did dangerous things to his mind. "She's the only person I know who might have the answers. The swindle took place on some property her father owned on Devil's Ridge."

Neva's lower lip trembled and her dark eyes accused him of crimes better left unspoken. Trask had used Victoria Wilson to convict her father; Neva doubted that Tory would be foolish enough to trust him again. "And you think that talking with Tory will clear this up?" She waved the letter in her hand as if to emphasize her words. "This is a prank, Trask. Nothing more. Leave it alone." She fell back into the rocker still clenching the letter and tucked her feet beneath her.

Trask silently damned himself for all the old wounds he was about to reopen. He reached forward, as if to stroke Neva's bent head, but his fingers curled into a fist of frustration. "I wish I could, Neva," he replied as he gently removed the letter from her hand and reached for the suede jacket he'd carelessly thrown over the back of the couch several hours earlier. He hooked one finger under the collar and tossed the jacket over his shoulder. "God, I wish I could."

"You and your damned ideals," she muttered. "Nothing will bring Jason back. But this…vendetta you're on…could hurt my son."

"Even if what I find out is the truth?"

Neva closed her eyes. She raised her hand and waved him off. She knew there was no way to talk sense to him when he had his mind made up. "Do what you have to do, Trask," she said wearily. "You will anyway. Just remember that Nicholas is the one who'll suffer." Her voice was low; a warning. "You and I—we'll survive. We always do. But what about Nick? He's in school now and this is a small town, a very small town. People talk."

Too much, Trask thought, silently agreeing. *People talk too damned much.* With an angry frown, he turned toward the door.

Neva heard his retreating footsteps echoing down the hall, the door slamming shut and finally the sound of an engine sparking to life then rumbling and fading into the distance.

CHAPTER TWO

As DUSK SETTLED over the ranch, Tory was alone. And that's the way she wanted it.

She sat on the front porch of the two-story farmhouse that she had called home for most of her twenty-seven years. Rough cedar boards, painted a weathered gray, were highlighted by windows trimmed in a deep wine color. The porch ran the length of the house and had a sloping shake roof supported by hand-hewn posts. The house hadn't changed much since her father was forced to leave. Tory had attempted to keep the house and grounds in good repair...to please him when he was released. Only that wouldn't happen. Calvin Wilson had been dead for nearly two years, after suffering a painful and lonely death in the penitentiary for a crime he didn't commit. All because she had trusted Trask McFadden.

Tory's jaw tightened, her fingers clenched over the arm of the wooden porch swing that had been her father's favorite. Guilt took a stranglehold of her throat. If only she hadn't believed in Trask and his incredible blue eyes—eyes Tory would never have suspected of anything less than the truth. He had used her shamelessly and she had been blind to his true motives, in love enough to let him take advantage of her. *Never again,* she swore to herself. *Trusting Trask McFadden was one mistake that she wouldn't make twice!*

With her hands cradling her head, Tory sat on the varnished slats of the porch swing and stared across the open fields toward the mountains. Purple thunderclouds rolled near the shadowy peaks as night fell across the plateau.

Telling herself that she wasn't waiting for Trask, Tory slowly rocked and remembered the last time she had seen him. It had been in the courtroom during her father's trial. The old bitterness filled her mind as she considered how easily Trask had betrayed her…

THE TRIAL HAD already taken over a week and in that time Tory felt as if her entire world were falling apart at the seams. The charges against her father were ludicrous. No one could possibly believe that Calvin Wilson was guilty of fraud, conspiracy or *murder,* for God's sake, and yet there he was, seated with his agitated attorney in the hot courtroom, listening stoically as the evidence against him mounted.

When it had been his turn to sit on the witness stand, he had sat ramrod stiff in the wooden chair, refusing to testify in his behalf.

"Dad, please, save yourself," Tory had begged on the final day of the trial. She was standing in the courtroom, clutching her father's sleeve, unaware of the reporters scribbling rapidly in their notepads. Unshed tears of frustration and fear pooled in her large eyes.

"I know what I'm doin', Missy," Calvin had assured her, fondly patting her head. "It's all for the best. Trust me…"

Trust me.

The same words that Trask had said only a few days before the trial. And then he had betrayed her completely. Tory paled and watched in disbelief and horror as Trask took the stand.

He was the perfect witness for the prosecution. Tall, good-looking, with a proud lift of his shoulders and piercing blue eyes, he cut an impressive figure on the witness stand, and his reputation as a trustworthy lawyer added to his appeal. His suit was neatly pressed, but his thick gold-streaked hair remained windblown, adding to the intense, but honest, country-boy image he had perfected. The fact that he was the brother of the murdered man only added sympathy from the jury for the prosecution. That he had gained his information by engaging in a love affair with the accused's daughter didn't seem to tarnish his testimony in the least. If anything, it made his side of the story appear more poignantly authentic, and the district attorney played it to the hilt.

"And you were with Miss Wilson on the night of your brother's death," the rotund district attorney suggested, leaning familiarly on the polished rail of the witness stand. He stared at Trask over rimless glasses, lifting his bushy brown eyebrows in encouragement to his star witness.

"Yes." Trask's eyes held Tory's. She was sitting behind her father and the defense attorney, unable to believe that the man she loved was slowly, publicly shredding her life apart. Keith, who was sitting next to her, put a steadying arm around her shoulder, but she didn't feel it. She continued to stare at Trask with round tortured eyes.

"And what did Miss Wilson confide to you?" the

D.A. asked, his knowing eyes moving from Trask to the jury in confidence.

"That some things had been going on at the Lazy W...things she didn't understand."

"Could you be more specific?"

Tory leaned forward and her hands clutched the railing separating her from her father in a death-grip.

The corner of Trask's jaw worked. "She—"

"You mean Victoria Wilson?"

"Yeah," Trask replied with a frown. "Tory claimed that her father had been in a bad mood for the better part of a week. She...Tory was worried about him. She said that Calvin had been moody and seemed distracted."

"Anything else?"

Trask hesitated only slightly. His blue eyes darkened and delved into hers. "Tory had seen her father leave the ranch late at night, on horseback."

"When?"

"July 7th."

"Of this year—the night your brother died?"

The lines around Trask's mouth tightened and his skin stretched tautly over his cheekbones. "Yes."

"And what worried Miss Wilson?"

"Objection," the defense attorney yelled, raising his hand and screwing up his face in consternation as he shot up from his chair.

"Sustained." Judge Miller glared imperiously at the district attorney, who visibly regrouped his thoughts and line of questioning.

The district attorney flashed the jury a consoling smile. "What did Miss Wilson say to you that led you to believe that her father was part of the horse swindle?"

Trask settled back in his chair and chewed on his lower lip as he thought. "Tory said that Judge Linn Benton had been visiting the ranch several times in the past few days. The last time Benton was over at the ranch—"

"The Lazy W?"

Trask frowned at the D.A. "Yes. There was a loud argument between Calvin and the judge in Calvin's den. The door was closed, of course, but Tory was in the house and she overheard portions of the discussion."

"Objection," the defense attorney called again. "Your honor, this is only hearsay. Mr. McFadden can't possibly know what Miss Wilson overheard or thought she overheard."

"Sustained," the judge said wearily, wiping the sweat from his receding brow. "Mr. Delany…"

The district attorney took his cue and his lips pursed together thoughtfully as he turned back to Trask and said, "Tell me what you saw that convinced you that Calvin Wilson was involved in the alleged horse switching."

"I'd done some checking on my own," Trask admitted, seeing Tory's horrified expression from the corner of his eye. "I knew that my brother, Jason, was investigating an elaborate horse swapping swindle."

"Jason told you as much?"

"Yes. He worked for an insurance company, Edward's Life. Several registered Quarter Horses had died from accidents in the past couple of years. That in itself wasn't out of the ordinary, only two of the horses were owned by the same ranch. What was suspicious was the fact that the horses had been insured so heavily. The company didn't mind at the time the policy was taken out, but wasn't too thrilled when the horse died and the claim had to be paid.

"Still, like I said, nothing appeared out of the ordinary until a company adjuster, on a whim, talked with a few other rival companies who insured horses as well. When the computer records were cross-checked, the adjuster discovered a much higher than average mortality rate for highly-insured Quarter Horses in the area surrounding Sinclair, Oregon. Jason, as a claims investigator for Edward's Life, was instructed to check it out the next time a claim came in. You know, for fraud. What he discovered was that the dead horse wasn't even a purebred Quarter Horse. The mare was nothing more than a mustang, a range horse, insured to the teeth."

"How was that possible?"

"It wasn't. The horse was switched. The purebred horse was still alive, kept on an obscure piece of land in the foothills of the Cascade Mountains. The way Jason figured it, the purebred horse would either be sold for a tidy sum, or used for breeding purposes. Either way, the owner would make out with at least twice the value of the horse."

"I see," the D.A. said thoughtfully. "And who owned this piece of land?"

Trask paused, the corners of his mouth tightening. "Calvin Wilson."

A muffled whisper of shock ran through the courtroom and the D.A., while pretending surprise, smiled a bit. Tory thought she was going to be sick. Her face paled and she had to swallow back the acrid taste of deception rising in her throat.

"How do you know who owned the property?"

"Jason had records from the county tax assessor's office. He told me. I couldn't believe it so I asked his daughter, Victoria Wilson."

Tory had to force herself not to gasp aloud at the vicious insinuations in Trask's lies. She closed her eyes and all the life seemed to drain out of her.

"And what did Miss Wilson say?"

"That she didn't know about the land. When I pressed her she admitted that she was worried about her father and the ranch; she said that the Lazy W had been in serious financial trouble for some time."

The district attorney seemed satisfied and rubbed his fleshy fingers together over his protruding stomach. Tory felt as if she were dying inside. The inquisition continued and Trask recounted the events of the summer. How he had seen Judge Linn Benton with Calvin Wilson on various occasions; how his brother, Jason, had almost concluded his investigation of the swindle; and how Calvin Wilson's name became linked to the other two men by his damning ownership of the property.

"You mean to tell me that your brother, Jason, told you that Calvin Wilson was involved?"

"Jason said he thought there might be a connection because of the land where the horses were kept."

"A connection?" the district attorney repeated, patting his stomach and looking incredulously at the jury. "I'd say that was more than 'a connection.' Wouldn't you?"

"I don't know." Trask shifted uneasily in his chair and his blue eyes narrowed on the D.A. "There is a chance that Calvin Wilson didn't know exactly what was happening on the land as it is several miles from the Lazy W."

"But what about the mare that was switched?" the D.A. prodded. "Wasn't she registered?"

"Yes."

"And the owner?"

"Calvin Wilson."

"So your brother, Jason McFadden, the insurance investigator for Edward's Life, thought that there might be a connection?" the D.A. concluded smugly.

"Jason was still working on it when the accident occurred." Trask's eyes hardened at the injustice of his brother's death. It was just the reaction the district attorney had been counting on.

"The accident which took his life. Right?"

"Yes."

"The accident that was caused by someone deliberately tampering with the gas line of the car," the D.A. persisted.

"Objection!"

"Your honor, it's been proven that the engine of Jason McFadden's car had been rigged with an explosive device that detonated at a certain speed, causing sparks to fly into the gas line and explode in the gas tank. What I'm attempting to prove is how that happened and who was to blame."

The gray-haired judge scowled, settled back in his chair and stared at the defense attorney with eyes filled with the cynicism of too many years on the bench. "Overruled."

The D.A. turned to face Trask.

"Let's go back to the night that Victoria Wilson saw

her father leave the ranch. On that night, the night of July 7th, what did you do?"

Trask wiped a tired hand around his neck. "After I left Tory, I waited until Calvin had returned and then I confronted him with what Jason had figured out about the horse swapping scam and what I suspected about his involvement in it."

"But why did you do that? It might have backfired in your face and ruined your brother's reputation as an insurance investigator."

Trask paused for a minute. The courtroom was absolutely silent except for the soft hum of the motor of the paddle fan. "I was afraid."

"Of what?"

Trask's fingers tightened imperceptibly on the polished railing. "I was afraid for Jason's life. I thought he was in over his head."

"Why?"

"Jason had already received an anonymous phone call threatening him, as well as his family." Trask's eyes grew dark with indignation and fury and his jaw thrust forward menacingly. "But he wouldn't go to the police. It was important to him to handle it himself."

"And so you went to see Calvin Wilson, hoping that he might help you save your brother's life."

"Yes." Trask glared at the table behind which Tory's father was sitting.

"And what did Calvin Wilson say when you confronted him?"

Hatred flared in Trask's eyes. "That all the problems were solved."

At that point Neva McFadden, Jason's widow, broke down. Her small shoulders began to shake with the hysterical sobs racking her body and she buried her face in her hands, as if in so doing she could hide from the truth. Calvin Wilson didn't move a muscle, but Tory felt as if she were slowly bleeding to death. Keith's face turned ashen when Neva was helped from the courtroom and his arm over Tory's shoulders tightened.

"So," the D.A. persisted, turning everyone's attention back to the witness stand and Trask, "you thought that because of your close relationship with Calvin Wilson's daughter, that you might be able to reason with the man before anything tragic occurred."

"Yes," Trask whispered, his blue eyes filled with resignation as he looked from the empty chair in which Neva had been sitting, to Calvin Wilson and finally to Tory. "But it didn't work out that way…"

TORY CONTINUED TO rock in the porch swing. A gentle breeze rustled the leaves of the aspen trees and whispered through the pines…just as it had on the first night she'd met him. All her memories of Trask were so vivid. Passionate images filled with love and hate teased her weary mind. Falling in love with him had been too easy…but then, of course, he had planned it that way, and she had been trapped easily by his deceit. Thank God she was alone tonight, she thought, so that she had time to think things out before she had to face him again.

It had taken a lot of convincing to get Keith to leave the ranch, but in the end he had gone into town with some of the single men who worked on the Lazy W. It was a muggy Saturday night in early summer, and Keith had decided that he would, against his better judgment, spend a few hours drinking beer and playing pool at the Branding Iron. It was his usual custom on Saturday evenings and Tory persuaded him that she wanted to be left alone. Which she did. If what Keith had been saying were true, then she wanted to meet Trask on her own terms, without unwanted ears to hear what promised to be a heated conversation.

The scent of freshly mown hay drifted on the sultry breeze that lifted the loose strands of hair away from her face. The gentle lowing of restless cattle as they roamed the far-off fields reached her ears. She squinted her eyes against the gathering night. Twilight had begun to color the landscape in shadowy hues of lavender. Clumps of sagebrush dappled the ground beneath the towering ponderosa pines. Even the proud Cascades loomed darkly, silently in the distance, a cold barrier to the rest of the world. *Except that the world was intruding into her life all over again.* The rugged mountains hadn't protected her at all. She had been a fool to think that she was safe and that the past was over and done.

The faint rumble of an engine caught Tory's attention. *Trask.*

Tory's heart began to pound in anticipation. She felt the faint stirrings of dread as the sound came nearer. He'd come back. Just as he'd promised and Keith had warned. A thin sheen of sweat broke out on her back and between her breasts. She clenched her teeth in renewed determination and her fingers clenched the arm of the swing in a death grip.

The twin beams of headlights illuminated the stand of aspen near the drive and a dusty blue pickup stopped in front of her house. Tory took in a needed breath of air and trained her eyes on the man unfolding himself from the cab. An unwelcome lump formed in her throat.

Trask was just as she had remembered him. Tall and lean, with long well-muscled thighs, tight buttocks, slim waist and broad chest, he looked just as arrogantly athletic as he always had. His light brown hair caught in the hot breeze and fell over his forehead in casual disarray.

So much for the stuffy United States senator image, Tory thought cynically. His shirt was pressed and clean, but open-throated, and the sleeves were pushed over his forearms. The jeans, which hugged his hips, looked as if they had seen years of use. *Just one of the boys...* Tory knew better. She couldn't trust him this night any more than she had on the day her father was sentenced to prison.

Trask strode over to the porch with a purposeful step and his eyes delved into hers.

What he encountered in Tory's cynical gaze was hostility—as hot and fresh as it had been on the day that Calvin Wilson had been found guilty for his part in Jason's death.

"What're you doing here?" Tory demanded. Her voice was surprisingly calm, probably from going over the scene a thousand times in her mind, she thought.

Trask climbed the two weathered steps to the porch, placed his hands on the railing and balanced his hips against the smooth wood. His booted feet were crossed in front of him. He attempted to look relaxed, but Tory noticed the inner tension tightening the muscles of his neck and shoulders.

"I think you know." His voice was low and familiar. It caused a prickling sensation to spread down the back of her neck. Looking into his vibrant blue eyes made it difficult for her not to think about the past that they had shared so fleetingly.

"Keith said you were spreading it around Sinclair that you wanted to see me."

"That's right."

"Why?"

His eyes slid away from her and he studied the starless sky. The air was heavy with the scent of rain. "I thought it was time to clear up a few things between us."

The memory of the trial burned into her mind. "Impossible."

"Tory—"

"Look, Trask," she said, her voice trembling only slightly, "you're not welcome here." She managed a sarcastic smile and gestured toward the pickup. "And I think you'd better leave before I tell you just what a bastard I think you are."

"It won't be the first time," he drawled, leaning against the post supporting the roof and staring down at her. His eyes slid lazily down her body, noting the elegant curve of her neck, the burnished wisps falling free of the loose knot of auburn hair at the base of her neck, the proud carriage of her body and the fire in her eyes. She was, without a doubt, the most beautiful and intelligent woman he had ever known. Try as he had to forget her, he had failed. Distance and time hadn't abated his desire; if anything, the feelings stirring within burned more torridly than he remembered.

He had the audacity to slant a lazy grin at her and Tory's simmering anger began to ignite. Her voice seemed to catch in her throat. "Leave."

"Not yet."

Righteous indignation flared in her eyes. "Leave, damn you..."

"Not until we get—"

"Now!" Her palm slapped against the varnished wooden arm of the swing and she pushed herself upward. "I don't want you ever to set foot on this ranch again. I thought I made that clear before, but either you have an incredibly short memory, or you just conveniently ignored out last conversation."

"Just for the record; I haven't forgotten anything. And that was no conversation," he speculated. "A war zone maybe, a helluva battle perhaps, but not idle chitchat."

"And neither is this. I don't know why you're here, Trask, and I don't really give a damn."

"You did once," he said softly, his dark eyes softening.

The tone of his voice pierced into her heart and her self-righteous fury threatened to escape. "That was before you used me, senator," she said, her voice a raspy whisper. One slim finger pointed at his chest. "Before you took everything I told you, turned it around and testified against my father!"

"And you still think he was innocent," Trask said, shaking his head in wonder.

"I know he was." Her chin raised a fraction and she impaled him with her flashing gray-green eyes. "How does it feel to look in the mirror every morning and know that you sent the wrong man to prison?" Hot tears touched the back of her eyes. "My father sat alone, slowly dying, the last few years of his life spent behind bars, all because of your lies."

"I never perjured myself, Tory."

Her lips pursed together in her anger. "Of course not. You were a lawyer. You knew just how to answer the questions; how exactly to insinuate to the jury that my father was part of the conspiracy; how to react to make the jury think that he was there the night that Jason found out about the swindle, how he inadvertently took part in your brother's death. Not only did you blacken my father's name, Trask, as far as I'm concerned, you took his life just as certainly as if you had thrust a knife into his heart." She took a step backward and placed her hand on the doorknob. Her fingers curled over the cold metal and her voice was edged in steel. "Now, get off this place and don't ever come back. You may be a senator now, maybe even respected by people who are only privy to your public image, but as far as I'm concerned you're nothing better than an egocentric opportunist who used the publicity surrounding his brother's death to get him elected!"

Trask's eyes flashed in the darkness. He took a step closer to her, but the hatred in her gaze stopped him dead in his tracks. "I only told the truth."

Rage stormed through her veins, thundered in her mind. Five long years of anger and bewilderment poured out of her. "You sensationalized this story, used it as a springboard to get you in the public eye, crushed everyone you had to so that you would get elected." The unshed tears glistened in her eyes. "Well, congratulations, senator. You got what you wanted."

With her final remarks, she opened the door and slipped through it, but Trask's hand came sharply upward and caught the smooth wood as she tried to slam the door in his face. "You've got it all figured out——"

"Easy to do. Now please, get off my land and out of my life. You destroyed it once, isn't that enough?"

Something akin to despair crossed his rugged features, but the emotion was quickly disguised by determination. "No."

"No?" she repeated incredulously. *Oh, God, Trask, don't put me through this again...not again.* "Well once was enough for me," she murmured.

"I don't think so."

"Then you don't know me very well. I'm not the glutton for punishment I used to be." She pushed harder on the door, intent on physically forcing him out of her life.

"I wouldn't be so sure about that."

"What!"

"Look at you—you're still punishing yourself, blaming yourself for your father's conviction and death."

The audacity of the man! She felt her body begin to shake. "No, Trask. As incredible as you might find all this, I blame *you*. After all, you were the one who testified against my father..."

"And you've been hating yourself ever since."

"*I* can look in the mirror in the morning. *I* can live with myself."

"Can you?" His skepticism echoed in the still night air.

"I don't see any reason for discussing any of this. I've told you that I want you out of my life."

"And I don't believe it."

Once again she tried to slam the door, but his broad shoulder caught the hard wood. "You've got one incredible ego, senator," she said, wishing there was some way to put some distance between her body and his.

"You were waiting for me," he accused, his eyes sliding from her face down her neck, past the open collar of her blouse to linger at the hollow of her throat.

"Of course I was."

"Alone."

She was gripping the edge of the door so tightly that her fingers began to ache. "I didn't want the gossip to start all over again. Keith told me that you were looking for me, so I decided to wait. I prefer to keep my conversations with you private. You know, without a judge, jury or the press looking over my shoulder, ready to use every word against me."

His eyes slid downward, noticing the denim skirt and soft apricot-colored blouse. "So why did you get dressed up?"

"Don't flatter yourself, senator. I usually take a shower after working with the horses all day. The way I dress has nothing to do with you." Her eyes narrowed slightly. "So why don't you just take yourself and that tremendous ego of yours out of here? If you need a wheelbarrow to carry it there's one in the barn."

He shoved his body into the doorway, wedging himself between the door and the jamb. Tory was strong, she put all of her weight against the door, but she was no match for the powerful thrust of his shoulders as he pushed his way into the darkened hallway. "You're going to hear what I have to say whether you like it or not."

"No!"

"You don't have much of a choice."

"Get out, Trask." Her words sounded firm, but inwardly she wavered; the desperation she had noticed earlier flickered in his midnight-blue eyes. As much as she hated him, she still felt a physical attraction to him. *God, she was a fool*.

"In a minute."

She stepped backward and placed her hands on her hips. Her breath was expelled in a sigh of frustration. "Since I can't convince you otherwise, why don't you just say what you think is so all-fired important and then leave."

He eyed her suspiciously and walked into the den.

"Wait a minute—"

"I need your help."

Tory's heart nearly stopped beating. There was a thread of hopelessness in his voice that touched a precarious part of her mind and she had to remind herself that he was the enemy. He always had been. Though Trask seemed sincere she couldn't, wouldn't let herself believe him. "No way."

"I think you might change your mind."

"You've got to be kidding," Tory whispered.

She followed him into the den, her father's den, and swallowed back her anger and surprise. Trask had placed a hand on the lava rock fireplace and his head was lowered between his shoulders. How familiar it seemed to have him back in the warm den her father had used as an office. Knotty pine walls, worn comfortable furniture, watercolors of the Old West, Indian weavings in orange and brown, and now Trask, leaning dejectedly against the fireplace, looking for all the world as if he truly needed her help, made her throat constrict with fond memories. *God, how she had loved this man*. Her fist curled into balls of defeat.

"I'm not kidding, Tory." He glanced up at her and she read the torment in his eyes.

"No way."

"Just listen to me. That's all I ask."

Anger overcame awe. "I can't help you. I won't."

His pleas turned to threats. "You'd better."

"Why? What can you do to me now? Destroy my reputation? Ruin my family. Kill my father? You've already done all that, there's nothing left. You can damned well threaten until you're blue in the face and it won't affect me...or this ranch."

In the darkness his eyes searched her face, possessively reading the sculpted angle of her jaw, the proud lift of her chin, the tempting mystique of her intelligent gray-green eyes. "Nothing's left?" he whispered, his voice lowering. One finger reached upward and traced the soft slope of her neck.

Tory's heart hammered in her chest. "Nothing," she repeated, clenching her teeth and stepping away from his warm touch and treacherous blue eyes.

He grimaced. "This has to do with your father."

She whirled around to face him. "My father is dead." Shaking with rage she pointed an imperious finger at his chest. "Because of you."

His jaw tightened and he paced the length of the room in an obvious effort to control himself. "You'd like to believe that I was responsible for your father's death, wouldn't you?"

All of the anguish of five long years poured out of her. "You were. He could have had the proper medical treatment if he hadn't been in prison—"

"It makes it easier to think that I was the bad guy and that your father was some kind of a saint."

"All I know is that my father would never have been a part of anything like murder, Trask." She was visibly shaking. All the old emotions, love, hate, fear, awe and despair, churned inside her. Tears stung her eyelids and she fought a losing battle with the urge to weep.

"Your father was a desperate man," he said quietly.

"What's that supposed to mean?"

"Desperate men make mistakes, do things they wouldn't normally do." The look on his face was pensive and worried. She noticed neither revenge nor anger in his eyes. *Trask actually believed that her father had been nothing better than a common horse thief.*

"You're grasping at straws. My father was perfectly fine."

Trask crossed the room, leaned an arm on the mantel and rubbed his chin. All the while his dusky blue eyes held hers. "The Lazy W was losing money hand over fist." She was about to protest but he continued. "You know it as well as anyone. When you took over, you were forced to go to the bank for additional capital to keep it running."

"Because of all the bad publicity. People were afraid to buy Quarter Horses from the Lazy W because of the scandal."

"Right. The scandal. A simple scam to make money by claiming that the purebred Quarter Horses had died and offering as proof bodies of horses who resembled the blue bloods but weren't worth nearly as much. No one around here questioned Judge Benton's integrity, especially when his claims were backed up by the local veterinarian, George Henderson. It was a simple plan to dupe and defraud the insurance companies of thousands of dollars and it would never have come off if your father hadn't provided the perfect hiding spot for the purebreds who hadn't really met their maker. It all boiled down to one helluva scandal."

"I can't believe that Dad was involved in that."

"The horses were found on his property, Tory." Trask frowned at her stubborn pride. "You're finding it hard to believe a lot of things these days, aren't you?" he accused, silently damning himself for the torture he was putting her through. "Why didn't your father defend himself when he had the chance, on the witness stand? If he was innocent pleading the fifth amendment made him look more guilty than he was."

A solitary tear slid down her cheek. "I don't want to hear any more of this…"

"But you're going to, lady. You're going to hear every piece of incriminating evidence I have."

"Why, Trask?" she demanded. "Why now? Dad's dead—"

"And so is Jason. My brother was murdered, Tory. Murdered!" He fell into a chair near the desk. "I have reason to believe that one of the persons involved with the horse swindle and Jason's death was never brought to justice."

Her eyes widened in horror. "What do you mean?"

"I think there were more than three conspirators. Four, maybe five…who knows? Half the damned county might have been involved." Trask looked more haggard and defeated than she had ever thought possible. The U.S. senator from Sinclair, Oregon had lost his luster and become jaded in the past few years. Cynical lines bracketed his mouth and his blue eyes seemed suddenly lifeless.

Tory's breath caught in her throat. "You're not serious."

"Dead serious. And I intend to find out who it was."

"But Judge Benton, he would have taken everyone down with him—no one would have been allowed to go free."

"Unless he struck a deal, or the other person had something over on our friend the judge. Who knows? Maybe this guy is extremely powerful..."

Tory shook her head, as if in so doing she could deny everything Trask was suggesting. "I don't believe any of this," she said, pacing around the room, her thoughts spinning crazily. *Why was Trask dredging all this up again. Why now? Just when life at the Lazy W had gotten back to normal...* "And I don't want to. Nothing you can do or say will change the past." She lifted her hands over her head in a gesture of utter defeat. "For God's sake, Trask, why are you here?"

"You're the only one who can help me unravel this, Tory."

"And I don't want to."

"Maybe this will change your mind." He extracted a piece of paper from his wallet and handed it to her. It was one of the photocopies of the letter he'd received.

Tory read the condemning words and her finely arched brows pulled together in a scowl of concentration. "Who sent you this?" she demanded.

"I don't know."

"It came anonymously?"

"Yes. To my office in Washington."

"It's probably just a prank."

"The postmark was Sinclair, Oregon. If it's a prank, Tory, it's a malicious one. And one of your neighbors is involved."

Tory read the condemning words again:

One of your brother's murderers is still free. He was part of the Quarter Horse swindle involving Linn Benton, Calvin Wilson and George Henderson.

"But who would want to dig it all up again?"

Trask shook his head and pushed his fingers through his hair. "Someone with a guilty conscience? Someone who overheard a conversation and finally feels that it's time to come clean? A nosy journalist interested in a story? I don't know. But whoever he is, he wants me involved."

Tory sank into the nearest chair. "And you couldn't leave it alone."

"Could you?"

She smiled bitterly and studied the letter in her hand. "I suppose not. Not if there was a chance to prove that my father was innocent."

"Damn it, Tory!" Trask exclaimed. "Calvin had the opportunity to do that on the witness stand. He chose to hide behind the fifth amendment."

Tory swallowed as she remembered her father sitting in the crowded courtroom. His thick white hair was neatly in place, his gray eyes stared straight ahead. Each time the district attorney would fire a question at him, Calvin would stoically respond that he refused to answer the question on the basis that it might incriminate him. Calvin's attorney had been fit to be tied in the stifling courtroom. The other defendants, Linn Benton, a prominent circuit court judge and ringleader of the swindle and George Henderson, a veterinarian and local rancher whose spread bordered the Lazy W to the north, cooperated with the district attorney. They had plea bargained for shorter sentences. But, for reasons he wouldn't name to his frantic daughter, Calvin Wilson accepted his guilt without a trace of regret.

"Face it, Tory," Trask was saying. "Your father was involved for all the right reasons. He was dying of cancer, the ranch was in trouble financially, and he wouldn't be able to take care of either you or your brother. He got involved with the horse swindle for the money…for you. He just didn't expect that Jason would find out about it and come snooping around." He walked to the other side of the room and stared out the window at the night. "I never wanted to think that your father was involved in the murder, Tory. I'd like to believe that he had no idea that Jason was onto him and the others. But I was there, I confronted the man and he looked through me as if whatever I said was of no significance." Trask walked across the room and grabbed Tory's shoulders. His face was twisted in disbelief. *"No significance! My brother's life, for God's sake, and Calvin stood there like a goddamn wooden Indian!"*

Tory tried to step away. "Not murder, Trask. My father wouldn't have been involved in Jason's death. He…" Her voice broke. "…couldn't."

"You don't know how much I want to believe you."

"But certainly—"

"I don't think your father instigated it," he interjected. "As a matter of fact, it's my guess that Benton planned Jason's 'accident' and had one of his henchmen tamper with the car."

"And Dad had to pay."

"Because he wouldn't defend himself."

She shook her head. "Against your lies." His fingers tightened over the soft fabric of her blouse. Tension charged the hot night air and Tory felt droplets of nervous perspiration break out between her shoulders.

"I only said what I thought was the truth."

The corners of her mouth turned bitterly downward and her eyes grew glacial cold. "The truth that you got from me."

His shoulders stiffened under his cotton shirt, and his eyes drilled into hers. "I never meant to hurt you, Tory, you know that."

For a fleeting moment she was tempted to believe him, but all the pain came rushing back to her in a violent storm of emotion. She felt her body shake with restraint. "I trusted you."

He winced slightly.

"I trusted you and you used me." The paper crumpled in her hand. "Take this letter and leave before I say things that I'll regret later."

"Tory…" He attempted to draw her close, but she pulled back, away from his lying eyes and familiar touch.

"I don't want to hear it, Trask. And I don't want to see you again. Now leave me alone—"

A loud knock resounded in the room and the hinges on the front door groaned as Rex Engels let himself into the house.

"Tory?" the foreman called. His steps slowed in the hallway, as if he was hesitant to intrude.

"In here." Tory was relieved at the intrusion. She stepped away from Trask and walked toward the door. When Rex entered he stopped and stared for a moment at Trask McFadden. His lips thinned as he took off his dusty Stetson and ran his fingers over the silver stubble on his chin. At five foot eight, he was several inches shorter than Trask, but his body was whip-lean from the physical labor he imposed on himself. Rugged and dependable, Rex Engels had been with the Lazy W for as long as Tory could remember.

The foreman was obviously uncomfortable; he shifted from one foot to the other and his eyes darted from Tory to Trask and back again.

"What happened?" Tory asked, knowing immediately that something was wrong and fearing that Keith was in the hospital or worse...

"I got a call from Len Ross about an hour ago," Rex stated, his mouth hardening into a frown. Tory nodded, encouraging him to continue. Ross was a neighboring rancher. "One of Ross's boys was mending fence this afternoon and he noticed a dead calf on the Lazy W."

Tory's shoulders slumped a little. It was always difficult losing livestock, especially the young ones. But it wasn't unexpected; it happened more often than she would like to admit and it certainly didn't warrant Rex driving over to the main house after dark. There had to be something more. Something he didn't want to discuss in front of Trask. "And?"

Rex rubbed his hand over his neck. He looked meaningfully at Trask. "The calf was shot."

"What?" Tory stiffened.

"From the looks of it, I'd guess it was done by a twenty-two."

"Then you saw the calf?" Trask cut in, his entire body tensing as he leaned one shoulder against the arch between den and entryway.

"Yep."

"And you don't think it was an accident?" Tory guessed.

"It's not hunting season," the foreman pointed out, moving his gaze to Trask in silent accusation. "And there were three bullet holes in the carcass."

Tory swallowed against the sickening feeling overtaking her. First Trask with his anonymous letter and the threat of dredging up the past again and now evidence that someone was deliberately threatening her livestock. "Why?" she wondered aloud.

"Maybe kids…" Rex offered, shifting his gaze uneasily between Tory and Trask. "It's happened before."

"Hardly seems like a prank," Trask interjected. There were too many unfortunate coincidences to suit him. Trask wasn't a man who believed in coincidence or luck.

Rex shrugged, unwilling to discuss the situation with the man who had sent Calvin Wilson to prison. He didn't trust Trask McFadden and his brown eyes made it clear.

Once the initial shock had worn off, Tory became furious that someone would deliberately kill the livestock. "I'll call Paul Barnett's office when we get back," she said.

"Get back?"

"I want to see the calf." Her gray-green eyes gleamed in determination; she knew that Rex would try to protect her from the ugly sight.

"There's not much to see," Rex protested. "It's dark."

"And this is my ranch. If someone has been deliberately molesting the livestock, I want to know what I'm up against. Let's go."

Rex knew there was no deterring her once she had set her mind on a plan of action. In more ways than one,

Victoria was Calvin's daughter. He looked inquiringly at Trask and without words asked, what about him?

"Trask was just leaving."

"Not yet," Trask argued. "I'll come with you."

"Forget it."

"Listen to me. I think that this might have something to do with what we were discussing."

The anonymous letter? Her father's imprisonment? The horse swindle of five years ago? "I don't see how—" she protested.

"It won't hurt for me to take a look."

He was so damned logical. Seeing no reasonable argument, and not wanting to make a scene in front of Rex, Tory reluctantly agreed. "I don't like this," she mumbled, reaching for her jacket that hung on a wooden peg near the door and bracing herself for the unpleasant scene in the fields near the Ross property.

"Neither do I."

The tone of Trask's voice sent a shiver of dread down Tory's spine.

Rex cast her a worried glance, forced his gray Stetson onto his head and started for the door. As Tory grabbed the keys to her pickup she wondered what was happening to her life. Everything seemed to be turning upside down. All because of Trask McFadden.

CHAPTER THREE

TRASK SAT ON the passenger side of the pickup, his eyes looking steadily forward, his pensive gaze was following the disappearing taillights of Rex's truck.

Tory's eyebrows were drawn together in concentration as she attempted to follow Rex. Her fingers curled around the steering wheel as she tried to maneuver the bouncing pickup down the rutted dirt road that ran the length of the Lazy W toward the mountains.

The tension within the darkened interior of the pickup was thick enough to cut with a knife. Silence stretched tautly between Tory and Trask and she had to bite her tongue to keep from screaming at him that she didn't want him forcing himself back into her life.

She downshifted and slowed to a stop near the property line separating the Lazy W from Len Ross's spread.

"Over here," Rex announced when she shut off the engine, grabbed a flashlight out of the glove box and jumped from the cab of the truck. Trask held apart the strands of barbed wire, which surrounded the pastures, as she wrapped her skirt around her thighs, climbed through the fence and followed the beam of Rex's flashlight. Trask slid through the fence after her. Though he said nothing, she was conscious of his presence, his long legs taking one stride to every two of her smaller steps.

The first large drops of rain began to fall just as Tory approached the crumpled heap near a solitary pine tree. The beam of Rex's flashlight was trained on the lifeless white face of the calf. Dull eyes looked unseeingly skyward and a large pink tongue lolled out of the side of the heifer's mouth.

"Dear God," Tory whispered, bending over and touching the inert form. Her stomach lurched uncomfortably as she brushed the flies from the curly red coat of the lifeless animal. Living on the ranch as she had for most of her twenty-seven years, Tory was used to death. But she had never been able to accept the unnecessary wanton destruction of life that had taken the small Hereford. It was all so pointless. Her throat tightened as she patted the rough hide and then let her hands fall to her sides.

Rex ran his flashlight over the calf's body and Tory noticed the three darkened splotches on the heifer's abdomen. Dried blood had clotted over the red and white hairs. Tory closed her eyes for a second. Whoever had killed the calf hadn't even had the decency to make it a clean kill. The poor creature had probably suffered for several hours before dying beneath the solitary ponderosa pine tree.

"What about the cow—the mother of the calf?"

"I took care of her," Rex stated. "She's with the rest of the herd in the south pasture."

Tory nodded thoughtfully and cocked her head toward the dead calf. "Let's cover her up," she whispered. "I've got a tarp in the back of the truck."

"Why?" Rex asked, but Trask was already returning to the pickup for the tarp.

"I want someone from the sheriff's office to see the calf and I don't want to take a chance that some scavenger finds her. A coyote could clean the carcass by morning," Tory replied, as she stood and dusted off her skirt. In the darkness, her eyes glinted with determination. "Someone did this—" she pointed to the calf "—deliberately. I want that person found."

Rex sucked in his breath and shook his head. "Might not be that easy," he thought aloud.

"Well, we've got to do something. We can't just sit by and let it happen again."

Rex shook his head. "You're right, Tory. I can't argue with that. Whoever did this should have to pay, but I doubt if having someone from the sheriff's office come out will do any good."

"Maybe not, but at least we'll find out if any of the other ranchers have had similar problems."

Rex forced his hands into the pockets of his lightweight jacket and pulled his shoulders closer to his neck as the rain began to shower in earnest. "I'll check all the fields tomorrow, just to make sure that there are no other surprises."

"Good."

Rex glanced uneasily toward the trucks, where Trask was fetching the tarp. "There's something else you should know," the foreman said. His voice was low, as if he didn't want to be overheard.

Tory followed Rex's gaze. "What?"

"The fence…someone snipped it. Whoever did this—" he motioned toward the dead calf "—didn't bother to climb through the fence, or use the gate. No, sir. They clipped all four wires clean open."

Tory's heart froze. Whoever had killed the calf had done it blatantly, almost tauntingly. She felt her stomach quiver with premonition. Things had gone from bad to worse in the span of a few short hours.

"I patched it up as best I could," Rex was saying with a frown. "I'll need a couple of the hands out here tomorrow to do a decent job of it."

"You don't think this is the work of kids out for a few kicks," Tory guessed.

Rex shrugged and even in the darkness Tory could see him scowl distractedly. "I don't rightly know, but I doubt it."

"Great."

"You don't have anyone who bears you a grudge, do you?" Rex asked uncomfortably.

"Not that I know of."

"How about someone who still has it in for your pop? Now that he's gone, you'd be the most likely target." He thought for a minute, as if he was hesitant to bring up a sore subject. "Maybe someone who's out to make trouble because of the horse swindle?"

"I don't think so," Tory murmured. "It's been a long time...over five years."

"But McFadden is back. Stirring up trouble..." If Rex meant to say anything more, he didn't. Trask reappeared with the heavy tarp slung over his shoulder. Without a word the two men covered the small calf and lashed the tarp down with rope and metal stakes that Trask had brought from the truck.

"That about does it," Rex said, wiping the accumulation of rain from the back of his neck once the unpleasant job had been completed. "It would take a grizzly to rip that open." He stretched his shoulders before adding, "Like I said, I'll check all the fences and the livestock myself, in the morning. I'll let you know if anything looks suspicious." Rex's concerned gaze studied Trask for a tense second and Tory saw the muscles in Trask's face tighten a bit.

"I'll talk to you in the morning," Tory replied.

"'Night," Rex mumbled as he turned toward his truck.

"Thanks for checking it out, Rex."

"No problem." Rex pushed his hat squarely over his head. "All part of the job."

"Above and beyond the call of duty at ten o'clock at night."

"All in a day's work," Rex called over his shoulder.

Tory stood beside Trask and watched the beam of Rex's flashlight as the foreman strode briskly back to the truck.

"Come on," Trask said, placing his arm familiarly around her shoulders. "You're getting soaked. Let's go."

Casting a final despairing look at the covered carcass, Tory walked back to the pickup with Trask and didn't object to the weight of his arm stretched over her shoulders. This night, when her whole world was falling apart, she felt the need of his strength. She supposed her contradictory feelings for him bordered on irony, but she really didn't care. She was too tired and emotionally drained to consider the consequences of her renewed acquaintance with him.

"I'll drive," Trask said.

"I can—"

"I'll drive," he stated again, more forcefully, and she reached into her pocket and handed him the keys, too weary to argue over anything so pointless. He knew the back roads of the Lazy W as well as anyone. He had driven them often during the short months of their passionate but traitorous love affair. How long ago that happy carefree time in her life seemed now as they jostled along the furrowed road.

Trask drove slowly back to the house. The old engine of the truck rumbled through the dark night, the wipers pushed aside the heavy raindrops on the windshield, and the tinny sound of static-filled country music from an all-night radio station drifted out of the speakers.

"Who do you think did it?" Trask asked as he stopped the truck near the front porch.

"I don't have any idea," Tory admitted with a worried frown. "I don't really understand what's going on. Yesterday everything was normal: the worst problem I had to deal with was a broken combine and a horse with laminitis. But now—" she raised her hands helplessly before reaching for the door handle of the pickup "—it seems that all hell has broken loose." She looked toward him and found his eyes searching the contours of her face.

"Tory—" He reached for her, and the seductive light in his eyes made her heartbeat quicken. His fingers brushed against the rain-dampened strands of her hair and his lips curved into a wistful smile. "I remember another time," he said, "when you and I were alone in this very pickup."

A passionate image scorched Tory's mind. Just by staring into Trask's intense gaze she could recall the feel of his hands against her breasts, the way her skin would quiver at his touch, the taste of his mouth over hers. "I think we'd better not talk or even think about that," she whispered.

His fingers lingered against her exposed neck, warming the wet skin near the base of her throat. "Can't we be together without fighting?" he asked, his voice low with undercurrents of restrained desire.

After all these years, Trask still wanted her; or at least he wanted her to think that he still cared for her— just a little. Maybe he did. "I...I don't know."

"Let's try."

"I don't think I want to," she admitted, but it was too late. She watched with mingled fascination and dread as his head lowered and his mouth closed over hers, just as his hand pressed against her shoulder, pulling her against his chest. She was caught up in the scent of him; the familiar odor of his skin was dampened with the rain and all of her senses reawakened with his touch.

The warmth of his arms enveloped her and started the trickle of desire running in her blood. Warm lips, filled with the smoldering lust of five long years, touched hers and the tip of his tongue pressed urgently against her teeth.

I can't let this happen, she thought wildly, pressing her palms against his shoulders and trying to pull out of his intimate embrace. When he lifted his head from hers, she let her forehead fall against his chin. Her hands remained against his shoulders and only her shallow breathing gave her conflicting emotions away. "We can't start all over, you know," she said at length, raising her head and gazing into his eyes. "It's not as if either of us can forget what happened and start over again."

"But we don't have to let what happened force us apart."

"Oh, Trask, come on. Think about it," Tory said snappishly, although a vital but irrational part of her mind wanted desperately to believe him.

"I have. For five years."

"There's no other way, Trask. You and I both know it." Before he could contradict her or the illogical side of her nature could argue with her, she opened the door of the truck and dashed through the rain and across the gravel drive to the house.

She was already in the den when Trask entered the room. He leaned insolently against the archway. The rain had darkened his hair to a deep brown and the shoulders of his wet shirt clung to his muscles. Standing against the pine wall, his arms crossed insolently over his chest, his brilliant eyes delving into hers, he looked more masculine than she ever would have imagined. Or wanted. "What are you running from?" he asked.

"You...me...us." She lifted her hands into the air helplessly before realizing how undignified her emotions appeared. Then, willing her pride back into place, she wrapped her arms around herself and settled into the chair behind her father's desk. She hoped that the large oak table would put distance between her body and his—give her time to get her conflicting emotions back into perspective.

Trask looked bone-weary as he sauntered around the den and, uninvited, poured himself a healthy drink from the mirrored bar near the fireplace. He lifted the bottle in silent offering, but Tory shook her head, preferring to keep her wits about her. Her reaction to Trask was overwhelming, unwelcome and had to be controlled. She couldn't let herself be duped again. What was it they always said? Once burned, twice shy? That's the way it had to be with Trask, she tried to convince herself. He'd used her once. Never again.

He strode over to the window, propping one booted foot against a small stool, sipping his drink and staring out at the starless night. Raindrops slid in twisted paths down the panes.

"This ever happened before?" Trask asked. He turned and leaned against the windowsill, one broad hand supporting most of his weight.

"What?"

"Some of your livestock being used for target practice."

Her eyes narrowed at the cruel analogy. "No."

Swirling the amber liquor in his glass, he stared at her. "Don't you think it's odd?"

"Of course."

Trask shook his head. "More than that, Tory. Not just odd. What I meant is that it seems like more than a coincidence. First this letter—" he pointed to the anonymous note still lying face up crumpled on a small table "—and now the calf."

Tory felt the prickling sensation of dread climb up her spine. "What are you getting at?"

"I think the dead calf is a warning, Tory."

"What!"

"Someone knows I'm here looking for the person that was unconvicted in the original trial for Jason's murder. I've made no bones about the fact that I intended to visit you. The calf was a message to stay away from me."

Tory laughed nervously. "You're not serious...."

"Dead serious."

Tory felt the first stirrings of fear. "I think you've been in Washington too long, senator," she replied. "Too many subcommittees on underworld crime have got you jumping at shadows. This is Sinclair, Oregon, not New York City."

"I'm not kidding, Tory." His eyes glittered dangerously and he finished his drink with a scowl. "Someone's trying to scare you off."

"It was probably just a prank, like Rex said."

"Rex didn't believe that and neither do you."

"You know how kids are: they get an idea in their heads and just for kicks—"

"They slaughter a calf?" he finished ungraciously. Anger flashed in his eyes and was evident in the set of his shoulders. "Real funny: a heifer with three gunshot wounds. Some sense of humor."

"I didn't say it was meant to be funny."

His fist crashed violently into the windowsill. "Damn it, Tory, haven't you been listening to a word I've said? It's obvious to me that someone is trying to scare you off!"

"Then why not send me a letter...or phone me? Why something as obscure as a dead calf? If you ask me, you're grasping at straws, trying to tie one event to the other just so that I'll help you in this...this wild-goose chase!" Realizing that he only intended to continue the argument, she reached for the phone on the corner of the desk.

Trask's eyes were blazing and the cords in his neck

protruded. He was about to say something more, but Tory shook her head, motioning for him to be silent as she dialed the sheriff's office and cradled the receiver between her shoulder and her ear. "No, Trask, what you're suggesting doesn't make any sense. None whatsoever."

"Like hell! If you weren't so damned stubborn—"

"Deputy Smith?" Tory said aloud as a curt voice answered the phone. "This is Tory Wilson at the Lazy W." Tory held up her hand to silence the protests forming on Trask's tongue. As quickly as possible, she explained everything that had occurred from the time that Len Ross's hands had noticed the dead animal.

"We'll have someone out in the morning," the deputy promised after telling her that no other rancher had reported any disturbances in the past few weeks. Tory replaced the phone with shaking hands. Her brows drew together thoughtfully.

"You're beginning to believe me," Trask deduced. He was still angry, but his rage was once again controlled.

"No—"

"You'd better think about it. Has anything else unusual happened around here?"

"No...wait a minute. There was the combine that broke down unexpectedly and I do have a stallion with laminitis, but they couldn't be connected...never mind." *What was she thinking about? Governor's condition and the broken machinery were all explainable problems of running the Lazy W. The malicious incident involving the calf—that was something else again.* She forced a fragile smile. "Look, Trask, I think you'd better leave."

"What about the letter?" he demanded, picking up
the small piece of paper and waving it in her face. "Are
you going to ignore it, too?"

"I wouldn't take it too seriously," she allowed, lifting her shoulders.

"No?"

"For God's sake, Trask, it isn't even signed. That
doesn't make much sense to me. Why wouldn't the person who wrote it want to be identified, that is if he has
a logical authentic complaint? If the man who wrote
this note wanted you to do something, why didn't he
bother to sign the damned thing?"

"Maybe because he or she is afraid. Maybe the person who was involved with the swindle and avoided
justice got away because he's extremely powerful—"

"And maybe he just doesn't exist." She eyed the
grayish sheet of paper disdainfully. "That could be
a letter from anyone, and it doesn't necessarily mean
it's true."

"Tory—" His eyes darkened at her obstinacy.

"As I said before, I think it's time you left."

He took a step nearer to her, but she held up her
hand before motioning toward the letter. "I can't help
you with this. I have enough tangible problems here
on the ranch. I don't have time to deal with fantasies."

Trask watched as she forced the curtain of callous
disinterest over her beautiful features. The emerald-
green eyes, which had once been so innocent and loving, turned cold with determination. "Oh, God, Tory,
is this what I did to you?" he asked in bewilderment.
"Did what happened between us take away all your
trust? All your willingness to help? Your concern for

others as well as yourself?" He was slowly advancing upon her, his footsteps muffled by the braided rug.

Tory's heart pounded betrayingly at his approach. It pulsed rapidly in the hollow of her throat and Trask's intense gaze rested on the revealing cleft.

"I've missed you," he whispered.

"No—"

"I didn't mean for everything between us to end the way it did."

"But it did. Nothing can change that. You sent my father to prison."

"But I only told the truth." He paused at the desk and hooked a leg over the corner as he stared down at her.

"Let's not go over this again. It's been too long, Trask. Too many wounds are still fresh." She swallowed with difficulty but managed to meet his stare boldly. "I've hated you a long time," she said, feeling her tongue trip over the lie she had held true for five unforgiving years.

"I don't believe it."

"You ruined me single-handedly."

"Your father did that." He leaned forward. He was close enough to touch her, but he stopped just short and stared down into her eyes. Eyes that had trusted him with her life five years earlier. "What did you expect me to do? Lie on the witness stand? Would you have preferred not knowing about your father?"

She couldn't stand it anymore; couldn't return his self-righteous stare. "He was innocent, damn it!" Her fists curled into knots of fury and she pushed herself up from the chair.

"Then why didn't he save himself, tell his side of the story?"

"I don't know." Her voice trembled slightly. "Don't you think I've asked myself just that question over and over again?" She felt his arms fold around her, draw her close, hold her body against his as he straightened from the desk. She heard the steady beating of his heart, felt the warmth of his breath caress her hair and she knew in a blinding flash of truth that she had never stopped loving him.

"If there were another man involved in the horse swindle, don't you want to see him accused of the crime?"

"So he could be put behind bars like my father."

"Oh, Tory," he said, releasing a sigh as his arms tightened around her. "How can you be so damned one-sided? You used to care what happened to people..."

"I still do."

"But not to the extent that you're willing to help me find out who was involved in my brother's murder and the Quarter Horse swindle."

She felt herself sag against him. *It would be so nice just to forget about what happened. Pretend that everything was just as it had been on the night she'd met Trask McFadden before her life had become irrevocably twisted with his.* "I just don't know if it will do any good. For all you know that letter could be phony, the work of someone who gets his jollies by stirring up trouble."

"Like the dead calf?"

Tory ran her fingers through her hair. "You don't know that the two incidents are related."

"But we won't find out unless we try." He held her closer and his breath whispered through her hair. "Just give it a chance, Tory. Trust me."

The same old words. Lies and deceit. Rolling as easily off his tongue as they had in the past. All the kindness in her heart withered and died.

She extracted herself from his embrace and impaled him with her indignant green-eyed stare. "I can't help you, Trask," she whispered. "You're on your own this time." She reached for the copy of the note and slowly wadded it into a tight ball before tossing the damning piece of paper into the blackened fireplace.

Trask watched her actions and his lips tightened menacingly. "I'm going to find out if there was any truth to that letter," he stated emphatically. "And I'm going to do it with or without your help."

Though her heart was pounding erratically, she looked him squarely in the eye. "Then I guess you're going to do it alone, aren't you, senator?"

Looking as if he had something further to say, Trask turned on his heel and walked out of the room. The front door slammed behind him and the engine of his pickup roared to life before fading in the distance.

"You bastard," Tory whispered, sagging against the windowsill. "Why can't I stop loving you?"

CHAPTER FOUR

FOR SEVERAL HOURS after Trask had left the ranch, Tory sat on the window seat in her bedroom. Her chin rested on her knees as she stared into the dark night. Raindrops pelted against the panes, drizzling against the glass and blurring Tory's view of the lightning that sizzled across the sky to illuminate the countryside in its garish white light. To the west, thunder rolled ominously over the mountains.

So Trask had come back after all. Tory frowned to herself and squinted into the darkness. *But he hadn't come back for her,* as he had vowed he would five years past. This time he had returned to Sinclair and the Lazy W because he needed her help to prove that another man was part of the Quarter Horse swindle as well as involved in Jason McFadden's premeditated death.

With tense fingers she pushed the hair out of her eyes. Seeing Trask again had brought back too many dangerous memories. Memories of a younger, more carefree and reckless period of her life. Memories of a love destined to die.

As she looked through the window into the black sky, Tory was reminded of a summer filled with hot sultry nights, the sweet scent of pine needles and the familiar feel of Trask's body pressed urgently against hers.

She had to rub her hands over her arms as she remembered the feel of Trask's hard muscles against her skin, the weight of his body pinning hers, the taste of his mouth...

"Stop it," she muttered aloud, pulling herself out of her wanton reverie. "He's the man that sent Dad to prison, for God's sake. Don't be a fool—not twice."

She walked over to the bed and tossed back the quilted coverlet before lying on the sheets and staring at the shadowed ceiling. Her feelings of love for Trask had been her Achilles' heel. She had trusted him with every breath of life in her body and he had used her. Worse than that he had probably planned the whole affair; staging it perfectly. And she'd been fool enough to fall for his act, hook, line and sinker. But not again.

With a disconsolate sigh, she rolled onto her side and stared at the nightstand. In the darkness she could barely make out the picture of her father.

"Oh, Dad," Tory moaned, twisting away from the picture. "I wish you were here." Calvin Wilson had been an incredibly strong man who had been able to stand up to any adversity. He had been able to deal with the loan officers of the local banks when the ranch was in obvious financial trouble. His calm gray eyes and soft-spoken manner had inspired the local bankers' confidence when the general ledgers of the Lazy W couldn't.

He had stood stoically at the grave site of his wife of fifteen years without so much as shedding a tear. While holding his children close he had mourned silently for the only woman he had truly loved, offering strength to his daughter and young son.

When he had faced sentencing for a crime he hadn't committed he hadn't blinked an eye. Nor had he so much as flinched when the sentence of thirty years in prison had been handed down. He had taken it all without the slightest trace of fear. When he'd found out that he was terminally ill with a malignant tumor, Calvin Wilson had been able to look death straight in the eye. Throughout his sixty-three years, he had been a strong man and a loving father. Tory knew in her heart that he couldn't have been involved in Jason McFadden's murder.

Then why didn't he stand up for himself at the trial?

If he had spoken out, told his side of the story, let the court hear the truth, even Trask's damning testimony would have been refuted and maybe Calvin Wilson would be alive now. And Trask wouldn't be back in Sinclair, digging up the past, searching for some elusive, maybe even phantom, conspirator in Jason's death.

And now Trask had returned, actually believing that someone else was involved in his brother's death.

So it all came back to Trask and the fact that Tory hadn't stopped loving him. She knew her feelings for him were crazy, considering everything they had been through. She loved him one minute, hated him the next and knew that she should never have seen him again. He could take his wild half-baked theories, anonymous letters and seductive smile straight back to Washington where they all belonged. Surely he had better things to do than bother her.

"Just leave me alone, Trask," Tory said with a sigh. "Go back to Washington and leave me alone…I don't want to love you any more…I can't…"

THE NEXT MORNING, after a restless night, Tory was making breakfast when Keith, more than slightly hung over, entered the kitchen. Without a word he walked to the refrigerator, poured himself a healthy glass of orange juice and drank it in one swallow. He then slumped into a chair at the kitchen table and glared up at Tory with red-rimmed eyes.

"Don't tell me you're dehydrated," Tory said, with a teasing lilt in her voice.

"Okay, I won't. Then you won't have to lecture me."

"Fair enough." From the looks of it Keith's hangover was punishment enough for his binge, Tory thought, and she had been the one who had insisted that he go into town last night. If he were suffering, which he obviously was, it was partially because of her insistence that he leave the ranch. She flipped the pancakes over and decided not to mention that Keith hadn't gotten home until after three. He was over twenty-one now, and she didn't have to mother him, though it was a hard habit to break considering that the past five years she had been father, mother and sister all rolled into one.

"How about some breakfast?" she suggested, stacking the pancakes on a plate near a pile of crisp bacon and placing the filled platter on the table.

"After a few answers."

"Okay." Tory slid into the chair facing him and poured syrup over her stack of hotcakes. "Shoot."

"What have to decided to do about McFadden?" Keith asked, forking a generous helping of bacon onto his plate.

"I don't know," Tory admitted. She took a bite from a strip of bacon. "Maybe there's nothing I can do."

"Like hell. You could leave."

"Not a chance, we went over this yesterday." She reached for the coffeepot and poured each of them a cup of coffee.

"McFadden will come here."

"He already has."

"What!" Keith's face lost all of its color. "When?"

"Last night. While you were in town."

Keith rubbed his palm over the reddish stubble on his chin. "Damn, I knew something like this would happen."

"It wasn't that big of a deal. We just talked."

Keith looked at his older sister as if she had lost her mind. "You did what?" he shouted, rising from the breakfast table.

"I said I talked with him. How else was I supposed to find out what he wanted?"

Keith's worried eyes studied her face. "So what happened to the woman who, just yesterday afternoon, was going to bodily throw Trask McFadden off her land if he set foot on it. You know, the lady with the ready rifle and deadly aim?"

"Now, wait a minute—" Tory's face lost all of its color and her eyes narrowed.

"Weren't you the one who suggested that we point a rifle at his head and tell him to get lost?"

"I was only joking…"

"Like hell!" Keith sputtered before truly seeing his sister for the first time that morning. A sinking realization hit him like a ton of bricks. "Tory, you're still in love with him, aren't you? I can't believe it! After what he did to you?" Keith stared at his sister incredulously before stalking over to the refrigerator and pouring himself a large glass of milk. "This isn't happening," he said, as if to console himself. "This is all just a bad dream…"

"I'm not in love with him, Keith," Tory said, tossing her hair over her shoulder and turning her face upward in order to meet Keith's disbelieving gaze.

"But you were once."

"Before he testified against Dad."

"Goddamn," Keith muttered as he sucked in his breath and got hold of himself. His large fist curled in frustration. "I knew he'd show up the minute I left the ranch. What did he want?"

"My help."

"Your what? I can't believe it. After what he put you through? The nerve of that bastard!" He took a long swig from his glass with one hand, then motioned to his sister. "Well, go on, go on, this is getting better by the minute."

"He thinks that there may have been someone else involved in Jason's murder and the horse swindle."

"Are you kiddin'?" Keith placed his empty glass on the counter and shook his head in disbelief. "After all this time? No way!"

"That's what I told him."

"But he didn't buy it?"

"I'd say not."

"Great! The dumb bastard will probably drag all of it up again. It'll be in the papers and everything." Keith paced between the table and the back door. He squinted against the bright morning sunshine streaming through the dusty windowpanes and looked toward the barn. "Dad's name is sure to come up."

"Sit down and eat your breakfast," Tory said, eyeing Keith's neglected plate.

Keith ignored her. "This is the last thing we need right now, you know. What with all the problems we're having with the bank…" He swore violently, balled one fist and smashed it into his other palm. "I should never have left you last night, I knew it, damn it, I knew it!" His temper threatened to explode completely for a minute before he finally managed to contain his fury. Slowly uncurling his fist, he regained his composure and added with false optimism, "Oh, well, maybe McFadden got whatever it was he wanted off his chest and now it's over."

Tory hated to burst Keith's bubble, but she had always been straight with her brother, telling him about the problems with the ranch when they occurred. There was no reason to change now. "I don't know that it's over."

"What's that supposed to mean?"

"I don't think Trask is going to let up on this. He seemed pretty determined to me." Tory had lost all interest in her breakfast and pushed her plate aside. Unconsciously she brushed the crumbs from the polished maple surface of the table.

"But why? What's got him all riled up after five years?" Keith wondered aloud. "His term as a senator isn't up for another couple of years, so he isn't looking for publicity…"

"He got a letter."

Keith froze. He turned incredulous gray eyes on his sister. "Wait a minute. The man must get a ton of mail. What kind of a letter got under his skin?"

"An anonymous one."

"So what?"

No time like the present to drop the bomb, she sup

posed. With a feeling of utter frustration she stood, picked up her plate and set it near the sink. "If you want to read it, there's a copy in the den, in the fireplace."

"In the fireplace! Wonderful," Keith muttered sarcastically as he headed through the archway that opened to the short hallway separating the living room, kitchen, dining room and den.

"Hey, what about this breakfast?" Tory called after him.

"I'm not hungry," Keith replied, from somewhere in the vicinity of the den.

"Great," Tory muttered under her breath as she put the uneaten pancakes and bacon on another plate. "Tomorrow morning it's cold cereal for you, brother dear." With a frown at the untouched food, she opened the door to the back porch and set the plate on the floorboards. Alex, the ranch's ancient Border collie, stood on slightly arthritic legs and wagged his tail before helping himself to Keith's breakfast.

"Serves him right," Tory told the old dog as she petted him fondly and scratched Alex's black ears. "I'm glad someone appreciates my cooking."

Tory heard Keith return to the kitchen. With a final pat to Alex's head, she straightened and walked into the house.

Keith was standing in the middle of the kitchen looking for all the world as if he would drop through the floor. He was holding the crumpled and now slightly blackened piece of paper in his hands and his face had paled beneath his tan. He set the paper on the table and smoothed out the creases in the letter. "Holy shit."

"My sentiments exactly."

"So how does he think you could help him?" Keith asked, his eyes narrowing in suspicion.

"I don't know. We never got that far."

"And this—" he pointed down at the paper "—is why he wanted to see you?"

"That's what he said."

Keith closed his eyes for a minute, trying to concentrate. "That's a relief, I guess."

Tory raised an inquisitive brow. "Meaning?"

Keith smiled sadly and shook his head. "That I don't want to see you hurt again."

"Don't worry, brother dear," she assured him with a slightly cynical smile, "I don't intend to be. But thanks anyway, for the concern."

"I don't want to be thanked, Tory. I just want you to avoid McFadden. He's trouble."

Tory couldn't argue the point. She turned on the tap and started hot water running into the sink. As the sink filled she began washing the dishes before she hit Keith with the other bad news. "Something else happened last night."

"I'm not sure I want to know what it is," Keith said, picking up his coffee cup and drinking some of the lukewarm liquid. With a scowl, he reached for the pot and added some hot coffee to the tepid fluid in his cup.

"You probably don't."

He poured more coffee into Tory's empty cup and set it on the wooden counter, near the sink. "So what happened?"

"There was some other nasty business yesterday," Tory said, ignoring the dishes for the moment and wiping her hands on a dish towel. As she picked up her cup she leaned her hips against the edge of the wooden counter and met Keith's worried gaze.

"What now?" he asked as he settled into the cane chair near the table and propped his boots on the seat of another chair.

"Someone clipped the barbed wire on the northwest side of the ranch, came in and shot one of the calves. Three times in the abdomen. A heifer. About four months old."

Keith's hand hesitated over the sugar bowl and his head snapped up. "You think it was done deliberately?"

"Had to be. I called the sheriff's office. They're sending a man out this morning. Rex is spending the morning going over all of the fence bordering the ranch and checking it for any other signs of destruction."

"Just what we need," Keith said, cynicism tightening the corners of his mouth. "Another crisis on the Lazy W. How'd you find out about it?"

"One of Len Ross's men noticed it yesterday evening. Len called Rex and he checked it out."

"What about the rest of the livestock?"

"As far as I know all present and accounted for."

"Son of a bitch!" Keith forgot about the sugar and took a swallow of his black coffee.

"Trask thinks it might be related to that," she pointed to the blackened letter.

"Trask thinks?" Keith repeated, his eyes narrowing. "How does he know about it?"

"He was here when Rex came over to tell me about it."

Keith looked physically pained. "Lord, Tory, I don't know how much more of your cheery morning news I can stand."

"That's the last of the surprises."

"Thank God," Keith said, pushing himself up from the table and glaring pointedly at his older sister. "You're on notice, Tory."

She had to chuckle. "For what?"

"From now on when I decide to stay on the ranch rather than checking out the action at the Branding Iron, I'm not going to let you talk me out of it."

"Is that so? And how would you have handled Trask when he showed up on the porch?"

"I would have taken your suggestion yesterday and met him with a rifle in my hands."

"This isn't 1840, you know."

"Doesn't matter."

"You can't threaten a United States senator, Keith."

"Just you watch," Keith said, reaching for his Stetson on the peg near the back door. "The next time Mc-Fadden trespasses, I'll be ready for him." With those final chilling words, he was out the back door of the house and heading for the barn. Tory watched him with worried eyes. Keith's temper had never had much of a fuse and Trask's presence seemed to have shortened it considerably.

It was her fault, she supposed. She should never have let Keith see the books. It didn't take a genius to see that the Lazy W was in pitiful financial shape, and dredging up the old scandal would only make it worse. But Keith had asked to see the balance sheets, and Tory had let him review everything, inwardly pleased that he had grown up enough to care.

DEPUTY WOODWARD ARRIVED shortly after ten. Tory had been in the den writing checks for the month-end bills when she had heard the sound of a vehicle approaching and had looked out the window to see the youngest of Paul Barnett's deputies getting out of his car. Slim, with a thin mustache, he had been hired in the past year and was one of the few deputies she had never met. Once, while in town, Keith had pointed the young man out to her.

When the chimes sounded, Tory put the checkbook into the top drawer of the desk and answered the door.

"Mornin'," Woodward said with a smile. "I'm looking for Victoria Wilson."

"You found her."

"Good. I'm Greg Woodward from the sheriff's office. From what I understand, you think someone's been taking potshots at your livestock."

Tory nodded. "Someone has. I've got a dead calf to prove it."

"Just one?"

"So far," Tory replied. "I thought maybe some of the other ranchers might have experienced some sort of vandalism like this on their ranches."

The young deputy shook his head. "Is that what you think it was? Vandalism?"

Tory thought about the dead calf and the clipped fence. "No, not really. I guess I was just hoping that the Lazy W hadn't been singled out."

Woodward offered an understanding grin. "Let's take a look at what happened."

Tory sat in the passenger seat of the deputy's car as he drove down the rutted road she had traveled with Trask less than twelve hours earlier. The grooves in the dirt road were muddy and slick from the rain, but

Deputy Woodward's vehicle made it to the site of the clipped fence without any problem.

Rex was already working on restringing the barbed wire. He looked up when he saw Tory, frowned slightly and then straightened, adjusting the brim of his felt Stetson.

As Deputy Woodward studied the cut wire and corpse of the calf, he asked Tory to tell him what had happened. She, with Rex's help, explained about Len Ross's call and how she and Rex had subsequently discovered the damage to the fence and the calf's dead body.

"But no other livestock were affected?" Woodward asked, writing furiously on his report.

"No," Rex replied, "at least none that we know about."

"You've checked already?"

"I've got several men out looking right now," Rex said.

"What about other fences, the buildings, or the equipment for the farm?"

"We have a combine that broke down last week, but it was just a matter of age," Tory said.

Woodward seemed satisfied. He took one last look at the calf and scowled. "I'll file this report and check with some of the neighboring ranchers to see if anything like this has happened to anyone else." He looked meaningfully at Tory. "And you'll call, if you find anything else?"

"Of course," Tory said.

"Does anyone else know what happened here?" the young man asked, as he finished his report.

"Only two people other than the ranch hands," Tory replied. "Len Ross and Trask McFadden."

The young man's head jerked up. "Senator McFadden?"

Tory nodded and offered a confident smile she didn't feel. Greg Woodward was a local man. Though he had probably still been in high school at the time, he would have heard of Jason McFadden's murder and the conspiracy of horse swindlers who had been convicted. "Trask was visiting last night when Rex got the news from Len and came up to the house to tell me what had happened."

"Did he make any comments—being as he was here and all—or did he think it was vandalism?"

Tory's mind strayed to her conversation with Trask and his insistence that the animal's death was somehow related to the anonymous letter he had received. "I don't know," she hedged. "I suppose you'll have to ask him—"

"No reason to bother the senator," Rex interjected, his eyes traveling to Tory with an unspoken message. "He doesn't know any more than either of us."

Deputy Woodward caught the meaningful glance between rancher and foreman but didn't comment. He had enough sense to know that something wasn't right at the Lazy W and that Senator McFadden was more than a casual friend. On the drive back with Tory, Woodward silently speculated on the past scandal and what this recently divulged information could mean.

When the deputy deposited Tory back at the house, she felt uneasy. Something in the young man's attitude had changed when she had mentioned that Trask had been on the ranch. *It's starting all over again,* she thought to herself. *Trask has only been in town two days and the trouble's starting all over again. As if she and everyone connected with the Lazy W hadn't suffered enough from the scandal of five years past.*

TORY PARKED THE pickup on the street in front of the feed store in Sinclair. So far the entire day had been a waste. Deputy Woodward hadn't been able to ease her mind about the dead calf; in fact, if anything, the young man's reaction to the news that Trask knew of the incident only added to Tory's unease.

After Deputy Woodward had gone, Tory had attempted to do something, anything to keep her mind off Trask. But try as she might, she hadn't been able to concentrate on anything other than Trask and his ridiculous idea—no, make that conviction—that another person was involved in the Quarter Horse swindle as well as his brother's death.

He's jumping at shadows, she told herself as she stepped out of the pickup and into the dusty street, but she couldn't shake the image of Trask, his shoulders erect in controlled, but deadly determination as he had stood in her father's den the night before. She had witnessed the outrage in his blue eyes. *"He won't let up on this until he has an answer,"* she told herself with a frown.

She pushed her way into the feed store and made short work of ordering supplies for the Lazy W. The clerk, Alma Ray, had lived in Sinclair all her life and had worked at Rasmussen Feed for as long as Tory could remember. She was a woman in her middle to late fifties and wore her soft red hair piled on her head. She had always offered Tory a pleasant smile and thoughtful advice in the past, but this afternoon Alma's brown eyes were cold, her smile forced.

"Don't get paranoid," Tory cautioned herself in a whisper as she stepped out of the feed store and onto the sidewalk. "It's not as if this town is against you, for God's sake. Alma's just having a bad day—"

"Tory."

At the sound of her name, Tory turned to face Neva McFadden, Jason's widow. Neva was hurrying up the sidewalk in Tory's direction and Tory's heart sank. She saw the strain in Neva's even features, the worry in her doe-brown eyes. Images of the courtroom and Neva's proud face twisted in agony filled Tory's mind.

"Do you have a minute?" Neva asked, clutching a bag of groceries to her chest.

It was the first time Neva McFadden had spoken to Tory since the trial.

"Sure," Tory replied. She forced a smile, though the first traces of dread began to crawl up her spine. It couldn't be a coincidence that Neva wanted to talk to her the day after Trask had returned to the Lazy W. "Why don't we sit down?" She nodded in the direction of the local café, which was just across the street from the feed store.

"Great," Neva said with a faltering smile.

Once they were seated in a booth and had been served identical glasses of iced tea, Tory decided to take the offensive. "So, what's up?"

Neva stopped twirling the lemon in her glass. "I wanted to talk to you about Trask."

"I thought so. What about him?"

"I know that he went to see you last night and I have a good idea of what it was about," Neva stated. She hesitated slightly and frowned into her glass as if struggling with a weighty decision. "I don't see any reason to beat around the bush, Tory. I know about the letter Trask received. He showed me a copy of it."

"He showed it to me, too," Tory admitted, hiding her surprise. She had assumed that Trask hadn't spoken to anyone but her. It wouldn't take long for the gossip to start all over again.

"And what do you think about it?" Neva asked.

Tory lifted her shoulders. "I honestly don't know."

Neva let out a sigh and ignored her untouched drink. "Well, I do. It was a prank," Neva said firmly. "Just someone who wants to stir up the trouble all over again."

"Why would anyone want to do that?"

"I wish I knew," Neva admitted, shaking her head. The rays of the afternoon sun streamed through the window and reflected in the golden strands of her hair. Except for the lines of worry surrounding her eyes, Neva McFadden was an extremely attractive woman. "I wish to God I knew what was going on."

"So do I."

Neva's fingers touched Tory's forearm. She bit at her lower lip, as if the next words were awkward. "I know that you cared for Trask, Tory, and I know that you think he…"

"Used me?"

"Yes."

"It was more than that, Neva," Tory said, suddenly wanting this woman who had borne so much pain to understand. "Trask betrayed me and my family."

Neva stiffened and she withdrew her hand. "By taking care of his own."

"He lied, Neva."

Neva shook her head. "That's not the way it was. He just wanted justice for Jason's death."

"Justice or revenge?" Tory asked and could have kicked herself when she saw the anger flare in Neva's eyes.

"Does it matter?"

Tory shrugged and frowned. "I suppose not. It was a horrible thing that happened to Jason and you. And… and I'm sorry for…everything…I know it's been hard for you; harder than it's been for me." Her mouth suddenly dry, Tory took a long drink of the cold tea and still felt parched.

"It's over," Neva said. "Or it was until Trask came back with some wild ideas about another person being involved in Jason's death."

"So you think the letter was a prank."

"Of course it was."

"How can you be sure?"

Neva avoided Tory's direct gaze. "It's been five years, Tory. Five years without a husband or father to my son."

All the feelings of remorse Tory had felt during the trial overcame her as she watched the young woman battle against tears. "Neva, I'm sorry if my family had any part in the pain you and Nicholas have felt."

"Your father was involved with Linn Benton and George Henderson. I know you never believed that he was guilty, Tory, but the man didn't even stand up for himself at the trial."

Tory felt as if a knife, five years old and dull, had been thrust into her heart. "I don't see any reason to talk about this, Neva. I've already apologized." Tory pushed herself up from the table. "I think I should go."

"Don't! Sit down, Tory," Neva pleaded. "Look, I didn't mean to start trouble. God knows that's the last thing I want. The reason I wanted to talk to you is because of Trask."

Tory felt her heart begin to pound. She took a seat on the edge of the booth, her back stiff. "So you said."

"Don't get involved with him again, Tory. Don't start believing that there was more to what happened than came out in the trial."

"I know there was more," Tory stated, feeling a need to defend her father.

"I don't think so. And even if there was, what would be the point of dredging it all up again? It won't bring Jason back to life, or your father. All it will do is bring the whole sordid scandal back into the public eye."

Tory leaned back and studied the blond woman. There was more to what Neva was suggesting than the woman had admitted. Tory could feel it. "But what if the letter Trask received contains part of the truth? Don't you want to find out?"

"No." Neva shook her head vehemently.

"I don't understand—"

"That's because you don't have a child, Tory. You don't have a six-year-old son who needs all the protection I can give him. It's bad enough that he doesn't have a father, but does he have to be reminded, taunted, teased about the fact that his dad was murdered by men in this town that he trusted?"

"Oh, Neva—"

"Think about it. Think long and hard about who is going to win if Trask continues his wild-goose chase;

no one. Not you, Tory. Not me. And especially not Nicholas. He's the loser!"

Tory chose her words carefully. "Don't you think your son deserves the truth?"

"Not if it costs him his peace of mind." Neva lifted her chin and her brown eyes grew cold. "I know that you don't want another scandal any more than I do. And as for Trask, well—" she lifted her palms upward and then dropped her hands "—I hope that, for both your sakes, you don't get involved with him again. Not just because of the letter. I don't think he could handle another love affair with you, Tory. The last time almost killed him." With her final remarks, Neva reached for her purse and sack of groceries and left the small café.

"So much for mending fences," Tory muttered as she paid the small tab and walked out of the restaurant. After crossing the street, she climbed into her pickup and headed back to the Lazy W. Though she had never been close to Neva, not even before Jason's death, Tory had hoped that someday the old wounds would heal and the scars become less visible. Now, with the threat of Trask opening up another investigation into his brother's death, that seemed impossible.

As Tory drove down the straight highway toward the ranch, her thoughts turned to the past. Maybe Neva was right. Maybe listening to Trask would only prove disastrous.

Five years before, after her father's conviction, Tory had been forced to give up her dream of graduate school to stay at the Lazy W and hold the ranch together. Not only had the ranch suffered financially, but her brother, Keith, who was only sixteen at the time, needed her support and supervision. Her goal of becoming a veterinarian as well as her hopes of becoming Trask McFadden's wife had been shattered as easily as crystal against stone.

When Calvin had been sent to prison, Tory had stayed at the ranch and tried to raise a strong-willed younger brother as well as bring the Lazy W out of the pool of red ink. In the following five years Keith had grown up and become responsible, but the ranch was still losing money, though a little less each year.

Keith, at twenty-one, could, perhaps, run the ranch on his own. But it was too late for Tory. She could no more go back to school and become a veterinarian than she could become Trask McFadden's wife.

CHAPTER FIVE

THE BUILDINGS OF the Lazy W, made mostly of rough-hewn cedar and fir, stood proudly on the flat land comprising the ranch and were visible from the main highway. Tory wheeled the pickup onto the gravel lane that was lined with stately pines and aspen and led up to the house.

Purebred horses grazed in the fields surrounding the stables, whole spindly legged foals romped in the afternoon sunlight.

Tory's heart swelled with pride for the Lazy W. Three hundred acres of high plateau held together by barbed wire and red metal posts had been Tory's home for all of her twenty-seven years and suddenly it seemed that everyone wanted to take it away from her. Trask, with his damned investigation of the horse swindle of five years ago, was about to ruin her credibility as a Quarter Horse breeder by reminding the public of the shady dealings associated with the Lazy W.

Tall grass in the meadow ruffled in the summer breeze that blew across the mountains. White clouds clung to the jagged peaks of the Cascades, shadowing the grassland. This was the land she loved and Tory would fight tooth and nail to save it—even if it meant fighting Trask every step of the way. He couldn't just come marching back into her life and destroy everything she had worked for in the past five years!

Tory squinted against the late-afternoon sun as she drove the pickup into the parking lot near the barn and killed the engine. The warm westerly wind had removed any trace of the rainstorm that had occurred the night before and waves of summer heat shimmered in the distance, distorting the view of the craggy snow-covered mountains.

She pushed her keys into the pocket of her jeans and walked to the paddock where Governor was still separated from the rest of the horses. Eldon, one of the ranch hands, was dutifully walking the bay stallion.

"How's our patient?" Tory asked as she patted Governor on the withers and lifted his hoof. Governor snorted and flattened his ears against his head. "Steady, boy," Tory murmured softly.

"Still sore, I'd guess," the fortyish man said with a frown. His weathered face was knotted in concern.

"I'd say so," Tory agreed. "Has he been favoring it?"

"Some."

"What about his temperature?" Tory asked as she looked at the sensitive tissue within the hoof.

"Up a little."

She looked up and watched Governor's ribs, to determine if his breathing was accelerated, but it wasn't.

"I'll call the vet. Maybe Anna should have a look at it."

"Wouldn't hurt."

She released Governor's hoof and dusted her hands on her jeans. "I'll see if she can come by tomorrow; until then we'll just keep doing what we have been for the past two days."

"You got it."

Tory, with the intention of pouring a large glass of lemonade once she was inside the house, walked across the gravel parking area and then followed a worn path to the back porch. Alex was lying in the shady comfort of a juniper bush. He wagged his tail as she approached and Tory reached down to scratch the collie behind his ears before she opened the door to the kitchen.

"Tory? Is that you?" Keith yelled from the vicinity of the den when the screen door banged shut behind her.

"Who else?" she called back just as she heard his footsteps and Keith entered the homey kitchen from the hall. His young face was troubled and dusty. Sweat dampened his hair, darkening the strands that were plastered to his forehead. "You were expecting someone?" she teased while reaching into the refrigerator for a bag of lemons.

"Of course not. I was just waiting for you to get back."

"That sounds ominous," she said, slicing the lemons and squeezing them on the glass juicer. "I'm making lemonade, you want some?"

Keith seemed distracted. "Yeah. Sure," he replied before his gray eyes darkened. "What took you so long in town?"

Tory looked up sharply. Keith hadn't acted like himself since Trask was back in Oregon. "What is this, an inquisition?"

"Hardly." Keith ran a hand over his forehead, forcing his hair away from his face. "Rex and I were just talking…about what happened last night."

"You mean the calf?" she asked.

"Partially." Keith had taken the wooden salt shaker off the table and was pretending interest in it.

Tory felt her back stiffen slightly as she poured sugar and the lemon juice into a glass pitcher. "And the rest of your discussion with Rex centered on Trask, is that it?"

"Right."

At that moment Rex walked into the room. He fidgeted, removed his hat and worked the brim in his gnarled fingers.

"How about a glass of lemonade?" Tory asked, as much to change the direction of the conversation as to be hospitable.

"Sure," the foreman responded. A nervous smile hovered near the corners of his mouth but quickly faded as he passed a hand over his chin. "I thought you'd like to know that all of the horses and cattle are alive and accounted for."

Relief seeped through Tory's body. So the calf was an isolated incident—so much for Trask's conspiracy theories about vague and disturbing warnings in the form of dead livestock. "Good. What about any other signs of trouble?"

Rex shook his head thoughtfully. "None that I could see. None of the animals escaped through that hole in the fence, and we couldn't find any other places where the fence was cut or tampered with."

Tory was beginning to feel better by the minute. The dark cloud of fear that had begun to settle over her the evening before was slowly beginning to dissipate. "And the fence that was damaged has been repaired?"

"Yep. Right after you brought the deputy out to look at the calf. Did it myself."

"Thanks, Rex."

"All part of the job," he muttered, avoiding her grateful glance.

"Well, then, I guess the fact that the rest of the livestock is okay is good news," Tory said, wincing a little as she remembered the unfortunate heifer. Neither man responded. "Now, I think we should take some precautions to see that this doesn't happen again."

Rex smiled slightly. "I'm open to suggestion."

"Wait a minute, Tory," Keith cut in abruptly as Tory turned back to the pitcher of lemonade and began adding ice water to the cloudy liquid. "Why are you avoiding the subject of McFadden?"

"Maybe I'm just tired of it," Tory said wearily. She had hoped to steer clear of another confrontation about Trask but knew the argument with her brother was inevitable. She poured the pale liquid into three glasses filled with ice and offered a glass to each of the men.

"McFadden's not going to just walk away from this, you know," Keith said.

"I know."

"Then for Pete's sake, Tory, we've got to come up with a plan to fight him."

"A plan?" Tory repeated incredulously. She had to laugh as she took a sip of her drink. "You're beginning to sound paranoid, Keith. A plan! People who make up plans are either suffering from overactive imaginations or are trying to hide something. Which are you?"

"Neither. I'm just trying to avoid another scandal, that's all," Keith responded, his eyes darkening. "And maybe save this ranch in the process. The last scandal nearly destroyed the Lazy W as well as killed Dad, or don't you remember?"

"I remember," Tory said, some of the old bitterness returning.

"Look, Sis," Keith pleaded, his voice softening a little. "I've studied the books and worked out some figures. The way I see it, the Lazy W has about six months to survive. Then the note with the bank is due, right?"

"Right," Tory said on a weary sigh.

"The only way the bank will renew it is if we can prove that we can run this place at a profit. Now you're close, Tory, damned close, but all it takes is for all the old rumors to start flying again. Once people are reminded of what Dad was supposedly involved in, we'll lose buyers as quickly as you can turn around, and there go the profits."

"You don't know that—"

"I sure as hell do."

Tory shifted and avoided Keith's direct stare. She knew what he was going to say before the words were out.

"The only way the Lazy W can stay in business is to sell those Quarter Horses you've been breeding. You know it as well as I do. And no one is going to touch those horses with a ten-foot pole if they think for one minute that the horses might be part of a fraud. The reputation of this ranch is…well, shady or at least it was, all because of the Quarter Horse scam five years ago. If all the publicity is thrown into the public eye again, your potential buyers are going to dry up quicker than Devil's Creek in a hot summer."

"And you think that's what will happen if Trask is allowed to investigate his anonymous letter?"

"You can count on it."

Tory's eyes moved from the stern set of Keith's

jaw to Rex. "You've been awfully quiet. What do you think?"

"I think what I always have," Rex said, rubbing his chin. "McFadden is trouble. Plain and simple."

"There's no doubt about that," Tory thought aloud, "but I don't know what any of us can do about it."

"Maybe you can talk him out of dredging everything up again," Keith suggested. "However, I'd like it better if you had nothing to do with the son of a bitch."

Tory glared at her younger brother. "Let's leave reference to Trask's parentage and any other ridiculous insults out of this, okay? Now, how do you know he'll be back?"

"Oh, he'll be back all right. He's like a bad check; he just comes bouncing back. As sure as the sun comes up in the morning, McFadden will be back."

Tory shook her head and frowned into her glass. She swirled the liquid and stared at the melting ice. "So if he returns to the Lazy W, you want me to try and persuade him to ignore the letter and all this nonsense about another man being involved in the Quarter Horse swindle and Jason's death. Have I got it right?"

"Essentially," Keith said.

"Not exactly an intricate plan."

"But the only one we've got."

Tory set her glass on the counter and her eyes narrowed. "What if the letter is true, Keith? What if another person was involved in Jason's death, a man who could, perhaps, clear Dad's name?"

Keith smiled sadly, suddenly old beyond his years. "What's the chance of that happening?"

"'Bout one in a million, I'd guess," Rex said.

"Less than that," Keith said decisively, "considering that McFadden wouldn't be trying to clear Dad's name. He's the guy who put Dad in the prison in the first place, remember? I just can't believe that you're falling for his line again, Sis."

Tory paled slightly. "I'm not."

"Give me a break. You're softening to McFadden and you've only seen him once."

"Maybe I'm just tired of everyone trying to manipulate me," Tory said hotly. She stalked across the room and settled into one of the chairs near the table. "This whole thing is starting to reek of a conspiracy or at the very least a cover-up!"

"What do you mean?" Keith seemed thoroughly perplexed. Rex avoided Tory's gaze and stared out the window toward the road.

"I mean that I ran into Neva McFadden at the feed store. She wanted to talk to me, for crying out loud! Good Lord, the woman hasn't breathed a word to me since the trial and today she wanted to talk things over. Can you believe it?"

"'Things' being Trask?" Keith guessed.

"Right." Tory smiled grimly at the irony of it all. Neva McFadden was the last person Tory would have expected to beg her to stay away from Trask and his wild theories.

"You know that she's in love with him, don't you?" Keith said and noticed the paling of Tory's tanned skin. Whether his sister denied it or not, Tory was still holding a torch for McFadden. That thought alone made Keith's blood boil.

"She didn't say so."

"I doubt if she would: at least not to you."

"Maybe not," Tory whispered.

"So anyway, what did she want to talk about?"

"About the same thing you're preaching right now. That Trask's anonymous letter was just a prank, that we should leave the past alone, that her son would suffer if the scandal was brought to the public's attention again. She thought it would be wise if I didn't see Trask again."

"Too late for that," Rex said, removing his hat and running his fingers through his sweaty silver hair as he stared through the window. His thick shoulders slumped and his amiable smile fell from his face. "He's coming down the drive right now."

"Great," Keith muttered.

Tory's heart began to pound with dread. "Maybe we should tell him everything we discussed just now."

"That would be suicide, Tory. Our best bet is to convince him that his letter was nothing more than a phony—"

A loud rap on the door announced Trask's arrival. Keith let out a long breath of air. "Okay, Sis, you're on."

Tory's lips twisted cynically. "If you're looking for an Oscar-winning performance, you're going to be disappointed."

"What's that supposed to mean?" Keith asked warily.

"Haven't you ever heard the expression 'You catch more flies with honey than with vinegar'?" Without further explanation, she walked down the short corridor, ignored the round of swearing she heard in the kitchen and opened the front door.

Trask was about to knock again. His fist was lifted to his shoulder and his jaw was set angrily. At the sight of Tory, her gray-green eyes sparkling with a private joke, he was forced to smile and his angular features softened irresistibly. When Senator McFadden decided to turn on the charm, the effect was devastating to Tory's senses, even though she knew she couldn't trust him.

"I thought maybe you were trying to give me a not-so-subtle hint," Trask said.

Tory shook her head and laughed. "Not me, senator. I'm not afraid to speak my mind and tell you you're not welcome."

"I already knew that."

"But you're back." She leaned against the door, not bothering to invite him inside, and studied the male contours of his face. Yes, sir, the senator was definitely a handsome man, she thought. Five years hadn't done him any harm—if anything, the added maturity was a plus to his appearance.

"I hoped that maybe you'd reconsidered your position and thought about what I had to say."

"Oh, I've thought about it a lot," Tory replied. "No one around here will let me forget it."

"And what have you decided?" Cobalt-blue eyes searched her face, as if seeing it for the first time. Tory's heart nearly missed a beat.

"Why don't you come inside and we'll talk about it?" Tory stepped away from the door allowing him to pass. Keith and Rex were already in the den and when Trask walked through the archway, the tension in the room was nearly visible.

"It takes a lot of guts for you to come back here," Keith said. He walked over to the bar and poured himself a stiff drink.

"I said I would," Trask responded. A confident grin contrasted with the fierce intensity of his gaze.

"But I can't believe that you honestly expect Tory or anyone at the Lazy W to help you on…this wild-goose chase of yours."

"I just want to look into it."

"Why?" Keith demanded, replacing the bottle and lifting the full glass to his lips.

Trask crossed his arms over his chest. "I want to know the truth about my brother's death."

Keith shook his head. "So all of a sudden the testimony at the trial wasn't enough. The scandal wasn't enough. Sending an innocent man to jail wasn't enough. You want more."

"Only the truth."

Keith's jaw jutted forward. "It's a little too late, don't ya think, McFadden? You should have been more interested in the truth before taking that witness stand and testifying against Calvin Wilson."

"If your father would have told his side of the story, maybe I wouldn't be here right now."

"Too late for second-guessing, McFadden," Keith said, his voice slightly uneven. "The man's dead."

An uncomfortable silence filled the room. Rex shifted restlessly and pushed his Stetson over his eyes. "I've got to get home," he said. "Belinda will be looking for me." He headed toward the door and paused near the outer hallway. "I'll see ya in the morning."

"Good night, Rex," Tory said just as the sound of the front door slamming shut rattled through the building.

"I think maybe you should leave, too," Keith said, taking a drink of his Scotch and leaning insolently against the rocks of the fireplace. He glared angrily at

Trask and didn't bother to hide his contempt. "We're not interested in hearing what you have to say. You said plenty five years ago."

"I didn't perjure myself, if that's what you're insinuating."

"I'm not insinuating anything, McFadden. I believe in telling it straight out."

"So do I."

"Then you'll understand when I ask you to leave and tell you that we don't want any part of your plans to drag up all the scandal about the horse swindle again. It won't do anyone a bit of good, least of all the people on this ranch. You'll have to find another way to get elected this time, senator."

Trask leaned a hip against the back of a couch and turned his attention away from Keith to Tory. His blue eyes pierced hers. "Is that how you feel?" he demanded.

Tory looked at Trask's ruggedly handsome face and tried to convince herself that Trask had used her, betrayed her, destroyed everything she had ever loved, but she couldn't hide from the honesty in his cold blue stare. He was dangerous. As dangerous as he had ever been, and still Tory's heart raced at the sight of him. She knew her fascination for the man bordered on lunacy. "I agree with Keith," she said at last. "I can't see that opening up this whole can of worms will accomplish anything."

"Except make sure that a guilty party is punished."

"So you're still looking for retribution," she whispered, shaking her head. "It's been five years. Nothing is going to change what happened. Neva's right. Nothing you can do or say will bring Jason back."

"Neva?" Trask repeated. "You've been talking to

her?" His features froze and the intensity of his stare cut Tory to the bone.

"Today, she ran into me on the street."

"And the conversation just happened to turn to me." The corners of his mouth pulled down.

Tory's head snapped upward and her chin angled forward defiantly. "She's worried about you, senator, as well as about her son. She thinks you're on a personal vendetta that will do nothing more than open up all the old wounds again, cause more pain, stir up more trouble."

Trask winced slightly and let out a disgusted sound. "I'm going to follow this through, Tory. I think you can understand. It's my duty to my brother. He was murdered, for God's sake! Murdered! And one of the men responsible might still be free!

"The way I see it, you have two options: you can be with me or against me, but I'd strongly suggest that you think about all of the alternatives. If your father was innocent, as you so self-righteously claim, you've just gotten the opportunity to prove it."

"You would help me?" she asked skeptically.

"Don't believe him, Tory," Keith insisted, walking between Tory and Trask and sending his sister pleading glances. "You trusted him once before and all he did was spit on you."

Trask's eyes narrowed as he focused on Tory's younger brother. "Maybe you'd better just stay out of this one, Keith," he suggested calmly. "This is between your sister and me."

"I don't think—"

"I can handle it," Tory stated, her gaze shifting from Trask to Keith and back again. Her shoulders were squared, her lips pressed together in determination. Fire sparked in her eyes.

Keith understood the unspoken message. Tory would handle Trask in her own way. "All right. I've said everything I needed to say anyway." He pointed a long finger at Trask. "But as far as I'm concerned, McFadden, you have no business here." Keith strode out of the room, grabbed his hat off the wooden peg in the entry hall, jerked open the front door and slammed it shut behind him.

Trask watched Keith leave with more than a little concern. "He's got more of a temper than you did at that age."

"He hates you," Tory said simply.

Trask smiled wryly and pushed his fingers through his hair. "Can't say as I blame him."

"I hate you, too," Tory lied.

"No, no you don't." He saw that she was about to protest and waved off her arguments before they could be voiced. "Oh, you hate what I did all right. And, maybe a few years back, you did hate me, or thought that you did. But now you know better."

"I don't know anything of the kind."

"Sure you do. You know that I haven't come back here to hurt you and you know that I only did what I did five years ago because I couldn't lie on the witness stand. The last thing I wanted to do was send your dad to prison—"

Tory desperately held up a palm. "Stop!" she demanded, unable to listen to his lies any longer. "I—I don't want to hear any more of your excuses or rationalizations—"

"It's easier to hate me, is that it?"

"No—yes! God, yes. I can't have you come in here and confuse me and I don't want to be a part of this… investigation or whatever you want to call it. I don't care about anonymous letters."

"Or dead calves?"

"One has nothing to do with the other," she said firmly, though she had to fight to keep her voice from trembling.

Trask studied his hands before lifting his eyes to meet her angry gaze. "I think you're wrong, Tory. Doesn't it strike you odd that everyone you know wants you to avoid me?"

She shook her head and looked at the ceiling. "Not after the hell you put me through five years ago," she whispered.

"You mean that it hasn't crossed your mind that someone is deliberately trying to keep you out of this investigation for a reason?"

"Such as?"

"Such as hiding the guilty person's identity."

"I can't be involved in this," Tory said, as if to convince herself. She had to get away from Trask and his damned logic. When she was around him, he turned her mind around. She began walking toward the door but stopped dead in her tracks when he spoke.

"Are you afraid of the truth?"

"Of course not!" She turned and faced him.

He pushed himself away from the couch. "Then maybe it's me."

"Don't be ridiculous," she said, but as he advanced upon her, she saw the steadfastness of his gaze. It dropped from her eyes to her mouth and settled on the rising swell of her breasts. "I'm not afraid of you,

Trask. I never have been. Not even after what you did to me."

He stopped when he was near her and his eyes silently accused her of attempting to deceive him. When he reached forward to brush a wayward strand of hair away from her face, his fingertip touched her cheek, but she didn't flinch. "Then maybe you're afraid of yourself."

"That's nonsense."

"I don't think so." His fingers wrapped around her nape and tilted her head upward as he lowered his head and captured her lips with his. His mouth was warm and gentle, his tongue quick to invade her parted lips. Memories of hot summer nights, star-studded skies and bodies glistening with the sheen of perfect afterglow filled her mind. How easily she could slip backward…

The groan from deep in his throat brought her crashing back to a reality as barren as the desert. He didn't love her, had never loved her, but was attempting once again to use her. As common sense overtook her, Tory tried to step backward but the arms surrounding her tightened, forcing her body close.

"Let go of me," she said, her eyes challenging.

"I don't think so. Letting you go was the biggest mistake I've ever made and believe me, I've made my share. I'm not about to make the same mistake twice."

"You may have made a lot of mistakes, Trask, but you didn't have a choice where I was concerned. I swore that I'd never let you hurt me again, and it's a promise to myself that I intend to keep."

The warm hands at the base of her spine refused to release her. Instead they began to slowly massage her, and through the thin fabric of her cotton blouse, she could feel Trask's heat. It seeped through the cloth and warmed her skin, just as it had in the past.

His lips caressed her face, touching the sensitive skin of her eyelids and cheeks.

"I can't let this happen," she whispered, knowing that she was unable to stop herself.

Her skin began to flush and the yearnings she had vowed dead reawakened as his mouth slid down her throat and his hands came around to unbutton her blouse. As the fabric parted Tory could feel his lips touching the hollow of her throat and the swell of her breasts.

"Trask, please…don't," she said, swallowing against the desire running wildly in her blood.

His tongue circled the delicate ring of bones at the base of her throat while his hands opened her blouse and pushed it gently off her shoulders. "I've always loved you, Tory," he said as he watched her white breasts rise and fall with the tempo of her breathing.

Her rosy nipples peeked seductively through the sheer pink lace of her bra and the swelling in his loins made him say things he would have preferred to remain secret. "Love me," he pleaded, lifting his gaze to her green eyes.

"I…I did, Trask," she replied, trying to think rationally. She reached for the blouse that had fallen to the floor, but his hand took hold of her wrist. "I loved you more than any woman should love a man and… and I paid for that love. I will never, never make that mistake again!"

The fingers over her wrist tightened and he jerked her close to his taut body. With his free hand he tilted her face upward so that she was forced to stare into his intense blue eyes. "You can come up with all the reasons and excuses you want, lady, but they're all a pack of lies."

"You should know, senator. You wrote the book on deceit."

His jaw whitened and his lips twisted cynically. "Why don't you look in the mirror, Tory, and see the kind of woman you've become: a woman who's afraid of the truth. You won't face the truth about your father and you won't admit that you still care for me."

"There's a big difference between love and lust."

"Is there?" He cocked a thick brow dubiously and ran his finger down her throat, along her breastbone to the front clasp of her bra. "What we felt for each other five years ago, what would you call that?"

"All those emotions were tangled in a web of lies, Trask. Each one a little bigger than the last. That's how I've come to think of what we shared: yesterday's lies." He released her slowly and didn't protest when she reached for her blouse and slipped it on.

"Then maybe it's time to start searching for the truth."

"By reopening the investigation into your brother's death?"

"Yes. Maybe if we set the past to rest, we could think about the future."

Tory let out a disgusted sound. "No way, senator. You know what they say, 'You can never go back.' Well, I believe it. Don't bother to tease me with vague promises about a future together, because I don't buy it. Not anymore. I've learned my lesson where you're concerned. I'm not as gullible as I used to be, thank

God." She stepped away from him and finished buttoning her blouse.

His lips tightened and he pinched the bridge of his nose with his fingers, as if trying to thwart a potential headache. "Okay, Tory, so you aren't interested in a relationship with me—the least you can do is help me a little. If you really believe your father's name can be cleared, I'm offering you the means to do it."

"How?"

"I want to go up to Devil's Ridge tomorrow."

The request made her heart stop beating. Devil's Ridge was a piece of land not far from the Lazy W. It had once been owned by her father and Calvin had willed the forty acre tract in the foothills of the Cascades to Keith. Devil's Ridge was the parcel of land where the Quarter Horses were switched during the swindle; the piece of land that had proved Calvin Wilson's involvement in the scam.

"Tory, did you hear me?"

"Yes."

"Will you come with me?"

No! I can't face all of the scandal again. "If you promise that no one else will know about it." Tory saw the questions in his eyes and hastened to explain. "I don't want any publicity about this, until you're sure of your facts, senator."

"Fair enough." He studied her face for a minute. "Are you with me on this, Tory?"

"No, but I won't hinder you either," she said, tired of arguing with Trask, Keith, Neva and the whole damned world. "If you want permission to wander around Devil's Ridge, you've got it. And I'll go with you."

"Why?"

"Because I want to keep my eye on you, senator."

"You still don't trust me, do you?" he asked.

"I can't let myself." *It's my way of protecting myself against you.*

A cloud of anguish darkened his eyes but was quickly dispersed. "Then I'll be here around noon tomorrow."

"I'll be waiting."

He had started toward the door, but turned at the bittersweet words. "If only I could believe that," he said before opening the door and disappearing through it.

Tory watched his retreating figure through the glass. The late-afternoon sun was already casting lengthening shadows over the plains of the Lazy W as Trask strode to his pickup and, without looking backward, drove away.

"WHAT BUSINESS IS it of yours?" Trask demanded of his sister-in-law. She was putting the finishing touches on a birthday cake for Nicholas, swirling the white frosting over the cake as if her brother-in-law's tirade was of little, if any, concern. "Why did you confront Tory?"

"It is my business," Neva threw back coolly as she surveyed her artwork and placed the knife in the empty bowl. When she turned to face Trask, her small chin was jutted in determination. "We're talking about the death of *my* husband, for God's sake. And you're the one who brought me into it when you started waving that god-awful note around here yesterday afternoon."

"But why did you try to convince Tory to stay out of it? She could help me."

Neva turned world-weary brown eyes on her brother-in-law. "Because I thought she might be able to get through to you. You don't listen to many people, Trask. Not me. Not your advisors in Washington. No one. I thought maybe there was a chance that Tory might beat some common sense into that thick skull of yours."

"She tried," Trask admitted.

"But failed, I assume."

"This is something I have to do, Neva." Trask placed his large hands on Neva's slim shoulders, as if by touching he could make her understand.

With difficulty, Neva ignored the warmth of Trask's fingers. "And damn the consequences, right? Your integrity come hell or high water." She wrestled free of his grip.

"You're blowing this way out of proportion."

"Me?" she screamed. "What about you? You get one crank letter and you're ready to tear this town apart, dig up five-year-old dirt and start battling a new crusade." She smiled sadly at the tense man before her. "Only this time I'm afraid you'll get hurt, Don Quixote; the windmills might fight back and hurt you as well as your Dulcinea."

"Whom?"

"Dulcinea del Toboso, the country girl whom Don Quixote selects as the lady of his knightly devotion. In this case, Victoria Wilson."

"You read too much," he said.

"Impossible."

Trask laughed despite the seriousness of Neva's stare. "Then you worry too much."

"It comes with the territory of being a mother," she said, picking up a frosting-laden beater and offering it to him. "Someone needs to worry about you."

He declined the beater. "I get by."

She studied the furrows of his brow. "I don't know, Trask. I just don't know."

"Just trust me, Neva."

The smile left her face and all of the emotions she had been battling for five long years tore at her heart. "I'd trust you with my life, Trask. You know that."

"Neva—" He took a step closer to her but she walked past him to the kitchen window. Outside she could watch Nicholas romp with the puppy Trask had given him for his birthday.

"But I can't trust you with Nicholas's life," she whispered, knotting her fingers in the corner of her apron. "I just can't do that and you have no right to ask me." Tears began to gather in her large eyes and she brushed them aside angrily.

Trask let out a heavy sigh. "I'm going up to Devil's Ridge tomorrow."

"Oh, God, no." Neva closed her eyes. "Trask, don't—"

"This is something I have to do," he repeated.

"Then maybe you'd better leave," she said, her voice nearly failing her. Trask was as close to a father to Nicholas as he could be, considering the separation of more than half a continent. If she threw Trask out, Nicholas would never forgive her. "Do what you have to do."

"What I have to do is stay here for Nicholas's birthday party."

Neva smiled through her tears. "You're a bastard, you know, McFadden; but a charming one nonetheless."

"This is all going to work out."

"God, I hope so," she whispered, once again sneak-

ing a glance at her dark-haired son and the fluff of tan
fur with the beguiling black eyes. "Nicholas worships
the ground you walk on, you know."

Trask laughed mirthlessly. "Well, if he does, he's the
only one in town. There's no doubt about it, I wouldn't
win any popularity contests in Sinclair right now."

"Oh, I don't know, you seem to have been able to
worm your way back into Tory's heart."

"I don't think so."

"We'll see, senator," Neva mused. "I think Victoria
Wilson has never gotten you out of her system."

CHAPTER SIX

ANNA HUTTON LIFTED Governor's hoof and examined it carefully. Her expert fingers gently touched the swollen tissues and the bay stallion, glistening with nervous sweat, snorted impatiently. "Steady, there," she murmured to the horse before lifting her eyes to meet Tory's worried gaze. "I'd say your diagnosis was right on the money, Tory," Anna remarked, as she slowly let the horse's foot return to the floor of his stall. "Our boy here has a case of acute laminitis. You know, girl, you should have been a vet." She offered Tory a small grin as she reached for her leather bag and once again lifted Governor's hoof and started cleaning the affected area.

"I guess I got sidetracked," Tory said. "So I'll have to rely on your expertise."

Anna smiled knowingly at her friend before continuing to work with Governor's hoof. The two women had once planned to go to graduate school together, but that was before Tory became involved with Trask McFadden and all of the bad press about Calvin Wilson and the Lazy W had come to light.

Tory's eyes were trained on Anna's hands, but her thoughts were far away, in a time when she had been filled with the anticipation of becoming Trask's wife. How willingly she had given up her career for him...

Glancing up, Anna noticed Tory's clouded expression and tactfully turned the conversation back to the horse as she finished cleaning the affected area. Governor flattened his dark ears to his head and shifted away from the young woman with the short blue-black hair and probing fingers. "You might want to put him in a special shoe, either a bar shoe or a saucer; and keep walking him. Have you applied any hot or cold poultices or put his hoof in ice water?"

"Yes, cold."

"Good, keep doing that," Anna suggested, her eyes narrowing as she studied the stallion. "I want to wait another day and see how he's doing tomorrow, before I consider giving him adrenaline or antihistamines."

"A woman from the old school, huh?"

"You know me, I believe the less drugs the better." She patted the horse on the shoulder. "He's a good-looking stallion, Tory."

"The best," Tory replied, glancing affectionately at the bay. "We're counting on him."

"As a stud?"

"Uh-huh. His first foals were born this spring."

"And you're happy with them?"

Tory nodded and smiled as she held open the stall gate for her friend. "I've always loved working with the horses, especially the foals."

Anna chuckled and shook her head in amazement as the two women walked out of the stallion barn and into the glare of the brilliant morning sun. "So you decided to breed Quarter Horses again, even after what happened with your father. You're a braver woman than I am, Victoria Wilson."

"Or a fool."

"That, I doubt."

"Keith thought raising horses again was a big mistake."

"So what does he know?"

"I'll tell him you said that."

"Go ahead. I think it takes guts to start over after the trial and all the bad publicity…"

"That was all a horrible mistake."

Anna placed her hand on Tory's arm. "I know, but I just thought that you wouldn't want to do anything that might…you know, encourage all the old rumors to start up again. I wouldn't."

"You can't run away from your past."

"Especially when our illustrious Senator McFadden comes charging back to town, stirring it all up again."

Tory felt her back stiffen but she managed a tight smile as they walked slowly across the gravel parking lot. "Everyone has to do what they have to do. Trask seems to think it's his duty to dig it all up again…because of Jason."

One of Anna's dark brows rose slightly. "So now you're defending him?"

"Of course not!" Tory said too quickly and then laughed at her own reaction. "It's just that Trask's been here a couple of times already," she admitted, "and, well, just about everyone I know seems to think that I shouldn't even talk to him."

"Maybe that's because you've led everyone to believe that you never wanted to see him again. After all, he did—"

"Betray me?"

"Whatever you want to call it." Anna hesitated a moment, biting her lips as if contemplating the worth of her words. "Look, Tory. After the trial, you were pretty messed up, bitter. It's no wonder people want to protect you from that kind of hurt again."

"I'm a grown woman."

"And now you've changed your mind about Trask?"

Tory shook her head and deep lines of worry were etched across her brow. "It's just that—"

"You just can't resist the guy."

"Anna!"

"Oh, don't look so shocked, Tory. In my business it's best to say the truth straight out. You know that I always liked Trask, but that was before he nearly destroyed my best friend."

"I wasn't destroyed."

"Close enough. And now, just when it looks like you're back on your feet again, he comes waltzing back to Sinclair, stirring up the proverbial hornet's nest, digging up dead corpses and not giving a damn about who gets hurt, including you and Neva. It tends to make my blood boil a bit."

"So you don't think I should see him."

Anna smiled cynically. She stopped to lean against the fence and gaze at the network of paddocks comprising the central core of the Lazy W. "Unfortunately what I think isn't worth a damn, unless it's about your livestock. I'm not exactly the best person to give advice about relationships, considering the fact that I've been divorced for almost a year myself." She hit the top rail of the fence with new resolve. "Anyway, you didn't ask me here to talk about Trask, and I've got work to do."

"Can't you stay for a cup of coffee?" Anna was one of Tory's closest friends; one of the few people in Sinclair who had stood by Tory and her father during Calvin's trial.

Anna squinted at the sun and cocked her wrist to check her watch. "I wish I could, but I'm late as it is." She started walking to her van before turning and facing Tory. Concern darkened her brown eyes. "What's this I hear about a calf being shot out here?"

"So that's going around town, too."

Anna nodded and shrugged. "Face it, girl. Right now, with McFadden back in town, you're big news in Sinclair."

"Great," Tory replied sarcastically.

"So, what happened with the calf?"

"I wish I knew. One of Len Ross's hands saw the hole in the fence and discovered the calf. We don't know why it was shot or who did it."

"Kids, maybe?"

Tory lifted her shoulders. "Maybe," she said without conviction. "I called the sheriff and a deputy came out. He was going to see if any of the other ranchers had a similar problem."

"I hope not," Anna said, her dark eyes hardening. "I don't have much use for people who go around destroying animals."

"Neither do I."

Anna shook off her worried thoughts and climbed into the van. The window was rolled down and she cast Tory one last smile. "You take care of yourself, okay?"

"I will."

"I'll be back tomorrow to see how old Governor's doing."

"And maybe then you'll have time for a cup of coffee."

"And serious conversation," Anna said with mock gravity. "Plan on it."

"I will!"

With a final wave to Tory, Anna put the van in gear and drove out of the parking lot toward the main road.

AN HOUR LATER Tory sat in the center of the porch swing, slowly rocking on the worn slats, letting the warm summer breeze push her hair away from her face and bracing herself for the next few hours in which she would be alone with a man she alternately hated and loved.

Trask arrived promptly at noon. Fortunately, neither Keith nor Rex were at the house when Trask's Blazer ground to a halt near the front porch. Though Tory felt a slight twinge of conscience about sneaking around behind her brother's back, she didn't let it bother her. The only way to prove her father's innocence, as well as to satisfy Trask, was to go along with him. And Keith would never agree to work with Trask rather than against him.

What Tory hadn't expected or prepared herself for was the way her pulse jumped at the sight of Trask as he climbed out of the Blazer. No amount of mental chastising seemed to have had any effect on the feeling of anticipation racing through her blood when she watched him hop lithely to the ground and walk briskly in her direction. His strides were long and determined and his corduroy pants stretched over the muscles of his thighs and buttocks as he approached. A simple shirt with sleeves rolled over tanned forearms and a Stetson pushed back on his head completed his attire. *Nothing to write home about,* she thought, but when she gazed into his intense blue eyes she felt trapped and her heart refused to slow its uneven tempo.

"I thought maybe you would have changed your mind," Trask said. He mounted the steps and leaned against the rail of the porch, his long legs stretched out before him.

"Not me, senator. My word is as good as gold," she replied, but a defensive note had entered her voice; she heard it herself, as did Trask. His thick brows lifted a bit.

"Is it? Good as gold that is?" He smiled slightly at the sight of her. Her skin was tanned and a slight dusting of freckles bridged her nose. The reckless auburn curls had been restrained in a ponytail, and she was dressed as if ready for a long ride.

"Always has been." She rose from the swing and her intelligent eyes searched his face. "If you're ready—" She motioned to the Blazer.

"No time like the present, I suppose." Without further comment, he walked with her to his vehicle, opened the door of the Blazer and helped her climb inside.

"What happened to Neva's pickup?" Tory asked just as Trask put the Blazer in gear.

"I only used it yesterday because this was in the shop."

"And Neva let you borrow her truck?"

"Let's say I persuaded her. She wasn't too keen on the idea."

"I'll bet not." She tapped her fingers on the dash and a tense silence settled between them.

The road to Devil's Ridge was little more than twin ruts of red soil separated by dry blades of grass that scraped against the underside of the Blazer. Several times Trask's vehicle lurched as a wheel hit a pothole or large rock hidden by the sagebrush that was slowly encroaching along the road.

"I don't know what you hope to accomplish by coming up here," Tory finally said, breaking the smothering silence as she looked through the dusty windshield. She was forced to squint against the noonday glare of the sun that pierced through the tall long-needled ponderosa pines.

"It's a start. That's all." Trask frowned and downshifted as they approached a sharp turn in the road.

"What do you think you'll find?" Tory prodded.

"I don't know."

"But you're looking for something."

"I won't know what it is until I find it."

"There's no reason to be cryptic, y'know," she pointed out, disturbed by his lack of communication.

"I wasn't trying to be."

Tory pursed her lips and folded her arms across her chest as she looked at him. "You just think that you're going to find some five-year-old clue that will prove your theories."

"I hope so."

"It won't happen, senator. The insurance investigators and the police sifted through this place for weeks. And that was right after the indictments…" Her voice drifted off as she thought about those hellish days and nights after her father had been arrested. All the old feelings of love and hate, anger and betrayal began to haunt her anew. Though it was warm within the interior of the Blazer, Tory shivered.

"It doesn't hurt to look around," Trask insisted. He stepped on the throttle and urged the truck up the last half mile to the crest of the hill.

"So this is where it all started," Tory whispered, her eyes moving over the wooded land. She hadn't set step on Devil's Ridge since the scandal. Parched dry grass, dusty rocks and sagebrush covered the ground beneath the pine trees. The land appeared arid, dryer than it should have for late June.

"Or where it all ended, depending upon your point of view," Trask muttered. He parked the truck near a small group of dilapidated buildings, and pulled the key from the ignition. The Blazer rumbled quietly before dying. "If Jason hadn't come up here that night five years ago, he might not have been killed." The words were softly spoken but they cut through Tory's heart as easily as if they had been thin razors.

She had been reaching for the handle of the door but stopped. Her hand was poised over the handle and she couldn't hold back a weary sigh. "I'm sorry about your brother, Trask. You know that. And though I don't believe for a minute that Dad was responsible for your brother's death, I want to apologize for anything my father might have done that might have endangered Jason's life."

Trask's eyes softened. "I know, love," he said, before clearing his throat and looking away from her as if embarrassed at how easily an endearment was coaxed from his throat. "Come on, let's look around."

Tory stepped out of the Blazer and looked past the few graying buildings with broken windows and rotting timbers. Her gaze wandered past the small group of paddocks that had been used to hold the purebred Quarter Horses as well as their not-so-blue-blooded counterparts. Five years before, this small parcel of land had been the center of a horse swindle and insur-

ance scam so large and intricate that it had become a
statewide scandal. Now it was nothing more than a
neglected, rather rocky, useless few acres of pine and
sagebrush with a remarkable view. In the distance to
the east, barely discernible to the naked eye were the
outbuildings and main house of the Lazy W. From her
viewpoint on the ridge, Tory could make out the gray
house, the barn, toolshed and stables. Closer to the
mountains she saw the spring-fed lake on the north-
western corner of the Lazy W. The green and gold
grassland near the lake was dotted with grazing cattle.

"Hard to believe, isn't it?" Trask said.

Tory jerked her head around and found that he was
staring at her. The vibrant intensity of his gaze made
her heartbeat quicken. "What?"

"This." He gestured to the buildings and paddocks
of the ridge with one hand before pushing his hat off his
head and wiping an accumulation of sweat off his brow.

"It gives me the creeps," she admitted, hugging her
arms around her breasts and frowning.

"Too many ghosts live here?"

"Something like that."

Trask smiled irreverently. His brown hair ruffled
in the wind. "I'll let you in on a secret," he said with a
mysterious glint in his eyes.

"Oh?"

"This place gives me the creeps, too."

Tory laughed in spite of herself. If nothing else,
Trask still knew how to charm her out of her fears.
"You'd better be careful, senator," she teased. "Admit-
ting something like that could ruin your public image."

Trask's smile widened into an affable slightly off-center grin that softened the square angle of his jaw. "I've

done a lot of things that could ruin my public image." His gaze slid suggestively down her throat to the swell of her breasts. "And I imagine that I'll do a few more."

Oh, Trask, if only I could trust you, she thought as she caught the seductive glint in his eyes and her pulse continued to throb traitorously. She forced her eyes away from him and back to the ranch.

"I wish we could just forget all this, you know," she said, still staring at the cattle moving around the clear blue lake.

"Maybe we can."

"How?"

"If it turns out to be a prank."

"And how will you know?" she asked, turning to face him again.

He shook his head. "I've just got to play it by ear, Tory; try my best and then…"

"And then, what? If you don't find anything here today, which you won't, what will you do? Go to the sheriff?"

"Maybe."

"But?"

"Maybe I'll wait and see what happens."

That sounded encouraging, but she felt a small stab of disappointment touch her heart. "In Washington?"

"Probably."

She didn't reply. Though she knew he was studying her reaction, she tried to hide her feelings. That she wanted him to stay in Sinclair was more than foolish, it was downright stupid, she thought angrily. The man had sent her father to jail, for God's sake. And now that Calvin was dead, Trask was back looking for another innocent victim. As she walked toward the largest of the buildings Tory told herself over and over again that she hated Trask McFadden; that she had only accompanied him up here to get rid of him once and for all, and that she would never think of him again once he had returned to Washington, D.C. Unfortunately, she knew that all of her excuses were lies to herself. She still loved Trask as passionately and as blindly as she had on the bleak night he had left her to chase down, confront and condemn her father.

"It would help me if I knew what I was looking for," she said.

"Anything that you think looks out of place. We can start over here," he suggested, pointing to the largest of the three buildings. "This was used as the stables." Digging his boots into the dry ground, her pushed with his shoulder against the door and it creaked open on rusty hinges.

Tory walked inside the musty structure. Cobwebs hung from the exposed rafters and everything was covered with a thick layer of dust. Shovels, rakes, an ax and pick were pushed into one corner on the dirt floor. Other tools and extra fence posts leaned against the walls. The two windows were covered with dust and the dried carcasses of dead insects, letting only feeble light into the building. Tory's skin prickled with dread. Something about the abandoned barn didn't feel right and she had the uneasy sensation that she was trespassing. Maybe Trask was right; all the ghosts of the past seemed to reside on the hilly slopes of the ridge.

Trask walked over to the corner between the two windows and lifted an old bridle off the wall. The leather reins were stiff in his fingers and the bit had rusted. For the first time since receiving the anonymous letter he considered ignoring it. The brittle leather in his hands seemed to make it clear that all he was doing was bringing back to life a scandal that should remain dead and buried.

He saw the accusations in Tory's wide eyes. God, he hadn't been able to make conversation with her at all; they'd both been too tense and at each other's throats. Confronting the sins of the past had been harder than he'd imagined; but that was probably because of the woman involved. He couldn't seem to get Victoria Wilson out of his system, no matter how hard he tried, and though he'd told himself she was trouble, even an adversary, he kept coming back for more.

In the past five years Trask's need of her hadn't diminished, if anything it had become more passionate and persistent than before. Silently calling himself the worst kind of fool, he looked away from Tory's face and continued his inspection of the barn.

Once his inspection of the stable area had been accomplished, he surveyed a small shed, which, he surmised, must have been used for feed and supplies. Nothing.

The last building was little more than a lean-to of two small, dirty rooms. One room had served as observation post; from the single window there was a view of the road and the Lazy W far below. The other slightly larger room was for general use. An old army cot was still folded in the corner. Newspapers, now yellowed, littered the floor, the pipe for the wood stove had broken near the roof line and the few scraps of paper that were still in the building were old wrappers from processed food.

Tory watched as Trask went over the floor of the

cabin inch by inch. She looked in every nook and cranny and found nothing of interest. Finally, tired and feeling as if the entire afternoon had been a total waste of time, she walked outside to the small porch near the single door of the shanty.

Leaning against one of the rough cedar posts, she stared down the hills, through the pines to the buildings of the Lazy W. Her home. Trask had single-handedly destroyed it once before—was she up here helping do the very same thing all over again? *History has a way of repeating itself,* she thought to herself and smiled cynically at her own stupidity for still caring about a man who would as soon use her as love her.

Trask's boots scraped against the floorboards and he came out to the porch. She didn't turn around but knew that he was standing directly behind her. The warmth of his breath fanned her hair. For one breathless instant she thought that his strong arms might encircle her waist.

"So what did you find, senator?" she asked, breaking the tense silence.

"Nothing," he replied.

The "I told you so" she wanted to flaunt in his face died within her. When she turned to face him, Tory noticed that Trask suddenly looked older than his thirty-six years. The brackets near the corners of his mouth had become deep grooves.

"Go ahead, say it," he said, as if reading her mind.

She let out a disgusted breath of air. "I think we're both too old for those kinds of games, don't you?"

He leaned against the building and crossed his arms over his chest. "So the little girl has grown up."

"I wasn't a little girl," she protested. "I was twenty-two…"

"Going on fifteen."

"That's not nice, senator."

"Face it, Tory," he said softly. "You'd been to college, sure, and you'd worked on the ranch, but in a lot of ways—" he touched her lightly on the nape of her neck with one long familiar finger, her skin quivered beneath his touch "—you were an innocent."

She angled her head up defiantly. "Just because I hadn't known a lot of men," she began to argue.

"That wasn't it, and you know it," Trask said, his fingers stopping the teasing motion near her collar. "I was talking about the way you looked up to your father, the fact that you couldn't make a decision without him, your dependency on him."

"I respected my father, if that's what you mean."

"It went much further than that."

"Of course it did. I loved him." She took one step backward and folded her arms over her chest. "Maybe you don't understand that emotion very well, but I do. Simple no-holds-barred love."

"It went beyond simple love. You worshiped him, Tory; put the man on such a high pedestal that he was bound to fall; and when you discovered that he was human, that he did make mistakes, you couldn't face it. You still can't." His blue eyes delved into hers, forcing her to return their intense stare.

"I don't want to hear any of this, Trask. Not now."

"Not ever. You just can't face the truth, can you?"

A quiet anger had begun to invade her mind. It started to throb and pound behind her eyes. "I faced the truth a long time ago, senator," she said bitterly. "Only the man that I worshiped, the one that I placed on the pedestal and who eventually fell wasn't my father."

Trask's jaw tightened and his eyes darkened to a smoldering blue. "I did what I had to do, Tory."

"And damn the consequences?"

"And damn the truth."

There was a moment of tense silence while Tory glared at him. Even now, despite her anger, she was attracted to him. "I think we'd better go," she said. "I'm tired of arguing with you and getting nowhere. I promised to bring you up here so you could snoop around and I've kept my end of the bargain."

"That you have," he said, rubbing his hands together to shake off some of the dust. "Okay, so we found nothing in the buildings—I'd like to walk around the corral and along the road."

"I don't see why—"

"Humor me," he insisted. "Since we've already wasted most of the afternoon, I'd like to make sure that I don't miss anything." He saw the argument forming in her mind. "This way we won't have to come back."

And I won't have to make excuses to Keith or Rex, Tory thought. "All right, senator," she agreed. "You lead, I'll follow."

They spent the next few hours walking the perimeter of the land, studying the soil, the trails through the woods, the fence lines where it was still intact. Nothing seemed out of the ordinary to Tory and if Trask found anything of interest, he kept it to himself.

"I guess Neva was right," Trask said with a grimace.

"About what?"

"A lot of things, I suppose. But she thought coming up here would turn out to be nothing more than a wild-goose chase."

"So now you're willing to concede that your anonymous letter was nothing more than a prank?"

Trask pushed his hat back on his head and squinted thoughtfully up at the mountains. "I don't know. Maybe. But I can't imagine why."

"So you're not going to give it up," Tory guessed. "The diligent hard-working earnest Senator McFadden won't give up."

"Enough already," Trask said, chuckling at the sarcasm in Tory's voice. "Why don't we forget about the past for a while, what d'ya say?"

"Hard to do, considering the surroundings."

"Come on," Trask said, his anger having melted at the prospect of spending time alone with Tory now that what he had set out to do was accomplished. "I've got a picnic hamper that Neva packed; she'll kill me if we don't eat it."

"Neva put together the basket?" Tory asked, remembering Keith's comment to the effect that Neva was in love with Trask.

"Grudgingly," he admitted.

"I'll bet."

"Nicholas and I teamed up on her though."

"And she couldn't resist the charms of the McFadden men."

Trask laughed deep in his throat. "Something like that."

"This is probably a big mistake."

"But you'll indulge me?"

"Sure," she said easily. "Why not?" *A million reasons why not,* and she ignored all of them. The sun had just set behind the mountains and dusk had begun to shadow the foothills. An evening breeze carrying the heady scent of pine rustled through the trees.

After taking the cooler and a worn plaid blanket out of the back of the Blazer, Trask walked away from the buildings to a clearing in the trees near the edge of the ridge. From there, he and Tory were able to look down on the fields of the ranch. Cattle dotted the landscape and the lake had darkened to the mysterious purple hue of the sky.

"Bird's-eye view," she remarked, taking a seat near the edge of the blanket and helping Trask remove items from the cooler and arrange them on the blanket.

Trask sat next to her, leaning his back against a tree and stretching his legs in front of him. "Why did your father buy this piece of land?" he asked, while handing Tory a plate.

Tory shrugged. "I don't know. I think he intended to build a cabin for Mother…" Her voice caught when she thought of her parents and the love they had shared. As much to avoid Trask's probing stare as anything, she began putting food onto her plate. "But that was a long time ago, when they were both young, before Mom was sick."

"And he could never force himself to sell it?"

"No, I suppose not. He and Mom had planned to retire here, where they still could see the ranch and be involved a little when Keith took over."

"Keith? What about you?"

She smiled sadly and pretended interest in her meal. "Oh, you know, senator. I was supposed to get married and have a dozen wonderful grandchildren for them to spoil…" Tory heard the desperation in her voice and cleared her throat before boldly meeting his gaze. "Well, things don't always turn out the way you plan, do they?"

Trask's jaw tightened and his eyes saddened a little. "No, I guess not. Not always."

Trask was silent as he leaned against the tree and ate the meal that Neva had prepared. The homebaked bread, fried chicken, fresh melon salad and peach pie were a credit to any woman and Trask wondered why it was that he couldn't leave Tory alone and take the love that Neva so willingly offered him. Maybe it was because she had been his brother's wife, or, more honestly, maybe it was because no other woman affected him the way Tory Wilson could with one subtle glance. To distract himself from his uncomfortable thoughts, he reached into the cooler.

"Damn!"

"What?"

Trask frowned as he pulled out a thermos of iced tea. "I told Neva to pack a bottle of wine."

Tory looked at the platters of food. "Maybe next time you should pack your own lunch. It looks like she did more than her share, especially considering how she feels about what you're doing." After taking the thermos from his hands, she poured them each a glass of tea.

Trask didn't seem consoled and ignored his drink.

"We don't need the wine," Tory pointed out. "Maybe Neva knew that it would be best if we kept our wits about us."

"Maybe." Trask eyed Tory speculatively, his gaze centering on the disturbing pout of her lips. "She thinks I've given you enough grief as it is."

"You have."

Trask took off his hat and studied the brim. "You're not about to let down a bit, are you?"

"What do you mean?"

"Just that you're going to keep the old barriers up, all the time."

"You're the one intent on digging up the past; I'm just trying to keep it in perspective."

"And have you?"

Tory's muscles went tense. She took a swallow of her tea before answering. "I'm trying, Trask. I'm trying damned hard. Everyone I know thinks I'm crazy to go along with your plans, and I'm inclined to believe them. But I thought that if you came up here, poked around, did your duty, so to speak, that you'd drop it and the fires of gossip in Sinclair would die before another scandal engulfed us. I knew that you wouldn't just let go of the idea that another person was involved in your brother's death, and I also realized that if I fought you, it would just drag everything out much longer and fuel the gossip fires."

He set his food aside and wrapped his arms around his knees while studying the intriguing angles of Tory's face. "And that's the only reason you came up here with me?"

"No."

He lifted his thick brows, encouraging her to continue.

After setting her now empty plate on the top of the basket, she leaned back on her arms and stared at the countryside far below the ridge. "If by the slim chance you did find something, some clue to what had happened, I thought it might prove Dad's innocence."

"Oh, Tory…" He leaned toward her and touched her cheek. "I know you don't believe this, but if there were a way to show that Calvin had no part in the Quarter Horse swindle, or Jason's death, don't you think I'd be the first to do it?"

He sounded sincere and his deep blue eyes seemed to look through hers to search for her soul. God, but she wanted to believe him and trust in him again. He had been everything to her and the hand on her cheek was warm and encouraging. It conjured vivid images from a long-ago love. She had trouble finding her voice. The wind rustled restlessly through the branches overhead and Tory couldn't seem to concentrate on anything but the feel of Trask's fingers against her skin. "I…I don't know." She finished the cold tea and set her glass on the ground.

"My intention wasn't to crucify your father, only to tell my side of the story, in order that Jason's murderers were found out and brought to justice. If Calvin wasn't guilty, he should have stood up for himself—"

"But he didn't; and your testimony sent him to prison." She swallowed back the hot lump forming in her throat.

"Would it help you to know that I never, never meant to hurt you?" he asked, lowering his head and tenderly brushing his lips over hers.

"Trask—" The protest forming in her throat was cut off when his arms wrapped around her and he drew her close, the length of his body pressed urgently to hers.

"I've missed you, Tory," he admitted, his voice rough with emotions he would rather have denied.

"And I've missed you."

"But you still can't forgive me?"

She shook her head and for a moment she thought he would release her. He hesitated and stared into her pain-filled eyes. "Oh, hell," he muttered, once again pulling her close to him and claiming her lips with his.

His hands were warm against her back and through the fabric of her blouse she felt the heat of his fingers against her skin. Her legs were entwined with his and his hips pressed urgently to hers, pinning her to the ground as one of his hands moved slowly upward and removed the leather throng restraining her hair.

"God, you're beautiful," he whispered against her ear as he twined his fingers in her hair, watching the auburn-tinged curls frame her face in wild disarray. Slumberous green eyes rimmed with dark curling lashes stared up at him longingly. "I want you, Tory," he said, his breathing ragged, his heart thudding in his chest and the heat in his loins destroying rational thought. "I've wanted you for a long time."

"I don't know that wanting is enough, Trask," she whispered, thinking about the agonizing hours she had spent in the past five years wanting a man she couldn't have; wishing for a father who was already dead; desiring the life she had once had before fate had so cruelly ripped it from her.

"Just let me love you, Tory."

The words had barely been said when she felt Trask stiffen. He turned to look over his shoulder just as a shot from a rifle cracked through the still mountain air.

Tory's blood ran cold with fear and a scream died in her throat. Trask flattened himself over her body, protectively covering her as the shot ricocheted through the trees and echoed down the hillside. *Dear God, what was happening? The sound was so close!*

With the speed and agility of an athlete, Trask scrambled to his feet while jerking her arm and pulling her to relative safety behind a large boulder.

Tory's heart was hammering erratically as adrenaline pumped through her veins. She pushed her hair out of her eyes and discovered that her hands were shaking. "Oh, God," she whispered in desperate prayer.

"Are you okay?" His eyes scanned her face and body.

Her voice failed her but she managed to nod her head.

"You're sure?"

"Yes!"

"Who knows we're here?" Trask demanded, his hushed voice harsh, his eyes darting through the trees.

"No one—I didn't tell anyone," she replied.

"Well someone sure as hell knows we were here!"

"But—"

"Shh!" He clamped his hand over her mouth and raised a finger to his lips as he strained to hear any noise that might indicate the whereabouts of the assailant. Far down the hillside, the sound of hurried footsteps crackled through the brush. Tory's skin prickled with fear and her eyes widened until she realized that the footsteps were retreating, the sound of snapping branches becoming more distant.

Trask moved away from the protection of the boulder as if intent on tracking the assailant.

"Trask! No!" Tory screamed, clutching at his arm. "Leave it alone."

He tried to shake her off and turned to face her. "Someone's taking shots at us and I'm going to find out who."

"No wait! He has a rifle, you…you can't go. You don't have any way of protecting yourself!"

"Tory!"

"Damn it, Trask, I'm scared!" she admitted, holding his gaze as well as his arm. Her lower lip trembled and she had to fight the tears forming in her eyes. "You can't die, too," she whispered. "I won't let you!" He stood frozen to the spot. "I love you, Trask," Tory admitted. "Please, please, don't get yourself killed. It's not worth it. Nothing is!" Tory felt near hysteria as she clutched at his arm.

Trask stood stock still, Tory's words restraining him. "You love me?" he repeated.

"Yes!" Her voice broke. "Oh, God, yes."

"But you've been denying—"

"I know, I know. It's just that I don't want to love you."

"Because of the past."

"Yes."

"Then we have to find out the truth," he decided.

"It's not worth getting killed."

Trask's eyes followed the sound of the retreating footsteps and the skin whitened over his cheekbones as he squinted into the encroaching night. His one chance at finding the accomplice in Jason's murder had just slipped through his fingers. When silence once again settled on the ridge, he turned his furious gaze on Tory. His grip on her shoulders, once gentle, was now fierce.

"Who did you tell that we were here?" he demanded.

"No one!"

"But your brother and that foreman, Rex Engels, they knew we would be here this afternoon."

Tory shook her head and her green eyes blazed

indignantly. She jerked away from his fingers and scooted backward on the ground. "I didn't tell anyone, Trask. Not even Keith or Rex; they...neither one of them would have approved. As far as I know the only person who knew we were coming here today was Neva!"

The corners of Trask's mouth tightened and he glared murderously at Tory. "Someone set us up."

"And you think it was me?"

"Of course not. But it sure as hell wasn't Neva!"

"Why not? She didn't want you coming up here, did she? She doesn't want you to look into Jason's death, does she? Why wouldn't she do something to sabotage you?"

He walked away a few steps and rubbed the back of his neck. "That just doesn't make any sense."

"Well nothing else does either. The anonymous note, the dead calf and now this—" She raised her hands over her head. "Nothing is making any sense, Trask. Ever since you came back to the Lazy W, there's been nothing but trouble!"

"That's exactly the point, isn't it?" he said quietly, his mouth compressing into an angry line. "Someone's trying to scare you; warn you to stay away from me."

"If that's his intention, whoever he is, he's succeeded! I'm scared right out of my mind," she admitted while letting her head fall into her palm.

"What about the rest, Tory? That shot a few minutes ago was a warning to you to stay away from me!" He looked over his shoulder one last time.

"If that's what it was—"

"That's exactly what it was," he interjected. "Let's

go, before someone decides to take another potshot at us."

"You think that's what they were trying to do?"

"I'm certain of it."

"But maybe someone saw a rattlesnake, or was hunting."

"It's not deer season."

"Maybe rabbits—" She saw the look of disbelief on his face. "Or maybe the guy was a poacher...or someone out for target practice."

"It's nearly dark, Tory. I don't know about you, but I don't like being the bull's-eye."

From the look on Trask's rugged features, Tory could tell that he didn't believe her excuses any more than she did. He walked over to her and placed his hands upon her shoulders, drawing her close, holding her as he started walking back to the Blazer. "I'd like to believe all those pitiful reasons, too," he admitted.

"But you can't."

"Nope." He opened the door of the Blazer for her, helped her inside and climbed into the driver's seat. "No, Tory," he said, his voice cold. "Someone's trying to keep us apart, by scaring us with dead cattle and rifle shots."

"And that means there must be some truth to the letter," she finished for him.

"Exactly." He smiled a little remembering Tory's confession of love, started the Blazer, circled around the parking lot and started driving down the rutted lane back to the Lazy W.

CHAPTER SEVEN

"SO WHERE IS everyone?" Trask asked as he parked the truck near the barn.

"I don't know," Tory admitted uneasily. She got out of the Blazer and started walking toward the back of the dark house. The only illumination came from a pale moon and the security lamps surrounding the buildings of the ranch.

Trask was on Tory's heels, his footsteps quickening so that he could catch up with her. "What about your brother, where is he?"

If only I knew. "He and Rex were working on the broken combine this afternoon," she thought aloud, trying to understand why the ranch was deserted. "They probably went into town for a part, got held up and decided to stay for dinner..."

"Or he was up on the ridge with a rifle?" Trask suggested.

Tory turned quickly and couldn't disguise the flush of anger on her cheeks. "Don't start in about Keith, okay? He would never do anything that might jeopardize my life."

"You're sure about that?"

"As sure as I am about anything." Tory turned toward the house, dashed up the steps to the porch and unlocked the back door. She had trouble keeping her fingers steady as she worked with the lock. What was it Keith had said just yesterday? His words came back to her in chilling clarity.

"I would have met McFadden with a rifle in my hands...the next time McFadden trespasses, I'll be ready for him."

Tory's stomach knotted with dread and disgust. Trask had her thoughts so twisted that now she was doubting her own brother; the boy she had helped rear since their mother's death. Ignoring the hideous doubts crowding her mind, she flipped on the light and walked into the kitchen.

"What about the foreman?"

"Rex?"

"Yeah."

Tory almost laughed at the absurdity of Trask's insinuation. "You've got to be kidding! I've known Rex since I was a little girl—he'd do anything for the ranch. It's been his life. Dad hired him when Rex was down and out, when no other rancher in this state would touch him. Besides, neither Rex nor Keith knew where I was this afternoon."

Trask leaned against the cupboards, supporting his weight with his hands while Tory made a pot of coffee. Deep furrows etched his brow. "Why wouldn't anyone hire Rex?"

"You want to see all of the skeletons in the closet, don't you?"

"Only if it helps me understand what's going on."

"Well, forget it. Rex was in trouble once, when he was younger—before I was born. Dad hired him."

"What kind of trouble?" Trask persisted.

Tory frowned as she tried to remember. "I don't really know. Dad never talked about it. But once, when I was about eleven and I was supposed to be studying, I overheard Dad talking to Rex. It was something to do with Rex's past. It had to do with his ex-wife, I can't remember her name, it was something like Marlene or…Marianne, maybe. Something like that. Anyway, there was some sort of trouble between them, talk of him drinking and becoming abusive. She left Rex and no one would hire him."

"Except your dad."

"Right. And Rex has been with the Lazy W ever since."

"Without any trouble."

"Right."

Trask bit at his lower lip pensively. "I thought he was married."

"He is. He married Belinda about seven years ago."

"So he's above suspicion."

"Of course he is. He was the one who showed us the dead calf in the first place, remember?" She tapped her fingers on the counter impatiently. "Look, I don't like the thoughts that are going through your head. You're more than willing to start pointing fingers at anyone associated with the ranch, but no one here knew where we were going."

"We could have been followed," he said, rubbing the back of his neck and watching her movements.

She was about to pull some mugs down from the shelf, but hesitated and her slim shoulders slumped. "God, you're as bad as Keith," she muttered.

"What's that supposed to mean?"

"Just that the both of you have overactive, extremely fertile imaginations when it comes to each other. If you'd just sit down and try to straighten all of this out like adults instead of going for each other's throat, we'd all be a lot better off."

"I agree."

Trask grabbed a chair from the table, placed it on the floor and straddled it. He folded his arms over the back of the chair and rested his chin on his arms as he studied Tory.

"You agree?" she repeated incredulously.

"Of course. It just makes sense that if we all work together we can accomplish much more in a shorter space of time."

"And then you could finish this business and fly back to Washington," she thought aloud. Suddenly the future seemed incredibly bleak.

"Don't you want me to go?" he asked.

Swallowing a lump in her throat, she pushed her burnished hair from her face. "It doesn't really matter what I want," she whispered. "You've got an important job in Washington, people depend on you. There was a time when I would have begged you to stay…"

"And now?"

She winced, but decided to put her cards on the table. As the coffee finished perking and filled the room with its warm scent, she leaned one hip against the counter and stared into his deep blue eyes. "And now I think we're all better off if you go back to the capital, senator. I fell in love with you once and I won't let it happen again. Ever."

"What about what you said on the ridge?" he asked softly.

"I was scared; nothing more. I didn't want you to do anything foolish!"

"Tory—" He stood, but she cut off his next words.

"I don't want to hear it, Trask. Here—" She quickly poured them each a cup of coffee and tried to think of a way, any way, to change the course of the conversation. "Take your coffee and we'll drink it in the den."

"You can't ignore or deny what's happening between us."

"What's happening is that I'm trying to help you figure out if that note you received is a phony. That's all." She turned away from him and walked down the hall, hoping that her hands and voice would remain steady.

Once in the den she snapped on two lamps and walked over to the window. *Where was Keith?* She needed him now. Being alone with Trask was more than foolhardy, it was downright dangerous and seductive. She stood in front of the window and sipped her coffee as she looked across the parking lot to the shadowy barns.

Trask entered the room. She heard rather than saw him and felt the weight of his stare. His eyes never left her as he crossed the room and propped one booted foot on the hearth. "What are you afraid of, Tory?"

"I already told you, I'm not afraid...just confused. Everything in my life seems upside-down right now."

"Because of me?"

She let out a long sigh. "Yes."

"It will be over soon," he said. "Then your life will be back to normal—if that's what you want."

My life will never be the same again, Trask. "Good. I...I just want all this...nonsense to be over." She took a long sip of her coffee and set the empty mug on the windowsill. Her fingers had stopped shaking. "It's late. I think maybe you should leave."

"Maybe," he agreed, cocking a dark brow. "But I think it's time we settled some things between us." He reached over and snapped off the lamp on an end table. With only the light from the small brass lamp on the desk, the corners of the room became shadowed, more intimate.

Bracing herself, she turned and faced him. "Such as?"

He leaned back against the rocks of the fireplace and all of his muscles seemed to slacken. Defeat darkened his eyes. "Such as the fact that I've never gotten over you—"

"I told you, I don't want to hear this," she said, walking away from the window and shaking her head. "The past is over and done—it can't be changed or repeated. What happened between us is over. *You* took care of that."

"I love you, Tory," he said slowly, his voice low.

Tory stopped dead in her tracks. How long had she waited, ached, to hear just those words? "You don't understand the first thing about love, Trask. You never have."

"And you're always quick to misjudge me."

"You can't expect me to trust you, Trask, not after what happened to my father. It was all because of you."

Trask's face hardened and a muscle in the back of his jaw tightened. "Calvin is dead; I can't change that." He pushed away from the fireplace and crossed the room to stand before her. "Don't you think I wish he were alive? Don't you realize how many times I've punished myself, knowing that he died in prison, primarily because of my testimony?" His troubled eyes searched her face and he reached forward to grip her shoulders.

"Damn it, woman, I'd have given my right arm to hear his side of the story—only the man wouldn't tell it. It was as if he'd taken this vow of silence as some sort of penance for his crimes!" Trask's voice was low and threatening. "I've been through hell and back because of that trial!"

The grip on her arms was punishing, the conviction on Trask's face enough to cut her to the bone. "God, Trask, I wish I could believe you," she admitted, her voice trembling.

"But you can't."

"You betrayed me!"

He gave her a shake. Her hair fell over her eyes. "I told the truth on the witness stand. Nothing less. Nothing more." His voice was rising with his anger. "And your father didn't do a damned thing to save himself! Don't you think I've lain awake at night wondering what really happened on the night Jason was killed?" His face contorted with his rage and agony.

"I...I don't know..."

"Damn it, Tory! Believe it or not, I'm human. If you cut me, I bleed." He released her arms and let out a disgusted breath of air. Blue eyes seared through hers. "And, lady, you've cut me to ribbons..."

She let her face fall into her hands. Her entire body was shaking and the tears she would rather have forced back filled her eyes to spill through her fingers. "God, I wanted to trust you, Trask. I...I spent more than my share of sleepless nights wondering why did you use me? Why did you tell me you loved me? Why was I such a fool to believe all your lies...all your goddamned lies!" She began to sob and she felt the warmth of his arms surround her. "Let go of me," she pleaded.

"Never again." With one hand he snapped off the light on the desk. The room was suddenly shrouded in darkness. Only the pale light from a half-moon spilled through the windows. "Oh, love, I never used you. Never—"

"No…Trask…" His lips touched her hair, and his arms held her close. The heat of his body seemed to reach through her flesh and melt the ice in her heart. "I…I just loved you too much."

"Impossible."

"I know it's stupid," she conceded, letting the barriers that had held them apart slowly fall, "but I want to trust you again. God, I've wanted to be able to talk to you for so long; you don't know how many times I just wished that you were here, that I could talk to you."

"You should have called."

"I couldn't! Don't you see? You were my whole world once and you destroyed everything I'd ever loved. My father, my career, this ranch, and our love— everything."

"All because I told the truth."

"Your perception of the truth!"

"Tory, listen to me, you have to understand one thing: throughout it all I always loved you. I still do."

She felt the cold hatred within her begin to thaw and her knees went weak as she leaned against him, felt the strength of his arms, the comfort of his kiss. How many times had she dreamed and fantasized about being in Trask's arms again? "You love me Trask," she sniffed, slowly pulling out of his embrace and drying her eyes with her fingers, "when it's convenient for you. It was convenient for you five years ago when you were trying to help your brother with the horse swindle and it's convenient now, when you need my help." She stepped back and held his gaze. "I won't be used again, you know. Not by you."

"I wouldn't." His blue eyes were honest; the jut of his jaw firm with conviction. It was impossible not to believe him.

Tory cleared her throat. "Then what about Neva?"

"What about her?"

"Are you staying with her?" she asked, knowing the question was none of her business, but unable to help herself.

Trask's skin tightened over his cheekbones and his muscles tensed, but he didn't look away. "I did the first night. Since then, I've opened up the cabin on the Metolius River. It wasn't ready when I got into Sinclair," he began to explain and then let out an angry oath. "Hell, Tory, does it matter?" he demanded.

Her eyes turned cold. "Not really, I guess. I just like to know what or whom I'm up against. With you and that damned anonymous letter of yours, sometimes it's hard to tell."

"I'm not having an affair with my brother's widow, if that's what you want to know."

"It's none of my business."

"Like hell! Haven't you listened to a word I've said?" When she didn't respond, he curled a fist and slammed it into the wall near the desk, rattling a picture of an Indian war party. "Hell, woman, I'd be a liar to say that I've spent that past five years celibate, but I'm not involved with anyone right now except for you!" Once again his fingers captured her, winding comfortably behind her neck.

"We're not involved!"

With her indignation, his anger dissipated into the intimate corners of the room. Trask's smile was lazy and confident. "That's where you're wrong. We've been involved since the first time I laid eyes on you. Where was it? Rafting on the Deschutes River!"

"That was a long time ago," she murmured, recalling the wild ride down the white water. Though she had gone with another man, Trask's eyes hadn't left her throughout the day. Even then she'd seen the spark of seduction in his incredible blue gaze. Sitting on the raft, his tanned skin tight over lean corded muscles, his wet hair shining brown-gold in the summer sun, he didn't bother to hide his interest in her. And she fell. Lord, she fell harder than any sane person had a right to fall. She had met him later that night and within two weeks they'd become lovers. The irony of it all was that she had thought she would spend the rest of her life with him. *Only it didn't work out that way.*

"Let's not talk about the past."

He let go of her, holding her only with his eyes. "We have to sort this out."

"What's the point? Nothing will come of it." She felt the urge to back away but stood her ground. "I'll admit that I loved you once, but it's over. It's been over for a long time."

"Liar." He reached for her, drawing her body close to his. When his lips touched hers, and she tasted him, her resistance fled. Familiar yearnings awoke within the most feminine part of her, causing a bittersweet ache that only he could salve. Instead of pushing him away, she was leaning closer to him, her body reacting to the sensual feel of his hands on her skin, her blood pulsing with need as it rushed through her veins. "You want me," he whispered against her ear.

"No..."

"Let me love you."

Desire was heating her blood, thundering in her head, and the touch of his lips on her face and neck only made the throbbing need within her more painful. "I don't think—" she tried to say, but his lips cut off the rest of her objection.

She felt the warm invasion of his tongue and returned his kiss without restraint. When his lips moved downward to touch her neck and then slid still lower, she could do nothing but wait in anticipation. His tongue rimmed the hollow of her throat and she was forced to swallow against the want of him.

Suddenly, Trask released her, and Tory wanted to cry out against the bereft feeling she was left with. She watched as he strode to the den door and locked it, then moved toward her quickly banishing the cold feeling.

Warm hands outlined her ribs before reaching upward to mold a swollen breast. She felt her nipple tighten against the feel of his fingers and she let out a low moan of desire.

Slowly he removed her blouse, slipping each button through its hole and letting the fabric part to display her rounded breasts, swollen and bound only by the sheer white lace of her bra. His fingers teased the hardened nipple, and Tory leaned closer to him, the ache within her spreading throughout her body.

A primal groan escaped from his lips as he lowered himself to his knees and licked first one rose-tipped breast before suckling the other. The lace of the bra became moist and Trask's warm breath fanned the sheer fabric to send sharp electric currents through Tory's body. She closed her eyes and was blind to everything but the hunger for him. Her fingers twined in his hair.

The warmth of his hands pressed against the small of her back, bringing her closer to him, pressing more of her breast into his mouth. He groaned with the savage urgency of his lust, sucking hungrily from the white mound.

Scorching feelings of desire once awakened in Tory were impossible to smother. With each touch of his hand, Tory lost ground to the urges of her flesh. With each stroke of his tongue, the ache within her throbbed more painfully. With the heated pressure of his body against hers, she felt the urge to arch against him, demanding more of his sensual touch.

Five years she had waited for the feel of him, denying her most secret dreams and now the pain of those long empty nights alone was about to be rewarded. The scent of him was strong in her nostrils and the sound of his breathing filled her ears.

Her fingers curled in his hair as he removed her bra and took her naked breast in his mouth. She cradled his head to her body, holding on to him for dear life, knowing that her love for this man would never be returned and not caring about the consequences. This night, for a few short hours, he was hers—alone.

She moaned his name when his fingers sought the front opening of her jeans and touched the sensitive skin of her abdomen.

"Trask, please," she whispered hoarsely as his tongue traced the delicate swirl of her navel and he pulled her jeans and underwear off her body. Slowly she was pressed to the floor by the weight of his body.

The braided carpet felt coarse against her bare skin, but she didn't care.

She helped him remove his clothes and her fingers caressed the fluid muscles of his shoulders and chest. His body tensed beneath the tantalizing warmth of her touch.

Sweat dotted his brow; his restraint was obvious in the coil of his muscles. When Tory reached for the waistband of his pants, his abdominal muscles tightened. With all of the willpower he could muster, he stopped her by taking hold of her wrist and forced her chin upward with his other hand. His eyes searched hers. "I love you, Tory," he said, his voice rough. "I always have. But I want you to be sure about this… stop me now, if you have to, while it's still possible."

Closing her eyes against the flood of tears that threatened to spill, she tried to speak, to tell him how much she wanted him. Her lips quivered, but all the words she thought she should say wouldn't come.

Trask kissed her softly and wound his fingers in the thick auburn strands of her tousled hair. "If only I could make you happy," he murmured before capturing her lips in his and shifting his weight so that his body covered hers in a protective embrace.

As his flesh touched hers, his body heated until it glistened in a film of sweat. Her arms wound around his back and she clung to him as he became one with her, moving gently at first and then more quickly as her body responded to the familiarity of his touch. His hands massaged her breasts in the rhythm of his lovemaking.

"Oh, God," he whispered against her ear as the heat within her seemed to burst and he, too, surrendered.

"Tory," he called, his voice raspy. "Just love me again." And then he fell against her, his weight a welcome burden.

The tears that had been welling beneath her lids began to stream down her cheeks. "Shh," he whispered, "everything will be okay."

Slowly Trask rolled to his side and held her close to him. He kissed her and tasted the salt of her tears. For several minutes, they clung to each other in silence and Tory, her head pressed against his chest, listened to the steady beating of Trask's heart. Surrounded by his strength, she was lost in her feelings of love and despair for this man.

"Regrets?" he asked, once his breathing had slowed. Tenderly he brushed a tear from the corner of her eye.

"No…"

"But?"

Her voice trembled slightly. "I'm not sure that getting involved again is the smartest thing to do. But then I've made a lot of questionable decisions lately."

He propped himself on one elbow and stared down at her. His face was shadowed but even in the darkness Tory could see the seductive slash of his smile.

"Why not…get involved, that is?"

"I only agreed to see you because of the letter…and, well, having an affair with you now will only complicate things."

His grin slowly faded, and his hands caressed her bare shoulders. "I think you'd better say what you mean and quit beating around the bush."

Tory gathered her courage. The next words were difficult, but necessary. She couldn't continue to live in a crystal dreamworld that could shatter so easily. "All right, senator. What I'm trying to say is that I'm not comfortable with short-term affairs. You and I both know that when all of this…note business is cleared up, you'll be returning to Washington."

"You don't like dead-end relationships?"

"Exactly."

"You could come to Washington with me," he suggested. His arms tightened around her, holding her close to the contours of his body.

Tory almost laughed. She reached for her jeans. "And what would you do if I took you up on your offer?" she said. "I'm no more ready for the Washington social scene than you are to explain a mistress from Oregon."

"I was talking about a wife, not a mistress."

Tory's heart missed a beat and pain darkened her eyes. "Oh, Trask. Don't—"

"I asked you to marry me five years ago—remember?"

"That was before the trial."

"Forget the trial!" He jerked her roughly to him and she was forced to gaze into the intensity of his eyes.

"How can I? You're here, looking for another conspirator in your brother's death, for crying out loud!" She jerked on her jeans and reached for her blouse as all of the old bitterness returned to her heart. "And don't think that just because we made love you have to dangle a wedding ring in front of my nose. I fell for that trick once before—"

Trask's patience snapped. He took hold of her upper arms and refused to let go. "You're so damned self-righteous. I don't know how to make it any clearer to you that I love you. Asking you to marry me isn't a smoke screen for some dark ulterior motive. It's a proposal, plain and simple. I want you to be my wife and I was hoping that you could rise above the past and come to terms with your feelings as a mature adult woman!"

"I can."

He let go of her arms. "And?"

The lump in her throat swelled uncomfortably. "I love you even though I've been denying it, even to myself," she whispered. "I love you very much, but... but I'm not sure that I *like* you sometimes. As for marriage—we're a long way from making a decision like that."

Trask's back teeth ground together. "Have you been seeing someone else?"

Tory let out a disgusted sigh. "No. Not seriously."

"I heard that you were going to be married a couple of years back to some schoolteacher."

Tory smiled sadly with her confession. "It didn't work out." She turned away from him and began dressing. He watched as she slid her arms through the sleeves of her blouse.

"Why?"

Wasn't it obvious? "Because of you. As crazy as it sounds, senator, you're a hard act to follow." She smiled sadly at her own admission. How many times had she tried to deny, even to herself, that she still loved him?

"That's some consolation," he said, relief evident on his face. He had pulled on his cords, and pushed his arms through his shirt, but it was still gaping open, displaying in erotic detail, the muscles of his chest and abdomen. "I want you to consider my proposal."

"I think it's five years too late."

One dark brow quirked. "Better late than never, isn't that what they say?"

"'They' aren't always right."

Trask smiled cynically as he helped her to her feet. "Marry me, Tory. I need you."

"Not now, don't ask—"

"We put it off too long once before."

"I can't make a decision like this; not now, anyway. We've got too many things hanging over our heads. I...I need time, and so do you."

"You think that I'm caught up in the moment."

Her head snapped up. "I wouldn't be surprised."

"What would it take to convince you?"

"Time—enough time to put all of what happened behind us."

"Five years isn't enough?"

Tory smiled sadly. "Not when one party is interested in dredging it all up again."

He leaned forward, pushing his forehead against hers and locking his hands behind her shoulders. "I love you and I'm worried about you."

"I'm fine," she tried to assure him.

"Yeah, I can tell." He patted her gently on the buttocks. "So who would want to fill that gorgeous skin of yours full of buckshot?" he asked.

"No one was shooting at me."

His face became stern. "Whoever shot the calf wasn't playing around."

"I'm okay," she insisted but he didn't seem convinced. *"Really."*

"I think you should come and stay with me at the cabin. You'd be safer."

"I can't."

He rubbed his chin in frustration. "Look, Tory, I dragged you into this mess and now it seems to be getting dangerous. I feel responsible."

"You don't have to. I can look after myself."

"If another person was involved in the Quarter Horse swindle, he's also involved in murder, Tory. Jason's murder. There's no telling to what lengths he might go to protect himself. The dead calf and the potshot taken at us today are serious."

"Don't try to scare me; I'm already scared."

"Then?"

"I told you, I can handle it."

Impatiently Trask raked his fingers through his hair. "I want to keep an eye on you, but I have to go to Salem, to the penitentiary, tomorrow."

"To talk to George Henderson?"

"And Linn Benton."

Tory felt her throat constrict at the mention of her father's two "partners" in the horse swindle. "Do you think that's smart?"

Trask's eyes narrowed and in the darkness Tory could see the hardening of his jaw. "If someone else was involved, they'd know about it."

"And what makes you so sure they'd talk to you?"

"I already set up the meeting through the warden. Henderson and Benton are both up for parole in the next couple of years—your dad took most of the blame, you know. While he was handed down thirty years, they plea bargained for shorter sentences."

"It was never fair," she whispered.

"Because Calvin didn't even try to defend himself!" When she blanched he touched her lovingly on the chin. "Look, knowing the likes of Benton and Henderson, they won't want to stir up any trouble that might foul up their chances for parole."

"And you intend to throw your weight around, now that you're a senator and all."

"That's about the size of it."

"Isn't that unethical?"

"But effective."

She couldn't argue with his logic, though she didn't like the idea of involving Henderson and Benton. A small feeling of dread skittered down her spine. "When will you be back?"

"Tomorrow night. I'll come by here and let you know what happened."

"Good."

"Are you sure you won't come with me to the cabin?" he asked, pushing a wisp of hair out of her eyes. "It might be safer." Once again his eyes had darkened seductively.

"That depends upon what you call safe, senator," she said teasingly, trying to push aside her fears. "Besides, the Lazy W is home. I feel safer on this ranch than I do anywhere in the world. I've managed to make it by myself for five years. I think I'll be okay for the next twenty-four hours." She winked conspiratorially at him and he couldn't resist kissing her provocative pout.

Trask realized that there was no point in arguing further with Tory. Short of bodily carrying her to the Blazer and taking her hostage, there was no way of getting her to leave the ranch. "Just remember that I love you and that I expect you to take care of yourself."

She couldn't hide the catch in her voice. "I will."

He reached for his hat and forced it onto his head before kissing her once more and striding out of the house. Tory watched him from the window and smiled when she saw him tuck his shirttails into his cords. Then he climbed into the Blazer and roared down the lane.

"It's too easy to love you," she whispered as she mounted the stairs and headed to her bed…alone.

TRASK DROVE LIKE a madman. His fingers were clenched around the steering wheel of the Blazer and the stream of oaths that came from his mouth were aimed at his own stupidity.

He skidded to a stop at the main intersection in town and slammed his fist into the steering wheel. He was furious with himself. Inadvertently, because of his own damned impatience, he had placed Tory in danger.

"Damn it all to hell," he muttered, stripping the gears of the Blazer as he pushed the throttle and maneuvered through town. He drove without conscious thought to Neva's house. After parking the Blazer in the driveway, Trask strode to the front door and let himself in with his own key.

"Trask?" Neva called anxiously from her room. She tossed on her robe and hurried into the hallway. Trask was standing in the living room, looking as if he'd like to break someone's neck. "What are you doing here at this time of night?"

"I need to use your phone. There isn't one at the cabin."

"Go ahead." She pushed the blond hair away from her face and stared at the disheveled state of Trask's clothes and the stern set of his jaw. "You nearly scared me to death, you know."

"Sorry," he said without regret and paced between the living room and hallway. "I should have called."

"It's okay." She sighed and looked upward to the loft where her son was sleeping. "At least you didn't wake Nicholas...yet." She folded her arms over her chest and studied Trask's worried expression. "Are you going to tell me what's wrong or do I have to guess?"

"I'm really not sure."

"Don't tell me, Tory didn't go along with your plan."

"That wasn't it, no thanks to you." He frowned. In the past he'd been able to confide everything to Neva, but now things had changed; he sensed it. "Look, let me use the phone in the den and then we can talk."

"Okay. How about a cup of coffee?"

"How about a beer?"

Neva's brows shot upward. "That bad?"

"I don't know, Neva." He shook his head and the lines of worry near the corners of his eyes were more evident than they had been. "I just don't know." He walked through the kitchen to the small office where his brother had once planned to expose the biggest horse swindle in the Pacific Northwest.

Trask closed the door to the den and stared at the memorabilia that Neva had never managed to put away. A picture of Jason holding a newborn Nicholas was propped up on the desk. Jason's favorite softball glove and a ball autographed by Pete Rose sat on a bookcase next to all of the paperback thrillers Jason had intended, but never had time, to read. A plaque on the wall complemented the trophies in the bookcase; mementos of a life cut off much too early.

The desk chair groaned as Trask sat down, picked up the phone and punched out the number of the sheriff's department. After two rings the call was answered and Trask was told that Paul Barnett wasn't in the office, but would return in the morning.

"Great," Trask muttered. Rather than leave his name with the dispatcher, Trask hung up and drummed his fingers on the desk as he considered his alternatives. *You've been a fool*, he thought as he leaned back in the chair and put his fingers together tent style. *How could you have been so stupid?*

It was one thing to come back to Sinclair and start a quiet investigation; quite another to come back and flaunt the reasons for his return. Although he hadn't told anyone other than Neva and Tory about the anonymous letter, he hadn't hidden the fact that he was back in Sinclair for the express purpose of seeing Tory again. By now, half the town knew his intentions. The guilty persons could certainly put two and two together.

And so Tory was in danger, because of him. Trask took off his hat and threw it onto the worn leather couch. His mouth felt dry for the need of a drink.

The trouble was, Trask wasn't cut out for this cloak-and-dagger business. Never had been. Even the back-scratching and closed-door deals in Washington rubbed him the wrong way. As a junior senator, he'd already ruffled more than his share of congressional feathers.

With a grimace he pulled a copy of the anonymous letter out of his wallet and laid it on the desk while he dialed Paul Barnett's home number and waited. It took several rings, but a groggy-voiced Barnett finally answered.

The conversation was short and one-sided as Trask explained why he was in Sinclair and what had happened.

"I'll need to see the original note," Barnett said, once Trask had finished his story. All the sleep was out of the sheriff's voice. "I already sent one of my men out to check out the dead calf. As far as we can tell, it was an isolated incident."

"A warning," Trask corrected.

"Possibly."

"The same as the rifle shot this evening."

"I'll check into it, do what I can."

"Good. Tory's not going to like the fact that I called you. She wanted to keep things under wraps until we'd found what we were looking for."

"That's foolish of course, but I can't say as I blame her, considering what happened to her pa and the reputation of that ranch."

"What happened to Calvin and the ranch aren't important. Right now she needs protection. Whether she knows it or not," he added grimly.

"I don't have the manpower to have someone cover the Lazy W day and night, you know."

"I'll take care of that end. John Davis, a private investigator in Bend, owes me a favor—a big one."

"And you've called him?"

"I will."

"Good. And the note?"

"I'll bring it over within the hour."

"I'll be waiting."

Just as Trask hung up the phone, Neva knocked quietly on the door and entered the den. She offered Trask a mug filled with coffee. "We were out of beer," she lied.

Trask grinned at the obvious deception. "I don't need a mother, you know."

Neva leaned against the doorjamb and eyed him sadly. "Sometimes I wonder."

"I do all right."

"I read the papers, Trask. What do they call you? 'The young rogue senator from Oregon'?"

"Sometimes." He took a sip from the cup and let the warm liquid salve his nerves. "When are you going to take all this stuff—" he motioned to Jason's softball trophies and plaques "—down and put it away?"

"Maybe never."

Trask frowned and shook his head. "You're a young beautiful woman, Neva—"

"With a six-year-old son who needs to know about his father."

"Maybe he needs a new one."

Neva looked shocked. "He's a McFadden, Trask. Your brother's son. You want some stranger to raise him?"

"He'll always be a McFadden; but he could use some male influence."

"He has you," she said softly.

"I live in Washington."

"Until you don't get reelected."

Trask nearly choked on his coffee. "That's what I like to hear: confidence." Trask's eyes darted around the room and his smile faded. "You can't live in the past, Neva."

"I was going to say exactly the same thing to you."

Trask caught her meaningful glance and frowned into his cup before finishing his coffee in one swallow and setting the empty mug on the desk. "I've got to go."

"You could stay," she suggested, her cheeks coloring slightly. "Nicholas would be thrilled."

Trask shook his head, stood up, grabbed his hat and kissed Neva on the forehead. "Can't do it. I've got things to do tonight."

"And tomorrow?"

"I'll be in Salem."

Neva paled and sank into the nearest chair. Her fingers nervously gripped her cup. "I knew it," she said with a sigh. "You're going to see Linn Benton and George Henderson in the pen, aren't you?"

"Yes."

"Oh, Trask, why?" Doe-soft eyes beseeched him.

"It's important." He saw the tears of frustration fill her large eyes and he felt the urge to comfort her. "Look, Neva—"

She sniffed the tears aside and met his gaze. "It's all right, Trask. I'll manage. And when Nicholas wonders why all of his friends are pointing fingers at him and whispering behind his back, I'll tell him." Using the sleeve of her robe to dry her cheeks, she forced a frail smile. "Do what you have to do, senator. Don't worry about how it affects a six-year-old boy who worships the ground you walk on."

"You're not making this easy—"

"Damn it, Trask, I'm not trying to! I'd do anything I could to talk you out of this…madness."

Trask's eyes became incredibly cold. "How far would you go to protect your child?"

"As far as I had to."

"Regardless?"

"Nicholas's health, safety and well-being are my first concerns."

"And what about your health and safety?"

Neva smiled cynically. "I can't wait until you have a child, Trask. Then I'll ask you the same question."

"I just think you should put yourself first occasionally."

"Pearls of wisdom, senator. I'll think about them."

Trask paused at the door. "By the way, thanks for the picnic lunch today."

"You're welcome, I guess. Did you bring the cooler in?"

A picture of the empty cooler, scattered dishes and rumpled blanket filled his mind. In the urgency of the moment after the rifle shot had pierced the air, he had forgotten to retrieve anything. "No, uh, Tory wanted to clean it. I'll pick it up tomorrow and bring it back."

A spark of interest flickered in Neva's dark eyes. "So the picnic went well?"

For a reason he didn't understand, Trask lied to his sister-in-law for the first time in his life. No need to worry her, he thought, but he knew there was more to his evasive answer than he would acknowledge. "It was fine."

"And what did you find on Devil's Ridge?"

"Absolutely nothing." *Except a potential assassin.*

"But you're still going to Salem tomorrow," she said with a sigh. "You just can't let it drop, can you?"

"Not this time."

"Well go on." She waved him off with a limp hand. "You've got things to do, remember? Just be careful. Linn Benton, whether he's in prison or not, is still very powerful. He may have been stripped of his judicial robes, but he's still a wealthy and influential man with more than his share of friends, all of whom haven't forgotten that your testimony was instrumental in sending him to prison."

"Good night, Neva," Trask said, without waiting for a reply. There was none. He walked out the front door.

As he stepped off the porch and headed for the Blazer, he heard a noise and turned. Before he could see his assailant, Trask felt the thud of a heavy object strike the back of his head. Blinding lights flashed behind his eyes just as a knee caught him in the stomach and he fell forward onto the dry ground. Before he lost consciousness he heard a male voice that was vaguely familiar.

"Leave it alone, McFadden," it warned gruffly. Trask tried to stand, but was rewarded with another sharp kick in the abdomen. "You're out of your league, senator."

CHAPTER EIGHT

THE FIRST THING Trask remembered were hands, incredibly soft hands, holding his head. A woman's voice, filled with anguish and fear, was calling to him from a distance and there was pain, a pain so intense it felt as if it was splintering his head into a thousand fragments.

"Trask... Oh, dear God..." the woman cried out, nearly screaming with terror as she looked down on him. Moonlight caught in her silver hair, but the features of her face were blurred and indistinct. *"Trask!"*

His mouth felt cotton-dry and when he tried to speak the voice that he heard didn't sound like his own. "Neva?" He reached forward and his fingers touched her hair before his hand dropped to the ground. A blinding stab of pain shot through his brain when he tried to lift his head.

"Oh, God, Trask...are you all right?" Her fingers were exploring the lump on the back of his head and tears gathered in her large eyes. "I was afraid something like this might happen, but I just couldn't believe..."

He opened his eyes and tried to focus. It was dark, but the woman's face was definitely that of his sister-in-law. Propping himself on one elbow, he tried to push his body upright to stand, but the jarring pain in his ribs and abdomen made him suck in his breath and remain on the hard ground.

"What happened?" Neva demanded, looking at the beaten man with pitying eyes.

As if she could have prevented what happened, Trask thought dizzily and then discarded his annoying thought. Neva's head moved quickly from side to side, her eyes darting from one shadowed tree to another as if she half expected to discover the man who had attacked him lurking in the still night.

"Someone jumped me—" Trask began to explain.

"I knew it!" Her attention swung back to the injured man. "I knew that something like this would happen!" She let out a breath of despair and her shoulders slumped in resignation. As if finding an answer to an inner struggle, Neva clenched her fist in determination. "I'm going to call the police and then I'll get an ambulance for you."

"Hold on a minute," Trask ground out, again leveling himself up on one elbow. Sweat had broken out on his forehead and chest and several buttons were missing from his shirt. "I don't need an ambulance or the police…"

"You've been beaten, for God's sake!" she shrieked.

"Neva, get hold of yourself," he insisted as his groggy mind began to clear. *Tory! If anything had happened to her…*

With one hand he reached forward and held on to Neva's arm. "I've got to get into the house—to a phone," he stated. Disjointed but brutally clear images of Tory and what might have happened to her began to haunt him.

"You need a doctor."

"You're a nurse. Can't you just fix me up?"

She eyed him severely. "No. You need X-rays. And an examination by a doctor. You might have a concussion, maybe cracked ribs and God only knows what else." Gingerly she touched the deep cut along his jaw where his chin had crashed into the ground.

"I'll be fine," Trask said angrily, mentally cursing himself for not being more careful with Tory's safety. "Just help me up and get me into the house. Whoever did this to me may have gone after Tory."

"Tory?" Neva repeated, freezing.

"I don't have time to talk, damn it!" A dozen hideous scenarios with Tory as the unwitting victim filled his mind.

"Yes, sir," Neva snapped back at him, offering her body as support as he rose unsteadily. With her arm around his torso to brace him, Neva forced Trask to lean on her as they walked up the steps to the front door. "Before you do anything else, I expect you to tell me exactly what happened."

"Later."

Once inside the house, she examined his head and offered him an ice pack. "Lucky for you you've got a thick skull," she murmured tenderly. "Now, what else?"

He motioned to his side. She took off his shirt and frowned at the purple bruise already discoloring his ribs. "Someone doesn't like you poking around," she decided.

"No one likes me poking around," he said with what was an attempt at a smile. "Not even you."

"Maybe you should take this warning seriously," she suggested.

"Can't do it, Neva."

"Oh, Trask, why not?"

"I'll explain once I make a few calls—"

"Mom?" Nicholas was standing on the landing of the stairs to the loft. His blue eyes rounded at the disheveled and battered sight of Trask sprawled over the couch in the living room.

"Nick, I thought you were asleep." Neva's eyes flickered with fear before darting from Trask to her son and back again. Her gaze silently implored Trask to keep the truth from Nicholas.

The young boy ignored his mother and his eyes clouded with worry. "What happened, Uncle Trask?"

"Would you believe a barroom brawl?" Trask asked, forcing a painful grin.

"Naw." Nicholas stuck out his lower lip pensively and looked at his mother. "Is that really what happened?"

Neva shrugged.

"Sort of," Trask intervened, sensing Neva's discomfiture. "We good guys always have to be on the lookout, you know."

Nicholas came down the last few steps. The boy's eyes were round with excitement and hero worship for his uncle. "Mom? Did Uncle Trask get into a fight?"

"I don't really know," Neva said nervously.

"So where's the other guy?"

"He took off," Trask said, attempting levity. "He'd had enough I guess."

"Because you beat him?" Nicholas sat on the edge of the couch.

Trask had to laugh and the pain in his ribs seared through his body. "Unfortunately the other guy got the better of me."

Nicholas frowned petulantly while stepping closer to the couch and surveying his uncle. "But the good guys are always supposed to win."

"Only on television," Trask replied, ruffling the boy's coarse hair. "Or if they get help from their friends." Trask's eyes moved from Nicholas to Neva. She paled slightly and tried to avoid his gaze.

"Come on, Nick. You can have a piece of pie and a glass of milk. Then you've got to go back to bed. Uncle Trask has to make some phone calls." She placed the telephone on the coffee table and carefully stepped over the cord. "Here, take these," she said to Trask, offering him aspirin and a glass of water.

"Thanks."

"But I want to stay up." Nicholas turned pleading eyes on his uncle.

"You'd better do what your mom says," Trask suggested.

"But it's not fair!"

"Nothing ever is," Neva replied softly, thinking of Jason's early death and the men who were responsible for his murder as she guided Nicholas into the kitchen and waited while he ate his pie.

When Nicholas had finished eating, over his loud protests, Neva put him back into bed. She watched the boy until his breathing became regular and he fell asleep with one arm tossed around the neck of the puppy Trask had given him for his birthday. Her throat tightened at the sight of her tousle-headed son sleeping so blissfully unaware of any of the suffering or malice in the world. How desperately she wanted to protect him.

As Nicholas started to snore, Neva could hear Trask

talking on the phone in the living room though most of the one-sided conversation was muffled.

"Damn!" Trask muttered as he slammed the receiver of the telephone back into the cradle. He had tried calling Tory twice, but no one at the Lazy W had bothered to answer the phone. Fortunately his other calls had gotten through. He ran his fingers through his hair and swung his feet over the edge of the couch.

"This has gone on long enough," Neva said tightly as she came down the stairs and took a seat in her favorite rocker. "The next time someone attacks you, it might be your life, senator…or maybe someone else's." Her voice cracked and her hands worked nervously in her lap. "I think you should call the sheriff. Let Paul Barnett do his job and wash your hands of this accomplice to the conspiracy theory right now."

"I already have," he said slowly as he watched her. For the first time since he had returned to Sinclair, Trask had an inkling of Neva's true fears and he finally understood her odd behavior.

With a groan, he stood. Neva started. "You should be lying down—in the guest room."

Trask walked over to her and, placing both hands on either arm of the wooden rocker, he imprisoned her in the chair. "Why don't you tell me what's really going on, Neva, what you're really afraid of?" he suggested, his voice cold. "Come on, level with me." His blue eyes pierced into hers.

"I'm afraid for you," she whispered.

"Not good enough."

"And for Nicholas." She rubbed her chin nervously and tried to avoid his stare. It was impossible as his face was only inches from hers.

"That's better."

Tears started to pool in her eyes. "The kids at school—"

"Are not what you're afraid of, are they? Someone's been threatening you and Nicholas."

"No…oh, God, no," she cried, desperation and fear contorting her face.

He placed one hand over hers. "Neva?"

There was silence, tense unbearable silence. Only the sound of the clock ticking over the mantel disturbed the quiet.

"Look, it's obvious that someone got to you and used Nicholas's safety as part of a threat. I just want a name, Neva."

"I don't know…"

Trask's fist coiled over her fingers. "Just one name!"

"Oh, Trask," she whispered, closing her eyes and slumping in the chair. "There is no name…." Her voice was shaking and she let her head drop into her hands. "Oh, God, Trask, I'm so scared," she whispered. He placed his arms around her and she tried in vain to stem the flow of her tears. Instead she began to sob against his shoulder. "I've been getting these calls— horrible calls—"

"From whom?"

"I don't know. Some man. He threatened me. Told me that if I didn't convince you to forget about the horse swapping swindle that…that…he'd take Nicholas from me…hurt him." She was shaking violently. "I was afraid to tell anyone."

White-hot rage raced through Trask's blood and all of his muscles tensed. "You should have told me," he ground out, pushing away from the chair.

"Probably," she admitted. "For the first time in my life I didn't know what to do. And the man insisted that I wasn't to tell you anything, or—" her anguished eyes searched Trask's bruised face "—or one of us would be hurt. And now look at you…look what he did…."

"Nothing's going to happen to Nicholas," Trask swore.

"How can you be sure—look what happened to you!"

Trask's eyes sparked blue fire. "I'll see to it that you're safe. Not only are we going to call Paul Barnett and tell him what's going on, I've got a friend, a private investigator, who'll put a twenty-four hour watch on you and Nicholas." He checked his watch. "Paul's probably already on his way to the Lazy W." Quickly he punched out the number of the sheriff's department and got hold of Deputy Woodward, who promised to come directly to Neva's house.

"I don't need to be watched," Neva stated, gathering her courage as Trask hung up and immediately re-dialed the phone.

"Don't argue with me, Neva," Trask nearly shouted just as the groggy voice of John Davis answered the phone. Again, Trask told his story and John promised to send a detective to Neva's home as well as have someone survey the comings and goings at the Lazy W.

"What are you planning?" Neva asked, once Trask had hung up the phone and was slipping his arms through his shirt.

"A deputy from the sheriff's department, a man by the name of Greg Woodward is coming over here tonight."

"No."

"Just listen to me, damn it. Woodward is going to take your statement and wait until one of John Davis's men arrives. Then he's going to meet me and Sheriff Barnett at the Lazy W."

"You're going back to see Tory?"

Trask's face hardened and his eyes darkened murderously. "If someone is dead set on discouraging me, I'd be willing to bet that the next person they'll approach is Tory."

Neva's mouth went dry. "What do you mean?"

"I mean simply that I'm worried about her. While we were at Devil's Ridge, someone took a shot at us."

"No!" Neva looked half-crazed with fear. Her face went deathly white and she glanced from Trask to the loft where Nicholas was sleeping so peacefully and back again. "I can't believe this is happening. All because of some damned note!"

"Believe it."

"Oh, dear Lord," she whispered.

There was a sharp knock at the door and Trask opened it to find Deputy Woodward on the doorstep. After assuring himself that Woodward had contacted the sheriff and was following Barnett's orders, Trask half ran to the Blazer, shoved the truck into gear and drove toward the Lazy W.

A THUNDEROUS NOISE awakened Tory. She sat bolt upright in bed until her groggy thoughts began to make sense and she realized that someone was pounding urgently at the front door. Probably Keith. He had a habit of losing his key....

She tossed on a robe and hurried down the stairs.

"I'm coming, I'm coming," she called. "Hold your horses."

"Thank God," she heard a male voice say and grinned when she realized it belonged to Trask.

Jerking the door open, she felt her smile widen for the man she loved. "Well, Senator McFadden, what brings you back to the Lazy W at this hour?"

As she stepped onto the front porch, she was swept into Trask's arms as he crushed her desperately to him. "Thank God, you're all right," he whispered against her wet hair. "If I ever lost you again…" His voice caught and the arms around her held on as if he expected her to disappear. "Where were you?" he demanded.

"When?"

"About twenty minutes ago." Still he held her tightly, almost deliberately.

"I was here."

"But I called. No one answered."

"I was here," she repeated. "Maybe you caught me when I was in the shower. I thought I heard the phone ring, but by the time I got to it, no one was there."

"Lord, Tory," he whispered, closing his eyes. "You had me half out of my mind with fear." He slowly pulled his head back and stared into her eyes. "Where's Paul Barnett?"

"The sheriff?" she asked incredulously. "Trask, what's going on? Do you have any idea what time it is? Why would Paul Barnett be here?"

"Because I asked him to come. He's supposed to be here, damn it!"

"Slow down, will you? You're talking like a lunatic!"

The light from the hallway spilled onto the front

porch and for the first time she noticed that his clothes were ripped and dirty and there were cuts below his right eye and on his chin. "Wait a minute," she said, drawing away and gently touching his beard-darkened jaw. "What in God's name happened to you?"

Trask's eyes fell on her face and then looked past her to the interior of the house. It was then she noticed his haggard expression and the fact that he walked with a slight limp. Worry crept into her voice. "Trask? What's going on?"

"Are you okay?"

"Looks like I should be asking you that one," she observed, concern making her voice rough. "Trask, what happened?"

"Our friend from the ridge caught up with me."

"What?"

Trask walked into the entry hall and began snapping on lights before he started looking into the corners of the rooms on the ground floor. Once a quick, but complete search of the lower level was accomplished, he started up the stairs and Tory followed him. "I was worried about you," he finally explained, once all the rooms and closets were searched. "Are you alone?"

"Yes. You could have asked me, y'know, instead of walking in here and tearing the place apart like some kind of madman."

He ignored her sarcasm. "Where's Keith?"

"I don't know," she admitted. "Sometimes he stays out late—"

"Son-of-a-bitch!" Trask stalked into the den. All of his muscles became instantly tense.

"Oh, no, Trask," Tory whispered, following him into the study and understanding his anger. She tried to ignore the tiny finger of dread slowly creeping up her spine. "You're not seriously trying to blame Keith for this—" she pointed at the disheveled state of his appearance "—are you?"

"I was hoping that he had an alibi."

Tory's eyes widened in horror. "You think Keith did this to you?"

"Maybe."

"Oh, Trask, no! You can't be serious!" she said, her voice shaking as she clamped a hand over her mouth and tried to pull herself together. Reading the anger in his eyes she slowly let her hands fall to her side. "But you're just guessing aren't you? I take it you didn't see who attacked you?"

"Didn't have time. It was dark."

Tory felt a little sense of relief. This was all a big mistake. Keith wouldn't rough somebody up, not even Trask McFadden. "Have you seen a doctor?"

"Neva examined me."

"Neva! Good Lord, have you been there, too?" Tory pushed her damp hair out of her eyes.

"That's where it happened."

Tory's eyes turned cold. Too much was happening and she couldn't think straight. "Wait a minute, slow down. Come into the kitchen and tell me exactly what happened and when and where and why." She started down the hallway, Trask right behind her.

"Why? That's the kicker, isn't it?"

Tory frowned as she took down two cups and made a pot of tea. Forcing her hands to remain steady, she poured the tea into the cups. "So tell me, what did Neva say?"

"Other than that I should be more careful?" Tory didn't crack a smile. "She thinks I'll live."

"Some consolation." She handed him a cup of tea and tried to force a grin as her eyes slid down his slightly bruised chin to the torn shirt that displayed all too vividly his muscled chest and discolored abdomen. "You look awful."

"That's a cut above the way I feel."

"I really think you should go to the emergency room, and get some X-rays."

"Later." He set down his cup and his eyes took her in; the tousled damp hair that hung in springy curls around a fresh face devoid of makeup, the gorgeous green eyes now dark with concern, and the soft heather-colored robe clinched loosely over her small waist. "God, I was worried about you," he admitted, rubbing his hand over his unshaven jaw.

"It looks like I should have been the one worrying."

He took the cup from her hands and pulled her toward him. Lowering his head, he caught her lips with his and let the fresh feminine scent of her fill his nostrils and flood his senses. "From now on, I'm not letting you out of my sight," he vowed against her ear before reluctantly releasing her.

"Is that a promise or a threat?"

His uneven, incredibly charming grin flashed white against his dark skin. "However you want to take it."

"I'll think about it and let you know what I decide."

Trask's face sobered and his fingers toyed with the lapel of her plush robe. "As much as I find the thought distasteful," he said with a frown as he kissed her forehead, "I think you should get dressed. I asked Sheriff Barnett to meet us here."

"Tonight?"

"Yeah." He stepped away from her and patted her firmly on the behind. "Look, I'll explain everything when Paul gets here, just go put on something—" he lifted his palms upward as he looked at her soft terry robe and the white silk gown that was visible when she walked "—something less erotic."

"I've never heard of a terry-cloth bathrobe being called erotic."

"Only because I've never seen you in one before."

Tory laughed and shook her head. Against her better judgment she walked upstairs and changed into a pair of cords and a sweater. She was braiding her hair into a single plait as she stood on the landing when she heard the knock at the front door.

"I'll get it," Trask said. He'd positioned himself at the bottom of the stairs and was watching with interest as Tory wrapped the rubber band around the tip of her braid.

"Suit yourself."

His teasing expression turned grim. "And I think you'd better try and track down your brother. There are a few questions he'll have to answer." With one last glance upward in her direction Trask opened the door.

Paul Barnett and Detective Woodward were standing on the front porch. Tory's fingers curled around the banister as she walked slowly down the stairs and faced all three men.

"Come in, sheriff...Deputy Woodward." She inclined her head toward each man and wondered if it was obvious to them how nervous she felt. Not since the trial had she been uncomfortable with the police, but this night, with Trask beaten and Keith missing, she felt a nervous sweat break out between her shoulder blades. "I was going to make a pot of coffee. I'll bring it into the den."

Barnett pursed his lips and nodded his agreement. He was a slightly paunchy man with wire-rimmed glasses, cold eyes and a hard cynical smile. "Anyone else here?"

"No."

"No hands on the ranch?"

"Not tonight."

"What about that kid brother of yours?" the sheriff pressed, his graying bushy eyebrows lifting with each of her negative responses.

Tory felt herself stiffen. "Keith isn't home. He's in town, I think."

"But you don't know?"

"No. Not for sure."

Barnett pressed his thin lips tightly together but didn't comment. When the three men went into the den, Tory escaped to the kitchen and put on a pot of coffee. She tried to ignore the fact that her hands as well as her entire body were trembling.

Where was Keith? Everyone wanted to talk to her brother and she had no idea where he was. It was late, damned late and unlike her brother to be out on a weeknight.

The grandfather clock in the entry hall chimed one o'clock. The hollow notes added to Tory's growing paranoia.

Drumming her fingers on the counter as the coffee perked, she considered using the phone and trying to track down her brother, but discarded the idea. He was twenty-one and able to make his own decisions. Or so she silently prayed.

The murmur of voices from the den caught her attention and her heart began to pound with dread. Quickly grabbing the glass carafe, four mugs, the sugar bowl and creamer, she set everything onto a woven straw tray and carried it into the den. Trask looked up from his position in her father's leather recliner and smiled reassuringly.

"Okay, now let me get this straight," Barnett was saying, his graying mustache working as he spoke. "You two went up on Devil's Ridge looking for some sort of clue that might lead you to the fourth man who was supposedly involved in the Quarter Horse swindle. Right?"

"Right," Trask replied.

Tory caught Barnett's inquisitive stare and nodded curtly to his unspoken question. "However, it could be a three-man conspiracy," she said. "I still don't believe that my father was involved."

"Be that as it may, Ms Wilson, your father was tried and convicted, so we'll have to assume that he was in on the swindle," Barnett said slowly before turning to Trask. "So, you believe the fourth man theory because of this piece of paper." He held up the anonymous letter, without waiting for a response. "And, you think that because you've been poking around looking for some proof to support the fourth man theory, one of the calves from the Lazy W was shot, and someone tried to shoot you as well, this afternoon—"

"I'm not sure they were shooting at us, maybe just trying to scare us," Trask interjected.

"Nevertheless, a shot was fired in your general direction."

"Yes."

"And when that didn't work, whoever it was that fired the rifle followed you to Neva McFadden's place and beat the tar out of you."

Trask frowned, nodded his head and rubbed his jaw pensively. "That's why I think it was a warning. If they had wanted me dead, I would have been. I had to have been an easy target coming out of Neva's house."

"So that's all of your story?"

"Except that someone's been calling Neva and harassing her, making threats against her son," Deputy Woodward added.

"What!" Tory's face drained of color and she almost dropped her coffee. She turned her wide eyes on Trask. "No—"

Trask's jaw hardened and his eyes turned as cold as blue ice. "That's why Neva tried to talk both me and you out of the investigation. She was afraid for Nicholas's life."

"This has gotten completely out of hand," Tory whispered, leaning against the pine-paneled wall.

"You should have called me," Barnett said, leveling his gaze at Trask, "instead of trying to investigate something like this on your own. Could have saved yourself a lot of grief as well as a beating."

"I was just trying to keep it quiet."

Barnett frowned. "We could have done a better job. In case you've forgotten, that's what my department gets paid to do. As it is, you've made one helluva mess of it."

Trask's lips twisted wryly. "Thanks."

After asking Tory questions that confirmed Trask's story about what happened on the ridge, the sheriff and his deputy finished their coffee, grabbed their notes and left.

"It gets worse by the minute," Tory confided, once she was alone with Trask.

"Barnett's right. I should have gone to the police in the beginning."

"And then the police would have flocked back here, the press would have found out about it and the scandal would have been plastered on the front pages of the local papers all over again."

"Looks like it's going to end up that way regardless."

"Nothing we can do about it now," she said with a sigh. Walking toward the recliner Tory searched Trask's face. His jaw was still strong, jutted in determination, but pain shadowed his blue eyes. The cuts on his face, though shallow, were slightly swollen and raw. "Are you okay? I could take you into Bend to the hospital."

"Not now."

"But your head—"

"It's fine. It'll wait until morning."

"Oh, senator," she said with a sad smile. "What am I going to do with you?"

His eyes slid seductively up her body to rest on the worried pout of her lips. "I can think of a dozen things…"

"Be serious."

"I am."

"Well, I'm not about to have you risk further injury." She glanced out the window and back at the clock. *Two-fifteen, and still no sign of Keith.* "Besides, it's late."

"Are you trying to give me a less than subtle hint?"

"I'm tired." She touched his head fondly. "You should be, too."

"I'm okay. Go to bed."

"And what about you?"

"I'm staying here."

"You can't—"

"Watch." He settled into the recliner and folded his hands over his chest.

"Trask. Think about it. You can't stay here. Keith will be home soon."

"That's who I'm waiting for."

"Oh, Trask." The rest of her response was cut off by the sound of an engine roaring up the driveway and the spray of gravel hitting the sides of the barn as the pickup ground to an abrupt halt.

"About time," Trask said, pushing himself upward.

Tory's heart was beating double time by the time that Keith opened the front door and strode into the den. His young face was set with fierce determination and he scowled at the sight of Trask.

"What's he doin' here?" Keith demanded of Tory, as he cocked an insolent thumb in Trask's direction.

"Why don't you ask me?" Trask cut in.

Turning, Keith faced Trask for the first time. It was then that he noticed the bruise on Trask's chin and his rumpled dirty clothing. "What the hell happened to you?"

"Why don't you tell me?" Trask hooked his thumbs in the belt loops of his jeans and leaned his shoulders against the fireplace. His intense gaze bored into Keith's worried face.

Keith immediately sobered. "What're you talking about?"

Trask's eyes narrowed. "Someone followed Tory and me up to Devil's Ridge this afternoon. Not only did this guy have a rifle, but he decided to use it by taking a shot at us."

"What?" Keith spun and faced his sister. "What's he talking about? Why would you go up to the ridge with him after what he did to you?" Keith became frantic and began pacing from the den to the hallway and back again. "I knew that McFadden couldn't wait to bring up all the dirt again!" He glanced over his shoulder at Trask. "What's he talking about—someone shooting at you? He's not serious—"

"Dead serious," Trask said tonelessly. "Then later, at Neva's place, someone decided to use the back of my head for batting practice."

Keith's face lost all of its color and his cocky attitude faded with his tan. "You're not kiddin' are ya?"

"Hardly," Trask said dryly, approaching the younger man in long sure strides. "And that same person has been calling my sister-in-law, threatening her to get me to stop this investigation." Keith looked as if he wanted to drop through the floor. "I don't suppose you know anything about that, do you?"

"I...I don't know anything."

"So where were you tonight?" Trask ground out.

"Tonight? You think I did it?" Keith seemed genuinely astounded. He looked pleadingly at Tory before stiffening at the sound of Trask's voice.

"Where were you?"

"I've been in town."

"Until two in the morning?"

"Yeah. Rex and I went into town, looking for a part for the combine. When we couldn't get it, I stayed at the Branding Iron for dinner and a few beers. Later I went over to Rex's place. He and several of the hands had a poker game going."

"And someone was with you all night?"

"For most of it." Keith's indignation flashed in his eyes. "Look, McFadden, I've done a lot of things in my life that I'm not particularly proud of, but what happened to you and Tory today has nothing to do with me."

"Why do I have difficulty believing you?"

"Because I've made no bones about the fact that I hate your guts." He pointed a condemning finger at Trask. "You nearly single-handedly destroyed everything my dad worked all of his life to achieve; you not only sent him to prison, but you took away all of his respectability by using his daughter and publicly humiliating her."

Trask's face hardened. A muscle worked in the corner of his jaw and his eyes narrowed fractionally. "I've made my share of mistakes," he admitted.

"Too many, McFadden. Too damned many! And tonight is just one more in the string. I didn't have anything to do with what happened to you tonight." He was shaking with rage. "Now I think it's about time you left."

Trask's eyes glittered with determination. "I'm not going anywhere, Wilson." He sat down in one of the chairs and propped the heels of his boots on the corner of the coffee table. "As a matter of fact, I intend to spend the rest of the night right here."

"Get out!"

"Not on your life."

Keith glared at his sister. "He's your problem," he spat out before stomping out of the den and treading heavily up the stairs to his room.

Tory took a seat on the arm of Trask's chair. "You were too hard on him, y'know," she reprimanded, her brow knotted in concern. "He's not involved in this."

"So he claims."

"You don't believe him," she said with a sigh.

"I don't believe anyone—" he looked into her worried eyes and smiled slightly "—except for you."

"Not too long ago you didn't trust me."

"Not you, lady; just your motives."

"Same thing."

Trask took her hand and pressed her fingers to his lips. "Not at all. But sometimes I think you'd lie to protect those closest to you."

She shook her head and smiled sadly. "Wrong, senator. Maybe I should have five years ago. Since Dad wouldn't say what happened, maybe I should have covered for him." She picked up a crystal paperweight from the desk and ran her fingers over the cut glass. "Maybe then he'd still be alive."

"And you'd be the criminal for perjuring yourself."

She frowned at her distorted reflection in the glass. "I guess there are no easy answers," she said, as she placed the paperweight on the corner of the desk. "You really don't have to stay, you know."

"Wouldn't have it any other way."

"It's ridiculous. Keith's here."

"Precisely my point." He looked up at her and wrapped his hand around her neck, drawing her lips to his. "I'm not taking any chances with your life."

"What about Neva and Nicholas?"

"A private investigator is with them."

"And you've assigned yourself to me as my personal bodyguard it that it?"

"Um-hm." He rubbed his lips gently against hers, then murmured, "I'm going to stick to you like glue."

"I just can't believe that anyone would want to hurt Nicholas or you."

He smiled wryly. "Believe it."

He pulled on her hand and she tumbled into the chair with him. Though he let out a sharp breath as her weight fell against his ribs, he grinned wickedly. "Maybe it would be best if I came to bed with you," he suggested, his breath touching her hair.

"I don't think so."

"Are you worried about what Keith and the rest of the hands will think?"

She shrugged. "A little, I guess."

"Hypocrite." He nuzzled her neck and she felt her blood begin to warm.

"There's nothing hypocritical about it, I'm just trying to use my head. We both need sleep. You can stay in the guest room. It's only a couple of doors down the hall from mine."

"I remember," he said softly, his voice intimate.

Tory had to look away from him to ignore the obvious desire smoldering in his eyes. *Who was she kidding? How many times had he stolen into her room in the past? He knew the ranch house like the back of his hand.*

"Where does Keith sleep?"

"He, uh, moved into Dad's room when Dad passed away."

"And the rest of the hands?"

"Usually go home. Once in a while someone will stay in the bunkhouse, but that's pretty rare these days."

"What about tonight or, say, the past week?"

"No one is staying on the ranch except Keith and myself."

"And Rex?"

"He has his own place, just north of Len Ross's spread. He and Belinda have lived there for over five years." *Five years!* Once again, Tory was reminded of the time when she was free to love Trask with all her heart. But that was before her world was destroyed by the horse swapping scam, Jason's murder and the trial.

She stood up and tugged on Trask's arm, hoping to break the intimacy that memories of the past had inspired. "Come on, mister, let me help you up the stairs." As he stood, she eyed him speculatively. "If you give me your clothes, I'll throw them in the wash so that you have something clean in the morning."

"Gladly," he agreed as they mounted the stairs.

"Just leave them in the hall outside your door."

"Whatever you say," he whispered seductively and a shiver of desire raced down her spine.

"What I say is that we both need some time to think about what happened today. Maybe then we can make some sense of it."

Trask's smile slid off his face. "None of this makes any sense," he admitted, grimacing against a sudden stab of pain.

A few minutes later Trask was in the guest room, his

clothes were in the washer and Tory was lying on her bed wondering if she would ever get to sleep, knowing that Trask was only two doors down the hall.

CHAPTER NINE

PALE LIGHT HAD just begun to stream into the bedroom when Tory heard the door whisper open. She rolled over to face the sound and focused her eyes on Trask as he approached the bed. He was wearing only a towel draped over his hips. A dark bruise discolored the otherwise hard muscles of his chest and the cut on his chin was partially hidden by his dark growth of beard. As he walked the towel gaped to display the firm muscles of his thighs moving fluidly with his silent strides.

"What're you doing?" she whispered, lifting her head off the pillow and rubbing her eyes.

"Guess."

The sight of him in the predawn light, a mischievous twinkle dancing in his blue eyes, his brown hair disheveled from recent slumber, made Tory's blood begin to race with anticipation.

But the purple bruise on his abdomen put everything into stark perspective. Someone didn't want Trask digging into the past and that person was willing to resort to brutal violence to stop Trask's investigation.

"What time is it?" she asked, pushing the disturbing thought aside.

"Five." He stopped near the bed and looked down at her, his gaze caressing the flush in her cheeks then meeting her questioning eyes. "I couldn't sleep very well," he admitted, his fingers working the knot on his towel. "Knowing you were in the same house with me has been driving me crazy."

"You're absolutely indefatigable...or is it insufferable? It's too early to decide which," she murmured, gazing up at him affectionately. "Last night someone tried to beat the living daylights out of you. There's a good chance you could have been killed and here you are—"

"Intent on seducing the woman I'm supposed to protect." He let the towel slide to the floor and sat on the edge of the bed. Bending slightly, he pushed the tousled auburn hair from her eyes and gently kissed her forehead. "Any complaints?"

"None, senator," she replied as he threw back the covers and settled into the bed, his naked body pressing urgently against the softer contours of hers.

"I could get used to a job like this," he said as he held her face in his hands and gazed into her slumberous eyes.

Happiness wrapped around Tory's heart. A cool morning breeze carrying the faint scent of new-mown hay ruffled the curtains as it passed through the open window. Morning birds had begun to chirp and from far in the distance came the familiar sound of lowing cattle. Lying with Trask in her bed as the first silvery rays of dawn seeped into the room seemed the most natural thing in the world. There was a peaceful solitude about dawn and Tory loved sharing that feeling with the only man she had ever loved.

His arms wrapped around her, pulling her close to him. The warmth and strength of his body was welcome protection. It felt good to lean on him again, she thought. Maybe there was a chance they could forget the pain of the past and live for the future. Looking into his eyes, Tory felt that there was nothing in the world that could possibly go wrong as long as he was beside her.

"God, I love you," he whispered as he lowered his head and kissed her almost brutally.

Through the sheer nylon nightgown, she felt his hands caress her skin. Deft fingers outlined each rib as they moved upward to mold around her breasts and Tory gasped at the raw desire laboring within her.

Her breast ached with the want of him, straining to be caressed by his gentle fingers. As he found one nipple and teased it to ripe anticipation, Tory moaned. The exquisite torment deep within her became white-hot as he lifted the nightgown over her head and slowly lowered himself alongside of her. His hands pressed against the small of her back as he took first one hard nipple into his mouth and after suckling hungrily for a time, he turned his attention to the other ripe bud and feasted again.

Tory's blood was pulsing through her veins, throbbing at her temples in an erratic cadence. Sweat moistened her body where Trask's flesh molded to hers. She could feel the muscles of Trask's solid thighs straining against hers and the soft hair on his legs rubbed her calves erotically, promising more of the impassioned bittersweet torment.

"I love you," she cried, all of her doubts erased by the pleasure of his body straining against hers. Painful emotions were easily forgotten with the want of him. Her fist clenched with forced restraint and her throat ached to shout his name as he slid lower and kissed the soft flesh of her abdomen, leaving a dewy trail from her breasts to her navel.

"I'm never going to let you go again," Trask vowed, his breath fanning her abdomen, his hands kneading the soft muscles of her back and buttocks as she lifted upward, offering herself to him. "Don't ever leave me, Tory."

"Never," she cried, the fires within her all-consuming in the need to be fulfilled, to become one, to surrender to her rampant desire for this one, proud man.

Slowly he drew himself upward and his hands twined in the wanton curls framing her face. His moist skin slid seductively over hers. "I'll keep you to that promise," he said, his voice rough and his blue eyes dark with passion. "Make love to me."

As she stared into his eyes, she reached forward, her arms tightening around his muscular torso. The warm mat of hair on his chest crushed her breasts as he rolled over her and his knees gently prodded her legs apart. "I want every morning to be like this one," he said as he lowered himself over her. His lips once again touched hers and she felt the warm invasion of his tongue just as he pushed against her and began the slow rhythmic dance of love.

Closing her eyes, Tory held him tightly, her fingers digging into the hard muscles of his back and shoulders as he moved over her in ever more rapid strokes. Her heart was thudding wildly in her rib cage. The warmth within her expanded around him and her breathing came in short gasps as Trask pushed her to the brink of ecstasy time and time again before the rippling tide of sweet fulfillment rushed over her and she felt his answering surrender.

Sweat dampened her curls as the warmth of afterglow caressed her. With Trask's strong arms wrapped around her, Tory felt there was nothing that they couldn't do, as long as they did it together.

She snuggled closer to him and Trask kissed her hair. "I meant it, you know," he insisted, his voice low. "About never letting you go."

"Good, because I'm going to hold you to it."

Silently they watched as the pale gray light of dawn faded with the rising sun. Clear blue sky replaced the early-morning haze.

Tory looked at the clock and groaned. "I've got to get up, senator. Rex usually gets here between six-thirty and seven."

"Why don't you call him and tell him to take the day off?"

Laughing at the absurdity of his request, she wiggled out of his arms. "It's easier to get a straight answer out of a politician than it is to get Rex to take a day off," she said teasingly.

"You're feeling particularly wicked this morning aren't you?" But he was forced to chuckle.

"And what about you? Are you going to take the day off and forget about going to visit Linn Benton and George Henderson in the pen?"

His voice became stern. "Not on your life."

"That's what I was afraid of." Concern clouded her eyes as she rolled off the bed and reached for the robe draped over a bedpost at the foot of the bed. "It wouldn't surprise me if they were behind what happened to you last night."

Tenderly rubbing his jaw, Trask shook his head. "They're in prison, remember?"

"Yeah, but Linn Benton's got more than his share of friends." She shivered involuntarily and cinched the belt of her robe more tightly around her waist.

"So do I."

"I don't think friends in Washington count. They can't help you here," she thought aloud. Mentally shaking herself, she then tried to rise above the worries that had been with her ever since Trask had forced himself back in her life with his damned anonymous letter.

As she stared at the man she loved, she had to smile. His brown hair was tousled, his naked body was only partially hidden by the navy-blue sheet and patchwork quilt and his seductive blue eyes were still filled with passion. "I'll go throw your clothes in the dryer."

"Don't bother. I already did. They're probably dry by now."

"You mean that you went creeping around this house this morning with only a towel around you?"

"I wasn't creeping. And the only people here are you and Keith." His grin widened and amusement sparked in his eyes. "Besides I know where the utility room is. Believe it or not, I have done my own laundry on occasion."

"Hmph. I suppose you have." With a shake of her head, Tory went downstairs and into the kitchen. After starting the coffee, she walked into the adjoining utility room and removed Trask's clothes from the dryer. As he had predicted, the jeans and shirt were warm and dry. She draped them over her arm, climbed the stairs and returned to her room.

Trask was still lying on the four-poster, his head propped up with both pillows, a bemused grin making his bold features appear boyishly captivating. Tory's heart beat more quickly just at the sight of him.

"There you go, senator," she said, tossing the clothes to him.

"Can't I persuade you to come back to bed?"

"Not this morning. I'm a working woman, remember?"

"Excuses, excuses," he mumbled, but reached for his clothes. She sat on the edge of the bed while he pulled on his jeans and slipped his arms through the sleeves of his shirt.

"So tell me," she suggested, eyeing his bruised ribs and the cut on his chin. "Have you got any theories about who decided to use you as a punching bag?"

He looked up from buttoning his shirt. "A few."

"Care to share them?"

"Not just yet."

"Why not?"

"No proof."

"So what else is new?" she asked, leaning back against the headboard of the bed and frowning. Here, lying with Trask in the small room decorated in cream-colored lace, patchwork and maple, she had felt warm and secure. The worries of the night had faded but were now thrown back in her face, quietly looming more deadly than ever.

Trask stood and tucked in the tails of his shirt. "What's new?" he repeated. "Maybe a lot."

"This is no time to be mysterious."

"Maybe not," he agreed while cocking his wrist and looking at his watch. "But I've got to get out of here. I want to check on Neva and Nicholas, change clothes at the cabin and be in Salem by ten."

The thought of Trask leaving the ranch was difficult for Tory to accept. In a few short days, she had gotten used to his presence and looked forward to the hours she spent with him. The fact that he was leaving to face two of the men responsible for his brother's death made Tory uneasy. Though she knew that her father had been innocent, the ex-judge Linn Benton and his accomplice, George Henderson, had been and, in her opinion, still were ruthless men more than capable of murder.

"Look," he was saying as he walked to the door. "I want you to be careful, okay? I'll check with John Davis and make sure he has a man assigned to the Lazy W."

"I don't think that's necessary."

Trask's eyes glittered dangerously. "I hope not, but I'm a firm believer in the better-safe-than-sorry theory."

"Oh, yeah?" She stared pointedly at the cut on his chin and the bruise peeking out of his shirt. "Look where it's gotten you. And now you're going to talk to your brother's murderers!"

He frowned and crossed the room to hold her in his arms. Placing a soft kiss on the crown of her head he let out a long weary sigh. "Believe me, lady, someday this will all be behind us."

"You hope."

"I promise."

"Just don't tell me that in twenty years I'll look back at what we're going through now and laugh, 'cause I won't!"

He chuckled and hugged her fiercely. "Okay, I won't

lie to you, but I will promise you that we'll have plenty of stories that will entertain our grandchildren."

"That's a promise?" *Grandchildren and children. Trask's children.* At this point the possibility of marrying Trask and having his children seemed only a distant dream; a fantasy that she couldn't dare believe would come true.

"One I won't let you get out of." He lowered his head and captured her lips with his. "The sooner we get all of this mess behind us, the better. Then we can concentrate on getting married and filling the house with kids."

"Slow down, senator," she said, her love shining in her eyes. "First things first, don't you think? Oh, and if you want a cup of coffee, I'm sure it's perked."

He shook his head. "Haven't got time. I'll be back this afternoon."

"I'm counting on it."

"Maybe then I'll get a chance to talk to your foreman, Rex Engels."

Tory stiffened slightly. "Are you going to put him through the third degree, too?"

"Nothing so drastic," Trask promised. "I just want to ask him a few questions."

"About last night?"

"Among other things."

"You don't trust anyone, do you?"

"Just you," he said.

"Hmph," she muttered ungraciously and crossed her arms over her chest. "I'll tell Rex that you want to talk to him."

"Thanks." With a broad wink, he opened the door of her room and disappeared. She watched from the window as he walked out of the house, got into his Blazer and drove down the lane. A plume of gray dust followed in his wake and disturbed the tranquility of the morning. As the Blazer roared by the pasture, curious foals lifted their heads, pricking their ears forward at the noise while the mares continued to graze.

"When will it ever end?" Tory wondered aloud, taking one final look at the dew-covered grass and the rolling green pastures and dusty paddocks. With a thoughtful frown she turned away from the window and headed for the shower.

Tory was in the den balancing the checkbook when she heard Keith come down the stairs. He walked by the study without looking inside and continued down the hall to the kitchen.

"I'm in here," Tory called. When she didn't get a response, she shrugged and continued sorting through the previous month's checks. A few minutes later, Keith strode into the room, sipping from a cup of coffee.

He frowned as if remembering an unpleasant thought. "So where's our guest?"

"Trask already left for Salem."

Keith tensed. "Salem? Why?" His eyes narrowed and he lifted a hand. "Don't tell me: he plans on visiting Linn Benton and George Henderson in prison."

"That's the idea."

"He just won't let up on this, will he?"

"I doubt it. And now that the sheriff's department is involved, I would expect that Paul Barnett or one of his deputies will be out later to ask you questions."

"Just what I need," Keith said grimly and then changed the subject. "So how're you this morning?"

He threw a leg over one of the arms of the recliner, leaned back and studied his sister.

"As well as can be expected after last night."

Keith scowled into his cup. The lines of worry deepened around his eyes. "What McFadden said, about you being shot at, was it true?"

Tory let out a long breath. "Unfortunately, yes."

Keith's eyes clouded as he looked away from his sister. "And you think it has something to do with this anonymous note business, right?"

"I don't know," she admitted, taking off her reading glasses and setting them on the corner of the desk as she stared at her brother. "But it seems to me that it's more than a coincidence that the minute Trask comes into town, all the trouble begins."

"Has it ever occurred to you that Trask may have initiated all this hoopla just to get his name in the papers? You know, remind the voters that he's a hero."

"I don't think he hired someone to beat him up, if that's what you mean. And I don't think that he would let someone terrorize Neva or Nicholas—do you?"

Keith squirmed uncomfortably. "Maybe not."

"So how do you explain it?"

He looked straight into her eyes. "I can't, Sis. I don't have any clue as to why someone would take a shot at you or want to hurt Neva. And it scares me, it scares the hell out of me!"

"But maybe someone was just interested in hurting Trask?" she said. "The rest of us might just have gotten in the way. After all, he was the one that took the punches last night."

Keith's head snapped upward and his jaw tightened. "I hate the bastard. It's no secret. You know it and so does he." Keith's voice faded slightly and he hesitated before adding, "And I hate the fact that he's back here, getting you all messed up again, but I wouldn't beat him up or shoot at him, for crying out loud."

Tory tapped her pencil nervously on the desk. What she was about to say was difficult. "I'm sorry, Keith. But I can't seem to forget that the first day Trask came into town you were in a panic. You came out to the paddock to tell me about it, remember?" Tory's heart was hammering in her chest. She didn't like the role of inquisitor, especially not with Keith.

"I remember."

"And later you said something about pointing a gun at him if Trask tried to trespass."

Keith squeezed his eyes shut and rubbed the stiffness out of his neck. "That was all talk, Tory." He leaned back in the chair. "I just wish he'd leave us alone." After finishing his coffee, Keith stood. "I don't want to see you get hurt again. Everything that's happening scares me."

"I'm a big girl, Keith. I can take care of myself."

Keith offered his most disarming smile. "Then I'll try not to worry about you too much."

"Good." She let out a sigh of relief and felt the tension in her tight muscles ease. She believed everything Keith had told her and wondered why she had ever doubted him. "Oh, by the way, how did you do in the poker game last night?"

Keith's grin widened and he pulled out his wallet. When he opened it, he exposed a thick roll of bills tucked neatly in the side pocket. "I cleaned everyone's clock."

"That's a switch."

"Thanks for the vote of confidence."

"So how'd you get so lucky?"

Keith took his hat off a peg near the entry hall and jammed it onto his head. "Haven't you ever heard that poker is a game of skill, not luck?"

"Only from the winners."

Keith laughed as he walked out the front door. "I'll be on the west end of the ranch helping Rex clear out some brush."

"Will you be back for lunch?"

"Naw, I'll grab something later."

Keith left and Tory began drumming her fingers on the desk. Her brother had never won at poker in his life. Just when she was beginning to trust him, something he did seemed out of character. It worried her. It worried her a lot.

"Cut it out," she told herself, pushing her glasses onto her nose and studying the bank statement. "Trask's got you jumping at shadows." But she couldn't shake the unease that had settled in her mind.

IT WAS NEARLY one-thirty when Tory heard the sound of a vehicle coming down the drive. She had been leaning over the fence and watching the foals and mares as they grazed in the pasture. Shading her eyes against the glare of the afternoon sun, she smiled when she recognized Anna Hutton's white van.

Dusting her hands on her jeans, Tory met the van just as Anna parked it near the stables.

"How's our boy doing?" Anna asked as she hopped out of the van and grabbed her veterinary bag.

"Better than I'd expected. I took your advice about

the cold poultices and he's even putting a little weight on the leg this morning."

"Good." Anna grinned broadly. "See, I told you. Sometimes we don't have to resort to drugs."

"He's in the paddock around back," Tory said, leading Anna past the stables to the small enclosure where Governor was being walked by Eldon.

The stallion snorted his disapproval when he saw the two women and his black ears flattened to his head.

"So walking him hasn't proven too painful for him?" Anna asked, carefully studying the nervous horse.

"I don't think so," Tory replied. "Eldon?"

The ranch hand shook his head and his weathered face knotted in concentration. "He's been doin' fine. If I thought walkin' him was causing him too much pain, I wouldn't have done it, no matter what you said."

"It's great to have employees who trust your judgment," Tory commented when she read the amusement in Eldon's eyes.

Anna seemed satisfied. "Let's take a look at you," she said to the horse as she slid through the gate, patted Governor's dark shoulders and gently prodded his hoof from the ground. "Come on, boy," she coaxed. "You should be used to all of this attention by now."

After carefully examining Governor's hoof Anna released the horse's leg. "He looks good," she said to Tory. "Just keep doing what you have with the poultices. Keep walking him and consider that special shoe. I'll look in on him in another week."

"That's the best news I've had in two days," Tory admitted as Anna slipped through the gate and they began walking toward the house.

"I heard about what happened yesterday on Devil's Ridge," Anna commented.

Tory stopped dead in her tracks. "What? But how?"

With an encouraging smile, Anna met her friend's questioning stare. "You'd better be sure that your backbone is strong, Tory. All sorts of rumors are flying around Sinclair."

"Already? I don't see how—"

Anna placed her hand over Tory's arm. "Trask McFadden, excuse me, *Senator* McFadden is a famous man around these parts. What he does is news—big news. When someone attacks a man of his stature, it isn't long before the gossip mill gets wind of it and starts grinding out the information, indiscriminately mixing fact with fiction to distort the truth."

"But it only happened last night," Tory argued.

"And how many people knew about it?"

Tory smiled wryly and continued walking across the parking lot. "Too many," she admitted, thinking about Trask, Neva, Keith, the private investigator... The list seemed nearly endless.

"Then brace yourself; no doubt the press will be more than anxious to report what happened and how it relates to the horse swindle of five years ago as well as Jason McFadden's murder." Anna's voice was soft and consoling. "Your father's name, and his involvement in the scam, whether true or not, is bound to come up."

Tory let out a long breath of air. "That's just what I was trying to avoid." The afternoon sun felt hot on the back of her neck and the reddish dust beneath the gravel was stirred up by the easterly breeze.

"Too late. The handwriting's on the wall."

Tory lifted her chin and her eyes hardened. Involuntarily her slim shoulders squared. "Well, what's done is done, I suppose. At least you've given me fair warning. Now, how about staying for a late lunch?"

"It sounds heavenly," Anna admitted, pleased that Tory had seemed to buck up a little and was ready to face the challenge of the future. "I thought you'd never ask!"

Tory laughed and found that she looked forward to Anna's company and sarcastic wit. She needed to think about something other than the mysterious happenings on the ranch and it had been a long time since she and Anna had really had a chance to talk.

"THAT WAS DELICIOUS," Anna stated, rolling her eyes as she finished her strawberry pie. "Denver omelet, spinach salad and pie to boot. Whenever you give up ranching, you could become a chef. It's a good thing I don't eat here more often or I'd gain twenty pounds."

"I doubt that," Tory said, pleased with the compliment nonetheless. "You'll never gain weight, not with the work schedule you demand of yourself."

"That's my secret," Anna said. "I never have time to eat."

Chuckling softly the two women cleared the dishes from the table and set them in the sink. "So we've talked about what happened here yesterday, and about my plans for the ranch, and about Governor's condition. Now, tell me about you. How're you doin'?"

Anna's dark eyes clouded. "Things have been different since Jim moved out." She held up a strong finger, as if to remind herself. "However, despite it all, I've survived."

"If you don't want to talk about it…"

Anna forced a sad smile. "There's nothing much to talk about. I was involved with starting my own veterinary practice. I worked long hours and was exhausted when I got home. I resented the fact that he expected me to be the perfect wife, housekeeper, you-name-it, and he got bored with listening to my dreams, I guess. I kind of ignored him and I guess he needed a woman. So I really can't blame him for taking up with someone else, can I?"

"I would," Tory said firmly. "It seems to me that if two people love each other, they can work things out."

"It's not always that easy."

Tory thought of her own situation with Trask. The love they shared had always been shrouded in deceit. "Maybe you're right," she finally admitted. "But I don't see why you should have to go around carrying all this guilt with you."

Frowning thoughtfully, Anna rubbed her thumb over her index finger. "Maybe I carry it because I was brought up to believe that a woman's place is in the home, having babies, washing dishes, enjoying being her husband's best friend." She leaned against the counter and stared out the window. "But I got greedy. I wanted it all: husband, home, children and a fascinating career. I didn't mean to, but somehow I lost Jim in the shuffle."

"Easy to do—"

"Too easy. But I've learned from my mistakes, thank you, and you should, too."

"What's that supposed to mean?"

Anna laughed grimly. "That I'm about to poke my nose in where it doesn't belong."

"Oh?"

"Look, Tory. I know you never got over Trask." Anna saw the protest forming on Tory's lips and she warded it off with a flip of her wrist. "There's no use denying it; you love him and you always have, regardless of all that mess with your dad. It's written all over your face.

"And, despite what happened in the past, I think Trask's basically a decent man who loves you very much. What happened with your dad was unfortunate and I was as sad as anyone when Trask took the stand against Calvin. But that was five years ago and it's over." She took a deep breath. "So, if Trask is the man you love, then you'd better do your damnedest to let him know it."

Tory couldn't hide the stunned expression on her face. "That's the last piece of advice I would have expected from you," she replied.

"I had a chance to think about it last night. Let me tell you, if fate dealt me another chance with Jim, I'd make sure that I held on to him."

"How? By giving up your practice and independence?"

Anna shook her head. "Of course not. By just being a little less stubborn and self-righteous. I still believe that you can have everything, if you work at it. But you have to give a little instead of taking all the time."

"But that works two ways," Tory thought aloud.

"Of course. But if you're both willing, it should be possible." Anna looked up at the clock on the wall and nearly jumped out of her skin. "Geez, is it really three? Look, Tory, I've got to cut this session short, if you don't mind. I'm supposed to be in Bend at four."

"I'm just glad you stopped by."

"Anytime you're willing to cook, I'm ready to eat. Thanks for lunch!" Anna was out the back door in a flash and nearly bumped into Keith as he was walking through the door to the back porch.

"Excuse me," Anna called over her shoulder, while running down the two wooden steps to the path that led to the front of the house.

Keith, his eyes still fastened on Anna's retreating back came into the kitchen and threw the mail down on the table. Dust covered him from head to foot and sweat darkened the strands of his hair. Only the creases near his eyes escaped the reddish-brown dust. He placed his hat on the peg near the back door and wiped the back of his hand over his face, streaking the brown film. "I suppose I missed lunch," he said, eyeing the dishes in the sink.

"I suppose you did," Tory replied. "Anna and I just finished."

"I saw her take off." He stretched the knots out of his back. "I have to go into town and pick up the part for the combine. Then I'll go talk to Paul Barnett—you did say that he wanted to see me?"

Tory nodded.

"After that I'll probably stay in town for a couple of hours and have a few beers at the Branding Iron. Do you think I could con you into making me a sandwich or something while I get cleaned up?"

"Do I look like a short order cook?" she asked testily. "Didn't I ask you if you'd be back for lunch this morning before you left?"

"Please?"

Keith could be so damned charming when he chose to be, Tory thought defensively. She managed a stiff smile. "Okay, brother dear, I'll see what I can scrape together, but I'm not promising gourmet."

"At this point I'd be thrilled with peanut butter and jelly," Keith admitted as he sauntered out of the kitchen and up the steps. In a few minutes, Tory could hear the sounds of running water in the shower upstairs.

By the time that Keith returned to the kitchen, some twenty minutes later, he'd showered, shaved and changed into clean clothes.

"I hardly recognized you," Tory said teasingly. She placed a platter of ham sandwiches next to a glass of milk on the table. It was then she saw the mail. Quickly pushing aside the magazines and catalog offers, she picked up the stack of envelopes and began to thumb through them.

"Bills, bills and more…what's this?" Tory stopped at the fifth envelope. The small white packet was addressed to her in handwriting she didn't recognize. There was no return address on the envelope but the letter was postmarked in Sinclair. Without much thought, she tore open the envelope. A single piece of paper was enclosed. On it, in the same unfamiliar handwriting that graced the envelope was a simple message:

STAY AWAY FROM MCFADDEN

"Oh, dear God!" Tory whispered, letting the thin white paper fall from her hands onto the table.

"What?" Keith set down his sandwich and grabbed the letter before staring at the threat in disbelief. As the message began to sink in, his anger ignited and his face became flushed. He tossed the letter onto the table. "That does it, Tory, I'm not going to listen to any more of your excuses. When McFadden gets back here you tell him that you're out of this investigation of his!"

"I think it's too late for that." She was shaken but some of her color had returned.

"The hell it is! Damn it, Tory. He was beaten. Neva's been getting threatening phone calls. You were shot at, for crying out loud! Shot at with a rifle! What does it take to get it through your thick head that whoever is behind this—" he pointed emphatically at the letter "—is playing for keeps!"

"We can't back out, the police are involved and the whole town knows what's happening."

"Who gives a rip? We're talking about our lives, for God's sake!" His fist curled angrily and the muscles of his forearms flexed with rage. "All of this has got to stop!" Pounding the table and making the dishes rattle, Keith pushed his chair backward and stood beside the door. Leaning heavily against the frame he turned pleading gray eyes on his sister. "You can make him stop, y'know. You're the only one he'll listen to."

"Not when he's set his mind to something."

"Then unset it, Tory!" He turned his palms upward and shook his hands. "What does it take to get through to you?"

Tory looked down at the note lying face up on the table and she trembled. For a moment she considered Keith's suggestion, but slowly her fear gave way to anger. "I won't be threatened," she said, "or compromised. Whoever sent this must have a lot to lose. I wonder what it is?"

"Well, I don't!" Keith nervously pushed his hair away from his face. "I wish this whole nightmare would just end."

"But it won't. Not unless we find the truth," she said.

"Oh, God, Tory, you're such a dreamer. You always

have been. That's how McFadden tricked you the first time and now you've let him do it to you again. You're so caught up in your romantic fantasies about him that you don't see the truth when it hits you in the face!"

Tory leaned against the refrigerator. "Then maybe you'll be so kind as to spell it out for me."

"He's using you, Tory. All over again. I just never thought you'd be dumb enough to fall for it!"

With his final angry words tossed over his shoulder, Keith stalked out of the room leaving Tory feeling numb. Within a few moments, she heard the sound of the pickup as it roared down the lane before squealing around the corner to the open highway.

For the rest of the afternoon, Tory waited for Trask to return as he had promised. She tried to make herself busy around the house, her anxiety increasing with each hour that passed without word from him. As the day darkened with the coming of night, Tory began to worry. What, if anything, had he found out from Linn Benton and George Henderson?

Both men had to hate him. Trask's testimony had sealed their fate and sent them both to prison. What if they were somehow involved in his beating and the threatening calls to Neva?

When the phone rang at ten o'clock, Tory felt relief wash over her. It had to be Trask.

She answered the telephone breathlessly. "Hello?"

"Tory? It's Neva." Tory's heart fell through the floor. "I was wondering—actually hoping—that you'd heard from Trask." All of Tory's fears began to crystallize.

"I haven't seen him since this morning," she admitted.

"I see." There was a stilted silence. "Do you know if he went to Salem?"

"That's where he was headed when he left here."

"Damn." Neva waited a second before continuing.

"Maybe he went to the cabin," Tory suggested hopefully, though she already guessed the answer.

"I was already there, about an hour ago. His Blazer's gone and no one answered the door. I have a key and let myself in. I'm sure he hasn't been there since early this morning."

Tory's heart began to pound with worry. "And I assume that he hasn't called you?"

"No."

"Have you called the sheriff?"

"Not yet."

"What about the investigator, John what's-his-name?"

"Davis," Neva supplied. "He knows I'm worried. He's already contacted a couple of his men."

Tory slid into a nearby chair and felt the deadweight of fear slumping her shoulders. "So what do we do now?"

"Nothing to do but wait," Neva replied. "You'll call if you hear from him?"

"Of course." Tory hung up the phone and a dark feeling of dread seemed to seep in through the windows and settle in her heart. Where was Trask? The question began to haunt her.

Dear God, please let him be all right!

CHAPTER TEN

THE ROAD FROM the Willamette Valley was narrow. It twisted upward through the Cascades like some great writhing serpent intent on following the natural chasm made by the Santiam River. With sheer rock on one side of the road and the deep ravine ending with rushing white water on the other, the two lane highway cut across the mountains from the Willamette Valley to central Oregon.

At two in the morning, with only the beams from the headlights of the jeep to guide him, Trask was at the wheel of his Blazer heading east. And he was dead-tired. He had spent all of the morning and most of the afternoon at the penitentiary asking questions and getting only vague answers from the low-lifes Henderson and Benton.

Trask's hands tightened over the steering wheel as he thought about the ex-judge's fleshy round face. Even stripped of his judicial robes and garbed in state-issued prison clothes, Linn Benton exuded a smug untouchable air that got under Trask's skin.

Linn Benton had been openly sarcastic and when Trask had asked him about another person being involved in the horse swindle, the judge-turned-inmate had actually had the audacity to laugh outright. Trask's slightly battered condition and obvious concern about what had happened five years past seemed to be a source of amusement to the ex-judge. Trask had gotten nowhere with the man, but was more convinced than ever that somehow Linn Benton was pulling the strings from inside the thick penitentiary walls. But who was the puppet on the outside?

George Henderson had been easier to question. The ex-vet had been shaking in his boots at the thought of being questioned by a man whose brother he had helped kill. But whether Henderson's obvious anxiety had been because of Trask's stature as a senator, or because of previous threats he may have received from his prison mate, Linn Benton, Trask couldn't determine.

With an oath, Trask downshifted and the Blazer climbed upward toward Santiam Pass.

All in all, the trip hadn't been a complete waste of time, Trask attempted to console himself. For the first time he was certain that Linn Benton was still hiding something. And it had to be something that he didn't expect Trask to uncover, or the rotund prisoner wouldn't have smirked so openly at his adversary. It was as if Benton were privy to some private irony; an irony Trask couldn't begin to fathom.

"But I will." Trask squinted into the darkness and made a silent vow to get even with the men who had killed his brother. If another person was involved in Jason's death, Trask was determined to find out about it and see to it that the person responsible would pay.

For over six hours, Trask had been in the Multnomah County Library in Portland. He had searched out and microfilmed copies of all of the newspaper clippings about the horse swindle and Jason's murder, hoping to find something, anything that would give him a hint of what was happening and who was behind the series of events starting with the anonymous letter. If only the person who had written the letter would show his face…tell his side of the story…let the truth be known once and for all…then justice could be served and Trask could put the past behind and concentrate on a future with Tory.

THE NIGHT SEEMED to have no end. Tory heard Keith come in sometime after midnight. She tossed and turned restlessly on the bed, alternately looking at the clock and staring out the window into the dark night sky. *What could have happened to Trask?* she wondered for what had to be the thousandth time. *Where was he? Why hadn't he called?*

She finally slept although fitfully and when the first streaks of dawn began to lighten the room, Tory was relieved to have an excuse to get out of bed and start the morning chores. If she had had to spend another hour in bed staring at the clock, she would have gone out of her mind with worry about Trask.

She had changed, showered and started breakfast before she heard Keith moving around in his room upstairs.

Coffee was perking and the apple muffins were already out of the oven when Keith sauntered into the kitchen. She turned to face her brother and he lifted his hands into the air as if to ward off a blow. "Truce, Sis?" he asked, grinning somewhat sheepishly.

The corners of Tory's lips curved upward and her round eyes sparkled with affection for her brother.

"You know I don't hold a grudge. Well, at least not against you."

"Or Trask McFadden," he pointed out, walking to the stove and pouring them each a cup of coffee.

"I think five years was enough," Tory said.

"For sending Dad to prison where he died? Give me a break!" He offered her a mug of steaming coffee, which she accepted, but she felt her smile disintegrate.

Tory set the basket of muffins on the table and tried to ignore Keith's open hostility toward Trask. "Did you say something about a truce?"

"A truce between you and me. Not with McFadden!" Keith frowned, sat down in his regular chair and reached for a muffin. "By the way, where is he this morning?"

"I don't know," she admitted, biting nervously at her lower lip and trying to hide the fact that she was worried sick about him. She glanced nervously at the clock. It was nearly seven.

"Did he visit Benton and Henderson yesterday?" Keith had his knife poised over the butter, but his eyes never left his sister's anxious face. It was evident from the circles under her eyes and the lines near the corners of her mouth that she hadn't been able to sleep.

"I don't know that either. No one's seen or heard from him since he left here yesterday morning."

Keith set the knife aside. "So you're worried about him, right?"

"A little."

"He can handle himself."

"I wish I could believe that," Tory said.

"But you can't? Why not?"

"Think about it," Tory said with a sigh. "His brother

was murdered for what he knew, Trask was beaten up the night before last and someone shot at him on Devil's Ridge." Her voice trembled slightly and she took a long swallow of coffee. "I think I have a reason to be worried." She glanced nervously out the window before taking a seat at the table. "If I don't hear from him this morning, I'm calling Paul Barnett."

"Maybe Trask's with Neva," Keith said as gently as he could.

Tory felt the sting of Keith's remark and she paled slightly. "He wasn't with Neva," she whispered. "Neva called here last night. She's worried, too."

"Look, Tory," Keith cajoled. "A United States senator doesn't just vanish off the face of the earth. He'll be back flashing that politician's smile of his. The man's a survivor, for crying out loud."

Tory didn't answer. She swirled the coffee in her mug and silently prayed that this time Keith was right.

The sound of Rex's pickup caught her attention. Still wrapped in her own worried thoughts, Tory poured the foreman a cup of coffee without really thinking about it. By the time that Rex came in through the back door, she had already added a teaspoon of sugar to the cup.

"'Mornin'," Rex greeted, noting the lines of worry disturbing the smooth skin of Tory's brow.

"How about some breakfast?" Tory asked.

Rex eyed the muffins and the sliced fruit on the table. "Looks good, but no thanks." He patted his flat abdomen. "Already ate with Belinda." He paused for a moment and shook his head. "I just wanted to let you know that I fixed the combine late yesterday afternoon and that I'm planning to cut the yearling calves from the herd today. There's a rancher who lives in

Sisters and he's interested in about thirty head. He'll be here around eleven." Rex pushed the brim of his hat farther up on his forehead as he accepted the cup of coffee Tory offered. He warmed his gnarled fingers around the ceramic mug. "He might want to look at the horses, too."

Tory managed a smile. "Good. You can show him the mares and the foals as well as the yearlings."

Keith didn't bother to hide his surprise. He frowned, causing a deep groove in his forehead between his eyebrows. "You plan on selling some of the mares?"

"Maybe. If the price is right."

Her brother leaned back in his chair and his eyes narrowed thoughtfully. "Because you know that once this scandal hits the papers no one, even if his life depends on it, will buy a Quarter Horse from the Lazy W."

"That's exaggerating a little, I think. But the note from the bank is due soon and we'll need all the cash we can get."

"Don't remind me."

"I'll try not."

"Okay," Rex said, noticing the simmering hostility between brother and sister. "I'll show the man from Sisters around, see if I can get him interested in any of the horses."

"I thought you wanted to keep the mares another year at least and wait until the foals were born," Keith persisted.

Tory pursed her lips and shook her head. "I think we'd better go with the bird in the hand theory." She leveled her concerned eyes at Rex. "If the buyer wants any of the mares, they're for sale."

"What about stallions?" Rex asked.

Tory clenched her teeth. "They're for sale, too. For the right price."

"Even Governor?" Rex asked.

"All of them," Tory whispered.

"Tory, I can't let you do this—" Keith began to interrupt and looked as if he wanted to say more, but Tory cut him off.

"I don't think we've got a choice. I have a meeting with the bank scheduled for the end of next week, and for once I'd like to show that the Lazy W has a positive cash flow. You were right when you first told me we'd have to sell—it just took a while for it to sink in. Selling some of the cattle and a few horses might get us out of the red for the month of June. Even if it's only one month, it would say a lot and help me convince the loan officer to lend us more operating capital."

"Hmph! How was I to know you'd listen to me for once?" Keith replied. Then, not having an argument against her logic, but worried just the same, Keith set down his empty coffee cup, got up from the table and explained that he would be working with some of the men who were cutting hay.

Rex and Keith walked out of the house together. Tory was left alone with the dirty dishes as well as her worries about what may have happened to Trask.

TWO HOURS LATER, as she was finishing feeding the horses and wondering which, if any of the stock, would sell to the buyer from Sisters, she heard the sound of Trask's Blazer rumbling down the drive. Her heart seemed to leap inside her. She looked out the dusty window of the stables to confirm what her ears had told her and a smile grew from one side of her face to the other as she watched Trask's vehicle stop near the house. He got out of the Blazer and stretched, lifting his hands over his head, and making his flat abdomen appear almost concave with the unconscious, but erotic movement. He was dressed in worn cords and a shirt with the sleeves pushed up to his elbows. The sight of him brought tears of relief to Tory's eyes.

He started for the house, but she pounded on the window of the stables. Trask turned, squinted against the sun and his wonderful slightly crooked smile stole over his jaw when he noticed her. That was all the encouragement she needed. Without caring that they might be seen, Tory ran out of the stables and straight into his arms. He held her so tightly that her feet were pulled from the ground as he spun her around.

Bending his head, Trask kissed her passionately, sending warm bursts to every point in her body.

"What happened to you?" she asked breathlessly, once the lingering kiss was over. His arms were still around her, locking her body next to his, pressing her curves against the hard muscles of his thighs and torso. "I was worried to death!"

"I should have called," he admitted, kissing her forehead and letting the faint scent of lilacs from her hair fill his nostrils. All of the frustrations that had knotted the muscles in the back of his neck since visiting the penitentiary seemed to melt away just at the sight of Tory's enigmatic smile and the feel of her warm body pressed eagerly to his.

"At the very least you should have called! You had Neva and me out of our minds with worry."

"Neva, too, huh?" he asked with a frown.

"What did you expect would happen when you disappeared?"

"I had no idea I was so popular," he said with a smile and she laughed, her hands still clutching his shoulders. Through the light cotton fabric of his shirt, she could feel the corded strength of his muscles tightening around her as he kissed her once again before lifting his head. His blue eyes smoldered with aroused passion.

"Why didn't you come back last night?" she managed to ask, though her thoughts were centered on the feel of his body pressed tightly against her.

"It didn't cross my mind that it would take all day and half the night to finish what I'd set out to do. I didn't get back to the cabin until two-thirty and even if I had a phone there, I wouldn't have called. I thought you'd already be in bed." That thought brought a seductive curve to his lips.

"I was!" she retorted trying to sound angry and failing. She lovingly traced the rugged set of his jaw with a finger. "I was in bed tossing and turning and wondering what horrible fate had come to you." Unconsciously she touched the cut on his chin. "You don't have a great track record for keeping yourself safe, you know. I stared at the ceiling and the clock all night long."

"I'm sorry," he said, refusing to release her and grinning broadly. His blue eyes twinkled with the morning light and he kissed her finger when it strayed near his mouth. Her breath caught in her throat at the feel of his tongue on her fingertip. "You paint a very suggestive picture, y'know," he whispered hoarsely. "I would have done just about anything to be with you last night." Familiarly his hands slid up her back, drawing her still closer to him, letting her feel the need rising within him. Instantly her body began to react and as his head dipped again, she parted her lips, anxious for the taste of him. How right it felt to be held in his arms with the warmth of the morning sun at her back.

"Maybe we should make up for lost time," he suggested against her ear.

She had to clear her throat and force herself to think rationally. The feel of Trask's body pressed urgently against hers made it difficult to think logically. "Later, senator," she said, trying to ignore the sweet rush of desire flooding her veins. "I've got work to do and I want to hear everything you found out yesterday."

"Can't it wait?" His breath fanned her ear.

She swallowed with difficulty and the feel of his palms pressed against the small of her back made refusing him incredibly difficult. Tory was tempted to say "yes" but she couldn't forget the threatening letter she had received just the day before. "I don't think so," she replied, reluctantly slipping out of his embrace and taking his hand to lead him toward the house. "You're not the only one who has something to say."

For the first time he noticed the trace of worry in her gray-green eyes. "Something happened last night?"

They were approaching the path leading to the back of the house. Alex, who had been lying under his favorite juniper bush, tagged along behind them and slid through the screen door when Tory opened it.

"Yesterday," Tory clarified. She poured them both a cup of coffee, placed a plate of leftovers on the floor for Alex's breakfast and retrieved the note from a drawer in her father's desk in the den.

Trask's eyes narrowed and glittered dangerously as she studied the single sheet of paper. "This has gone too far," he muttered. His fists clenched in frustrated rage and the muscles of his forearms flexed. "First Neva was threatened, and now you."

"Apparently someone has something to hide."

"And he'll go to just about any lengths to keep his secret hidden." Trask let out a long sigh and leaned against the counter. "Have you talked to the sheriff?"

"Not yet."

"What about any of John Davis's men?"

Tory shook her head. "The one man assigned to the ranch keeps a pretty low profile. He's only been inside the house a couple of times, but several of the hands have commented about his presence."

Trask's head snapped upward. "And what have you told them?"

"That I'm trying to prevent another one of the calves from being shot, you know, protecting the livestock."

"And they bought that story?" His dark brows raised suspiciously.

Tory shrugged. "I doubt it. The hands are too smart to be conned. They know when someone is trying to pull the wool over their eyes and can see through lies, just about any lie. Though they don't go poking around in my business, it's hard to ignore the fact that a United States senator showed up here, sporting a rather ugly cut on his chin. Especially since there was a scandal he was involved in a few years ago." She looked pointedly at Trask. "It hasn't helped that the rumors and gossip are already flying around Sinclair like vultures over a dying animal. So you see, it's really too much to expect the hands to think that the only reason a detective is on the ranch is to protect the cattle."

"I suppose so." He looked down at the letter again. "I don't like this, Tory."

She shuddered and took a sip of her coffee. "Neither do I."

Trask wearily pushed the hair from his face and began to pace across the kitchen floor.

"Cut that out," Tory admonished softly and then explained. "Pacing drives me nuts."

"You really are on edge aren't you?"

"I think we both are. Why don't you call Neva and let her know that you're all right? Then you can sit down and tell me everything that happened yesterday with the judge and his accomplice."

Trask reluctantly agreed and while he was on the phone to Neva and Paul Barnett, Tory fixed him a breakfast of muffins, fresh fruit and scrambled eggs. She was just placing the eggs on a platter when Trask walked back into the kitchen.

"You're spoiling me," he accused with a devilish twinkle in his eyes.

"And you love it." She looked up and pointed at a chair near the table. "Now, sit, senator, and tell me everything there is to know about Linn Benton."

Trask slid into his chair and began eating. "Benton seemed to think it was a joke that I was there, but Henderson was scared spitless. I think Henderson would have talked, but he was afraid that Linn Benton would find out."

"So you didn't learn anything you didn't already know?"

"Nothing specific," Trask admitted. "But I've got a gut feeling that somehow Linn Benton is involved in what's happening here. He was so amused by the whole thing, especially the fact that someone had beat the hell out of me." Puzzled lines etched across Trask's forehead.

"But you can't figure out exactly what he's doing or with whom, right?"

He looked away from her and his blue eyes grew as cold as the morning sky in winter. "I'm working on it. John Davis is checking out Benton's friends and the people that still work for him on his ranch near Bend, and after I was through at the penitentiary, I drove to Portland and did some research."

"What kind of research?"

"I made copies of all the newspaper accounts of what happened five years ago. Everything I could find on Jason's murder as well as the Quarter Horses and the swindle."

Tory felt her back stiffen. "But you were at the trial, heard and gave testimony. You already knew what happened; at least you thought you did."

"But I wanted to get a new perspective on the scam. I thought I could find it in the press accounts of the investigation and the trial."

"You must have read all those articles a hundred times," she whispered.

"I did five years ago under…a lot of stress and conflicting emotions," he said quietly. He finished his breakfast and again noticed the threatening letter. "So who do you think sent you this?" He pointed to the single white sheet of paper.

"I don't know."

"But surely you could hazard a guess," he coaxed.

"The only people I can think of are Linn Benton and George Henderson because we already know that they were involved. Benton has powerful allies outside of the penitentiary, people who are still on his payroll or owe him favors—"

The front door opened with a bang. "Tory?" Keith's anxious voice echoed through the house.

"In the kitchen," she called out to him.

"Thank God you're here," he said, striding to the back of the house and stopping short when he met Trask's cool stare. "I've got a bone to pick with you, McFadden."

Trask smiled wryly. "Another one?"

"Rex found another calf—shot just like the last one," Keith said, his face twisted with worry. He jerked his hat off his head, tossed it carelessly onto the counter and slid into the chair facing Trask.

Tory's slim shoulders slumped. Yesterday the note, today another calf...when would it end. "Where is it?" she asked.

"Rex found it on the south side of the pasture, near the lake. He's already taken care of the carcass."

"What was he doing in that pasture?" Trask asked.

"He works here, damn it!" Keith replied, his fist coiling angrily. "He was laying irrigation pipe—why the hell am I explaining all this to you?"

Tory held up her hands, forestalling the fight before it got started. "The calf was shot just like the other one?"

"Right. Near as we can tell, someone jumped the fence, picked out a victim and blasted it."

Tory felt her blood run cold. She looked at Trask and noticed that every muscle in his face had hardened.

"This all happened because of you," Keith pointed out as he leaned against his elbows on the table and rubbed a dirty hand over his brow, leaving streaks of dust on his face. "Everything was going along okay until you started poking around here."

A muscle in the corner of Trask's jaw began to work convulsively and he set his coffee cup on the table. When he stood, he towered over Keith and felt older than his thirty-six years. "I know that because I returned to Sinclair, I've put the ranch in danger. Believe me, it wasn't intentional."

"Hmph." Keith stared insolently up at the man who was responsible for all of the pain in his life. Tory's brother had to close his eyes and shake the feeling of dread that had overtaken him in the last few days.

"You don't have to worry about what's happening—"

"Like hell!" Keith's head snapped upward. "Another calf's been killed and we got this…this threat, for crying out loud!"

"I'll take care of it."

"Like the way you took care of Dad?" Keith demanded.

Tory's stomach was in knots. "I don't think bringing up the past will help—"

"Hell, Tory, that's what this is all about—the past—or have you forgotten?"

"Of course not!"

"Maybe we should all just cool off," Trask suggested, staring pointedly at Keith.

The silence in the kitchen was so thick Tory could feel the weight of it upon her shoulders. When Rex came through the back door, she was glad for the excuse of pouring the foreman a cup of coffee.

"We lost another one," Rex stated, frowning slightly

at the sight of Trask in the house. He took off his Stetson and ran his hand over his forehead.

"Keith told us about it," Tory said.

"What are your theories about how it was killed?" Trask asked, leaning his elbows against the counter, stretching his legs in front of him before crossing his ankles and folding his arms over his chest. Though he tried to appear casual, Tory noticed the grim set of his jaw and the determination in his eyes.

Rex shrugged and accepted the cup of coffee Tory offered. "Don't really know."

"Surely you must have some thoughts about what happened?"

Rex stared at Trask over the rim of his cup. "All I know is that the trouble started when you arrived."

Trask's eyebrows cocked. "So you think it was more than a coincidence?"

"I'd stake my life on it."

"Tell me, Rex," Trask cajoled and Tory was reminded of the one time she had seen him working as a lawyer in the courtroom. Her blood chilled at the memory. It had been two or three months before the scandal involving her father had been discovered. Trask's country-boy charm and affable smile had won him the confidence of everyone in the courtroom, including a few of the prosecution's witnesses. He coaxed one woman, a witness for the prosecution, into saying something the D.A. would rather have remained secret. Dread began to knot in Tory's stomach as Trask began to question Rex in his soft drawl. "Tell me how long you've been with the Lazy W."

"More years than I'd want to count," Rex replied,

returning Trask's stare without flinching. "What're you getting at, McFadden?"

Trask overlooked the question. "And why did Calvin hire you?"

Tory felt the air in the room become thick with suspicion. "Trask—"

"What's this got to do with anything?" Keith demanded.

The foreman disregarded Keith's interruption and drained his cup, never once taking his eyes off Trask. "Calvin needed help with the Lazy W, I guess. And I needed a job."

"And you've stayed all these years."

"Yep."

"Even after Calvin died." Trask made it sound as if Rex's loyalty were some sort of crime.

"I'm too old to jump from spread to spread."

"Trask," Tory interjected, her voice wavering slightly. "There's no need for this. Rex doesn't have to explain himself."

"Just a few friendly questions," Trask replied coldly.

Tory wondered what had happened to the warm caring man he had been only moments before.

"Well, let me ask you a few," Keith cut in. "You seem to be pointing fingers at nearly everyone you meet, McFadden. But what about you? How do we know that the letter you brought here isn't a phony? How do we know that you haven't been the one calling Neva, sending threatening letters to Tory or shooting the calves?"

If Trask was outraged, he managed to hide it. His lips twisted into a grim smile but his eyes became as cold as the deepest well at midnight.

"And you think I took a shot at myself, too?" Trask returned.

"You could have hired someone to fire a shot when you were up on Devil's Ridge. After all, you were the only one who knew you'd be up there. As for what happened to you—" Keith's palm flipped upward as he pointed to the discoloration under Trask's eye "—you could have hired that done as well, for authenticity's sake!"

"You know, Wilson, you have one hell of an imagination," Trask said with genuine amusement. "Why would I bother?"

"I think your motives are pretty obvious. Sure it looks like you're on the up and up; that way you could worm your way back into Tory's heart, not to mention the fact that you'd look good to the press. All the rumors and publicity that are bound to spring from your investigation aren't going to hurt your career, are they? And they'll serve to remind the voting public of the reason you were elected in the first place, proving beyond a shadow of a doubt that you're still the hard-nosed, filled-with-integrity candidate you were four years ago!"

"I just want to find out if another man was involved in Jason's death."

"You've got your vengeance and more," Keith said. "Because my father wasn't involved with Linn Benton or George Henderson."

"Then why didn't he say so, declare his innocence? He had his chance."

"I…I don't know," Keith said, his cocky attitude slipping a little.

"So we're back to square one, aren't we?" Trask

thought aloud. "Well, not for long. I intend to figure out what happened back then." Trask's eyes glittered so fiercely that Tory felt a needle of fear pierce her heart.

"And what if your anonymous letter is a phony? How about that?" Keith persisted. "Then you've brought us all this trouble for no reason."

"I don't think so."

"Neither do I," Tory said with conviction as she looked at the cut on Trask's face.

"Oh, God, Tory, you can't believe him, not again!"

"It sure takes a helluva lot to convince you, Wilson," Trask said tiredly before returning his gaze to Tory. The warmth returned to his eyes. "Look, I'm going to be gone for a few days, do some checking around. But I'll be back. And, while I'm gone, one of John Davis's men will be here." He looked pointedly at Rex and Keith before letting his gaze fall back on Tory. "I think you should call Paul Barnett and report what happened to the calf."

"I will," she promised.

"Here we go again," Keith muttered as he grabbed his hat and walked out the door.

Rex shifted uncomfortably before wiping his hand nervously over his brow. "I just want to clear the air," he said.

"About what?"

"The reasons I came to the Lazy W."

"Rex, you don't have to—"

"I've got nothing to hide, Tory. I couldn't get work anywhere because of my first wife. She claimed that I...that I'd get angry with her, drink too much and... rough her up." Rex closed his eyes and sadly shook his head. "Marianne swore that on several occasions I'd beat her; but it just wasn't so. The only time I slapped her was after a particularly bad fight and, well, she had a butcher knife, said she was going to use it on me if I came near her. I took the knife away from her and slapped her. She filed charges against me."

"Which were later dropped," Trask added.

"You knew all about it?" Rex asked with a grimace.

Trask nodded and Tory felt sick inside that Rex had been forced to bare his soul.

"Even though I was aquitted, no one would give me work."

"Except for Calvin Wilson."

Rex's chin jutted outward. "I've been here ever since." He set down his cup and started toward the door. "I'll be in the stables if you want me," he said to Tory. "The buyer from Sisters still wants thirty head of cattle."

Still slightly numb from the scene she had just witnessed, Tory found it difficult to concentrate on the work at hand. Her eyes offered Rex a silent apology. "What about horses?"

Rex frowned and shook his head. "He said he'll wait to decide about the horses, though he looked at a couple of yearlings that he liked." Forcing his hat onto his head, Rex walked out the back door. Tory didn't have to question him any further. She knew that the sale of the horses wasn't completed because of the Quarter Horse swindle her father was supposedly involved in five years ago. Even though it had happened long ago and her father was dead, people remembered, especially now that Trask was back. So the paranoia of the past had already started interfering with the future.

When she heard Trask move toward the door, she

impaled him with her eyes. "That was uncalled for, senator," she rebuked.

"What?"

"You didn't have to humiliate Rex. Especially since you knew all the answers anyway. That's called baiting, senator, and I don't like it. It might work in Washington, D.C., but I won't have it here, on the Lazy W, used against my employees."

"I just wanted to see if he would tell the truth."

Hot injustice colored Tory's cheeks. "And did he pass the test?" she demanded.

"With flying colors."

"Good. Then maybe you'll quit harassing everyone who works on this ranch and concentrate on Linn Benton or whoever else might have a grudge against your brother."

"I didn't mean to upset you," he said softly.

"You don't mean to do a lot of things, but you do them anyway, despite anyone else's feelings."

"Not true, Victoria," he countered, coming up to her and placing his hands over her shoulders, his blue eyes searching hers. His fingers gently massaged the tense muscles near the base of her neck, warming her skin. "I'm always concerned about you and what you feel."

"You weren't five years ago."

A shadow of pain crossed his eyes. "I only told what I thought was the truth and you still can't forgive me, can you?"

She closed her eyes against a sudden unwanted feeling that she would break down and cry. "It…it was very hard to sit by and know that Dad was dying…alone in some god-awful jail cell all because of what I told you."

"It's not your fault that you overheard Linn Benton discussing plans with your father."

"But it's my fault that you found out about it," she whispered.

Trask frowned and took her into her arms, but the response he got was cold and distant. "You can't keep blaming yourself."

She let out a tired sigh. "I try not to."

He hesitated a minute. "Are you okay?" She nodded mutely and took hold of her emotions to force the tears backward.

"Good." He kissed her softly on the forehead. "I've got to go. I'll be back in a couple of days."

"Where are you going?"

"I wish I knew," he admitted. "I'll start by visiting John Davis in Bend and showing him all these clippings. Maybe he can come up with something; a new angle. I'll be back...soon."

"I'm counting on it, senator," she whispered before he gathered her into his arms and kissed her with all of the passion that had fired his blood since the first time he had seen her. His tongue caressed and mated with hers and she leaned against him, her knees becoming soft. Once again she was caught up in the storm of emotions that raged within her each time she was near him, and when he finally released her, she felt empty inside.

Tory stood on the back porch and watched him leave. When his Blazer was out of sight, she tried to think of anything but Trask and his reasons for returning to the Lazy W.

Pouring hot coffee into her cup, she walked into the den and sat at the desk, intending to concentrate on preparing a financial statement to take to the bank later in the week.

But the numbers were meaningless and her mind wandered. She found her thoughts returning to the conversation she had overheard between her father and Linn Benton five years ago…in this very study.

THE SUMMER NIGHT had been breathlessly hot and humid. Tory had come downstairs for a glass of lemonade when she heard the muted whispers behind the closed doors to the study. Her father's den had never been off limits, but that night, the night that Linn Benton had stormed into the house, everything changed and the pieces of the argument that drifted to her ears caught her attention and made her hesitate on the lowest step.

"Don't be so goddamned sanctimonious," the judge had said in his high-pitched wheezing tone. "You're in this up to your neck, Wilson."

Tory slipped down the final step and stood frozen in the entry hall, eavesdropping on a conversation she wished later that she had never overheard.

"I should never have gotten involved with you," her father replied brusquely.

"Too late for second thoughts now."

"If it weren't for the kids…" Her father's voice had drifted off and her heart grew cold. Calvin was entangled with Linn Benton because of her brother and her. Her father was doing something he didn't believe in just to support his children! She reached for the door, but the self-satisfied laughter of Linn Benton made her withdraw her hand. Tory realized that it would be better if she waited until she could speak to her father alone before confronting him.

The rest of the angry conversation was muted and she only heard parts of it, just enough to know that whatever the two men were arguing about wasn't aboveboard. She silently worried in the outer hall before going upstairs and pacing the floorboards of her room.

When she heard the judge's car roar down the drive, she raced down the stairs, intent on confronting her father and begging him to abandon whatever it was that involved Linn Benton.

But Calvin was no longer in the study. The door to the den was open, and thick cigar smoke still lingered in the air. Two half-empty glasses of whisky sat neglected on the desk.

"Dad?" she called, starting for the kitchen and glancing out the window just in time to see her father reining his favorite gelding out of the stables and kicking the horse into a full gallop in the moonlight. Head bent against a mounting summer wind, Calvin Wilson raced through the pastures toward the mountains and Devil's Ridge.

Tory ran to the front door, jerked it open and let the hot dusty wind inside. *"Dad!"* she called again, this time screaming at the top of her lungs from the front porch. Either Calvin didn't hear her voice over the sound of his horse's racing hoofbeats and the whistling wind, or he chose to ignore her.

Tory was just about to follow him when Trask arrived. She was already leading a mare from the stables as his truck approached. Tory's nerves shattered with fear for her father's life and she quickly explained about the strange conversation she had overheard to the man she loved and trusted with all of her heart.

Trask muttered an angry oath and his eyes blazed with angry lightning.

His jaw set with furious resolve and with only a few abrupt commands telling her to stay on the ranch and wait for his call, Trask wheeled his jeep around and followed Calvin through the open fields. Like a fool she had trusted him and obeyed, keeping her lonely vigil through the night, pacing in the den, praying that the phone would ring and end her fears.

Early the next morning, when Trask finally returned, she learned the horrible truth: Jason McFadden had been found dead—the result of a monstrous plot conceived by Linn Benton, George Henderson, and, according to Trask, her own father. Tory was numb with disbelief when she learned that Calvin Wilson had been charged with murder.

CHAPTER ELEVEN

NEARLY TWO QUIET weeks had passed when Trask found himself staring into the self-satisfied smile of the private investigator. Trask was sitting in one of the soft leather chairs near the desk, but his body had gone rigid.

"You found out *what*?" Trask demanded, staring at the private investigator in disbelief.

"Just what I told you," John Davis replied, settling back in his chair and casually lighting a cigarette. Behind him, through the second-story window of his office, was a bird's-eye view of the bustling downtown area of the city of Bend.

"Damn!" Trask's fist coiled and he slapped it into his other palm. His dark brows drew together.

"I thought you wanted the truth."

"I did. I did." Trask sounded as if he were trying to convince himself. "It's just that… Hell, I don't know." His thoughts were jumbled and confused. The past couple of weeks had eased by in a regular routine. Fortunately there had been no more threatening letters, dead calves or violence. He had spent most of his time with Tory on the Lazy W. The days had been pleasant; the nights filled with passionate exhilaration. And now this unexpected news from John Davis was about to change all that. The damned thing was that it was exactly what he had been asking for.

"You're sure about this," Trask said, already knowing the answer as he stared at the damning report in John's hands.

The private investigator stubbed out his cigarette and studied his client through thick lenses. "Positive, and even if you're entertaining thoughts about keeping it quiet, I can't. I've got some responsibility to the law, y'know." He tossed the neatly typed report across the desk.

"As well as your clients."

"Doesn't matter. If you want to keep something the size of this quiet, Trask, you'll have to use every bit of senatorial pull you have in this state. Even that might not be enough."

"I didn't say I wanted to keep it quiet."

"Good. Now, if you're worried about your career once the truth is known..." The young man shrugged and smiled.

"I don't give a damn about my career!"

"Still the rogue senator, right?"

Trask's face tensed and his eyes dropped to the damning document lying on the polished mahogany of the desk. He picked it up and folded it neatly into the manila envelope John offered. "This is going to be one hell of a mess," he thought aloud.

"But it will be over," John replied. The investigator's voice sounded like a trumpet of doom.

"Yes, I suppose it will," Trask replied. "I guess I should thank you." He placed the thick envelope in his jacket pocket and tossed the coat over his arm.

"I guess maybe you should," John replied with a smile, though his eyes remained sober.

Trask strode out of the office feeling as if the weight of the world had been placed upon his shoulders. *So Tory had been right all along: Calvin Wilson had been innocent! But not so her younger brother, Keith.* And that news would destroy her. No doubt she would blame Trask.

Trask's blood began to boil with anger when he thought about how many times Keith had lied through his teeth, not only to Trask, but to Tory as well. Letting out a descriptive curse, Trask walked down the short flight of stairs to the ground floor. According to John Davis's report, which the investigator had double-checked, Keith Wilson and not Calvin Wilson had been involved in the Quarter Horse swindle five years past. All Trask's testimony at the original trial had been in error. Calvin Wilson had only been trying to protect his teenaged son from prosecution.

"Crazy old fool," Trask muttered as he walked out of the building and climbed into his Blazer. He threw the truck into gear and let out a stream of oaths against himself and the whole vile mess that Linn Benton had conceived. The aftermath of the ex-judge's illegal scam was ruining the lives of the only people he really cared about. Tory, Neva and Nicholas had all been innocent victims of a plot so malicious it had included the murder of his brother.

Trask's mouth twisted downward and he could feel his jaw clench at the stupidity of Keith Wilson. All of Tory's precious trust would be shattered when she found out the truth about her brother and that Trask had helped send her father, an innocent man, to prison.

"Damn it, Wilson," he swore, as if Calvin were in the Blazer with him. "Why couldn't you have said something before being so goddamned noble!"

TORY WALKED OUT of the bank and into the blazing heat of midafternoon. Her head throbbed and the muscles in the back of her neck ached. For the past two hours she had explained the profit and loss statements, as well as going over the assets and liabilities of the Lazy W to a disinterested young loan officer.

"I'll let you know," the bored young man had said. "But I can't make any promises right now. Your loan application, along with the financial statements and a status report of your current note with the bank will have to be reviewed by the loan committee as well as by the president of the bank."

"I see," Tory had replied, forcing a discouraged smile. She knew, whether the young man admitted it or not, that he was peddling her nothing more than financial double-talk. The Lazy W didn't have a snow-ball's chance in hell of receiving more funds from this particular bank. "And how long will it take before I can expect an answer?" Tory had asked.

"The loan committee meets next Thursday."

"Fine." She had stood, shook the banker's soft hand and walked out of the building, certain that the Lazy W would have to secure operating capital from another source.

After stopping by Rasmussen Feed for several sacks of oats and bran for the horses, Tory made her weekly visit to the grocery store and bought a local newspaper along with her week's supply of groceries. Once the sacks were loaded in the pickup, she glanced at the headlines on the front page of the paper.

The article was small, but located on page one. In five neatly typed paragraphs it reported that Senator Trask McFadden was back in Sinclair looking into the possibility that there may have been a fourth conspirator in his brother's death as well as the Quarter Horse swindle of five years past. The *Sinclair Weekly* promised a follow-up story the next week.

"Wonderful," Tory muttered with a groan, tossing the newspaper aside and heading back to the Lazy W.

The past two weeks had been quiet and Tory had ignored her earlier doubts about the past to the point that she had let herself fall completely and recklessly in love with Trask all over again. There had been no threats or violence and oftentimes Tory would allow herself to forget the reason that Trask had come back to Sinclair. She had even managed not to dwell on the fact that he would be leaving for Washington D.C. very shortly.

Though she was still worried about the threats of violence that seemed to have accompanied him back to the Lazy W, Tory had thought less and less about them as Trask's wounds had healed and there hadn't been any further incidents. Unfortunately, the *Sinclair Weekly* decided to stir things up.

Just let me love him without the rest of the world intruding, she silently prayed.

Of course her hopes were in vain. With the article in the newspaper, everything came crashing back to reality. No longer could she ignore the real reason Trask had returned to Sinclair. Nor could she forget that he would leave as soon as he had finished his investigation.

And then what? she asked herself. *What about all his words of love, promises of marriage? Is that what you want? To be married to a United States senator who lives in Washington D.C.? And what if he isn't sincere? What if this has all been an adventure for him— nothing more. He left you once before. Nothing says he can't do it again.*

"But he won't," she said as she parked the pickup near the back door. "He won't leave me and he'll never betray me again!" Hearing her own voice argue against the doubts in her mind, she experienced a sudden premonition of dread.

Tory unpacked the groceries and after changing from the linen business suit she had worn to meet with the bank's loan officer, she drove the pickup to the stables, unloaded the heavy sacks of grain and stacked them in the feed bins against the wall.

Her eyes wandered lovingly over the clean wooden stalls, and she noted the shining buckets that were hung near the mangers. The smell of horses, leather and saddle soap combined with the sweet scent of oats and freshly cut hay. Tory gazed through the window. Against the backdrop of long-needled pines, Governor was grazing contentedly, his laminitis nearly cured. A distant sound caught his attention. He lifted his graceful dark head and pricked his ears forward, before pawing the ground impatiently and tossing his head to the sky. Tory's heart swelled with pride as she watched the magnificent stallion, a horse she had cared for since he was a fiery young colt.

She walked outside and closed the door of the stables behind her. Her eyes scanned the horizon and the rolling fields leading toward the craggy snowcapped mountains. What would she do if she lost the Lazy W? Leaning against the fence she could feel her brows draw together. The thought of losing the ranch was sobering and her small chin lifted in defiance against the fates that sought to steal her home and livelihood from her.

I can't, she thought to herself, slowly clenching her fists. *No matter what else happens, I can't lose this ranch.* Tory had always believed that where there was a will, there was a way. So it was with the Lazy W. She would find a way to keep the ranch, no matter what. Livestock could be sold, as well as pieces of machinery, if need be. And there were several parts of the ranch that could be parceled off without really affecting the day-to-day operations. The fields used for growing hay could be sold and she could buy the hay she needed from other ranchers. And there was always Devil's Ridge. Though Keith now owned that parcel, it could be sold or mortgaged.

She leaned on the fence and sighed. If things had gone differently, Devil's Ridge would now be where her father and mother would have retired and Keith would be running the ranch. Tory could have married Trask, and had several precious children to love…

"Stop it," she muttered to herself, slapping the fence post and dismissing her daydreams. "If wishes were horses, then beggars would ride."

Trying to shake the mood of desperation that had been with her since leaving the bank, Tory saddled her favorite palomino mare and mounted the spirited horse. After walking through the series of paddocks surrounding the stables, she urged the small horse into a gallop through the fields surrounding the main build-

ings of the ranch. Tory really didn't know where she
was going, but she felt compelled to get away from the
problems at the Lazy W.

The mare was eager to stretch her legs and Tory
leaned forward in the saddle, encouraging the little
horse. The only sounds she could hear were the thudding of the mare's hooves against the summer-hard
ground and the pounding of her own heart. As the
palomino raced toward the lake in the largest pasture,
Tory felt the sting of the wind tangle her hair and force
tears to her eyes. As if stolen by the wind, the pres-
sures of running the ranch ebbed from Tory's mind
and she gave herself up to the breathless exhilaration
of the horse's sprint.

"You're just what I needed," she confided to the
mare as she slowly reined the horse to a stop. Tory slid
out of the saddle and let the horse drink from the clear
lake. The late-afternoon sky reflected on the spring-fed
pond and the scent of newly mown hay drifted over the
land. *Her land.* The land both she and her father had
worked to keep in the family.

While the mare grazed nearby, Tory propped her
back against a solitary pine tree and stared at the horizon to the west. Misty white clouds clung to the up-
permost peaks of the craggy snow-covered mountains
in the distance. Closer, in the forested foothills, the distinct rocky spine of Devil's Ridge was visible.

Despite her earlier vows to herself, Tory's thoughts
centered on the ridge and the afternoon she had spent
with Trask just a few short weeks before.

Trask. His image flitted seductively through her
mind.

He was the one man she should hate but couldn't.

Despite the deceit of the past and the uncertainty of the future, Tory loved him with all of her heart. The past few weeks even Keith seeemd to have thawed and for the first time Tory thought there was actually a chance of a future with the man she loved. She tossed a pebble into the lake and watched the ever-widening circles spread over the calm water.

So what about the anonymous note, the dead calves, the rifle shot on Devil's Ridge, the threats? her persistent mind nagged.

With lines of concern creasing her brow, Tory plucked a piece of grass from the ground and twirled it in her fingers. *When all of this is behind us,* she thought, envisioning Trask's face, *then there will be time for you and me. Alone. Without the doubts. Without the lies...*

The sound of an approaching horse caught Tory's attention. The mare lifted her head and nickered softly to the approaching horse and rider before grazing again.

Tory shielded her eyes from the sun with her hand and recognized a large buckskin gelding and the man astride the horse. A smile eased over her features at the sight of Trask riding the gelding. Dressed in jeans and a cotton shirt, bareheaded to the sun, he looked as comfortable in the saddle as he did in a Senate subcommittee.

Tory forced herself to her feet and dusted her hands together as Trask dismounted and tethered the gelding near Tory's mare. "I was just thinking about you," she admitted, her lips lifting into a welcoming smile. "How did you know where to find me?"

"One of the hands, Eldon—at least I think that's his name—" Tory nodded. "He saw you leave and told me which direction to take after saddling the buckskin for me."

"So much for privacy," she murmured.

"I didn't think you'd mind." He walked over to her and gently pulled her against him. Immediately she felt her body respond and the dormant stirrings of desire begin to waken deep in her soul.

"I don't, senator. Not much, anyway," she said teasingly, cocking her head upward to gaze at him. The late-afternoon sun caught in her hair, streaking the tangled auburn strands with fiery highlights of gold.

When she looked deep into his eyes she noticed the worry lingering in his gaze. The tautness of his skin as it stretched over his cheekbones and the furrow of his brow made her sense trouble. "Something's wrong," she said, feeling her throat constrict with dread.

He tried to pass off her fears with a patient smile, but his blue eyes remained intense, dark with a secret. "I was just thinking that it's about time we got married."

"What!" Though what he was saying was exactly what she wanted to hear, she couldn't hide the astonishment in her eyes.

"Don't look so shocked," he said coaxingly, kissing her tenderly on the forehead and squeezing his eyes shut against the possibility that he might never hold her again. "You know that it's something I've been talking about for the past three weeks."

"Wait a minute. What's going on? I thought we had an understanding that we had to get things settled between us. What about the note and the dead calves and your theory about another person being involved in the Quarter Horse swindle—"

"None of that will change." His voice was calm, his jaw hard with determination.

It was then that real fear gripped her throat. "You know something, don't you?" she asked, with the blinding realization that he was hiding something from her. She pulled away from his embrace and felt her heart thud with dread.

The pain in his eyes was nearly tangible and the lines near his mouth were grim with foreboding. "I want you to marry me, as soon as possible."

"But there has to be a reason."

"How about the fact that I can't live without you."

"Level with me, Trask."

"I am. I want to spend the rest of my life with you and I thought you wanted the same."

"I do…but something isn't right. I can see it in your eyes. What happened?" she demanded.

Trask pushed his hands through his hair and his broad shoulders slumped. "I just came from John Davis's office," he admitted.

John Davis. The private investigator. Tory's voice trembled slightly. "And?"

"And he came up with some answers for me."

"Answers that I'm not going to like," she surmised, taking in a deep breath.

"Yes."

"About Dad?"

"No."

Trask turned and met her confused gaze. "John Davis did some digging, thorough digging. He even went back to the penitentiary to double-check with George Henderson about what he'd discovered. George decided to come clean."

"About what?"

"Your father was innocent, Tory. Just as you believed."

So that was it! Trask's guilt for condemning an innocent man to prison was what was bothering him. Relief washed over her in a tidal wave and tears of happiness welled in her eyes. If only her father were still alive he could be a free man. "But that's wonderful news," she said, stepping closer to him.

The look he sent her could have cut through steel. "There's more. Your father wasn't involved with Linn Benton and George Henderson but someone else was."

She froze and the first inkling of what he was suggesting penetrated her mind. "Who?"

"Your brother, Tory. Keith was an integral part of the horse swindle."

Tory didn't move. She let the words sink in and felt as if her safe world was spinning crazily away from her. Cold desperation cloaked her heart. "But that's impossible. Keith was only sixteen. He didn't even know Judge Benton or…George…"

"He knew George Henderson, Tory. George was the local vet. He'd been out to the ranch more times than you can remember. He liked your brother. Keith had even gone hunting with him on occasion."

"But he was just a boy," she said, feeling numb inside. "It just doesn't make any sense, none of it."

"Why do you think Keith reacted so violently to my return to Sinclair?"

"He has reason to hate you."

"And fear me."

Tory's mind was clouded with worried thoughts, pieces of the puzzle that weren't fitting together. She walked away from Trask, pushed her hands into the back pockets of her jeans and stared into the lake, not noticing the vibrant hue of the water. The gentle afternoon breeze lifted her hair from her face. "I don't believe you," she whispered. "If Keith had been involved with Linn Benton and George Henderson, it all would have come out at the trial."

"Unless your father paid for your brother's crime."

"No!" She whirled to face him. Her eyes were wide with new understanding and fear.

"Why else wouldn't Calvin defend himself?" He reached forward and grabbed her upper arms, his fingers digging into the soft flesh. She was forced to stare past the anger of his eyes to the agony in his soul. "Your father sacrificed himself, Tory. So that your brother wouldn't have to go to some correctional institution or prison."

"No! I won't believe it!" A thousand emotions raged within her: love, hate, anger, fear and above all disbelief. "You're grasping at straws because that investigator found out that Dad was innocent."

"God, woman, do you think I made this up?" he asked, his voice cracking with emotion. "Do you think I enjoy watching you fall apart? Do you think I wanted to come out here and tell you that I was wrong, that I'd made some horrible mistake about your father and that your only living relative was the real criminal?"

She placed her head in her hands and closed her eyes. "I don't know, Trask."

"Marry me," he said, desperately trying to hold on to the love they had shared. "Don't think about anything else, just marry me."

"Oh, God, are you crazy?" she threw back at him,

her chest so tight she could barely breath. "After what you just told me, you want to marry me." Her eyes became incredibly cold.

"I don't want to lose you again," he said, his fingers clutching her upper arms in a death grip.

Again she buried her face in her hands trying hopelessly to make some sense of what he was telling her, trying not to let her feelings of love for this man color her judgment. She swallowed with difficulty before lifting her eyes and meeting his stormy gaze. "I...I just can't believe any of this."

"Can't or won't?"

"Same thing," she pointed out, feeling suddenly alone in an alien world of lies and deception. "I won't believe it and I can't. Keith was with me at the trial, helped me here at the ranch. He's grown into a good man and now you're trying to make me believe that he was capable of swindling the public, being a part of a gruesome murder and letting my father go to prison in place of him? How would you feel if I'd just said the same thing to you." Tory was shaking, visibly fighting to keep from breaking down.

"I don't know," he admitted, his voice harsh, "because I've lived the past five years without my brother."

"It's all happening again," Tory whispered, swallowing back the lump forming in her throat. "Just like before." She felt as if her heart was slowly being shredded by a destiny that allowed her to love a man who only wanted to hurt her. "And you're the one to blame." She shook her head and let the tears run freely. "I suppose you think that Keith beat you up, shot the calves and wrote threatening notes to both me and Neva?"

"I don't know," Trask said. "But I wouldn't rule it out."

"And what does your crackerjack ace detective think?" she asked, her voice filled with sarcasm.

"He knows he's found out the truth. He knows that some of the testimony of the original trial was faulty at best and maybe downright lies at the worst."

"Including yours?" she asked. Trask's jaw hardened and his eyes glittered dangerously, but Tory couldn't help the outrage overtaking her. *Keith. A criminal!* It couldn't be. She wouldn't sit still and let her only brother be given the same sentence as her innocent father. She had to fight back against the fates that were continually at odds with her happiness. "And I suppose Mr. Davis feels obligated to set the record straight."

"It's his job."

She smiled bitterly through her tears. "And what about you, senator? Is it your duty as well?"

"I've only wanted two things in my life: the truth and one other thing."

"I don't want to hear it," she whispered.

"You can't hide from it, Tory. I want you. All of you. No matter what else happens, I want you to be with me for the rest of my life." He lifted his head proudly and she realized just how difficult confronting her had been for him.

Her heart felt as if it were breaking into a thousand pieces. "Then why do you continue to try and ruin me?" she choked out, her eyes softening as she looked past the pain in his. "Must we always be so close and yet so distant?"

He reached for her, but she drew away. Her eyes were filled with tears and she didn't care that they ran down her cheeks and fell to her chest. "Please, just trust me," he asked so softly that she barely heard the words.

"I don't know if that's possible," she replied. She straightened her spine and attempted to tell herself that she could live without him. She had before. She would again, despite the gripping pain in her chest. "I…I think we should go back to the house." She turned toward the mare but the sound of his voice stopped her dead in her tracks.

"Victoria?" he said and she pivoted to face him. "I'll always love you."

She squeezed her eyes tightly shut, as if in so doing she could deny the painful words. *How desperately she had loved Trask and now she wished with all of her heart that she could hate him.*

They rode back to the house in silence, each wrapped in private and painful thoughts. Though dusk was gathering over the meadows, painting the countryside in vibrant lavender hues and promising a night filled with winking stars and pale light from a quarter moon, Tory didn't notice.

Keith's pickup was parked near the barn. Tory's heart began to race at the thought of the confrontation that was about to take place. She silently prayed that just this once Trask was dead wrong.

After Eldon offered to unsaddle and cool the horses, Tory walked with Trask back to the house. They didn't touch or speak and the tight feeling in Tory's chest refused to lessen.

"About time you showed up," Keith shouted down the stairs when he heard Tory walk into the house. "I'm starved." The knot in the bottom of her stomach tightened at the sight of her brother as he came down the stairs. His shirt was still gaping open and he was towel-drying his hair. "What say we go into Bend and catch a movie and then we'll go to dinner—my treat…" His voice faded when he saw Trask. He lowered the towel and smiled grimly. "I guess you probably have other plans." He stopped at the bottom step and noticed her pale face. "Hey, what's wrong?"

"There's something Trask wants to ask you about," Tory said, her voice quavering slightly.

"So what else is new?" Keith cast an unfriendly glance at Trask before striding into the kitchen.

"It's a little different this time," Trask remarked, following the younger man down the short hallway.

"Oh yeah? Good." Keith chuckled mirthlessly to himself. "I'm tired of the same old questions." He seemed totally disinterested in Trask's presence and he rummaged in the refrigerator for the jug of milk.

Alex was whining at the back door and Keith let the old collie into the house. "What's the matter, boy?" he asked, scratching the dog behind the ears. "Hungry?"

The sight of her brother so innocently petting the dog's head tore at Tory's heart. "Keith—" Tory's words froze when she noticed Rex's pickup coming down the drive.

"What?"

"Maybe we should talk about this later," she said.

"Talk about what?" Keith poured a large glass of milk, then drank most of it in one swallow.

"About what happened five years ago," Trask stated.

"I thought you said you had come up with some new questions."

"I have." The edge to Trask's voice made Keith start.

"Not now—" Tory pleaded, desperation taking a

firm hold of her. She had already lost her father and the thought of losing Keith the same way was unbearable.

Though he felt his stomach tighten in concern as he studied the pale lines of Tory's face, Trask ignored her obvious dread, deciding that the truth had to be brought into the open. "No time like the present, I always say." He watched with narrowed eyes as the foreman climbed out of his pickup and started walking toward the house. "Besides, Rex should be part of this."

"Part of what?" For the first time Keith noticed the worry in his sister's eyes. "What's going on?" he insisted. "Don't tell me we got another one of those damned notes!"

"Not quite."

"Oh, Keith," Tory whispered, her voice cracking.

Rex rapped on the back door and entered the kitchen. His eyes shifted from Tory to her brother before settling on Trask and he felt the electric tension charging the air. "Maybe I should come back later——" he said, moving toward the door.

"No." Trask swung a chair around and straddled the back. "I think that you can help shed a little light on something I've discovered."

"You're still going at it, aren't you?" the foreman accused. He lifted his felt hat from his head and worked the wide brim between his gnarled fingers. "You're worse than a bull terrier once you get your teeth into something."

"Trask's private investigator has come up with another theory about what happened five years ago," Tory explained, her worried eyes moving to her brother.

Keith bristled. "What do you mean 'another theory'?"

"John Davis seems to think that your father was innocent," Trask said, silently gauging Keith's reaction.

"Big deal. We've been telling you that for years."

"But you wouldn't tell me who Calvin was protecting."

"What!" Keith's face slackened and lost all of its
color.

Tory felt as if her heart had just stopped beating.

"John Davis seems to think that your father was
covering for you; that you were the man called 'Wilson' that was involved with Linn Benton and George
Henderson."

"Wait a minute—" Rex cut in.

Tory's eyes locked with the foreman's anxious gaze.
Oh, my God, he knows what happened, she realized
with a sickening premonition of dread. Her chest felt
tight and she had to grip the counter for support.

"What do you know about this?" Trask turned furious eyes on the foreman.

"Keith wasn't involved with the likes of Henderson
and Benton," the foreman said, his face flushed, his
grizzled chin working with emotion.

"Davis can prove it," Trask said flatly.

Dead silence.

"How?" Tory asked.

Trask took the envelope from his jacket and tossed
it onto the table. "Someone, a man who worked for
Linn Benton when he was judge, saw Keith. George
Henderson verified the other guy's story."

"No!" Tory screamed, her voice catching on a sob.
Not Keith, too. She wouldn't, couldn't lose him.

"Back off, McFadden," Rex threatened, his eyes

darting to the rifle mounted over the door before returning to Trask.

Keith's shoulders slumped and he looked up at the ceiling. "No, Rex, don't. It's over—"

"Shut up!" the foreman snapped, his cold eyes drilling into Trask and his gnarled hands balling into threatening fists. "You just couldn't leave it alone, could you?"

"Why are you standing up for him? Were you involved, too?" Trask suggested.

"Save it, Rex," Keith said, his eyes locking with those of his sister. "He obviously knows everything." Keith's hands shook as he opened the envelope and skimmed through the contents of John Davis's report.

"Not everything. Maybe you can fill in a few of the missing blanks."

"Oh, God, Keith," Tory said, shaking her head, her voice strangling in her throat. "You don't have to say anything."

"It's time, Sis. I knew it the minute McFadden showed up here. I let Dad cover for me because I was young and scared. I don't have those excuses to hide behind any more."

"Please," she whispered.

"You promised your father," Rex reminded Keith.

"And it was a mistake. A mistake that you and I have had to live with for five years," Keith said. "I know what it's done to me and I can see what's happening to you."

"You were in on it, too?" Trask said, his voice stone-cold.

"No, he wasn't involved," Keith said.

"Wait a minute," Tory said, realizing that Keith was

about to confess to a man who would ultimately want to see him sent to prison. "You don't have to say anything that might incriminate you—you should talk to a lawyer...."

"Forget it, Tory. It's time I said what's on my mind. Even if McFadden hadn't come back, I would have told the truth sooner or later. It wasn't fair for Dad to take the rap for me, or for Dad to expect Rex to protect me."

A deathly black void had invaded her heart and she felt as if her world was crumbling apart, brick by solid brick. *All because of Trask.*

"What happened?" Trask asked persistently. Every muscle in his body was tight from the strain of witnessing what this confrontation was doing to Tory. Maybe he'd been wrong all along, he thought, maybe, as Keith and Neva had so often suggested, he should have forgotten it all and just fallen in love with Tory again. As it was, she was bound to hate him. He could read it in her cold gray-green eyes.

"George Henderson approached me," Keith was saying. "He asked me if I would help him with some horses he wanted hidden up on Devil's Ridge. All I had to do was keep quiet about it and make sure that no one went up to the ridge. I was stupid enough to agree. When I found out what was going on, how he and Linn Benton were switching expensive Quarter Horses for cheaper ones, I told George I wanted out. George might have gone for it, but the judge, he wouldn't let me out of the deal...told me I was an accomplice, even if an unwitting one. And he was right. No doubt about it, the judge knew the law from both sides. And I did know that something shady was going on. I just didn't realize how bad it was…or…or that it could mean a stiff jail sentence."

"So you were in over your head," Trask said without emotion.

Keith nodded and Tory's eyes locked with her brother's dull gaze before he looked ashamedly away from her.

"But you could have come to me or to Dad," Tory said, feeling dead inside. *First her father and now Keith!* Her chest felt so tight she had to fight to stand on her feet. Closing her eyes, she leaned against the wall for support.

"No way could I have come to Dad or you. How could I let you know how bad I got suckered, or that I had let someone use our property to conduct illegal business? I was already a failure as far as Dad was concerned; you were the responsible one, Sis."

"We were a family, Keith," she moaned. "We could have helped you—"

"What about the horses? The ones from the Lazy W?" Trask cut in, knowing that he had to get this inquisition over fast before Keith could think twice about it. And Tory. God, he wished there was a way to protect and comfort her.

"I switched the horses," Keith admitted. "I figured that I was in too far to back out. If I didn't agree, Benton promised to tell Dad."

Trask's fingers rubbed together and a muscle in the back of his jaw clenched and unclenched in his barely concealed rage. "So what about my brother?" he asked, his voice low and cold.

"I had no idea that Jason was on to us," Keith said, his gray eyes filled with honesty. "I knew that Benton and Henderson were worried about being discovered but I didn't know anything about the insurance company investigation or your brother's role as an investigator."

"He's telling the truth," Rex admitted, wearily sliding into a chair and running his hands through his thinning hair.

"But what about the conversation that Tory overheard?"

Tory's disbelieving eyes focused on Rex.

"It was part of the ruse. Staged for your benefit," Rex said, returning Tory's discouraged stare. "Once Linn Benton approached your father and told him about Keith, Calvin was determined as hell to sacrifice himself instead of his boy. He had to make everyone, including you, Tory, believe that he had been a part of the swindle. He didn't know anything about the plot to kill Jason McFadden. That was Linn Benton's idea."

Tears had begun to stream down Tory's face. She swiped at them with the back of her hand, but couldn't stem the uneven flow from her eyes. She shuddered from an inner cold. "So Dad wouldn't testify on the stand because he wanted to protect Keith?"

"That's right," Keith said, tears clouding his vision. Angrily he sniffed them back.

"Your dad knew he was dying of cancer; it was an easy decision to sacrifice himself in order that his son go free," Rex explained.

"And you went along with it," Tory accused, feeling betrayed by every person she had ever loved.

"I owed your dad a favor—a big one."

Tory took in a shuddering breath. "I don't want to

hear any more of this," she said with finality. "And I don't want to believe a word of it."

"We can't hide behind lies any longer," Keith said, squaring his shoulders. "I'll call Sheriff Barnett tonight."

"Wait!" Tory held up her hand. "Think about what you're doing, Keith. At least consider calling a lawyer before you do anything else!"

Keith came over to her and touched her shoulders. "I've thought about this too long as it is. It's time to do something—"

"Please…" she begged, clinging to her brother as if by holding on to him she could convince him of the folly of his actions.

Keith smiled sadly and patted her back. "If it makes you feel any better I'll call a lawyer, just as soon as I talk Barnett into coming out here and taking my statement."

"I wish you wouldn't—" Rex said.

"You're off the hook," Keith said, releasing his sister and walking from the kitchen and into the den. Tory sat in a chair near the doorway and refused to meet Trask's concerned gaze.

"So you were the one who shot the calves, right?" Trask asked the foreman once Keith had left the room.

Rex frowned and lifted his shoulders. He couldn't meet Tory's incredulous gaze. "I thought you would stop the damned investigation if you discovered any threats to Tory."

"So you sent the note?" Tory asked.

"I'm not proud of it," Rex admitted, "but it was all I could think of doing." His chin quivered before he raised his eyes to meet Tory's wretched stare. "I

promised your old man, Tory. You have to believe I
never meant to hurt you or the ranch…I…I just wanted
to do right by your dad." His voice cracked and he
had to clear his throat. "Your father hired me when
no one else in this town would talk to me." He turned
back to Trask. "I just wish it would've worked and you
would've gone back to Washington where you belong
instead of stirring up the lives of good decent people
and making trouble."

Tory's head was swimming in confusion. So Keith
had been involved in the Quarter Horse swindle and
her father had only tried to protect his young son. And
Rex, feeling some misguided loyalty to a dying man,
had kept the secret of Keith's involvement. Even the
foreman's fumbling attempts to deter Trask were in response to a debt that had been paid long ago.

"I reckon I'd better talk to the sheriff as well," Rex
said, forcing his hat back on his head and walking
down the hall to the den where the soft sound of Keith's
voice could be heard.

Trask got out of the chair and walked over to Tory.
He reached for her but she recoiled from him. Not only
had Trask put her father in jail five years earlier, but
now he was about to do the same to her brother.

"Tory—"

"Don't!" She squared her shoulders, stood, shook
her head and looked away from him while her stomach
twisted into painful knots. *How could this be happening?* "I don't want to hear reasons or excuses or anything!" Cringing away from him she backed into the
kitchen counter.

"This had to come out, y'know."

"But you didn't have to do it, did you? You didn't

have to drag it all out into the open and destroy everything that's mattered to me. First my father and now my brother. God, Trask, when you get your pound of flesh, you just don't stop, do you? You want blood and tears and more blood." Tears ran freely down her cheeks. "I hope to God you're satisfied!"

Trask flinched and the rugged lines of his face seemed more pronounced. He ran his fingers raggedly through his windblown hair and released a tired sigh. "I wish you'd believe that I only wanted to love you," he whispered.

"And I wish you'd go to hell," she replied. "I'd ask you if you intend to testify against my brother, but I already know the answer to that one, don't I?"

His lips tightened and the pain in his eyes was overcome by anger. "I had a brother once, too. Remember? And he was more than a brother. He was a husband and a father. And he was murdered. *Murdered*, Tory. Keith knew all about it. He just didn't have the guts to come clean."

"That's all changed now, hasn't it? Thanks to you."

"I didn't want it to end this way," he said, stepping closer to her, but she threw up her hands as if to protect herself. He stopped short.

"Then you should never have started it again. Face it, senator, if there was ever anything between us, you've destroyed it. Forever!"

"There are still a lot of unanswered questions," he reminded her.

"Well, just don't come around here asking for my help in answering them," she retorted. "I'm not a glutton for punishment. I've had enough to last me a lifetime, thanks to you."

Trask stood and stared at her. His blue eyes delved into her soul. "I won't come back, Tory," he warned. "The next move is yours."

"Just don't hold your breath, senator," she whispered through clenched teeth before turning away from him. For a moment there was silence and Tory could feel that he wanted to say something more to her. Then she heard the sound of his retreating footsteps. They echoed hollowly down the hallway. In a few moments she heard the front door slam shut and then the sound of Trask's Blazer roaring down the lane.

"Oh, God," she cried, before clamping a trembling hand over her mouth. Tears began streaming down her face. "I love you, Trask. Damn it all to hell, but I still love you." The sobs broke free of her body and she braced herself with the counter.

"Get hold of yourself," she said, but the tears continued to flow and her shoulders racked with the sobs she tried to still. "I never want to see him again," she whispered, thinking of Trask and knowing that despite her brave words she would always love him. "You're a fool," she chastised herself, lowering her head to the sink and splashing water over her face, "a blind love-sick fool!"

Knowing that she had another investigation to face this night, for surely Sheriff Barnett and his deputy would arrive shortly, she tried to pull herself together and failed miserably. She leaned heavily against the counter and stared into the dark night. Far in the distance she saw the flashing lights of an approaching police car.

"This is it," she said softly to herself. "The beginning of the end…"

CHAPTER TWELVE

THE COURTROOM WAS small and packed to capacity. An overworked air-conditioning system did little to stir the warm air within the room.

Tory sat behind Keith. She tried to console herself with the fact that Keith was doing what he wanted, but her heart went out to her brother. He hadn't been interested in hiring an attorney, in fact, he had petitioned the court to allow him to represent himself. Even the district attorney was unhappy with the situation, but Keith had been adamant.

He looks so young, Tory thought as she studied the square set of her slim brother's shoulders and the proud lift of his jaw. *Just the way Dad had faced his trial.* Tory had to look away from Keith and swallow against the thick lump that had formed in the back of her throat.

The district attorney had already called several witnesses to the stand, the most prominent being George Henderson, who had been accompanied by a guard, when he testified. Not only did George tell the court that Keith, not his father, Calvin, had been in on the Quarter Horse swindle, but he also explained that Linn Benton had blackmailed Calvin into admitting to be a part of the scam.

According to Henderson, Linn Benton had been interested in recruiting Keith as a naive partner in order to have some leverage over Calvin Wilson and the Lazy W. Linn Benton knew that Calvin would never let his son go to prison and a deal was made. Calvin would accept most of the guilt in order to keep Keith's name out of the scam.

"Then what you're suggesting, Mr. Henderson," the soft-spoken D.A. deduced, "is that Calvin Wilson's only crime was that of protecting his son."

"Yes, sir," an aged Henderson replied from the stand. He had thinned considerably in prison and looked haggard. While he continuously rubbed his hands together, a nervous twitch near his eyes worked noticeably.

"And that Linn Benton was blackmailing Calvin Wilson with his son's life."

"That's about the size of it."

"Then Keith Wilson knew about the horse swindle."

"Yes."

Tory cringed, but Keith didn't flinch. A murmur of disapproving whispers filtered through the hot room.

"And he was aware of the deal struck between his father and Judge Linn Benton?"

Henderson nodded.

"You'll have to speak up, Mr. Henderson. The court reporter must be able to hear you. She can't record head movements," the elderly judge announced.

Henderson cleared his throat. "Yes, Keith Wilson knew about the blackmail and the deal," he rasped.

The district attorney paused and the courtroom became silent. "And did he know about the plan to kill Jason McFadden?"

George Henderson's wrinkled brow pulled into a scowl. "No."

"You're sure?"

"Yes," George answered firmly. He met Keith's stony gaze before looking away from him. "Benton did it all on his own. He only told me a few minutes before Jason McFadden's car exploded. By then it was too late to do anything about it." The old vet's shoulders slumped from the weight of five years of deceit.

"And why didn't you go to the police?"

"Because I was afraid," George admitted.

"Of being apprehended?"

"No." George shook his head and the twitch near his left eye became more pronounced. "I was afraid of crossing Linn Benton."

"I see," the district attorney said, sending a meaningful look to the jury. "No further questions."

Keith refused to cross-examine Henderson, as he had with all of the prosecution's witnesses. Tory felt sick inside. It was as if Keith had given up and was willing to accept his fate. For the past week, she had tried to get him to change his mind, hire an attorney and fight for his freedom, but her brother had been adamant, insisting that he was finally doing the "right" thing by his father.

"Don't worry about me," he had said just before the trial. "I'll be fine."

"I can't help but worry. You're acting like some sacrificial lamb—"

"That was Dad," Keith answered severely. "I'm just paying for what I did. It's my time."

"But I need you—"

"What you need is to run the ranch yourself, or better yet, make up with McFadden. Marry the guy."

"Are you out of your mind?" she had asked. "After

everything he's done? I can't believe you, of all people, are suggesting this."

Keith just shook his head. "I did hate him, Tory, but that was because of fear and guilt. I knew, despite what I said, that Trask wasn't responsible for Dad being sent to prison and dying. It was my fault. All McFadden ever wanted was the truth about his brother and you can't really blame him for that."

"How can you feel this way?" she asked incredulously.

"It's easy. I've seen how you are when you're around him. Tory, face it, you were happier than you'd been in years when he came back to Sinclair." His gray eyes held those of his sister. "You deserve that happiness."

Tears had formed in her eyes. "What about you?"

"Me, are you kiddin'?" he had joked, then his voice cracked. "I'll be having the time of my life."

"Seriously—"

"Tory, this is something I've got to do and you won't change my mind. So take my advice and be happy… with McFadden."

"He's responsible—"

Keith lifted a finger to her lips. "*I'm* responsible and it's time to pay up. Believe me, it's a relief that it's all nearly over."

Several other witnesses came to the stand, all painting the same picture that Keith was an ingrate of a son who had used his martyred father to protect himself.

When Trask was called to the stand, Tory felt her hands begin to shake. Until this point he had sat in the back of the courtroom and though Tory could feel his eyes upon her, she had never looked in his direction, preferring to stare straight ahead and watch the proceedings without having to face him or her conflicting emotions.

Trask seemed to have aged, Tory thought, her heart twisting painfully at the sight of him. He looked uncomfortable in his suit and tie. His rugged features seemed more pronounced, his cheeks slightly hollow, but the intensity of his vibrant blue eyes was still as bright as ever. When he sat behind the varnished rail of the witness stand, he looked past the district attorney and his eyes met Tory's to hold her transfixed. For several seconds their gazes locked and Tory felt as if Trask could see into her soul. Her throat tightened and her breath seemed trapped in her lungs.

"Senator McFadden," the D.A. was saying. "Would you describe in your own words why you came back to Sinclair and what you discovered?"

Trask tore his gaze away from Tory's and his voice was without inflection as he told the court about the series of events that had started with the anonymous letter he had received in Washington and had finally led to the arrest of Keith Wilson, as part of the Quarter Horse swindle that Trask's brother, Jason, was investigating when he was killed five years earlier.

Reporters were busy scribbling notes or drawing likenesses of the participants in the trial. The room was filled with faces of curious townspeople, many of whom Tory recognized. Anna Hutton sat with Tory, silently offering her support to her friend. Neva sat across the courtroom, her face white with strain. Several of the ranch hands were in the room, including Rex, who had already given his testimony. At Rex's side was his young wife, Belinda.

As Trask told his story, Tory sat transfixed. Though

it was stifling hot in the old courtroom with the high ceilings, Tory shuddered and experienced the icy cold sensation of *deja vu.* Trask's shoulders slumped slightly and the smile and self-assurance that had always been with him had vanished.

This has been hard on him, Tory thought, realizing for the first time since Keith had confessed that Trask did care what happened to her. He was a man driven by principle and was forced to stalk anyone involved in the murder of his brother. And if the situation were reversed, and Keith had been the man murdered, wouldn't she, too, leave no stone unturned in the apprehension of the guilty parties?

She twisted her handkerchief in her lap and avoided Trask's stare.

"So tell me, senator, how you found out that the defendant was part of the horse swindle."

"I had a private investigator, a man by the name of John Davis, look into it."

"And what did Mr. Davis find out?"

"That Keith Wilson, and not his father Calvin, was a partner to Linn Benton and George Henderson."

Tory felt sick inside as the questioning continued. The D.A. opened his jacket and rocked back on his heels. "Did Mr. Davis find out who sent you the first anonymous letter to Washington?"

"Yes."

Tory's eyes snapped up and she felt her breath constrict in her throat. *Who was responsible for bringing Trask back to Oregon? Who knew about Keith's involvement and wanted to see him go to prison?*

"The letter came from Belinda Engels," Trask

stated. Tory took in a sharp breath. "Belinda is the wife of Rex Engels, the foreman of the Lazy W."

"The same man who was sworn to secrecy by Calvin Wilson before he died?"

"Yes."

"Thank you, Senator McFadden. No more questions."

When Keith declined to cross-examine Trask, the senator was asked to step down. With his eyes fixed on Tory, Trask walked back to his seat, and Tory felt her heart start to pound wildly. Even now she couldn't look at him without realizing how desperately she loved him.

The district attorney called Belinda Engels to the stand and Tory watched in amazement as the young woman with the clear complexion and warm brown eyes explained that she had spent five years watching her husband's guilt eat at him until he became a shell of the man she had married.

"Then you knew about Keith Wilson's involvement in the horse swindle?"

"No," she said, looking pointedly at Keith. "I only knew that Rex was sure another man was involved. One night, not long after it happened, Rex woke from a horrible nightmare. Against his better judgment, he told me that he was covering for someone and that Calvin Wilson wasn't involved in the murder. I just assumed that the other man was someone connected to Linn Benton. I...I had no idea that he was Keith Wilson."

"And even though you knew that an innocent man was on trial five years ago, you didn't come forward with the information."

Belinda swallowed. "I…I thought that Rex might be charged with some sort of crime and I didn't think he'd be given a fair trial because of his past…with his ex-wife." Tory sitting silently, watched as the red-haired young woman struggled against tears.

"But you and your husband both knew that Calvin Wilson was innocent."

Belinda leveled her gaze at the district attorney. "My husband's a good honest man. He promised to keep Calvin's secret. I did the same."

Tory closed her eyes as she pictured her father and all of the suffering he had accepted for Keith's involvement with Linn Benton. Tears burned at the back of her eyes but she bravely pushed them aside.

The rest of the trial was a blur for Tory. She only remembered that Keith spoke in his own defense, explaining exactly what happened in the past and why. Since he had pleaded guilty to the charges, the only question was how stiff a sentence the judge would impose.

When Tory left the courtroom, her knees felt weak. She held her head high, but couldn't hide the slight droop of her shoulders or the shadows under her eyes. The past few weeks had been a strain. Not only had the trial loomed over her head, but she had been forced to deal with nosy reporters, concerned friends, and worst of all the absence of Trask in her life. She hadn't realized how difficult life would be without him. She had grown comfortable with him again in those first warm weeks of summer. Since he had discovered Keith's secret, there was a great emptiness within her heart, and life at the Lazy W alone was more than Tory could face at times.

Lifting her head over the whispers she heard in the outer hallway of the courthouse, she walked down the shiny linoleum-floored corridor, through the front doors and down the few concrete steps into the radiant heat of late July in central Oregon.

She stepped briskly, avoiding at all costs another confrontation with the press. At the parking lot, she stopped short. Trask was leaning against her pickup watching her with his harsh blue eyes.

After catching the breath that seemed to have been stolen from her lungs at the sight of him, Tory lifted her chin and advanced toward Trask. Her heart was pounding a staccato beat in her chest and her pulse jumped to the erratic rhythm, but she forced her face to remain emotionless.

Trask pushed his hands deep into his pockets, stretching his legs in front of him as he surveryed her. Dressed in a cool ivory linen suit, with her hair swept away from her face, Tory looked more like royalty or a sophisticated New York model than an Oregon rancher. He grimaced slightly when he noticed the coldness of her gaze as she approached. She stopped in front of him, her head slightly tilted to meet his gaze.

"Are you happy?" she asked, inwardly wincing at the cynicism in her words. She noticed him flinch.

His teeth clenched and a muscle worked in the corner of his jaw. The hot summer wind pushed his hair from his face, exposing the small lines etching his forehead. The sadness in his eyes touched a very small, but vital part of Tory's heart.

"No."

"At least satisfied, I hope."

He frowned and let out a long sigh of frustration. "Tory, look. I just wanted to say goodbye."

She felt a sudden pain in her heart. "You're…you're leaving for Washington," she guessed, surprised at how hard it was to accept that he would be on the other side of the continent. *If only she could forget him, find another man to love, someone who wouldn't destroy all she had known in her life.*

"The day after tomorrow."

She stiffened. "I see. You wanted to stick around for the sentencing, is that it?"

His face hardened, but the agony in his blue eyes didn't diminish and her feelings of love for him continued to do battle in her heart. Rex and Keith had been right all along. Trask had used her to promote himself and his damned political career. Already the papers were doing feature articles about him; painting him as some sort of martyred hero who had come back home to capture his brother's killers. *Only Keith hadn't killed anyone!*

"I just hoped that we could…" He looked skyward as if seeking divine guidance.

"I hope that you're not going to suggest that we be friends, senator. That's a little too much to ask," she said, but the trembling of her chin gave away her real feelings.

"I wish that there was some way to prove to you that I only did what I had to do, and that I didn't intend to hurt you." He lifted a hand toward her and she instinctively stepped backward.

"Don't worry about it. It won't happen again. All my family is gone, Trask. There isn't anyone else you can send to prison." She walked around to the driver's side of the truck and reached for the door handle, but Trask was there before her. His hand took hold of hers and for a breathless instant, when their fingers entwined, Tory thought there was a chance that she could trust him again. God, how she still loved him. Her eyes searched his face before she had the strength to pull away. "I have to go."

"I just want you to be careful, some things still aren't clear yet."

She shook her head at her own folly of loving him. "Some things will never be clear. At least not to me."

"Listen...I thought you'd want to know that I've instructed John Davis to keep watching the ranch."

"What!"

"I think there still may be trouble."

"That's impossible. It's all over, Trask."

"I don't think so."

"Call him off."

"What?"

"You heard me!" She pointed an angry finger at Trask's chest. "Tell Davis that I don't need anyone patrolling the ranch. Furthermore, I don't want him there. I just want to forget about this whole damned nightmare!" Her final words were choked out and she felt the tears she had managed to dam all day begin to flow.

"Tory..." His voice was soft, soothing. His fingers wrapped possessively over her arm.

"Leave me alone," she whispered, unable to jerk away. "And tell that private investigator of yours to back off. Otherwise I'll have the sheriff arrest him for trespassing."

"I just want you to be safe."

"And I want you out of my life," she lied, finally

pulling away and jerking open the door of the pickup. With tears blurring her vision, she started the truck and drove out of the parking lot, glancing in the rear-view mirror only once to notice the defeat in Trask's shoulders.

TORY HADN'T BEEN back at the Lazy W very long before the telephone rang. She had just stepped out of the shower and considered not answering the phone, but decided she couldn't. The call could possibly be from Keith.

Gritting her teeth against the very distinct possibility that the call was from another reporter, she answered the phone sharply.

"Hello?"

"Ms. Wilson?" the caller inquired.

Tory grimaced at the unfamiliar voice. "This is Victoria Wilson."

"Good. Don Morris with Central Bank."

The young loan officer! Tory braced herself for more bad news. "Yes?"

"I just wanted to let you know that the loan committee has seen fit to grant you the funds you requested."

Tory felt as if she could fall through the floor. The last thing she expected from the bank was good news. Nervously she ran her fingers through her hair. "Thank you," she whispered.

"No problem at all," the loan officer said with a smile in his voice. "You can pick up the check the day after tomorrow."

"Can you tell me something, Mr. Morris?" Tory asked cautiously. She didn't want to press her luck, but the bank's agreement to her loan didn't seem quite right. She felt as if she were missing something.

"Certainly."

"The last time I came to see you, you insisted that I didn't have enough collateral for another loan with the bank. What happened to change your mind?"

"Pardon me?" She could almost hear the banker's surprise.

"You haven't had a change of policy, have you?"

"No."

"Well?"

The young banker sighed. "Senator McFadden agreed to cosign on your note."

Tory's eyes widened in surprise. "What does Senator McFadden have to do with this?"

"He talked with the president of the bank and insisted that we lend you the money. The senator owns quite a chunk of stock in the bank, you know. And the president is a personal friend of his. Anyway, he insisted that he cosign your note."

Blood money! "And you agreed to it?"

"You did want the loan, didn't you? Ms. Wilson?"

"Yes…yes. I'll clear things up with the senator," she replied, her blood rising in her anger as she slammed down the phone. "Bastard," she whispered between clenched teeth.

It occurred to her as she towel-dried her hair and pulled on her jeans that Trask might have cosigned on the note to the bank as a final way of saying goodbye to her. After all, he did appear sincere when he said he hadn't wanted to hurt her.

"Oh, God, Trask, why can't we just let it die?" she wondered aloud as she took a moment to look out the window and see the beauty of the spreading acres of the ranch. As August approached the countryside had turned golden-brown with only the dark pines to add color and contrast to the gold earth and the blue sky. And Trask had given her the chance to keep it. It wasn't something he had to do. It was a gift.

"And a way of easing his conscience," she said bitterly, trying desperately to hate him.

Without really considering her actions, she ran outside and hopped into the pickup with the intention of confronting Trask one last time.

DUSK HAD SETTLED by the time that Tory reached Trask's cabin on the Metolius River. Even as she approached the single story cedar and rock building, she knew that Trask wasn't there. His Blazer was nowhere in sight and all of the windows and doors were boarded shut.

He'd already gone, Tory thought miserably, her heart seeming to tear into tiny ribbons. As she ran her fingers over the smooth wooden railing of the back porch, she couldn't help but remember the feel and texture of Trask's smooth muscles and she wondered if she would ever truly be free of him, or if she wanted that freedom.

With one last look at the small cabin nestled between the pines on the banks of the swift Metolius, Tory climbed back into her pickup and headed into Sinclair. On the outskirts of the small town, she turned down the road where Neva McFadden lived.

Trask's Blazer was parked in the driveway.

Maybe he had turned to Neva. Keith had said that Neva was in love with him. A dull ache spread through her at the thought of Trask with another woman, any other woman.

With her heart thudding painfully, Tory walked up the sidewalk and pounded on the front door. Almost immediately, Neva answered her knock.

"Trask!" she shouted before seeing Tory. The color drained from Neva's face. "Tory?" she whispered, shaking her head. "I thought that you might be Trask…" The blond woman's voice cracked and she had to place a hand over her mouth.

Tory felt her blood turn to ice water. "What happened? Isn't he here?" She lifted her hand and pointed in the direction of the Blazer but Neva only shook her head.

"I guess you'd better come in."

Neva led Tory into the house. "Where's Trask?" Tory asked, her dread giving way to genuine fear.

"I don't know. He…he and John Davis and Sheriff Barnett are looking for Nicholas."

Tory stood stock-still. When Neva lifted her eyes, they were filled with tears. "Where is Nicholas?" Tory asked.

"I…I don't know. Trask and I assume that he's been kidnapped."

"Kidnapped?" Tory repeated, as she leaned against the wall. "Why?"

"Because of the trial. Trask thinks Linn Benton is behind it."

"But how—?"

"I don't know. George Henderson told everything he knew about the swindle and that included some pretty incriminating things against Linn Benton. The blackmailing alone will keep him in the pen several more years," Neva said.

"Wait a minute, slow down. What about your son?"

"I came back from the trial and he was gone. There was just a note saying that I hadn't kept Trask from digging up the past and I'd have to pay."

"And you're sure that Nicholas didn't go to a friend's house?"

"Yes." Neva could stand the suspense no longer. Her tears fell freely down her face and her small body was racked with the sobs.

Tory wrapped her arms around the woman and whispered words she didn't believe herself. "It's going to be all right, Neva," she said. "Trask will find your son."

"Oh, God, I hope so! He's all I have left."

Gently Tory led Neva to the couch. "I think you should lie down."

"I can't sleep."

"Shh. I know, but you're a nurse; you've got to realize that the best thing to do is lie still. I'll…I'll make you some tea."

Neva reluctantly agreed. She sat on the edge of the couch, staring at the clock and wringing her hands with worry.

Tory scrounged around in Neva's kitchen and found the tea bags. Within a few minutes, she brought two steaming cups back to the living room.

"Thank you," Neva whispered, when Tory offered her the cup. She took a sip of the tea and set it on the arm of the couch, letting the warm brew get cold.

"They're going to kill Nicholas," she said firmly and tears ran in earnest down her cheeks.

"Don't talk that way—"

"I should never have told Trask. Oh, God—" Neva buried her face in her hands. "I'll never forgive myself if they hurt my baby—"

The knock on the door made Neva leap from the couch. "Oh, God, it's got to be Nicholas," she whispered, racing to the door to discover Deputy Woodward on the front steps.

"What happened?" she cried.

The grim deputy looked from one woman to the next. "We've found your boy, Mrs. McFadden."

Neva looked as if she would faint in relief. "Thank God. Is he all right?"

"I think so. He's in the hospital in Bend, just for observation. He appears unharmed. I'd be happy to drive you there myself."

"Yes, please," Neva said, reaching for her purse.

"Where's Trask?" Tory asked.

"Senator McFadden is in the hospital, too."

Tory felt sick inside and she paled. *What if something had happened to Trask? What if she could never see him again? What if he were dead?* Tory couldn't live without him.

Neva turned and faced the young deputy. "What happened?"

"The senator got into a fist fight with the man who kidnapped your son. It looks as if this guy might be the one that knocked Senator McFadden out and beat him up a few weeks ago—the guy who was shooting at you on Devil's Ridge."

"Who is he?" Tory demanded, fear and anger mingling in her heart.

"A man by the name of Aaron Hughs. He's the foreman of Linn Benton's spread, just north of Bend."

"And Hughs still works for him?"

"Appears that way." The deputy turned his attention to Neva. "Anyway, if it hadn't been for the senator, your boy would probably be across the state line by now. According to the sheriff, McFadden should be awarded some sort of medal."

"Then he's all right?" Tory asked.

"I think so."

"Thank God."

"How did you know where to find Nicholas?" Tory asked.

"Senator McFadden, he thought your son had to be somewhere on Linn Benton's ranch. As it turns out, he was right. The kid was tied to a chair in the kitchen."

A small cry escaped from Neva's lips. "Come on, let's go."

The trip to the hospital seemed to take forever. Tory closed her eyes and imagined Trask lying in a stark, white-sheeted hospital bed, beaten beyond recognition. *Oh, God, I've been such a fool,* she thought, knowing for the first time since Keith had been arrested that she would always love Trask McFadden. The few fleeting minutes that she had thought he might be dead had been the worst of her life.

Deputy Woodward took them into the hospital and straight into the emergency ward. Nicholas was sitting up on a stretcher looking white, but otherwise none the worse for wear. At the sight of his mother, he smiled and let out a happy cry.

Neva raced into his small arms and lifted him off

the portable bed. "Oh, Nicholas," she cried, her tears streaming down her face. "My baby. Are you all right?"

"I'm not a baby," the boy insisted.

Neva laughed at Nicholas's pout. "You'll always be my baby, whether you like it or not."

It was then that Tory noticed Trask. He was seated on a gurney, his legs dangling over the side. His hair was messed and there was a slight bruise on his chin, but other than that he appeared healthy.

Tory's heart leaped at the sight of him and tears of relief pooled in her eyes. Without hesitation, Tory walked up to him and stared into the intense blue of his eyes. She placed a hand lovingly against his face. "Thank God you're alive," she whispered, her voice husky with emotion.

"You thought my constituents might miss me?" he asked, trying to sound self-assured. The sight of her in the noisy emergency room had made his stomach knot with the need of her.

"It wasn't your constituents I was concerned about, senator. It was me. I'd miss you…more than you could ever imagine," she admitted.

He cracked a small smile. "How did you know I was here?"

"I came looking for you." She wrapped both of her arms around his neck.

His eyebrows shot up, encouraging her to continue. "Because you were going to beg me to marry you?"

"Not quite. I was going to give you hell about co-signing on my loan."

"Oh." He let out a long groan. "I thought maybe you'd finally come to your senses and realized what a catch I am."

Her smile broadened and the love she had tried to deny for many weeks lighted her eyes. "Now that you mention it, senator," she said, pressing her nose to his and gently touching the bruise on his jaw, "I think you're right. You need me around—just to make sure that you stay in one piece. Consider this a proposal of marriage."

"You're not serious?"

"Dead serious," she conceded. "I love you, Trask, and though I hate to admit it, I suppose I always have. If you can see your way clear to forgive me for being bull-headed, I'd like to start over."

His arms wrapped around her slender waist and he held her as if he was afraid she would leave him again. "What about Keith?" he asked softly.

"That's difficult," she admitted. "But he made his own mistakes and he's willing to pay for them. I only hope that he doesn't get a long sentence. I can't say that I feel the same about Linn Benton."

"I've already taken care of that. There are enough charges filed against him including blackmail and kidnapping to keep him in the penitentiary for the rest of his life.

"As for Keith, I talked to the judge. He's a fair man and I think he realizes that Keith was manipulated. After all, he was only sixteen when the Quarter Horse swindle was in full swing. That he finally turned himself in and confessed speaks well for him and he was absolved in the murder. My guess is that he'll get an extremely light sentence, or, if he's lucky, probation."

"That would be wonderful," Tory said with a sigh.

Trask slid off the bed and looked longingly into her eyes.

"Are you supposed to do that? Don't you have to be examined or something?"

"Already done. Now, what do you say if I find a way to get released from the hospital and you and I drive to Reno tonight and get married?"

"Tonight?" She eyed him teasingly. "Are you sure you're up to it?"

"A few cracked ribs won't slow me down." He nuzzled her neck. "Besides I'm not taking a chance that you might change your mind."

"Never," she vowed, placing her lips on his. "You're stuck with me for the rest of your life, senator."

"What about the Lazy W?"

"I guess I can bear to be away from it for a little while," she said. "Just as long as I know that we'll come back home after you've finished terrorizing Capitol Hill."

"That might be sooner than you know. I'm up for reelection pretty soon."

"And if I get lucky, you'll lose, right?"

Trask laughed and held her close. "If you get lucky, we'll be in Reno by morning," he whispered against her ear.

"Trask!" Neva, holding a tired Nicholas in her arms, ran up to her brother-in-law. "Thank you," she said, her joy and thanks in her eyes. Her smile trembled slightly. "Thank you for finding Nicholas."

Trask grinned at Nicholas and rumpled his hair. "Anytime," he said. "We good guys have to stick together, don't we?"

"Right, Uncle Trask. Come on, Mom, you promised me an ice-cream cone."

"That I did," Neva said, shaking her head. "Now all I have to do is find an all-night drive-in. Want to come along?"

"Please, Uncle Trask?" Nicholas's eyes were bright with anticipation.

Trask shook his head. "Another time, Nick." Trask looked meaningfully at Tory. "Tonight I've got other plans. Something that can't be put off any longer."

Neva's smile widened and she winked at Tory. "I'll see you later," she said. "Good luck." With her final remark, she packed her son out of the hospital.

"So now it's just you and me," Trask said. "The way it should have been five years ago."

"Senator McFadden?" A nurse called to him. "If you just sign here, you're free to go."

Trask signed the necessary forms with a flourish. "Let's get out of here," he whispered to Tory, gently pulling on her hand and leading her out of the building.

"You're sure about this, aren't you?" he asked, once they had crossed the parking lot and were seated in his Blazer.

"I've never been more sure of anything in my life," she vowed. "I've had a lot of time alone to think. And even though I tried to tell myself otherwise, even as late as this afternoon, I discovered that I loved you. There was a minute when I thought you were dead… and…I can't tell you how devastated I was. Thank God you're alive and we can be together."

He lifted his hands and held her face in both palms. "This is for life, you know. I won't ever let you go."

"And I won't be running, senator."

When his lips closed over hers. Tory gave herself up

to the warmth of his caress, secure in the knowledge that she would never again be without the one man she loved with all her heart.

* * * * *

DEVIL'S GAMBIT

CHAPTER ONE

TIFFANY HEARD THE back door creak open and then shut with a bone-rattling thud. *It's over,* she thought and fought against the tears of despair that threatened her eyes.

Hoping to appear as calm as was possible under the circumstances, she set her pen on the letter she had been writing and placed her elbows on the desk. Cold dread slowly crept up her spine.

Mac's brisk, familiar footsteps slowed a bit as he approached the den, and involuntarily Tiffany's spine stiffened as she braced herself for the news. Mac paused in the doorway. Tonight he appeared older than his sixty-seven years. His plaid shirt was rumpled and the lines near his sharp eyes were deeper than usual.

Tiffany knew what he was going to say before Mac had a chance to deliver his somber message.

"He didn't make it, did he?" she asked as her slate-blue eyes held those of the weathered ex-jockey.

There was a terse shake of Mac's head. His lips tightened over his teeth and he removed his worn hat. "He was a good-lookin' colt, that one."

"They all were," Tiffany muttered, seemingly to herself. "Every last one of them." The suppressed rage of three sleepless nights began to pound in her veins, and for a moment she lost the tight rein on her self-control. "Damn!" Her fist crashed against the desk before the weighty sadness hit and her shoulders slumped in defeat. A numb feeling took hold of her and she wondered if what was happening was real. Once again her eyes pierced those of the trainer and he read the disbelief in her gaze.

"Charlatan is dead," he said quietly, as if to settle the doubts in her mind. "It weren't nobody's fault. The vet, well, he did all he could."

"I know."

He saw the disappointment that kept her full lips drawn into a strained line. *She can't take much more of this,* he thought to himself. *This might be the straw that breaks the camel's back.* Everything that was happening to her was a shame—a damned shame.

"And don't you go blaming yourself," he admonished as if reading her thoughts. His crowlike features pinched into a scowl before he dropped his wiry frame into one of the winged side chairs positioned near the desk. Thoughtfully he scratched the rough stubble of his beard. He'd been awake for nearly three days, same as she, and he was dog-tired. At sixty-seven it wasn't getting any easier.

Tiffany tried to manage a smile and failed. What she felt was more than defeat. The pain of witnessing the last struggling breaths of two other foals had drained her. And now Charlatan, the strongest of the lot, was dead.

"It's just not fair," she whispered.

"Aye, that it's not."

She let out a ragged sigh and leaned back in the uncomfortable desk chair. Her back ached miserably and all thoughts of her letter to Dustin were forgotten.

"That makes three," she remarked, the skin of her flawless forehead wrinkling into an uncomfortable frown.

"And two more mares should be dropping foals within the next couple of weeks."

Tiffany's elegant jaw tightened. "Let's just hope they're healthy."

Mac pushed his hands through his thinning red hair. His small eyes narrowed suspiciously as he looked out the window at the group of large white buildings comprising Rhodes Breeding Farm. Starkly illuminated by the bluish sheen from security lights, the buildings took on a sinister appearance in the stormy night.

"We've sure had a streak of bad luck, that we have."

"It almost seems as if someone is out to get us," Tiffany observed and Mac's sharp gaze returned to the face of his employer.

"That it does."

"But *who* and *why*…and *how?*" Nothing was making any sense. Tiffany stretched her tired arms before dropping her head forward and releasing the tight clasp holding her hair away from her face. Her long fingers massaged her scalp as she shook the soft brown tresses free of their bond and tried to release the tension in the back of her neck.

"That one I can't answer," Mac replied, watching as she moved her head and the honey-colored strands fell to her shoulders. Tiffany Rhodes was a beautiful woman who had faced more than her share of tragedy. Signs of stress had begun to age her fair complexion, and though Tiffany was still the most regally beautiful and proud woman he knew, Mac McDougal wondered just how much more she could take.

"That's just the trouble—no one can explain what's happening."

"You haven't got any enemies that I don't know about?" It was more of a statement than a question.

Tiffany's frown was pensive. A headache was beginning to nag at her. She shrugged her shoulders. "No one that would want to ruin me."

"You're sure?"

"Positive. Look, we can't blame anyone for what's happened here. Like you said, we've just had a string of bad luck."

"Starting with the loss of Devil's Gambit four years ago."

Tiffany's eyes clouded in pain. "At least we got the insurance money for him," she whispered, as if it really didn't matter. "I don't think any of the foals will be covered, not once the insurance company gets wind of the problems we're having."

"The insurance money you got for Devil's Gambit wasn't half of what he was worth," Mac grumbled, not for the first time. Why had Ellery Rhodes been so careless with the most valuable stallion on the farm? The entire incident had never set well with Mac. He shifted uncomfortably on the chair.

"Maybe not, but I'm afraid it's all water under the bridge." She pushed the letter to Dustin aside and managed a weak smile. "It really doesn't matter anyway. We lost the horse and he'll never be replaced." She shuddered as she remembered the night that had taken the life of her husband and his most treasured Thoroughbred. Images of the truck and horse trailer, twisted and charred beyond recognition, filled her mind and caused her to wrap her arms protectively over her abdomen. Sometimes the nightmare never seemed to go away.

Mac saw the sadness shadow her eyes. He could have kicked himself for bringing up the past and reminding her of the god-awful accident that had left her a widow. The last thing Tiffany needed was to be constantly reminded of her troubles. *And now there was the problem with the foals!*

The wiry ex-jockey stood and held his hat in his hands. He'd delivered his message and somehow Tiffany had managed to take the news in stride. But then she always did. There was a stoic beauty and pride in Ellery Rhodes's widow that Mac admired. No matter how deep the pain, Tiffany Rhodes always managed to pull herself together. There was proof enough of that in her marriage. Not many women could have stayed married to a bastard the likes of Ellery Rhodes.

Mac started for the door of the den and twisted the brim of his limp fedora in his gnarled hands. He didn't feel comfortable in the house—at least not since Ellery Rhodes's death—and he wanted to get back to the foaling shed. There was still unpleasant work to be done.

"I'll come with you," Tiffany offered, rising from the desk and pursing her lips together in determination.

"No reason—"

"I want to."

"He's dead, just like the others. Nothing you can do."

Except cry a few wasted tears, Tiffany thought to herself as she pulled her jacket off the wooden hook near the French doors that opened to a flagstone patio.

Bracing herself against the cold wind and rain blowing inland from the coast, Tiffany rammed her fists into the pockets of her jacket and silently followed Mac down the well-worn path toward the foaling shed. She knew that he disapproved of her insistence on being involved with all of the work at the farm. After all, Ellery had preferred to leave the work to the professionals. But Tiffany wanted to learn the business from the ground up, and despite Mac's obvious thoughts that a woman's place was in the home or, at the very least, in the office doing book work, Tiffany made herself a part of everything on the small breeding farm.

The door to the shed creaked on rusty hinges as Tiffany entered the brightly lit building. Pungent familiar odors of clean straw, warm horses, antiseptic and oiled leather greeted her. She wiped the rain off her face as her eyes adjusted to the light.

Mac followed her inside, muttering something about this being no place for a woman. Tiffany ignored Mac's obvious attempt to protect her from the tragic evidence of Charlatan's death and walked with determination toward the short man near the opposite end of the building. Her boots echoed hollowly on the concrete floor.

Vance Geddes, the veterinarian, was still in the stall, but Felicity, the mare who just two days earlier had given birth to Charlatan, had already been taken away.

Vance's expression was grim and perplexed. Weary lines creased his white skin and bracketed his mouth with worry. He forced a weak smile when Tiffany approached him and he stepped away from the small, limp form lying in the straw.

"Nothing I could do," Vance apologized, regret and frustration sharpening his normally bland expression. "I thought with this one we had a chance."

"Why?" She glanced sadly at the dead colt and a

lump formed in her throat. Everything seemed so... pointless.

"He seemed so strong at birth. Stood up and nursed right away, not like the others."

Tiffany knelt on the straw and touched the soft neck of the still-warm foal. He was a beautiful, perfectly formed colt—a rich chestnut with one white stocking and a small white star on his forehead. At birth his dark eyes had been keenly intelligent and inquisitive with that special spark that distinguished Moon Shadow's progeny. Tiffany had prayed that he would live and not fall victim to the same baffling disease that had killed the other recently born foals sired by Moon Shadow.

"You'll perform an autopsy?" she asked, her throat tight from the strain of unshed tears.

"Of course."

After patting the soft neck one last time, Tiffany straightened. She dusted her hands on her jeans, cast one final searching look at the tragic form and walked out of the stall. "What about Felicity?"

"She's back in the broodmare barn. And not very happy about it. We had a helluva time getting her away from the foal. She kicked at John, but he managed to get her out of here."

"It's not easy," Tiffany whispered, understanding the anxious mare's pain at the unexplained loss of her foal. Tiffany looked around the well-kept foaling shed. White heat lamps, imported straw, closed-circuit television, all the best equipment money could buy and still she couldn't prevent the deaths of these last three foals.

Why, she wondered to herself. *And why only the offspring of Moon Shadow?* He had stood at stud for nearly eight years and had always produced healthy, if slightly temperamental, progeny. Not one foal had died. Until now. *Why?*

With no answers to her question, and tears beginning to blur her vision, Tiffany reluctantly left the two men to attend to the dead colt.

The rain had decreased to a slight drizzle, but the wind had picked up and the branches of the sequoia trees danced wildly, at times slamming into the nearby buildings. The weather wasn't unusual for early March in Northern California, but there was something somber and ominous about the black clouds rolling over the hills surrounding the small breeding farm.

"Don't let it get to you," Tiffany muttered to herself.

She shivered as she stepped into the broodmare barn and walked without hesitation to Felicity's stall.

The smell of fresh hay and warm horses greeted her and offered some relief from the cold night. Several mares poked their dark heads out of the stalls to inspect the visitor. Tiffany gently patted each muzzle as she passed, but her eyes were trained on the last stall in the whitewashed barn.

Felicity was still agitated and appeared to be looking for the lost foal. The chestnut mare paced around the small enclosure and snorted restlessly. When Tiffany approached, Felicity's ears flattened to her head and her dark eyes gleamed maliciously.

"I know, girl," Tiffany whispered, attempting to comfort the anxious mare. "It wasn't supposed to turn out like this."

Felicity stamped angrily and ignored the piece of apple Tiffany offered.

"There will be other foals," Tiffany said, wondering if she were trying to convince the horse or herself.

Rhodes Breeding Farm couldn't stand to take many more losses. Tears of frustration and anxiety slid down her cheeks and she didn't bother to brush them aside.

A soft nicker from a nearby stall reminded Tiffany that she was disturbing the other horses. Summoning up her faltering courage, Tiffany stared at Felicity for a moment before slapping the top rail of the stall and walking back to the house.

Somehow she would find the solution to the mystery of the dying foals.

THE FIRST INQUIRY came by telephone two days later. Word had gotten out about the foals, and a reporter for a local newspaper in Santa Rosa was checking the story.

Tiffany took the call herself and assured the man that though she had lost two newborn colts and one filly, she and the veterinarian were positive that whatever had killed the animals was not contagious.

When the reporter, Rod Crawford, asked if he could come to the farm for an interview, Tiffany was wary, but decided the best course of action was to confront the problem head-on.

"When would it be convenient for you to drive out to the farm?" she asked graciously, her soft voice disguising her anxiety.

"What about next Wednesday? I'll have a photographer with me, if you don't mind."

"Of course not," she lied, as if she had done it all her life. "Around ten?"

"I'll be there," Rod Crawford agreed.

Tiffany replaced the receiver and said a silent prayer that the two mares who were still carrying Moon Shadow's unborn foals would successfully deliver healthy horses into the world, hopefully before next Wednesday. A sinking feeling in her heart told her not to get her hopes up.

Somehow, she had to focus Rod Crawford's attention away from the tragedy in the foaling shed and onto the one bright spot in Rhodes Breeding Farm's future: Journey's End. He was a big bay colt, whose career as a two-year-old had been less than formidable. But now, as a three-year-old, he had won his first two starts and promised to be the biggest star Rhodes Farm had put on the racetrack since Devil's Gambit.

Tiffany only hoped that she could convince the reporter that the story at Rhodes Breeding Farm was not the three dead foals, but the racing future of Journey's End.

The reputation of the breeding farm was on the line. If the Santa Rosa papers knew about the unexplained deaths of the foals, it wouldn't be long before reporters from San Francisco and Sacramento would call. And then, all hell was sure to break loose.

THE DOORBELL CHIMED at nine-thirty on Wednesday morning and Tiffany smiled grimly to herself. Though the reporter for the *Santa Rosa Clarion* was a good half an hour early, Tiffany was ready for him. In the last four years she had learned to anticipate just about anything and make the most of it, and she wouldn't allow a little time discrepancy to rattle her. She couldn't afford the bad press.

Neither of the broodmares pregnant with Moon Shadow's offspring had gone into labor and Tiffany didn't know whether to laugh or cry. Her nerves were stretched as tightly as a piano string and only with effort did her poise remain intact. Cosmetics, for the most part, had covered the shadows below her eyes, which were the result of the past week of sleepless nights.

She hurried down the curved, marble staircase and crossed the tiled foyer to the door. After nervously smoothing her wool skirt, she opened the door and managed a brave smile, which she directed at the gentleman standing on the porch.

"Ms. Rhodes?" he asked with the slightest of accents.

Tiffany found herself staring into the most seductive gray eyes she had ever seen. He wasn't what she had expected. His tanned face was angular, his features strong. Raven-black hair and fierce eyebrows contrasted with the bold, steel-colored eyes staring into hers. There was a presence about him that spoke of authority and hinted at arrogance.

"Yes...won't you please come in?" she replied, finally finding her voice. "We can talk in the den...." Her words trailed off as she remembered the photographer. Where was he? Hadn't Crawford mentioned that a photographer would be with him this morning?

It was then she noticed the stiff white collar and the expensively woven tweed business suit. A burgundy silk tie was knotted at the stranger's throat and gold cuff links flashed in the early-morning sunlight. The broad shoulders beneath his jacket were square and tense and there was no evidence of a notepad, camera or tape recorder. Stereotyping aside, this man was no reporter.

"Pardon me," she whispered, realizing her mistake. "I was expecting someone—"

"Else," he supplied with a tight, slightly off-center smile that seemed out of place on his harsh, angular face. He wasn't conventionally handsome; the boldness of his features took away any boyish charm that might have lingered from his youth. But there was something about him, something positively male and sensual that was as magnetic as it was dangerous. Tiffany recognized it in the glint of his eyes and the brackets near the corners of his mouth. She suspected that beneath the conservative business suit, there was an extremely single-minded and ruthless man.

He extended his hand and when Tiffany accepted it, she noticed that his fingers were callused—a direct contradiction of the image he was attempting to portray.

"Zane Sheridan," he announced. Again the accent.

She hesitated only slightly. His name and his face were vaguely familiar, and though he looked as if he expected her to recognize him, she couldn't remember where she'd met him...or heard of him. "Please come in, Mr. Sheridan—"

"Zane."

"Zane," she repeated, slightly uncomfortable with the familiarity of first names. For a reason she couldn't put her finger on, Tiffany thought she should be wary of this man. There was something about him that hinted at antagonism.

She led him into the den, knowing instinctively that this was not a social call.

"Can I get you something—coffee, perhaps, or tea?" Tiffany asked as she took her usual chair behind the desk and Zane settled into one of the side chairs. Placing her elbows on the polished wood surface, she clasped her hands together and smiled pleasantly, just as if he hadn't disrupted her morning.

"Nothing. Thank you." His gray eyes moved away from her face to wander about the room. They observed all the opulent surroundings: the thick pile of the carpet, the expensive leather chairs, the subdued brass reading lamps and the etchings of Thoroughbreds adorning the cherry-wood walls.

"What exactly can I do for you?" Tiffany asked, feeling as if he were searching for something.

When his eyes returned to hers, he smiled cynically. "I was an acquaintance of your husband."

Zane's expression was meant to be without emotion as he stared at the elegant but worried face of Ellery Rhodes's widow. Her reaction was just what he had expected—surprise and then, once she had digested his statement, disbelief. Her fingers anxiously toyed with the single gold chain encircling her throat.

"You knew Ellery?"

"We'd met a few times. In Europe."

Maybe that was why his face and name were so familiar, but Tiffany doubted it. A cautious instinct told her he was lying through his beautiful, straight white teeth.

She was instantly wary as she leveled her cool blue gaze at him. "I'm sorry," she apologized, "but if we've met, I've forgotten."

Zane pulled at the knot of his tie and slumped more deeply and comfortably into his chair. "I met Ellery Rhodes before he was married to you."

"Oh." Her smile was meant to be indulgent. "And you're here because…?" she prompted. Zane Sheridan unnerved her, and Tiffany knew instinctively that the sooner he stated his business and was gone, the better.

"I'm interested in buying your farm."

Her dark brows arched in elegant surprise. "You're kidding!"

"Dead serious." The glint of silver determination in his eyes emphasized his words and convinced her that he wasn't playing games.

"But it's not for sale."

"I've heard that everything has a price."

"Well in this case, Mr. Sheridan, you heard wrong. The farm isn't on the market. However, if you're interested in a yearling, I have two colts that—"

"Afraid not. It's all or nothing with me," was the clipped, succinct reply. Apparently Zane Sheridan wasn't a man to mince words.

"Then I guess it's nothing," Tiffany replied, slightly galled at his self-assured attitude. Who the hell did he think he was, waltzing into her house uninvited, and offering to buy her home—Ellery's farm?

Just because he had been a friend of Ellery's—no, he hadn't said friend, just acquaintance.

It didn't matter. It still didn't give him the right to come barging in as if he owned the place. And there was more to it. Tiffany sensed that he was here for another reason, a reason he hadn't admitted. Maybe it was the strain in the angle of his jaw, or the furrows lining his forehead. But whatever the reason, Tiffany knew that Zane Sheridan was hiding something.

Tiffany stood, as if by so doing she could end the conversation.

"Let me know if you change your mind." He rose and looked past her to the framed portrait of Devil's

Gambit; the painting was mounted proudly above the gray stone fireplace.

Just so that Mr. Sheridan understood the finality of her position on the farm, she offered an explanation to which he really wasn't entitled. "If I change my mind about selling the place, I'll give Ellery's brother Dustin first option. He already owns part of the farm and I think that Rhodes Breeding Farm should stay in the family."

Zane frowned thoughtfully and rubbed his chin. "If the family wants it—"

"Of course."

Shrugging his broad shoulders as if he had no interest whatsoever in the Rhodes family's business, he continued to gaze at the portrait over the mantel.

"A shame about Devil's Gambit," he said at length.

"Yes," Tiffany whispered, repeating his words stiffly. "A shame." The same accident that had claimed the proud horse's life had also killed Ellery. Mr. Sheridan didn't offer any condolences concerning her husband, the man he'd said he had known.

The conversation was stilted and uncomfortable, and Tiffany felt as if Zane Sheridan were deliberately baiting her. But why? And who needed it? The past few weeks had been chaotic enough. The last thing Tiffany wanted was a mysterious man complicating things with his enigmatic presence and cryptic statements.

As she walked around the desk, shortening the distance between the stranger and herself, she asked, "Do you own any horses, Mr. Sheridan?" His dark brows quirked at the formal use of his surname.

"A few. In Ireland."

That explained the faint accent. "So you want to buy the farm and make your mark on American racing?"

"Something like that." For the first time, his smile seemed sincere, and there was a spark of honesty in his clear, gray eyes.

Tiffany supposed that Zane Sheridan was the singularly most attractive man she had met in a long while. Tall and whip-lean, with broad shoulders and thick, jet black hair, he stood with pride and authority as he returned her gaze. His skin was dark and smooth, and where once there might have been a dimple, there were now brackets of strain around his mouth. He had lived a hard life, Tiffany guessed, but the expensive tweed jacket suggested that the worst years had passed.

It would be a mistake to cross a man such as this, she decided. Zane Sheridan looked as if he were capable of ruthless retribution. This was evidenced in the tense line of his square jaw, the restless movement of his fingers against his thumb and the hard glint of determination in those steel-gray eyes. Zane was a man to reckon with and not one to deceive.

The doorbell rang, and Tiffany was grateful for the intrusion.

"If you'll excuse me," she said, taking three quick steps before pausing to turn in his direction.

"We're not through here."

"Pardon me?" Tiffany was taken aback. She expected him to show some civility and leave before Rod Crawford's interview. Instinctively Tiffany knew that having Zane in the same room with the reporter would be dangerous.

"I want to talk to you—seriously—about the farm."

"There's no reason, Mr.…Zane. You're wasting your time with me. I'm not about to sell."

"Indulge me," he suggested. He strode across the short distance separating them and touched her lightly on the arm. "Hear what I have to say, listen to what my offer is before you say no."

The doorbell chimed again, more impatiently this time.

"I really do have an appointment," she said, looking anxiously through the foyer to the front door. The grip on her arm tightened slightly.

"And I think you should listen to what I have to say."

"Why?"

He hesitated slightly, as if he weren't sure he could trust her and the skin tightened over his cheekbones. His rugged features displayed a new emotion. Anger and vengeful self-righteousness were displayed in the thrust of his jaw. All traces of his earlier civility had disappeared. Tiffany's heart began to pound with dread.

"Why are you here?" she asked again, her voice suddenly hoarse.

"I came to you because there is something I think that you should know."

"And that is?" Her heart was pounding frantically now, and she barely heard the doorbell chime for the third time.

"I'm not so sure that Devil's Gambit's death was an accident," he stated, gauging her reaction, watching for even the slightest trace of emotion on her elegant features. "In fact, I think there's a damned good chance that your horse is still alive."

CHAPTER TWO

THE COLOR DRAINED from Tiffany's face. "You...you think that Devil's Gambit might be alive?" she repeated, her voice barely a whisper. "You're not serious...."

But she could tell by Zane's expression that he was dead serious.

"Dear God," she whispered, closing her eyes. She wanted to dismiss what he was saying as idle conjecture, but he just didn't seem the type of man who would fabricate anything so bizarre. "I don't know if I can deal with this right now...." Devil's Gambit alive? But how? She'd been to the site of the accident, witnessed the gruesome truth for herself. Both the horse and the driver of the truck had been killed. Only Dustin had survived.

It was difficult to speak or to think rationally. Tiffany forced herself to look into Zane's brooding gaze and managed to clear her throat. "Look, I really do have an interview that I can't get out of. Please wait.... I...I want to talk to you. Alone." She extracted her arm from his grasp and made her way to the door. Her mind was running in crazy circles. What did he mean? Devil's Gambit couldn't possibly be alive. And Ellery—what about Ellery? Dear Lord, if what Zane was suggesting was true, there might be a chance that Ellery was still alive. But how? *Don't think like this,* she told herself. *What this man is suggesting can't possibly be true.*

Her knees were weak, and she leaned against the door for several seconds, trying to recover her lost equilibrium before the bell chimed for the fourth time. "Get hold of yourself," she murmured, but she was unable to disguise the clouds of despair in her eyes. Why now? Why did Zane Sheridan pick this time when everything at the breeding farm was in turmoil to enter her life with rash statements about the past? Forcing her worried thoughts to a dark corner of her mind, she straightened and braced herself for the interview.

With a jerk, she tugged on the brass handle and the door swung inward. Despite the storm of emotions raging within her, she forced what she hoped would appear a sincere and pleasant smile. Only the slightest trembling of her full lips hinted at her ravaged emotions.

"Mr. Crawford?" Tiffany asked the agitated young man slouching against a white pillar supporting the roof. "Please accept my apologies for the delay. My housekeeper isn't in yet and I had an unexpected visitor this morning." Her voice was surprisingly calm, her gaze direct, and she disguised the trembling in her fingers by hiding her hands in the deep pockets of her wool skirt.

The bearded, blond man eyed her skeptically, motioned to someone in the car and then handed her a card that stated that he was Rod Crawford of the *Santa Rosa Clarion.*

A petite, dark-haired woman climbed out of the car and slung a camera over one shoulder. Tiffany stepped away from the door to let the two people enter her home. In the distance she heard the familiar rumble of

Louise's old Buick. The noise was reassuring. Once the housekeeper took charge of the kitchen, some of the disorder of the morning would abate. *Except that Zane Sheridan was in the den, seemingly convinced that Devil's Gambit and, therefore, Ellery were still alive.*

"Could I offer you a cup of coffee…or tea?" Tiffany asked with a weak smile.

"Coffee—black," Crawford stated curtly, withdrawing a notepad from his back pocket.

Tiffany trained her eyes on the photographer. "Anything," the pleasant-featured woman replied. She flashed Tiffany a friendly grin as she extended her small hand. "Jeanette Wilkes." Jeanette's interested eyes swept the opulent interior of the house and she noted the sweeping staircase, gleaming oak banister, elegant crystal chandelier and glossy imported floor tiles. "I was hoping to get a couple of pictures of the farm."

"Wonderful," Tiffany said with a smile that disguised her inner turmoil. "Please, have a seat in the living room." She opened the double doors of the formal room and silently invited them inside.

"You have a beautiful home," Jeanette stated as she looked at the period pieces and the Italian marble of the fireplace with a practiced eye. Everything about the house was first class—no outward sign of money problems.

"Thank you."

"Is this where you work?" Crawford asked skeptically.

"No…"

"If you don't mind, Jeanette would like to get some shots of the inside of the farm as well as the outbuildings. You know, give people a chance to see whatever it is you do when you're working. Don't you have an office or something?" He eyed the formal living room's expensive formal furniture with obvious distaste.

"Of course." The last thing Tiffany could afford was any bad press, so she had to accommodate the nosy reporter. She decided she would have to find a way to get rid of Zane Sheridan. His story was too farfetched to be believed; and yet there was something forceful and determined about him that made her think the Irishman wasn't bluffing.

Zane was still in the den and Tiffany wanted to keep Rod Crawford, with his probing questions, away from the visitor with the Irish accent. If the two men with their different perspectives on what was happening at Rhodes Breeding Farm got together, the results would be certain disaster. Tiffany shuddered when she envisioned the news concerning Moon Shadow's foals and a rumor that Devil's Gambit was still alive being splashed across the front page of the *Santa Rosa Clarion*. The minute the combined reports hit the front page, she would have reporters calling her day and night.

Tiffany's mind was spinning miles a minute. What Zane had suggested was preposterous, and yet the surety of his gaze had convinced her that he wasn't playing games. But Devil's Gambit, alive? And Ellery? Her heart was beating so rapidly she could barely concentrate. She needed to talk to Zane Sheridan, that much was certain, just to find out if he were a master gambler, bluffing convincingly, or if he really did mean what he was saying and had the facts to back him up. But she had to speak to him alone, without the watchful eyes and ears of the press observing her.

Holding her back stiffly, she led Rod and Jeanette back through the foyer to the den, which was directly opposite the living room. Zane was standing by the fireplace, his eyes trained on the painting of the horse over the mantel. He had discarded his jacket and tossed it over the back of one chair, and the tight knot of his tie had been loosened. He looked as if he intended to stay. That was something she couldn't allow, and yet she was afraid to let him go. There were so many questions whirling in her mind. Who was he? What did he want? How did he know Ellery? Why did he want her to believe that Devil's Gambit might still be alive after four long years?

Without hesitation, Tiffany walked toward him. He turned to face her and his eyes were as cool and distant as the stormy, gray Pacific Ocean. If he had been lying a few moments before, he showed no trace of deceit. Yet his story couldn't possibly be true; either it was a total fabrication or he just didn't know what he was talking about.

The steadiness of his glare suggested just the opposite. Tiffany knew intuitively that Zane Sheridan rarely made mistakes. Cold dread took hold of her heart.

"Mr. Sheridan, would it be too much trouble to ask you to wait to finish our discussion?" she asked with an unsteady smile. *What if he wouldn't leave and caused a scene in front of the reporter from the* Santa Rosa Clarion? *His story was just wild and sensational enough to capture Rod Crawford's attention.*

Zane's eyes flickered to the other two people and quickly sized them up as reporters. Obviously something was going on, and the widow Rhodes didn't want him to know about it. His thick brows drew together in speculation.

"How long?"

"I'm not sure.... Mr. Crawford?"

"Call me Rod."

Tiffany made a hasty introduction, while the bearded man came to her side and shook Zane's outstretched hand. The image of the reporter's hand linked with Zane's made her uneasy.

"I don't know," Rod was saying, rubbing his bearded chin. "I suppose it will take...what?" He eyed Jeanette for input. "An hour, maybe two. I want to ask you some questions and then we need a quick tour of the buildings."

Tiffany's throat went dry. No matter how crazy Zane's story seemed, she had to talk to him, find out what he wanted and why he thought that Devil's Gambit might still be alive.

"I have a meeting at noon," Zane stated, his calculating gaze never leaving the worried lines of her face. There was something in Tiffany Rhodes's manner that suggested it would be to his advantage to stay. But he needed to be with her alone in order to accomplish everything he had planned for six long years. He'd given her the bait, and she'd swallowed it hook, line and sinker. The satisfaction he had hoped to find was sadly lacking, and he felt a twinge of conscience at the worry in her clouded eyes.

"Look, Ms. Rhodes—can we get on with it? We've got another story to cover this afternoon," Crawford interjected.

"Of course." Tiffany returned her attention to Zane's proud face. She hoped that she didn't sound nearly as desperate as she felt. "Could you come by tomorrow, or would it be more convenient to meet you somewhere?"

"I have to catch an early flight." His angular jaw was tense, his muscles rigid, but there was the glimmer of expectancy in his eyes. *He's enjoying this,* she thought and she had to work to control her temper. She couldn't blow up now, not with Rod Crawford in the room, but there was something infuriating in Zane's arrogant manner.

Trying not to sound condescending she asked, "Then tonight?" He couldn't just waltz into her life, make outrageous statements, and then disappear as if nothing had happened. She had to know the truth, or what he was attempting to portray as the truth. She wanted to forget about him and his wild imaginings, but she couldn't dismiss him as just another publicity seeker. What did he want—*really want* from her?

Zane's gray eyes narrowed a fraction. "All right. What time?"

"How about dinner—seven-thirty?"

"I'll be here."

He picked up his jacket and flung it over his arm. Tiffany escorted him to the door and let out a long sigh of relief when he was gone. At least he had no inkling why the reporter was there, although it wouldn't be too hard to figure out, especially once the article was printed. "Maybe he'll be back in Ireland where he belongs by then," she muttered with false optimism.

Louise was serving coffee and scones when Tiffany returned to the den. After accepting a cup of black coffee, Tiffany seated herself at her desk, feeling uncomfortably close to Rod Crawford, who sat across the desk. While Jeanette snapped a few "candid" shots of Tiffany at work, Rod began the interview.

"How long have you actually managed the farm?" he asked.

"About four years."

"Ever since your husband's death?"

Tiffany felt her back tighten. "That's right. Before that I helped Ellery on the farm, but he ran it."

"I don't mean to bring up a sore subject," the wily reporter went on, "but ever since you took over, you've had quite a few bad breaks."

Tiffany smiled grimly. "That's true, but I don't like to dwell on them. Right now I'm concentrating on Journey's End."

"The three-year-old, right?"

"Yes. He has all the potential of being one of the greatest horses of the decade."

Rod Crawford laughed aloud. "I doubt if you're all that objective about your own colt."

"Obviously you've never seen him run," Tiffany replied with a slow-spreading grin. The tense air in the room dissolved, as she talked at length about Journey's End's impressive career.

"What about the recent string of deaths in the foaling shed?" Rod asked when the conversation waned. Though Tiffany had been bracing herself for the question, she found no easy answer to it.

"Three foals died shortly after birth," she admitted.

"And you don't know why?" Skepticism edged Rod's question.

Tiffany shook her head. "So far the autopsies haven't shown anything conclusive, other than that the cause of death was heart failure."

Rod settled into his chair and poised his pencil theatrically in the air. "Were the foals related?"

Here it comes, Tiffany thought. "They had different dams, of course, but both colts and the filly were sired by Moon Shadow."

"And he stands at stud here, on the farm."

"Yes, although we're not breeding him...until all this is cleared up." Tiffany's hands were beginning to shake again, and she folded them carefully over the top of the desk.

"You think he might be the cause?"

"I don't know."

"Genetic problem?"

Tiffany pursed her lips and frowned thoughtfully. "I don't think so. He's stood for almost eight years, and until now he's proved himself a good sire. Devil's Gambit and Journey's End are proof of that."

"Moon Shadow was the sire of both stallions?"

"And many more. Some not as famous, but *all* perfectly healthy and strong horses."

"So, what with Journey's End's success, you must be getting a lot of requests for Moon Shadow's services."

"That's right. But we're turning them down, at least for a while, until we can prove that whatever is happening here is not a genetic problem."

"That must be costing you—"

"I think it's worth it."

"Then you must think he's the cause."

"I don't know what's the cause. It may just be coincidence."

Rod snorted his disbelief, and Tiffany had to press her hands together to keep from losing her temper. To Rod Crawford, Moon Shadow was just another story, but to Tiffany he was a proud stallion with an admirable reputation as a racehorse and a sire. She would do anything she had to—short of lying—to protect him and the reputation of the farm.

"Have you had him tested?" Rod asked.

"Moon Shadow?" When Rod nodded, Tiffany replied, "Of course. He's been given a complete physical, and we've taken samples of his semen to be analyzed."

"And?"

"So far, nothing."

Rod twirled his pencil nervously. "What about mares that were brought to Moon Shadow and then taken home?"

Tiffany felt a headache beginning to pound. "As far as I know, only the horses on this farm have been affected. However, it's still early in the year and there are several mares who haven't yet dropped their foals."

"Have you been in contact with the owners of the mares and explained the problem to them?"

"Mr. Crawford," Tiffany stated evenly, "I'm not certain there is a problem, or exactly the nature of it. I'm not an alarmist and I'm not about to warn other owners or scare them out of their wits. What I have done is written a letter inquiring as to the condition of the foals involved. I've had seven responses, and all of them indicate that they have beautiful, healthy horses. Two owners want to rebreed their mares to Moon Shadow."

Rod frowned. "And have you?"

"Not yet."

"Because you're afraid?"

"Because I want to be certain of what is happening before I do anything that might cause any stress or trauma to the horses or the owners." Tiffany looked him squarely in the eye. "This is more than a business for me. It's a way of life, and there's more at stake than money." Rod's blank stare told Tiffany that he didn't understand anything she was saying. Perhaps no one did. Rod Crawford, or anyone else for that matter, couldn't know about the agonizing years she had spent growing up in musty tack rooms and dingy stables where the smell of ammonia had been so strong it had made her retch. No one knew that the only comfort she had found as an adolescent child was in working with the Thoroughbreds her father had been hired to train.

Before her thoughts became too vivid and painful, Tiffany spread her hands expressively over the desk and forced a frail smile at the reporter. "Look, until I know for certain what exactly it is that's happening, I'm not about to make any rash statements, and I would appreciate your cooperation—"

Rod raised a dubious blond brow. "By withholding the story?"

"By not sensationalizing the deaths and *creating* a story. I agreed to this interview because I know of the *Clarion*'s reputation."

"I have to report the truth."

Tiffany smiled stiffly. "That's all I can ask for. Now, if you have any further questions about the horses involved, you can call Vance Geddes, the veterinarian who was with the mares when they delivered the foals."

"Fair enough," Rod replied.

Tiffany led the reporter and his assistant through the broodmare barn and the foaling shed, before returning outside to the brisk March air. While Rod asked questions, Jeanette took some outside shots of a field where mares grazed and spindly-legged foals ran in the shafts of late-morning sunlight.

Tiffany's face lifted with pride as she watched the dark foals run and shy behind the safety of their mothers' flanks. The newborns always held a special place in her heart. She loved to watch them stand and nurse for the first time, or run in the fields with their downy ears pricked forward and their intelligent eyes wide to the vast new world. Maybe that was why the deaths of the foals affected her so deeply.

"I'll send you a copy of the article," Rod promised just before he and Jeanette left.

"Thank you." Tiffany watched in relief as the sporty Mazda headed out the long drive. The interview hadn't been as bad as she had expected, but nonetheless, she felt drained from the ordeal.

After changing into comfortable jeans and a sweat-shirt, Tiffany returned to the den and pulled out the checkbook. But before she could concentrate on the ledgers, she let her eyes wander to the portrait of Devil's Gambit, the horse that Zane Sheridan insisted was alive.

"It can't be," she murmured to herself. Devil's Gambit had been a beautifully built colt with a short, sturdy back, and powerful hind legs that could explode into a full stride of uncanny speed and grace. Jet-black, with one distinctive white stocking, Devil's Gambit had taken the racing world by storm, winning all of his two-year-old starts by ever-increasing margins. As a three-year-old his career had taken off with a flour-ish, and he had been compared to such greats as Sec-retariat and Seattle Slew.

Then, a month before the Kentucky Derby, it had

all ended tragically. Devil's Gambit suffered a horrible death while being transported from Florida to Kentucky.

Tiffany had learned that Ellery had been driving and had apparently fallen asleep at the wheel. Dustin, his brother, had been a passenger in the truck. Miraculously, Dustin had survived with only minor injuries by being thrown out of the cab as the truck tumbled end over end, down an embankment, where it exploded into flames that charred beyond recognition the bodies of Ellery Rhodes and his fleet horse. Dustin's injuries had included a broken leg and minor concussion, which were treated at a local hospital. He had been out of the hospital in time to stand by Tiffany's side at Ellery's funeral.

Tiffany swallowed against the painful memory and shook her head. It had taken her several months to come to accept the death of her husband and his brave horse. And now a total stranger, a man by the name of Zane Sheridan, was trying to make her believe that it had all been a treacherous mistake.

But he didn't state that Ellery was alive, she reminded herself with a defeated smile, only Devil's Gambit. And when Zane had mentioned Ellery, it had been with a look of barely veiled contempt on his rugged black-Irish features.

What can it all mean? She slanted a glance at the portrait of Devil's Gambit and frowned. How could someone hide a horse of such renown? And who could have come up with such a scheme? And why? Certainly not for kidnapping ransom. *Get hold of yourself,* she cautioned, *you're letting your imagination run away with you, all because of some stranger's outlandish remarks.*

With a grimace she turned her attention back to the checkbook and finished paying the month-end bills. She wasn't exactly strapped for money, but each month her assets seemed to diminish. There was still a large, outstanding mortgage against the property, and several major repairs to the barns couldn't be neglected much longer.

If she regretted anything, it was allowing Ellery to build the expensive house. "You can't be a horse breeder unless you look the part," he had said with the confidence of one who understands the subtleties in life. "No one will bring their mares here if we don't *look* like we know what we're doing."

"It's not the house that counts, it's the quality of the stallions and the care of the horses," Tiffany had argued uselessly. In the end, Ellery had gotten his way. After all, it had only taken a quick signature at the bank—his signature—to get the loan to rebuild the house into a grand, Southern manor.

"This is California, not Kentucky," she had reminded him. "No one cares about this sort of thing." But her protests had fallen on deaf ears and Ellery had taken up wearing suits with patches on the sleeves and smoking a pipe filled with blended tobaccos.

The house was finished only six months before the accident. Since that time she had lived in it alone. It was beautiful and grand and mortgaged to the hilt. Ellery hadn't seen fit to purchase mortgage insurance at the time he took out the loan. "Money down the drain," he had commented with a knowing smile.

"I must have been out of my mind to have listened

to him," Tiffany thought aloud as she pushed the ledgers aside and stood. How many years had she blindly trusted him, all because he had saved her life? She shuddered when she remembered the time she had seen Ellery, his face contorted in fear, as he dived in front of the oncoming car and pushed her out of its path.

Maybe it had been gratitude rather than love that she had felt for him, but nonetheless they had been married and she had depended upon him. *And now there was a chance that he was still alive.* The thought made her heart race unevenly.

After grabbing her jacket, she sank her teeth into her lower lip, walked outside and turned toward the broodmare barn. A chilly wind was blowing from the west and she had to hold her hair away from her face to keep it from whipping across her eyes. Mac was leaning over the railing of one of the stalls in the barn. His sharp eyes turned in her direction when she approached.

"I was just about to come up to the house," he stated, a worried expression pinching his grizzled features.

"Something wrong?"

"No...but it looks like this lady here—" he cocked his head in the direction of the black mare restlessly pacing her stall "—is gonna foal tonight."

Instead of the usual expectation Tiffany always felt at the prospect of new life, she now experienced dread. The mare in question, Ebony Wine, was carrying another of Moon Shadow's foals.

"You're sure?" she asked, surveying the mare's wide girth.

"Aye. She's a week overdue as it is, and look." He

pointed a bony finger at the mare's full udder. "She's waxed over and beginning to drip."

"Has she starting sweating?"

"Not yet. It will be a while—sometime after midnight unless I miss my guess."

"But everything else looks normal?" Tiffany asked, her knowing gaze studying the restless horse.

"So far."

"Let me know when the time comes," Tiffany ordered, patting the mare fondly.

"You're not going to wait up again?"

"Of course I am."

Mac took off his hat and dangled it from his fingers as he leaned on the railing of the stall. "There's nothing you can do, you know. What will be, will be."

"You can't talk me out of this. I'll give Vance a call and ask him to come over." She took one last glance at the heavy-bellied mare. "Come up to the house and get me if anything goes wrong, or if it looks like the foal will be early."

Mac nodded curtly and placed his frumpy fedora back on his head. "You're the boss," he muttered, placing his hands in the back pockets of his trousers. "I'll be in the tack room if ya need me."

"Thanks, Mac." Tiffany walked outside but didn't return to the house. Instead, she let herself through a series of gates and walked through the gently sloping paddocks away from the main buildings.

When she neared the old barn, she halted and studied the graying structure. Once the barn had been integral to the farm, but the vacant building hadn't been used for years. Ellery had insisted that the horses needed newer, more modern facilities, and rather than put money into modernizing the old barn, he had erected the new broodmare barn and foaling shed.

The weathered building with the sagging roof was little more than an eyesore, and Tiffany realized that she should have had it torn down years before. Its only function was to store excess hay and straw through the winter.

She walked toward the barn and ignored the fact that blackberry vines were beginning to ramble and cling to the east wall. The old door creaked on rusty rollers as she pushed it aside and walked into the musty interior.

It took a few minutes for her eyes to adjust to the dim light. How many years had it been since she had first seen Ellery? She had been standing near the stalls, making sure that the horses had fresh water when he had startled her.

Before that fateful day, she had seen him only from a distance. After all, she was only a trainer's daughter. A nobody. Tiffany doubted that Ellery Rhodes realized that when he hired Edward Chappel, he took on Edward's eighteen-year-old daughter, as well.

Perhaps her mistake had been to stay with her father, but Edward Chappel was the only family she had known. Her mother, Marie, had abandoned them both when Tiffany was only five. She could remember little of Marie except that she had thick, golden hair and a beautiful but weary face that very rarely smiled.

Fragments of life with her mother had come to mind over the years. Tiffany remembered that Marie insisted that her daughter's hair always be combed and that her faded clothes always be neatly starched. And there was a tune…a sad refrain that Marie would sing when she helped Tiffany get dressed in the morning. Twenty years later, Tiffany would still find herself humming that tune.

The day that her mother had walked out of her life was still etched vividly in her mind. "You must remember that Mommy loves you very much and I'll come back for you," Marie had whispered to Tiffany, with tears gathering in her round, indigo eyes. "I promise, pumpkin." Then Marie had gathered her daughter close to her breast, as if she couldn't bear to walk out the door.

Tiffany had felt the warm trickle of her mother's tears as they silently dropped onto the crown of her head.

"Mommy, don't leave me. *Please....* Mommy, Mommy, don't go. I'll be good…Mommy, I love you, please…" Tiffany had wailed, throwing her arms around her mother's neck and then sobbing with all of her heart for hours after Marie's car had disappeared in a plume of dust.

Her father's face was stern, his shoulders bowed. "Don't blame her, Tiffy," he had whispered hoarsely, "it's all my fault, you know. I haven't been much of a husband."

Tiffany had never seen Marie Caldwell Chappel again.

At first she couldn't believe that her mother had left her, and each night she would stare out the window and pray that the tall man with the big car would bring her mother home. Later, in her early teens, Tiffany was angry that she didn't have a mother to help her understand the changes in her body and the new emotions taking hold of her. Now, as an adult, Tiffany understood that a woman who had been brought up with a taste for the finer things in life could never have been happy with Edward Chappel.

Edward had always been irresponsible, going from job to job, breeding farm to breeding farm, working with the animals he loved. But each time, just when Tiffany thought they had settled down for good and she had made one or two friends in the local school, he would lose his job and they would move on to a new town, a new school, a new set of classmates who would rather ignore than accept her. To this day, she had never made any close friends. She had learned long ago that relationships were fragile and never lasted for any length of time.

After Marie had left him, Edward had sworn off the bottle for nearly three years. Tiffany now realized that his abstinence was because of the hope that Marie would return to him rather than because of his new responsibility as a single parent.

When she was just eighteen and trying to save enough money to go to college, they'd moved to the Rhodes Farm. Edward was off the bottle again and he had promised his daughter that this time he would make good.

It was in this very barn that her life had changed. While she'd been softly talking to one of the yearlings, Ellery Rhodes had walked in on her.

"Who are you?" he'd asked imperiously, and Tiffany had frozen. When she'd turned to face him, the look on his even features was near shock.

"I'm Tiffany Chappel," she had replied, with a faltering smile.

"Ed's daughter?"

"Yes."

Ellery had been flustered. "I thought that you were just a little girl." His eyes moved from her face, down the length of her body and back again. An embarrassed flush crept up his neck. "Obviously, I was mistaken."

"Dad seems to think that I'm still about eleven," she explained with a shrug and turned back to the horses.

"How old are you?"

"Eighteen."

"Why aren't you out on your own?" It was a nosy question, but Ellery asked it with genuine concern in his gold eyes. His brows had pulled together and a thoughtful frown pulled at the corners of his mouth. For a moment Tiffany thought that he might fire her father because of her. Maybe Ellery Rhodes didn't like the idea of a girl—young woman—on his farm. Maybe one of the grooms had complained about a woman on the farm. She had already had more than her share of male advances from the stable boys.

Tiffany couldn't explain to her father's employer that she had to look after him, or that a good share of his work was done by her strong hands. Edward Chappel would be fired again. Instead she lied. "I'm only helping him out for a little while. Until I go back to college—"

Ellery's practiced eyes took in her torn sweatshirt, faded jeans and oversized boots. Tiffany knew that he saw through her lie, but he was too much of a gentleman to call her on it.

Two days later, she was called into his office. Her heart pounded with dread as she entered the old farmhouse and sat stiffly in one of the chairs near his desk.

Ellery looked up from a stack of bills he had been paying. "I've got a proposition for you, young lady," he stated, looking up at her and his gold eyes shining. "Your father has already approved."

"What do you mean?"

Ellery smiled kindly. It wasn't a warm smile, but it was caring. He explained that he had worked out a deal with her father. He liked the way she handled the horses, he claimed, and he offered to send her to school, if she promised to return to the farm and work off the amount of money her education would cost once she had graduated.

Tiffany had been ecstatic with her good fortune, and Edward, feeling that he had finally found a way to rightfully provide for his daughter, was as pleased as anyone.

She had never forgotten Ellery's kindness to her, and she had held up her part of the bargain. When she returned to the farm two years later, she found that her father was drinking again.

"You've got to leave," he said, coughing violently. The stench of cheap whiskey filled the air in the small room he had been living in on the farm.

"I can't, Dad. I've got a debt to pay."

Edward shivered, though he was covered by several thick blankets. "You should never have come back."

"Why didn't anyone tell me you were sick—"

Edward raised a feeble hand and waved away her concerns. "It wouldn't help anything now, would it? You were so close to finishing school, I didn't want you to know."

"I think you should be in a hospital."

Edward shook his head and another fit of racking coughs took hold of him. "I want you to leave. I've

got a little money. Get away from this farm, from Ellery Rhodes—"

"But he's been so good to me."

Her father's faded blue eyes closed for a second.
"He's changed, Tiff...." Another fit of coughing took
hold of him, and he doubled up in pain.

"I'm getting you to a hospital, right now."

Despite her father's protests, Tiffany managed to
get him out of the stifling room and to the main house.
When she knocked on the door, Stasia, the exotic-look-
ing woman Ellery was living with, answered the door.

"My father needs help," Tiffany said.

Stasia's full lips pulled into a line of disgust at the
sight of Tiffany and her father. Her dark eyes traveled
over Tiffany, and she tossed her hair off her shoulders.
"He needs to dry out—"

"He's sick."

"Humph."

Pulling herself to her full height, Tiffany looked the
older woman directly in the eye. "Please. Call Ellery."

"He's not here."

"Then find someone to help me."

Edward's coughing started again. His shoulders
racked from the pain. "I don't know why Ellery keeps
him around," Stasia muttered, as she reached for her
coat and begrudgingly offered to drive them into town.

Tiffany remained at her father's side for two days
until the pneumonia that had settled in his lungs took
his life.

"You stupid, lovable old fool," Tiffany had said,
tears running down her face. "Why did you kill yourself—why?" she asked, as her father's body was moved
from the hospital room to the morgue.

Refusing help from the hospital staff, Tiffany had run out of the building, blinded by tears of grief and guilt. If she hadn't gone away to school, if she had stayed on the farm, her father would still have been alive.

She didn't see the oncoming car as she crossed the street. She heard the blast from an angry horn, smelled the burn of rubber as tires screamed against the dry asphalt and felt a man's body push her out of the way of the station wagon.

The man who had saved her life was Ellery. He'd gathered her shaken form into his arms and muttered something about being sorry. She didn't understand why, and she didn't care. Ellery Rhodes was the only person she had ever known who had been kind to her with no ulterior motives.

Within two weeks, Stasia was gone and Ellery asked Tiffany to marry him.

Tiffany didn't hesitate. Ellery Rhodes was the first person she had met that she could depend on. He cared for her, and though he seemed distant at times, Tiffany realized that no relationship was perfect.

She wondered now if she had married him out of gratitude or grief. The love she had hoped would bloom within her had never surfaced, but she supposed that was because passionate, emotional love only existed in fairy tales.

Inexplicably, her thoughts returned to Zane Sheridan, with his knowing gray eyes and ruggedly hewn features. He was the last person she needed to complicate her life right now, and the idea that he could shed any light on what had happened to Devil's Gambit or Ellery was preposterous.

But what if there's a chance that Ellery's alive?

Without any answers to her questions, Tiffany headed back to the house to remind Louise that there would be a guest for dinner.

"YOU'RE ASKING THE impossible!" John Morris stated as he eyed his client over the clear rims of his reading glasses.

"It's a simple document," Zane argued, rubbing the back of his neck and rotating his head to relieve the tension that had been building ever since he had met Tiffany Rhodes. He'd known she was beautiful; he'd seen enough pictures of her to understand that her exotic looks could be any man's undoing. But he hadn't counted on the light of intrigue and mystery in her intense gaze or the serene beauty in the curve of her neck....

"A deed of sale for a breeding farm? You've got to be joking."

Zane's eyes flashed like quicksilver. He pulled at the bothersome knot in his tie and focused his eyes on the attorney. "Just get me a paper that says that for a certain amount of money—and leave that blank—I will purchase all of the assets and the liabilities of Rhodes Breeding Farm."

The lawyer let out a weary sigh. "You're out of your mind, Zane. That is if you want anything legal—"

"I want it to be binding. No loopholes. It has to be so tight that if the buyer decides she wants out of the deal, she has no legal recourse. None whatsoever." His square jaw tightened, and the thin lines near the corners of his eyes deepened with fresh resolve. Revenge was supposed to be sweet. So where was the satisfaction he had been savoring for nearly six years?

"You're asking the impossible. We're not talking about a used car, for God's sake."

"It can't be that difficult." Zane paced in the prestigious San Francisco lawyer's office and ran impatient fingers through his raven-black hair in disgust. "What about a quitclaim deed?"

The lawyer leaned back in his chair and held on to his pen with both hands. "I assume that you want to do this right."

"Of course."

"No legal recourse—right?"

"I already told you that."

"Then be patient. I'll draw up all the legal documents and do a title search…take care of all the loose ends. That way, once you've agreed upon a price, you can wrap it up and it *will* be binding. You can't have it both ways, not here anyway. You're not just talking about real estate, you know. There is personal property, equipment, the horses…."

"I get the picture." Zane stared out the window and frowned. The trouble was he wanted to get away from Tiffany Rhodes. Do what he had to do and then make a clean break.

There was something about the woman that got under his skin, and he didn't like the look of honesty in her slate-blue eyes. It bothered him. A lot. Whatever else he had expected of Ellery Rhodes's widow, it hadn't been integrity.

Zane shrugged as if to shake off the last twinges of guilt. "So how long will it take you?" he asked, hiding some of his impatience.

"Four weeks—maybe three, if we're lucky. I'll work out something temporary for the interim. Okay?"

"I guess it will have to be. Doesn't seem that I have much of a choice."

John drummed his fingers on the desk. "You're sure that this woman wants to sell? I've read a little about her. She seems to be...the plucky type. Not the kind to sell out."

"She just needs a little convincing."

John scowled at the blank piece of paper in front of him. "That sounds ominous—right out of a bad B movie."

Zane smiled despite his discomfiture. It was a rare smile, but genuine, and he flashed it on his friend in a moment of self-mockery. "I guess you're right."

"Aren't I always?"

"And humble, too," Zane muttered under his breath. "Come on, counselor, I'll buy you a drink."

"On one condition—"

Zane's brows quirked expectantly.

"That you quit calling me counselor. I hear enough of that in the courtroom."

"It's a deal."

John slipped his arms into his jacket and then straightened the cuffs before bending over his desk and pressing a button on the intercom. "Sherry, I'm going out for a few minutes with Mr. Sheridan. I'll be back at—" he cocked his wrist and checked his watch "—three-thirty."

John reached for the handle of the door before pausing and turning to face his friend. "There's just one thing I'd like to know about this transaction you requested."

"And that is?"

"Why the hell do you want to buy a breeding farm? I thought you learned your lesson in Dublin a few years back."

Zane's eyes grew dark. "Maybe that's exactly why I want it." With a secretive smile he slapped his friend fondly on the back. "Now, how about that drink?"

CHAPTER THREE

TIFFANY'S FINGERS DRUMMED restlessly on the desk as she stared at the portrait of Devil's Gambit. For so long she had believed that Ellery and his proud horse were dead. And now this man, this stranger named Zane Sheridan, insisted just the opposite. Her blue eyes were shadowed with pain as she studied the portrait of the horse. *Was it possible? Could Ellery still be alive?*

Shaking her head at the absurdity of the situation, she got up and paced restlessly, alternately staring at the clock and looking out the window toward the foaling shed. Ebony Wine would be delivering a foal tonight, Moon Shadow's foal. Would he be a normal, healthy colt or would he suffer the same cruel fate as three of his siblings?

She listened as the clock ticked off the seconds, and her stomach tightened into uneasy knots. Mac hadn't come to the house this afternoon, and Tiffany was beginning to worry. Between her anxiety for the unborn foal and worries about Zane Sheridan and his motives for visiting her, Tiffany's nerves felt raw, stretched to the breaking point.

Seven-thirty-five. Though Zane would arrive any minute, Tiffany couldn't sit idle any longer. She jerked her jacket off the wooden peg near the French doors and hurried outside, oblivious to the fact that her heels sank into the mud of the well-worn path. The darkness of the night was punctuated by the sharp wind that rattled the windowpanes and whistled through the redwoods.

Tiffany found Mac in the broodmare barn, examining the black mare. His face was grim, and Tiffany's heart nearly stopped beating.

"How's it going?" she asked, hoping that she didn't sound desperate.

Mac came to the outside of the stall and reached down to scratch Wolverine, the farm's border collie, behind the ears. Wolverine thumped his tail against the concrete floor in appreciation, but Tiffany had the impression that Mac was avoiding her gaze.

"So far so good," the ex-jockey replied, straightening and switching a piece of straw from one side of his mouth to the other. But his sharp brown eyes were troubled when they returned to Ebony Wine. The mare shifted uncomfortably in the large stall, and Tiffany noted that everything was ready for the impending birth. Six inches of clean straw covered the concrete floor, and a plastic bucket containing towels, antibiotics, scissors and other equipment necessary to help the mare give birth, had been placed near the stall.

"Might be a little earlier than I thought originally," Mac suggested. He took off his hat and straightened the crease with his fingers.

"Why?"

"This is her second foal. If I remember right, the last one came before midnight." He rammed the hat back on his head. "Could be wrong…just a feeling I've got."

"Have you called Vance?"

Mac nodded curtly. "He'll be here around eleven, earlier if we need him."

"Good."

Tiffany cast one final look toward the mare and then returned to the house. Wolverine padded along behind her, but she didn't notice. Her thoughts were filled with worry for the mare and anxiety about meeting Zane Sheridan again. He couldn't have picked a worse time to show up.

All afternoon her thoughts had been crowded with questions about him. Who was he? What did he want? How did he know Ellery? Why would he concoct such an elaborate story about Devil's Gambit being alive?

There was something about the man that was eerily familiar, and Tiffany felt that she had heard Ellery speak of him at least once. But it was long ago, before they were married, and she couldn't remember the significance, if there was any, of Ellery's remarks.

She had just returned to the house and stepped out of her muddied shoes when headlights flashed through the interior of the manor as if announcing Zane's arrival. "Here we go," she muttered to herself as she slipped on a pair of pumps and attempted to push back the tides of dread threatening to overtake her. "He's only one man," she told herself as the doorbell chimed. "One man with a wild imagination."

But when she opened the door and she saw him standing in the shadowy porch light, once again she experienced the feeling that Zane Sheridan rarely made mistakes. He was leaning casually against one of the tall pillars supporting the porch roof, and his hands were thrust into the front pockets of his corduroy slacks. Even in the relaxed pose, there was tension, strain in the way his smile tightened over his teeth, a coiled energy lying just beneath the surface in his eyes.

In the dim light, his mouth appeared more sensual than she had remembered and the rough angles of his face seemed less threatening. His jet-black hair was without a trace of gray and gleamed blue in the lamplight. Only his eyes gave away his age. Though still a sharp, intense silver, they were hard, as if they had witnessed years of bitterness. The skin near the corners of his eyes was etched with a faint webbing that suggested he had stared often into the glare of the afternoon sun.

"Sorry I'm late," he said, straightening as his bold gaze held hers.

"No problem," she returned and wondered what it was about him that she found so attractive. She'd never been a woman drawn to handsome faces or strong physiques. But there was an intelligence in Zane's eyes, hidden beneath a thin veneer of pride, that beckoned the woman in her. It was frightening. "Please come in."

I can't be attracted to him, she thought. *He can't be trusted. God only knows what he wants from me.*

He walked with her to the den. "I'm sorry for the interruption this morning—" she began.

"My fault. I should have called." A flash of a brilliant smile gleamed against his dark skin.

Tiffany didn't bother to wave off his apology. Zane's surprise appearance on her doorstep had thrown her day into a tailspin. It had been a wonder that she could even converse intelligently with the reporter from the *Santa Rosa Clarion* considering the bombshell that this man had dropped in her lap.

"Could I get you a drink?" she inquired as she

walked toward a well-stocked bar disguised in the bookcase behind her desk. Ellery had insisted on the most modern of conveniences, the bar being one of his favorites. Tiffany hadn't used it more than twice since her husband's death.

"Scotch, if you have it."

She had it all right. That and about every other liquor imaginable. "You never can guess what a man might drink," Ellery had explained with a knowing wink. "Got to be prepared...just in case. I wouldn't want to blow a potential stud fee all because I didn't have a bottle of liquor around." Ellery had laughed, as if his response to her inquiry were a joke. But he had filled the bar with over thirty bottles of the most expensive liquor money could buy. "Think of it as a tax deduction," he had joked.

"Oh, I'm sure I've got Scotch," she answered Zane. "It's just a matter of locating it." After examining a few of the unfamiliar labels, Tiffany wiped away some of the dust that had collected on the unused bottles. *What a waste.*

It didn't take long to find an opened bottle of Scotch. She splashed the amber liquor into a glass filled with ice cubes and then, with a forced smile, she handed Zane the drink. "Now," she said, her voice surprisingly calm, "why don't you tell me why you think Devil's Gambit is alive?"

After pouring herself a glass of wine, she took an experimental sip and watched Zane over the rim of her glass. "That is, if you haven't changed your mind since this morning."

A gray light of challenge flashed in his eyes and

his facade of friendly charm faded slightly. "Nothing's changed."

"So you still think that the horse is alive...and you're still interested in buying the farm, right?"

"That's correct."

Tiffany let out a ragged sigh and took a chair near the desk. "Please, have a seat."

Zane was too restless to sit. He walked over to the window and stared into the black, starless night. "I didn't mean to shock you this morning." Why the hell was he apologizing? He owed this woman nothing more than a quick explanation, and even that stuck in his throat. But there was something intriguing about her—a feminine mystique that touched a black part of his soul. Damn it all, this meeting was starting off all wrong. Ellery Rhodes's widow turned his thinking around. When he was with her, he started forgetting his objectives.

"Well, you did."

"Like I said—I should have called to make sure that we would have some time to talk."

Tiffany shifted uneasily in the chair. "We have all night," she said, and when a flicker of interest sparked in his eyes she quickly amended her statement. "Or however long it takes to straighten out this mess. Why don't you explain yourself?"

"I told you, I have reason to believe that Devil's Gambit is alive."

Tiffany smiled and shook her head. "That's impossible. I...I was at the scene of the accident. The horse was killed."

Zane frowned into the night. "*A* horse was killed."

"Devil's Gambit was the only horse in the trailer.

The other two horses that had been stabled in Florida were in another truck—the one that Mac was driving. They were already in Kentucky when the accident occurred." She ran trembling fingers through her hair as she remembered that black, tragic night. Once again she thought about the terror and pain that Ellery and his horse must have gone through in those last agonizing moments before death mercifully took them both. "Devil's Gambit died in the accident." Her voice was low from the strain of old emotions, and she had to fight against the tears threatening her eyes.

"Unless he was never in that truck in the first place."

Tiffany swallowed with difficulty. "What are you suggesting, Mr. Sheridan?"

"I think that Devil's Gambit was kidnapped."

"That's crazy. My husband—"

Zane's eyes flashed silver fire. "Was probably involved."

Tiffany stood on trembling legs, her hands flattened on the desk to support her. A quiet rage began to burn in her chest. "This conversation is absurd. Why would Ellery steal his own horse?"

Zane shrugged. "Money? Wasn't Devil's Gambit insured?"

"Not to his full value. After he won in Florida, we intended to increase the coverage, as he proved himself much more valuable than anyone had guessed. I had all the forms filled out, but before I could send them back to the insurance company as Ellery had suggested, I had to wait until I saw him again. Several of the documents required his signature." She shook her head at her own foolishness. "Why am I telling you all of this?" After releasing a weary sigh, she rapped her knuckles on the polished desk and clasped her hands behind her back.

"Because I'm telling you the truth."

"You think."

"I know."

Tiffany's emotions were running a savage gauntlet of anger and fear, but she attempted to keep her voice steady. "How do you know?"

"I saw your horse."

She sucked in her breath. "You saw Devil's Gambit? That's impossible. If he were alive, someone would have told me—"

"Someone is."

There was a charged silence in the air. "It's been four years since the accident. Why now?"

"Because I wasn't sure before."

Tiffany shook her head in denial, and her honey-colored hair brushed her shoulders. "This is too crazy—where did you see the horse? And how did you know it was Devil's Gambit? And what horse was killed in the trailer—and…and…what about my husband?" she whispered. "His brother Dustin was with him. Dustin knows what happened."

"Dustin claimed to be sleeping."

Tiffany flinched. How did this man, this virtual stranger, know so much about her and what had happened that night? If only she could remember what Ellery had said about Zane Sheridan. Ellery had spent some time in Ireland—Dublin. Maybe that was the connection. Zane still spoke with a slight brogue. Ellery must have known Zane in Dublin, and that's why he was here. Something happened in Ireland, years ago. Any other reason was just a fabrication, an excuse.

"Dustin would have woken up if the truck was stopped and the horses were switched. Dear God, do you know what you're suggesting?" Tiffany took a calming swallow of her wine and began to pace in front of the desk. Her thoughts were scattered between Zane, the tragic past and the tense drama unfolding in the foaling shed. "Ellery would never have been involved in anything so underhanded."

"Didn't you ever question what happened?" Zane asked suddenly.

"Of course, but—"

"Didn't you think it was odd that Dustin had taken sleeping pills? Wasn't he supposed to drive later in the night—switch off with Ellery so that they wouldn't have to stop?"

Tiffany was immediately defensive. "Dustin's an insomniac. He needed the rest before the Derby."

"The Derby was weeks away."

"But there was a lot of work—"

"And what about your husband? Why did he decide to drive that night? Wasn't that out of the ordinary?" Bitterness tightened Zane's features, and he clutched his drink in a death grip.

"He was excited—he wanted to be a part of it." But even to her, the words sounded false. Ellery had always believed in letting the hired help handle the horses. Before that night, he had always flown—first class—to the next racetrack.

Zane saw the doubts forming in her eyes. "Everything about that 'accident' seems phony to me."

"But there was an investigation—"

"Thorough?"

"I—I don't know.... I think so." At the time she had

been drowning in her own grief and shock. She had listened to the police reports, viewed the brutal scene of the accident, visited Dustin in the hospital and flown home in a private fog of sorrow and disbelief. After the funeral, Dustin's strong arms and comforting words had helped her cope with her loss.

"Were Ellery's dental records checked?"

Tiffany's head snapped up, and her eyes were bright with righteous defiance. "Of course not. Ellery was driving. Dustin was there. There didn't need to be any further investigation." Her eyes narrowed a fraction, and her voice shook when she spoke again. "What are you suggesting, Mr. Sheridan? That my husband is still alive—hiding from me somewhere with his horse?"

Zane impaled her with his silvery stare and then ran impatient fingers through his hair. "I don't know."

A small sound of disbelief came from Tiffany's throat and she had to lean against the desk for support. "I—I don't know why I'm even listening to this," she whispered hoarsely. "It just doesn't make any sense. Devil's Gambit is worth a lot more as Devil's Gambit—in terms of dollars at the racetrack and stud fees. Anything you've suggested is absolutely beyond reason." She smiled grimly, as if at her own foolhardiness. "Look, I think maybe it would be better if you just left."

"I can't do that—not yet."

"Why not?"

"Because I intend to convince you that your horse was stolen from you."

"That's impossible."

"Maybe not." Zane extracted a small manila envelope from his breast pocket and walked back to the desk. "There are some pictures in here that might change your mind." He handed Tiffany the envelope, and she accepted it with a long sigh.

There were three photographs, all of the same horse. Tiffany scanned the color prints of a running horse closely, studying the bone structure and carriage of the animal. The similarities between the horse in the photograph and Devil's Gambit were uncanny. "Where did you get these?" she asked, her breath constricting in her throat.

"I took them. Outside of Dublin."

It made sense. The horse, if he really was Devil's Gambit, would have to be hidden out of the country to ensure that no one would recognize or identify him. Even so, Zane's story was ludicrous. "This isn't Devil's Gambit," she said, her slate-blue eyes questioning his. "This horse has no white marks…anywhere." She pointed to the portrait above the fireplace. "Devil's Gambit had a stocking, on his right foreleg."

"I think the stocking has been dyed."

"To hide his identity?"

"And to palm him off as another horse, one of considerably less caliber."

"This is ridiculous." Tiffany rolled her eyes and raised her hands theatrically in the air. "You know, you almost convinced me by coming in here and making outlandish statements that I nearly believed. Heaven knows why. Maybe it's because you seemed so sure of yourself. But I can tell you without a doubt that this is not Devil's Gambit." She shook the prints in the air before tossing them recklessly on the desk. "Nothing you've said tonight makes any sense, nor is it backed up with the tiniest shred of evidence. Therefore I have to assume that you're here for another reason, such as the sale of the farm. My position hasn't altered on that subject, either. So you see, Mr. Sheridan, any further discussion would be pointless."

Louise knocked softly on the door of the den before poking her head inside. "Dinner's ready." She eyed Tiffany expectantly.

"I don't think—"

"Good. I'm starved," Zane stated as he turned his head in the housekeeper's direction. A slow-spreading, damnably charming grin took possession of his handsome face. Gray eyes twinkled devilishly, and his brilliant smile exposed a dimple on one tanned cheek.

"Whenever you're ready," Louise replied, seemingly oblivious to the tension in the room and returning Zane's smile. "I have to be getting home," she said apologetically to Tiffany, who nodded in response. Louise slowly backed out of the room and closed the door behind her.

"I didn't think you'd want to stay," Tiffany remarked, once Louise had left them alone.

"And miss a home-cooked meal? Not on your life."

Tiffany eyed him dubiously. "Something tells me this has nothing to do with the meal."

"Maybe I'm just enjoying the company—"

"Or maybe you think you can wear me down and I'll start believing all this nonsense."

"Maybe."

"There's no point, you know."

Zane laughed aloud, and the bitterness in his gaze disappeared for a second. "Try me."

"But we have nothing more to discuss. Really. I'm not buying your story. Not any of it."

"You're not even trying."

"I have the distinct feeling that you're attempting to con me, Mr. Sheridan—"

"Zane."

"Whatever. And I'm not up to playing games. Whether you believe it or not, I'm a busy woman who has more important things to do than worry about what could have happened. I like to think I deal in reality rather than fantasy."

Zane finished his drink with a flourish and set the empty glass down on the corner of the desk. "Then you'd better start listening to me, damn it. Because I'm not here on some cock and bull story." His thick brows lifted. "I have better things to do than spend my time trying to help someone who obviously doesn't want it."

"Help?" Tiffany repeated with a laugh. "All you've done so far is offer me vague insinuations and a few photographs of a horse that definitely is *not* Devil's Gambit. You call that help?"

Zane pinched the bridge of his nose, closed his eyes and let out a long breath. "If you weren't so blind, woman," he said, his black-Irish temper starting to explode.

"Look—"

Zane held up one palm and shrugged. "Maybe you just need time to think about all of this."

"What I don't need is someone to march into my life and start spewing irrational statements."

Zane smiled, and the tension drained from his face to be replaced by genuine awe of the woman standing near the desk. In the past six years, he'd imagined coming face to face with Ellery Rhodes's widow more often than he would like to admit, but never had he thought that she would be so incredibly bewitching. His mistake. Once before Ellery Rhodes and Zane Sheridan had been attracted to the same woman, and that time Zane had come out the loser, or so he had thought at the time. Now he wasn't so sure.

"Come on," he suggested, his voice becoming dangerously familiar. "I wasn't kidding when I said I was starved."

Tiffany backed down a little. "I won't change my mind."

With a nonchalant shrug, Zane loosened the knot of his tie and unbuttoned the collar of his shirt. His chin was beginning to darken with the shadow of a day's growth of beard, and he looked as if he belonged in this house, as if he had just come home from a long, tiring day at the office to share conversation and a drink with his wife.... The unlikely turn of her thoughts spurred Tiffany into action. As a slight blush darkened the skin of her throat, she opened the door of the den. Knowing it to be an incredible mistake, she led Zane past a formal dining room to a small alcove near the kitchen.

Louise had already placed the beef stew with gravy on the small round table.

"Sit," Tiffany commanded as she pulled out a bottle of wine and uncorked it before pouring the rich Burgundy into stemmed glasses. Zane did as he was bid, but his face registered mild surprise when Tiffany took the salads out of the refrigerator and set them on the table.

After Tiffany sat down, Zane stared at her from across a small maple table. "Your housekeeper doesn't live in?"

"No."

"But she manages to keep the place up?"

Tiffany released an uneasy laugh. "I'm not that messy. I do pick up after myself, even do my own laundry and cook occasionally," she teased. What must he think of her? That she was some princess who wouldn't get her fingers dirty? Did his preconceived notions stem from his relationship—whatever that was—with Ellery? "Actually, Louise only comes in twice a week. Today I asked her to come over because of the interview with Rod Crawford. I thought I might need another pair of hands. But usually I can handle whatever comes up by myself."

"That surprises me," Zane admitted and took a sip of his wine.

Tiffany arched her elegant dark brows. "Why?"

"Because of the house, I suppose. So formal."

"And here you are stuck in the kitchen, without the benefit of seeing the crystal and silver," Tiffany said with a chuckle. "Disappointed, Mr. Sheridan?"

His gray eyes drove into hers and his voice was low when he spoke. "Only that I can't persuade you to call me by my first name."

"I don't think I know you that well—"

"Yet." He raised his glass in mock salute and his flinty eyes captured hers. "Here's to an independent woman," he announced before taking another long drink.

She was more than a little embarrassed by the intimate toast, and after a few silent moments when she alternately sipped the wine and twirled the glass in her fingers, she decided she had to level with him. Against her wishes she was warming to him, and that had to stop. "Look, *Zane*. As far as I'm concerned, you're close enough to certifiably crazy that I doubt if I'll associate with you again," she said half-seriously as she poured them each another glass of wine and then began to attack her salad. "There's no reason for first names."

"I'm not crazy, Ms. Rhodes—"

"Tiffany." Gentle laughter sparkled in her eyes. "Just concerned, right?" Her smile faded and she became instantly serious. "Why? Why are you here, now, telling me all of this?"

"It took me this long to be sure."

"Then you'll understand why I'm having trouble accepting what you're suggesting as the truth. You've had four years to think about it. I just found out this morning."

Tiffany pushed her plate aside, crossed her arms over her chest and leveled serious blue eyes in his direction. "Let's quit beating around the bush," she suggested. "So what's in this for you? You don't impress me as the kind of man who would go traipsing halfway around the world just to set the record straight and see that justice is served."

"I'm not."

"I didn't think so."

"I have an interest in what happens here."

Dread began to hammer in her heart. "Which is?"

"Personal."

"What does that mean? A grudge—revenge—vendetta—what?" She leaned on one hand and pointed at him with the other. "This morning you said you knew Ellery. I got the impression then, and now again, that you didn't much like him." Her palm rotated in the air as she collected her scattered thoughts. "If you ask me, all this interest in my horse has to do with Ellery. What's the point, Mr. Sheridan? And why in the world would you want to buy this farm? There must be a dozen of them, much more profitable than this, for sale."

Zane set aside his fork and settled back in the chair. As he pondered the situation and the intelligent woman staring beguilingly at him, he tugged on his lower lip. "The reason I want this farm is because it should have been mine to begin with. That your husband got the capital to invest in this parcel of land was a…fluke."

"Come again," she suggested, not daring to breathe. What was he saying? "Ellery's family owned this land for years."

"I don't think so. The way I understand it, he was a tenant farmer until a few years ago. The two hundred thousand dollars that your husband put into this farm as a down payment—"

"Yes?" Tiffany asked.

"He stole it from me."

"Oh, dear God," Tiffany whispered, letting her head fall forward into her waiting hands. She didn't know whether to laugh or to cry. Obviously Zane thought he was telling the truth, and he didn't seem like a dangerous psychotic, but what he was saying was absolutely ridiculous. Ellery might have been many things, but Tiffany knew in her heart he wasn't a thief.

"I think it's time for you to leave, Mr. Sheridan," she said, her voice as cold as ice. "You've been saying some pretty wild things around here—things that could be construed as slander, and—"

Footsteps on the back porch interrupted her train of thought. Panic welled in Tiffany's mind and she snapped her head upward as the familiar boot steps drew near. Within a minute, Mac was standing in the kitchen, worrying the brim of his fedora in his fingers, his dark eyes impaling hers. "You'd better come, Missy," he said, his voice uncommonly low.

"Ebony Wine?"

"Aye."

"The foal is here?"

"Will be soon, and…" His eyes shifted from Tiffany to Zane and back again. Tiffany's heart began to thud painfully in her chest. She could read the silent message in Mac's worried gaze.

"No…" she whispered, pushing the chair back so hard that it scraped against the hardwood floor. Her fearful eyes darted to Zane. "If you'll excuse me, we have an emergency on our hands." She noticed the glimmer of suspicion in Zane's eyes, but didn't bother to explain. Time was too imperative.

In seconds she was away from the table and racing toward the den. "Have you called Vance?" she called over her shoulder.

Mac pushed his hat onto his head and nodded. "He's on his way. Damn, but I should have seen this coming. I'll meet you in the shed."

Tiffany kicked off her pumps, pulled on a pair of boots and yanked her jacket off the wooden hook. Mindless of the fact that she was dressed in wool slacks, angora vest and silk blouse, she opened the French doors and raced into the dark night. She had taken only three breathless strides, when she felt the powerful hand on her arm, restraining her in its hard grasp.

"What's going on?" Zane demanded as Tiffany whirled to face the man thwarting her. Her hair tossed wildly around her face, and even in the darkness Zane could see the angry fire in her wide eyes. He hadn't been able to decipher the silent messages passing from Mac to Tiffany in the kitchen, but Zane knew that something horrible was taking place and that Tiffany felt she could do something about it.

Tiffany didn't have time to argue. She was trying to free herself. "A mare's gone into labor."

"And that upsets you?"

She jerked her arm free of his imprisoning grasp. "There might be complications. If you'll excuse me—" But he was right beside her, running the short distance from the house to the foaling shed with her, his strides long and easy.

With a sinking feeling, Tiffany realized that there was no way she could hide her secret from him any longer, and she really didn't care. The only thing that mattered was the mare in labor and the unborn colt.

CHAPTER FOUR

THE SOFT OVERHEAD lights of the foaling shed were reflected in the sweat-darkened coat of Ebony Wine. As the mare paced restlessly in the stall, she alternately snorted in agitation and flattened her dark ears against her head in impatience.

Mac's arms were braced on the top rail of the gate to the foaling stall and his anxious brown eyes studied the horse. A matchstick worked convulsively in the corner of his mouth.

He spoke softly in quiet tones filled with years of understanding. "Simmer down, lady." His gravelly voice was barely audible as the distressed mare shifted under the intense pressure of an abdominal contraction.

Tiffany's heart was pounding more rapidly than her footsteps on the cold concrete floor as she walked rapidly down the length of the corridor to the foaling stall. The acrid smells of sweat and urine mingled with antiseptic in the whitewashed barn. One look at Mac's tense form told her that the birth of Ebony Wine's foal was going no better than he had expected.

Zane was at Tiffany's side, matching her short strides with his longer ones. His dark brows were drawn over his slate gray eyes. He kept his thoughts to himself as he tried to make head or tail of the tense situation. Something was very wrong here. He could feel it. Though it hadn't been stated, he had witnessed fear in Tiffany's incredible blue eyes when Mac had entered the kitchen and made the announcement that one of the mares had gone into labor. Zane had noticed something else in Tiffany's worried expression—determination and pride held her finely sculpted jaw taut, but worry creased her flawless brow. A sense of desperation seemed to have settled heavily on her small shoulders.

"Has her water broken?" Tiffany asked as she approached Mac and leaned over the railing of the stall.

Mac shook his head and ran bony fingers over the stubble on his jaw. "Not yet."

Ebony Wine was moving restlessly in the stall. Her sleek body glistened with sweat, and her ears twitched warily.

"Come on, lady," Mac whispered softly, "don't be so stupid. Lie down, will ya?"

"She didn't get off her feet the last time," Tiffany reminded the trainer.

"She'd better this time," Mac grumbled, "or we'll lose this one, sure as I'm standing here." He shifted the matchstick from one side of his mouth to the other. "Moon Shadow's colts need all the help they can get. Come on, Ebony, be a good girl. Lie down."

"Moon Shadow?" Zane asked. "He's the sire?"

Mac's troubled gaze shifted from the horse to Tiffany in unspoken apology. "That he is."

Zane's eyes narrowed as he studied the anxious mare. "Where's the vet?"

"He was at another farm—said he'd be here on the double," Mac replied.

At that moment, Ebony Wine's water broke and the amniotic fluid began cascading down her black legs.

"Looks like he might be too late," Zane observed wryly.

Without asking any further questions, he rolled up his shirt sleeves, walked to a nearby basin and scrubbed his arms and hands with antiseptic.

"What're you doing?" Tiffany demanded.

His gaze was steady as he approached her. "I'm trying to help you. I've spent most of my life with horses and seen enough foals being born to realize when a mare's in trouble. This lady here—" he cocked his dark head in the direction of the anxious horse "—needs a hand."

Mac looked about to protest, but Tiffany shook her head to quiet him. "Let's get on with it."

Ebony Wine stiffened as Mac and Zane entered the stall. Her eyes rolled backward at the stranger. Mac went to Ebony Wine's head and talked to the horse. "Come on, Ebony, girl. Lie down, for Pete's sake."

Zane examined the horse and the bulging amniotic sac beginning to emerge below her tail. "We've got problems," he said with a dark frown. "Only a nose and one leg showing. Looks as if one leg has twisted back on itself."

"Damn!" Mac muttered. His hands never stopped their rhythmic stroking of Ebony Wine's head.

Tiffany felt her heart leap to her throat. Moon Shadow's foals were having enough trouble surviving, without the added problems of a complicated birth. Against the defeat slumping her shoulders, Tiffany forced her head upward to meet the cruel challenge fate had dealt the mare. Her vibrant blue eyes locked with Zane's. "What do you want me to do?"

"Help with supplies." He pointed in the direction of the clean pails, scissors and bottles of antiseptic. "We've got to get that foal out of there, and my guess is that this lady isn't going to want our help."

The sound of the door to the foaling shed creaking open caught her attention and brought Tiffany's head around. Vance Geddes, his round face a study in frustration, let the door swing shut and hurried down the corridor to Ebony Wine's stall.

He took one look at the horse and turned toward the basin. "How long has she been at it?" he asked, quickly washing his hands.

"Over half an hour," Mac replied.

"And she won't lie down?"

"Not this one. Stubborn, she is."

"Aren't they all?" Vance's gaze clashed with the stranger attending to Ebony Wine. Zane responded to the unspoken question. "Zane Sheridan."

"'Evening," Vance said.

"I was here on other business, but I thought I'd help out. I've worked with Thoroughbreds all my life, and I think we've got problems here. One leg's twisted back. The foal's stuck."

"Great," Vance muttered sarcastically, entering the stall as quietly as possible. "Just what we need tonight." His eyes traveled over the mare. "How're ya, gal? Hurtin' a little?" he asked as he studied the glistening horse.

"How can I help?" Tiffany asked, forcing her voice to remain steady as she noticed the tightening of Vance's jaw.

"Be ready to hand me anything I might need," Vance replied and then positioned himself behind the mare to confirm what Zane had told him. "Damn." He shook his blond head and frowned. "All right, let's get him out of there."

Ebony Wine moaned as her womb contracted, and the foal remained stuck in the birth canal.

"This is gonna be touchy," Vance whispered, as warning to the tall man standing next to him.

Zane's body tensed and he nodded curtly, before he helped Vance carefully push the foal back into the mare so that there was less danger of breaking the umbilical cord and to give more room to coax the bent leg forward. Time was crucial, and both men worked quickly but gently, intent on saving the mare and her offspring.

Tiffany assisted with the towels and antiseptic, silently praying for the life of the unborn horse. Her throat was hot and tight with the tension in the confining stall. Sweat began to bead on Zane's forehead, and his intent eyes never left the mare. The muscles in his bronze forearms flexed as he worked on righting the foal. Tiffany's heart was hammering so loudly, it seemed to pound in her ears.

Ebony Wine pushed down hard with all the muscles of her abdomen. As the mare pushed, Vance and Zane stood behind her and pulled down steadily toward her hocks in rhythm with the birth contractions.

With the first push, the tiny hooves and the head of the foal emerged. On the second contraction, the mare gave a soft moan, and the men were able to pull the shoulders, the broadest part of a foal's body, through Ebony Wine's pelvis. Once the shoulders emerged, the rest of the foal followed.

The umbilical cord broke.

Zane dropped to the floor and, mindless of the fluid pooling at his knees, he ripped open the tough amniotic sac. Vance was beside him and worked on the colt's nose, so that it could breathe its first breaths of air.

Tiffany brought towels and held them near the foal so that Vance could take them as he needed them. Her eyes watched the little black colt's sides as she prayed for the tiny ribs to move. *Dear Lord, don't let him die. Please don't take this one, too.*

Because the colt had to be pulled out of the mare, the umbilical cord had broken early, and he was short-changed of the extra blood in the placenta that should have passed into his veins. Both men worked feverishly over the small, perfect body.

The foal's lips and eyelids looked blue as it lay wet and motionless in the straw.

"Oh, God, no," Tiffany whispered, as she realized that it had been far too long already since the birth. She dropped the towels and her small hands curled into impotent fists. "Not this one, too."

Ebony Wine nickered, ready to claim her foal. Mac gently held the frustrated mare as she tried to step closer to the unmoving black body lying on the floor of the stall.

Zane held his hands near the colt's nose to feel for breath. There was none. "He's not breathing," he whispered, looking up for a second at Tiffany before bending over the colt and pressing his lips to the nostrils, forcing air into the still lungs.

Vance knelt beside Zane, checking the colt for vital signs, while Zane fruitlessly tried to revive the colt.

"It's no use," Vance said at last, restraining Zane by

placing a hand on his shoulder. "This one didn't have a prayer going in."

"No!" Tiffany said, her voice trembling and tears building in her eyes. "He's got to live. He's got to!"

"Tiff…" Vance said wearily. The vet's voice trailed off. There were no adequate words of condolence. For a moment the only sounds in the building were the soft rain beating against the roof and the restless shifting of the mare's hooves in the straw.

Mindless of the blood and amniotic fluid ruining her clothes, Tiffany fell into the straw beside the inert body of the beautifully formed black colt. Her throat was swollen with despair, her eyes blurred with fresh tears. "You have to live, little one," she whispered in a voice filled with anguished desperation. She touched the foal's warm, matted coat. "Please…live."

Her fingers touched the small ears and the sightless eyes. "Don't die…."

"Tiffany." Zane's voice was rough but comforting as he reached forward and grabbed her shoulders. He felt the quiet sobs she was trying to control. "He was dead before he was born—"

Tiffany jerked herself free. "No!" Her hands were shaking as she raised them in the air. "He was alive and healthy and…"

"Stillborn."

That single word, issued softly from Zane's lips, seemed to echo against the rafters.

A single tear wove a solitary path down her cheek. Tiffany let her arms fall to her sides. "Oh, God," she whispered, pulling herself to her full height and shaking her head. Blood discolored her silk blouse, and straw stuck in her angora vest as well as her hair. "Not another one." Her small fist clenched and she pounded it on the rough boards of the stall. "Why? Why is this happening?" she demanded, hopelessly battling an enemy she couldn't see…didn't understand.

Ebony Wine snorted, and Tiffany realized she was disturbing the already distraught mare. She let her head drop into her palm, leaned against the wall and closed her eyes against the truth. *Why the foals? Why all of Moon Shadow's foals?*

"Come on, let's go back to the house," Zane suggested, placing his strong arms gently over her shoulders.

"I should stay," she whispered as cold reality began to settle in her mind. She felt a raw ache in her heart as she faced the tragic fact that another of Moon Shadow's foals was dead before it had a chance to live. It just wasn't fair; not to the mare, not to the farm, and not to the poor lifeless little colt.

"We'll take care of things," Mac assured her, giving Zane a look that said more clearly than words, "Get her out of here." Mac was holding the lead rope to Ebony Wine's halter, and the anxious horse was nickering to the dead foal.

"I'll make some coffee…up at the house," Tiffany murmured, trying to pull herself together. She was shaking from the ordeal but managed to wipe the tears from her eyes.

"Don't bother for me," Vance said, working with the afterbirth. "I'll stay with the mare until Mac can watch her and then I'll call it a night."

"Same goes for me." Mac's kind eyes rested on Tiffany. "You just take care of yourself, Missy. We'll handle the horses."

"But—"

"Shh, could be three, maybe four hours till I'm finished with this old gal here," Mac said, cocking his head sadly in the black mare's direction. "After that, I think I'll hit the hay. I'm not as young as I used to be, ya know, and the missus, she'll be looking for me." He winked at Tiffany, but the smile he tried to give her failed miserably.

Numbly, leaning against Zane's strong body, Tiffany slowly walked out of the foaling shed and into the night. The rain was still falling from the darkened sky. It splashed against the sodden ground, and the large drops ran through her hair and down her neck.

She felt cold all over, dead inside. Another of Moon Shadow's foals. Dead. Why? Her weary mind wouldn't quit screaming the question that had plagued her for nearly two weeks. She shuddered against the cold night and the chill of dread in her heart. Zane pulled her closer to the protective warmth of his body.

Hard male muscles surrounded her, shielded her from the rain as well as the storm of emotions raging in her mind. Lean and masculine, Zane's body molded perfectly over hers, offering the strength and security she needed on this dark night. For the first time in several years, Tiffany accepted the quiet strength of a man. She was tired of making decisions, weary from fighting the invisible demons that stole the lifeblood from innocent newborns.

The house was still ablaze with the lights she had neglected to turn off. Zane led her into the den and watched as she slumped wearily into the chair near the fireplace. The sparkle in her blue eyes seemed to have died with Ebony Wine's foal. Her arms were wrapped protectively over her breasts, and she stared sightlessly into the smoldering embers of the fire.

"I'll get you a drink," he offered, walking to the bookcase that housed the liquor.

"Don't want one."

He picked up a bottle of brandy before looking over his shoulder and pinning her with his intense gray gaze. "Tiffany, what happened?" he asked quietly. She continued to gaze dully at the charred logs in the stone fireplace. He repeated his question, hoping to break her mournful silence. "Just what the hell happened out there tonight?"

"We lost a colt," she whispered, tears resurfacing in her eyes.

"Sometimes that happens," he offered, waiting patiently for the rest of the story as he poured two small glasses of the amber liquor.

She lifted her gaze to meet his and for a moment he thought she was about to confide in him, but instead she shrugged her slim shoulders. "Sometimes," she agreed hoarsely as she watched his reaction.

How much could she trust this stranger? True, he had tried to help her with the unborn colt and in a moment of weakness she felt as if she could trust her life to him. But still she hesitated. She couldn't forget that he was here on a mission. Not only did he want to buy the farm, but he was filled with some insane theory about Devil's Gambit being alive.

Zane's stormy eyes glanced over her huddled form. Her soft honey-brown curls were tangled with straw and framed her elegantly featured face. Her tanned skin was pale from the ordeal. Dark, curling eyelashes couldn't hide the pain in her wide, innocent eyes.

She's seen more than her share of pain, Zane guessed as he walked over to her and offered the drink that she had declined.

"I don't want—"

"Drink it."

She frowned a little. "Just who do you think you are, coming in here and giving me orders?"

He smiled sternly. "A friend."

Tiffany found it difficult to meet the concern in his eyes. She remained rigid and ignored the glass in his outstretched hand.

With an audible sigh, Zane relented. Dealing with this beautiful woman always seemed to prove difficult. "All right, lady. Drink it. *Please.*"

Tiffany took the glass from his hand and managed an obligatory sip. The calming liquor slid easily down her throat, and as she sipped the brandy she began to warm a little. *Who was this man and why did he care?*

Zane walked over to the fireplace and stretched the tension out of his shoulders, before stoking the dying fire and finally taking a seat on the hearth. He propped his elbows on his knees and cradled his drink in his large hands.

She didn't follow his actions but kicked off her shoes, ignoring the mud that dirtied the imported carpet. Then she drew her knees under her chin as if hugging herself for warmth against an inner chill.

Zane's eyes never left her face. As he watched her he felt a traitorous rush of desire flooding his bloodstream and firing his loins. As unlikely as it seemed, he suddenly wanted Ellery Rhodes's beautiful widow and wanted her badly. The urge to claim her as his own was blinding. In a betraying vision, he saw himself kissing away the pain on her regal features, lifting the sweater vest over her head, slipping each button of her blouse through the buttonholes.

Zane's throat tightened as he imagined her lying beneath him, her glorious, dark-tipped breasts supple and straining in the moonlight....

"Stop it," he muttered to himself, and Tiffany looked upward from the flames to stare at him.

"Stop what?" she whispered, her eyes searching his.

Zane's desire was thundering in his ears, and he felt the unwelcome swelling in his loins. "Nothing," he muttered gruffly as he stood, walked across the room and poured himself another drink. He downed the warm liquor in one long swallow as if the brandy itself could quell the unfortunate urges of his body.

For God's sake, he hadn't reacted to a woman this way since Stasia. At the thought of his sultry Gypsy-like ex-wife, Zane's blood went ice-cold, and the effect was an instant relief. The ache in his loins subsided.

He set his glass down with a thud, jarring Tiffany out of her distant reverie. "Do you want to talk?" he asked softly, walking back across the close room to face her. He placed himself squarely before her, effectively blocking her view of the fire.

She shook her head and ran trembling fingers through her hair. "Not now..."

His smile was sad, but genuine. "Then I think you should get cleaned up and rest. It's after midnight—"

"Oh." For the first time that night, Tiffany was aware of her appearance. She looked down at her vest and saw the bloodstains discoloring the delicate gray wool. The sleeves of her pink blouse were rolled over her arms and stained with sweat and blood. She felt the urge to cry all over again when she looked up from her disheveled clothing and noticed the concern in Zane's gentle gray eyes.

Instead of falling victim to her emotions, she raised her head proudly and managed a stiff smile. "I'll be fine in the morning. This night has been a shock."

"Obviously."

"If you'll excuse me…"

When she rose from the chair, her knees felt unsteady, but she managed to stand with a modicum of dignity despite her disheveled appearance.

Zane picked up her barely touched glass. "I don't think you should be alone."

Involuntarily she stiffened. Ellery's words from long ago, just after her father had died, echoed in her mind. "You shouldn't be alone, Tiffany," Ellery had insisted. "You need a man to care for you." In her grief, Tiffany had been fool enough to believe him.

She lifted her chin fractionally. "I'll be fine, Mr. Sheridan," she assured him with a calm smile. "I've been alone for over four years. I think I can manage one more night."

He noticed the slight trembling of her fingers, the doubt in her clear blue eyes, and realized that she was the most damnably intriguing woman he had ever met.

"I'll stay with you."

"That won't be necessary."

"The mare's not out of the woods yet."

Tiffany hesitated only slightly. Zane's presence did lend a certain security. She remembered his quick, sure movements as he tried to revive Ebony Wine's dead colt. With a shake of her head, she tried to convince herself that she didn't need him. "Mac can take care of Ebony Wine."

"And it wouldn't hurt to have an extra pair of hands."

She was about to protest. She raised her hand automatically and then dropped it. "Don't get me wrong, Zane," she said softly, her tongue nearly tripping on the familiarity of his first name. "It's not that I don't appreciate what you've done tonight. I do. But the foal is dead." She shuddered and hugged her arms around her abdomen. "And Mac will attend to Ebony Wine." She shook her head at the vision of the dead little colt lying on the thick bed of straw. "I...I think it would be best if you would just leave for now. I know that we still have things to discuss, but certainly they'll wait until morning."

"I suppose." Zane glanced at the portrait of Devil's Gambit hanging proudly over the mantel. He had the eerie feeling that somehow the tense drama he had witnessed earlier in the foaling shed was linked to the disappearance of the proud stallion. *Impossible.* And yet he had a gut feeling that the two tragic events were connected.

As if Tiffany had read his thoughts, she shuddered. Zane was across the room in an instant. Tiffany wanted to protest when his strong arms enfolded her against him, but she couldn't. The warmth of his body and the protection of his embrace felt as natural as the gentle rain beating softly against the windowpanes. He plucked a piece of straw from her hair and tenderly let his lips press a soft kiss against her forehead. The gesture was so filled with kindness and empathy that Tiffany felt her knees buckle and her eyes fill with tears.

"I...I think you should go," she whispered hoarsely,

afraid of her response to his masculinity. *Damn him!* She wanted to lean on him. What kind of a fool was she? Hadn't she learned her lessons about men long ago from Ellery?

"Shh." He ignored her protests and led her gently out of the den, through the foyer and up the stairs. "Come on, lady," he whispered into her hair. "Give yourself a break and let me take care of you."

She felt herself melt inside. "I don't think, I mean I don't need—"

"What you need is to soak in a hot tub, wrap yourself in one of those god-awful flannel nightgowns and fall into bed with a glass of brandy."

It sounded like heaven, but Tiffany couldn't forget that the tenderness of the man touching her so intimately might be nothing more than a ploy to extract information from her. At this moment she was too tired to really give a damn, but she couldn't forget her earlier instincts about him. He was engaged in a vendetta of sorts; she could feel it in her bones. Try as she would, Tiffany couldn't shake the uneasy feeling that Zane Sheridan, whoever the hell he was, would prove to be the enemy.

Zane left Tiffany in the master bedroom. Once she was certain he had gone downstairs, she peeled off her soiled clothes, threw them in a hamper and walked into the adjacent bathroom.

As she settled into the hot water of the marble tub, her mind continued to revolve around the events of the past few weeks. If the first foal's death had been a shock, the second had been terrifying. Now two more foals by Moon Shadow had died mysteriously. Each foal had been only a few hours old, with the exception of Charlatan, who had survived for a few hope-filled days.

Just wait until Rod Crawford gets hold of this story, she thought as she absently lathered her body. The wire services would print it in a minute and she'd have more reporters crawling all over the place than she could imagine. If that wasn't enough, Zane Sheridan's theories about Devil's Gambit's fate would stir up the press and get them interested all over again in what was happening at Rhodes Breeding Farm. *And the scandal. Lord, think of the scandal!*

Tiffany sank deeper into the tub, and didn't notice that her hair was getting wet.

What about Zane Sheridan? Was he here as friend or foe? She sighed as she considered the roguish man who had helped her upstairs. One minute he seemed intent on some vague, undisclosed revenge, and the next his concern for her and the farm seemed genuine. *Don't trust him, Tiffany,* the rational side of her nature insisted.

"Men," she muttered ungraciously. "I'll never understand them." Her frown trembled a little as she thought about Ellery, the husband she had tried to love. Marrying him had probably been the biggest mistake of her life. The moment she had become Mrs. Ellery Rhodes, he seemed to have changed and his interest in her had faded with each passing day. "Dad warned you," she chided herself. "You were just too bullheaded to listen."

The distance between her and her husband had become an almost physical barrier, and Tiffany had foolishly thought that if she could bear Ellery a child, things might be different. He might learn to love her. *What a fool!* Hadn't she already known from her

own agonizing experience with her mother that relationships between people who loved each other were
often fragile and detached? In her own naive heart, she
had hoped that she would someday be able to reach
Ellery. Now, if what Zane Sheridan was saying were
true, Ellery might still be alive.

"Oh, God," she moaned, closing her eyes and trying to conjure Ellery's face in her mind. But try as
she would, she was unable to visualize the man she
had married. Instead, the image on her mind had the
forceful features on a virtual stranger from Ireland.
"You bastard," she whispered and wondered if she were
speaking to Zane or Ellery.

Her tense muscles began to relax as she rinsed the
soap from her body and then turned on the shower
spray to wash her hair.

Once she felt that all of the grime had been scrubbed
from her skin, she turned off the shower, stepped out
of the tub and wrapped herself in a bath sheet. After
buffing her skin dry, she grabbed the only nightgown
in the room, an impractical silver-colored gown of thin
satin and lace.

Just what I need, she thought sarcastically as she
slipped it over her head and straightened it over her
breasts. She smiled to herself, grabbed her red corduroy robe and cinched the belt tightly around her waist.
She was still towel-drying her hair when she stepped
into the bedroom.

As she did, her gaze clashed with that of Zane Sheridan.

"What are you doing here?" she asked, lowering
the towel and staring at him with incredulous slate-
blue eyes.

"I wanted to make sure that you didn't fall asleep in the tub."

She arched an elegant brow suspiciously. "Didn't you hear the shower running?" When a slow-spreading smile grew from one side of his face to the other, Tiffany's temper snapped. "I don't need a keeper, you know. I'm a grown woman."

His eyes slid over her body and rested on the gap in her overlapping lapels. "So I noticed."

Angrily, she tugged on the tie of her robe. "You're insufferable!" she spit out. "I could have walked in here stark naked."

"Can't blame a guy for hoping—"

"I'm in no mood for this, Zane," she warned.

He sobered instantly and studied the lines of worry on her beautiful face. "I know. I just thought I could get you to lighten up."

"A little difficult under the circumstances."

"You lost a foal. It happens."

Her lips twisted wryly. "That it does, Mr. Sheridan. That it does." She sat on the corner of the bed and supported herself with one straight arm while pushing the wet tendrils of hair out of her face with her free hand. "It's been a long day."

"I suppose it has." He strode across the room, threw back the covers of the bed and reached for a drink he had placed on the nightstand. "I checked on Ebony Wine."

Tiffany watched his actions warily. Why was he still here and why was she secretly pleased? She raised her head in challenge and ignored her rapidly pounding heart. "And?"

"You were right. Mac took care of her. She's a little confused about everything that went on tonight, still calling to the foal. But she's healthy. The afterbirth detached without any problem and Mac had already cleaned her up. He thinks she'll be ready to breed when she shows signs of foal heat, which should be the middle of next week. The veterinarian will be back to check her tomorrow and again before she goes into heat."

Tiffany nodded and accepted the drink he offered. "It's a little too much for me to think about right now," she admitted, swirling the brandy in her glass before taking a sip.

"It's the business you're in."

Tiffany stared into the amber liquor in her glass and moved her head from side to side. "And sometimes it seems like a rotten way of life."

Zane ran his hand around the back of his neck. "It's never easy to lose one, but it's the chance you take as a breeder."

"And the living make up for the dead?"

Zane frowned and shrugged. "Something like that. If it bothers you so much, maybe you should get out of the business," he suggested.

"By selling the farm to you?" Her eyes lifted and became a frigid shade of blue.

"I didn't think we would get into that tonight."

"You brought it up."

"I just voiced your concerns."

"Oh, God," she whispered, setting her unfinished drink aside. "Look, I'm really very tired and I can't think about all this tonight."

"Don't. Just try and get some sleep."

She managed a wan smile and walked around to

her side of the bed. "I guess I owe you an apology and a very big thank-you. I…really appreciate all the help you gave in the foaling shed."

Zane frowned. "For all the good it did."

Tiffany raised sad eyes to meet his questioning gaze. "I don't think there was anything anyone could have done."

"Preordained?"

She sighed audibly and shook her head. The wet hair swept across her shoulders. "Who knows?" She sat on the edge of the bed, her fingers toying with the belt holding her robe together. "Goodbye, Zane. If you call me in the morning, we can find another time to get together and talk about your hypothesis concerning Devil's Gambit and my husband."

"I'll be here in the morning," he stated, dropping into a chair facing the bed and cradling his drink in his hands.

"Pardon me?" she asked, understanding perfectly well what he meant.

"I'm staying—"

"You can't! Not here—"

"I just want to check with Mac once more, and then I'll sleep downstairs on the couch."

Visions of him spending the night in her house made her throat dry. She couldn't deny that he had been a help, but the thought of him there, in the same house with her, only a staircase away, made her uneasy. Her fingers trembled when she pushed them wearily through her hair. "I don't know," she whispered, but she could feel herself relenting.

"Come on, Tiff. It's after two. I'm not about to drive

back to San Francisco now, just to turn around and come back here in six hours."

Tiffany managed a smile. "I don't suppose that makes a whole lot of sense." Her blue eyes touched his. "You don't have to sleep in the den. There's a guest room down the hall, the first door to the left of the stairs."

He returned her hint of a smile and stood. For a moment she thought he was about to bend over the bed and kiss her. She swallowed with difficulty as their eyes locked.

Zane hesitated, and the brackets near the corners of his mouth deepened. "I'll see you in the morning," he said, his eyes darkening to a smoky gray before he turned out the lamp near the bed and walked out of the room.

Tiffany expelled a rush of air. "Oh, God," she whispered, her heart thudding painfully in her chest. "I should have made him leave." He was too close, his rugged masculinity too inviting.

Maybe he would come back to her room, or maybe he would sift through the papers in the den looking for something, anything, to prove his crazy theories. But all the important documents, the computer data disks and the checkbook were locked in the safe; even if Zane rummaged through the den, he would find nothing of value.

That's not why you're concerned, her tired mind teased. *What scares you is your response to him.* She rolled over and pushed the nagging thoughts aside. Despite all of her doubts, she was comforted that Zane was still with her. Somehow it made the tragedy of losing the foal easier to bear.

ZANE HIKED HIS quickly donned jacket around his neck and felt the welcome relief of raindrops slide under his collar. He needed time to cool off. Being around Tiffany, wanting to comfort her, feeling a need to make love to her until the fragile lines of worry around her eyes were gone, unnerved him. The last thing he had expected when he had driven to Rhodes Breeding Farm was that he would get involved with Ellery Rhodes's widow.

He heard the roar of an engine as he started to cross the parking lot. Turning in the direction of the sound, Zane walked toward Mac's battered truck. Mac rolled down the window as Zane approached. Twin beams from the headlights pierced the darkness, and the wipers noisily slapped the accumulation of rain from the windshield.

"Everything okay?"

"Aye," Mac replied cautiously. "The mare's fine."

"Good." Zane rammed his fists into the jacket of his coat. "What about the colt?"

"Vance will handle that." The wiry trainer frowned in the darkness. "He'll give us a report in a couple of days."

"Good." Zane stepped away from the truck and watched as Mac put the ancient Dodge pickup into gear before it rumbled down the driveway.

Wondering at the sanity of his actions, Zane unlocked his car and withdrew the canvas bag of extra clothes from the backseat. He always traveled with a change of clothes, his briefcase and his camera. He slung the bag over his shoulder and considered the briefcase. In the leather case were the papers his attorney had toiled over. According to John Morris, every document needed to purchase Rhodes Breeding Farm was now in Zane's possession. So why didn't owning the farm seem as important as it once had?

Zane cursed angrily and locked the briefcase in the car. Knowing that he was making a grave error, he walked back into the house, locked the doors and mounted the stairs. After throwing his bag on the guest bed, he took off his shoes and turned down the covers.

Then, on impulse, he went back to her room. He paused at the door and then strode boldly inside. His blood was thundering in his eardrums as he lowered himself into the chair near the bed. It took all of his restraint not to go to her.

Zane watched the rounded swell of her hips beneath the bedclothes, and the smoldering lust in his veins began to throb unmercifully. *You're more of a fool than you thought,* Zane chastised himself silently.

He noticed the regular rhythm of her breathing and realized that she had fallen asleep. The urge to strip off his clothes and lie with her burned in his mind. He fantasized about her response, the feel of her warm, sleepy body fitted to his, the agonizing glory of her silken fingers as they traced an invisible path down his abdomen....

A hard tightening in his loins warned him that his thoughts were dangerous; still he couldn't help but think of slowly peeling off her bedclothes and letting the shimmery nightgown peeking from the edges of her robe fall silently to the floor. He wanted to touch all of her, run his tongue over the gentle feminine curves of her body, drink in the smell of her perfume as he touched her swollen breasts....

Quietly he placed his drink on the table and walked over to the bed.

Tiffany moaned in her sleep and turned onto her back. In the dim light from the security lamps, with the rain softly pelting against the windows, Zane looked down at her. How incredibly soft and alluring she appeared in slumber. All traces of anxiety had left the perfect oval of her face. Her still-damp hair curled in golden-brown tangles around her shoulders and neck.

The scarlet robe had gaped open to display the silvery fabric of a gossamer gown and the soft texture of her breasts beneath. Tiffany shifted slightly and the hint of a dark nipple shadowed the silvery lace covering it.

Zane clenched his teeth in self-restraint. Never had he wanted a woman more, and he told himself that she was there for the taking. Hadn't he seen her vulnerability? Hadn't he witnessed the way she stared at him? Deep within her, there was a need to be taken by him; he could sense it.

He closed his eyes against the pain throbbing in his loins and dropped to his knees by the bed. "What have you done to me?" he whispered as he lovingly brushed a strand of hair from her eyes.

This woman was once the wife of Ellery Rhodes, a person he had intended to destroy. Zane couldn't help but wonder, as he stared into the sleep-softened face of Ellery Rhodes's widow, if just the opposite were true.

Would he be able to carry forth his plans of retribution, or would Ellery Rhodes's wife reap her sweet vengeance on him?

CHAPTER FIVE

WHEN TIFFANY OPENED her eyes she noticed that the first purple light of dawn had begun to filter into the room. With a muted groan, she stretched between the cool sheets and rolled over, intent on returning to sleep.

Her cloudy vision rested on the chair near the bed and her breath got lost somewhere in her throat.

Zane was in the room. The realization was like an electric current pulsing through her body, bringing her instantly awake. What was he doing here?

He was slumped back in the chair, his head cocked at an uncomfortable angle, his stocking feet propped against the foot of the bed. He had thrown a spare blanket over himself, but it had slipped to the floor. His unfinished drink sat neglected on the bedside table.

"You wonderful bastard," she whispered quietly, before a silent rage began to take hold of her. Why hadn't he left as he had promised? Why had he decided to stay here—in her bedroom? Conflicting emotions battled within her. On the one hand, she was pleased to see him. It was comforting to watch his beard-darkened face relaxed in quiet slumber. There was something slightly chivalrous in the fact that he had stayed with her on the pretense of caring for her. She supposed that in all honesty she should consider his actions a compliment, an indication that he cared for her—if only a little.

On the other hand, she was quietly furious that he would force himself so boldly into her life. Whatever it was that he wanted at Rhodes Breeding Farm, he obviously wanted very badly. Badly enough to pretend interest in Tiffany and her horses.

The smile that had touched the corners of her mouth began to fade. Zane stirred in the chair, and Tiffany knew that he would soon be awake. No better time than the present to take the bull by the horns! She slipped out of the bed and cinched her robe tightly under her breasts before planting herself in front of his chair.

"Liar!" she whispered loudly enough to disturb him.

The muscles in Zane's broad shoulders stiffened slightly. He grumbled something indistinguishable and his feet dropped to the floor as he tried to roll over.

"What the hell?" he mumbled, before opening his eyes. He awoke to find himself staring up at Tiffany's indignant blue gaze. Stretching in the uncomfortable chair, he tried to rub the stiffness from his neck and cramped shoulders. "What're you going on about?" he asked.

"You said you'd sleep downstairs or in the guest room."

A devilish grin stole across his features. "So I did."

Her blue eyes narrowed. "Don't you have any shame?"

"None." He pulled himself out of the chair and stretched his aching muscles. God, he hurt all over. It had been years since he'd slept sitting up; and never in his thirty-six years had he kept vigil on a beauti-

ful woman, a woman who obviously didn't appreciate his efforts.

"I should have known."

"Known what?" He rubbed his hands over the stubble of his beard and then threw his head back and rotated his neck to relieve the tension at the base of his
skull. "Don't you have any coffee around here?" he
asked once he'd stretched.

Tiffany crossed her arms self-righteously over her
breasts and glared up at her unwelcome visitor. She
was still wearing her robe, Zane noticed, though the
gap of the lapels had been pulled together when she
had tied the belt around her small waist. "Known you'd
end up here."

"It's too early in the morning for this outraged vir-
gin routine, Tiff," he said, rubbing the stubble on his
chin. "We're both adults."

Her lips pressed together in anger. "Virginity isn't
the issue."

He raised a brow in overt disbelief. "Then what is?
Morality?"

"Sanity," she shot back. "Your being in here bor-
ders on the insane. I don't know who you are, what
you want, where you live, why you're here in the first
place.... God, Zane, for all I know you could be married with a dozen kids."

His dark glare silenced her. "I'm not married," he
said gruffly.

"Good. Because I certainly wouldn't want some outraged wife calling me and demanding to talk to her
husband." He looked as if she had slapped him.

"I came in here to check on you last night and you're
acting as if I'm some kind of criminal, for God's sake."

She let out a ragged breath and her hands dropped to her sides. "It's just that I don't really know you," she said softly.

"Sure you do," he cajoled, his slate-colored eyes warming slightly when he noticed the flush of indignation on her cheeks.

Tiffany attempted to remain angry, but it was nearly impossible as she stared into Zane's incredible gray eyes. They were a reflection of the man himself, sometimes dark with anger, other times filled with a compelling intimacy that touched her heart and caused her pulse to jump. Slowly, by calculated inches, this man was working his way into her heart. She felt more vulnerable and naked than she had in years. The emotions beginning to blossom within her had to be pushed aside. She couldn't chance an involvement with him; it was far too dangerous.

Zane rubbed his eyes and stretched before smiling lazily. "Has anyone ever told you you're beautiful when you're angry?"

"Dozens," she returned sarcastically.

"Or that you're gorgeous when you wake up?"

Tiffany swallowed back a lump in her throat. "Not quite as many." She ran her long fingers through her knotted hair and slowly expelled a sigh. Arguing with him would get her nowhere. "I guess I haven't been very hospitable this morning," she conceded, lowering herself to a corner of the bed.

"Some people wake up in a bad mood."

"Especially if they find a stranger in their room?"

His gray eyes touched hers and his voice lowered to an intimate whisper. "We're not strangers."

Her elegant brows arched skeptically. "No?"

"No." He shook his head and frowned decisively.

"Then tell me," she suggested as one long, nervous finger began tracing the line of delicate stitching on the hand-pieced quilt. "Just how would you describe our relationship?"

A mischievous light gleamed in his eyes and his voice lowered suggestively. "How about two strong-willed people thrown mercilessly together by the cruel tides of fate?"

Tiffany couldn't help but laugh. "Seriously—"

"Seriously?" He sobered instantly. "Why don't we start as friends?"

She nodded silently to herself as if agreeing with an earlier-drawn conclusion. "Ah. Friends." Looking up, she found Zane staring intensely at her. "Friendship isn't formed in one night. Not when one of the 'friends' doesn't know anything about the other."

"Or suspects that he's holding out on her?"

She stiffened slightly. "Right." Folding her hands in her lap, she forced her eyes to meet the stormy gray of his. "You came here yesterday and announced that you intended to buy this farm. You also insisted that Devil's Gambit was alive. These aren't the usual kinds of statements to kick off an amiable relationship."

Before he could respond, she pointed an accusing finger up at him and continued, "And there's more to it than you've told me. I get the distinct impression you're here for other reasons, that you were probably involved with Ellery in the past and you're holding a grudge against him…or what used to be his before he died…."

Zane didn't deny it, but the mention of Ellery's name caused his face to harden. An unspoken challenge flashed from his eyes.

"My husband is dead——"

"You think." He rammed his fists into his pockets and walked over to one of the tall, paned windows. Leaning one shoulder against the window frame, he surveyed the farm. From his vantage point he could look past the white buildings near the house to the gently rolling hills in the distance. It was barely dawn. A gentle drizzle was falling, and wisps of fog had settled in the pockets between the hills to color the lush green meadows a hazy shade of blue.

Standing apart from the main buildings, its shape barely visible in the clinging fog, was the sagging skeleton of an old weather-beaten barn, the one structure on the farm that was in sharp contrast to the rest of the modern facilities. The old relic was out of sync with the times. Why had Ellery kept it?

Tiffany watched Zane with new fear taking hold of her heart. What was he saying? Did he really believe that Ellery could still be alive after all these years?

Her voice was suddenly hoarse and she was forced to clear her throat. "Look…"

He continued to stare at the rain-washed countryside.

"If you think that Ellery is alive, I want to know about it and I want to know now. This minute. No more stalls."

Zane lifted his hands dismissively. "I don't really know. The only thing I'm certain about is the horse."

"But you said——"

He whirled to face her, his burning hatred resurfacing in his eyes. "What I said was that I don't know what happened to your husband, but I wouldn't rule out the possibility that he could very well be alive and hiding out somewhere."

Tiffany's dark brows drew together, and she shook her head as if she could physically deny the doubts and fears beginning to plague her. "That doesn't make any sense!"

Zane's scathing eyes slowly traveled up her body to rest on her troubled face. He shook his head as if he couldn't begin to understand what was happening between himself and Ellery Rhodes's wife. "If your husband did leave you, then he's not only a crooked bastard, he's crazy to boot."

"You didn't much like him, did you?"

"I didn't like him at all." Zane uttered the words without any trace of emotion, as if he were simply stating a fact. He noticed the worry clouding her gaze, the weariness in the slump of her shoulders, and he silently wondered how such a beautiful woman could have linked up with the likes of Ellery Rhodes. Stasia's passion for money was understandable, but Tiffany? The bitter thought of Stasia heightened his curiosity and got the better of him. "Tell me, what kind of a marriage did you have?"

"Pardon me?"

"How was your relationship with Ellery?"

Searching gray eyes probed hers and seemed to pierce her soul. Just how much did this man want from her? "I don't think this is the time or the place—"

"Cut the bull, Tiffany."

"It's really none of your business—"

"Like hell! I just spent the night with you, lady, and I think that counts for something." His skin tightened over his cheekbones and his jaw hardened. An unspoken challenge flared in his intense gaze.

"Wait a minute. You didn't 'spend the night' with me. You merely sat in a chair in my room."

"Tell that to the rest of the people on the farm."

"I really don't give a rip what anyone else thinks, Zane," she replied, coloring only slightly. "What I do with my life is my own business."

He quirked a disbelieving brow.

"By the same token, I expect that you wouldn't go around to the workers and brag that you slept in the boss lady's room." Her heart was pounding wildly, but she managed to keep her voice steady.

Zane rammed fingers through his dark hair. "But I did."

"No reason to brag about it, especially since nothing happened."

"Not for any lack of wanting on my part," he admitted with a sigh of frustration. His eyes had darkened, and a tiny muscle worked furiously in the corner of his jaw. The tension that sleep had drained from his body resurfaced, and Tiffany realized for the first time just how badly this man wanted her. Her pulse jumped, and she had to force herself to stand and face him. Things were moving too rapidly, and she couldn't begin to deal with the bold desire written on Zane's rugged features.

"This conversation isn't getting us anywhere," she whispered, her voice becoming thick as her eyes lingered in the smoky depths of his. "I…I'm going to clean up and get dressed and then I'll fix you that cup of coffee. It's the least I can do since you helped out here last night…and were such a gentleman in the bargain." She motioned with a suddenly heavy hand toward the door of the room. "There's a bath down the hall, if you'd like to shave or change…."

He noticed her hesitation. "I brought a change of clothes."

"You did? Why?" Tiffany demanded. Had he intended to spend the night? Was he using her? If so, then why hadn't he tried to force himself upon her last night? Surely he had sensed her attraction to him. Zane Sheridan was a very fascinating man, and it had been a long time since she had been with a man…so very long.

"I thought I was going straight to the airport from here," he replied, abruptly bringing her back to the present.

She flushed from her wanton thoughts and smiled. "I see. Then I'll meet you downstairs later."

Without any further protests, Zane left the room. Tiffany waited until she heard him on the stairs, then she slowly closed the door to the bedroom and locked it.

A few minutes later she heard water running in the guest bathroom at the other end of the hall, and she smiled. "You're a fool," she whispered to herself as she stripped off the vibrant red robe, flung it carelessly on the foot of the bed and walked into her private bathroom. "A stranger just spent the night in your room, and if you had your way, he would be back here in a minute making furious, passion-filled love to you."

After turning on the shower, she shook her head and smiled at her unfamiliar and traitorous thoughts. "Tiffany, my friend," she warned her reflection in the steamy mirror, "this fascination with Zane Sheridan can only spell trouble."

Dropping her silvery nightgown on the floor, she stepped into the hot spray of water.

AFTER BRAIDING HER hair into a single plait, applying just a little makeup and dressing in her favorite pair of faded jeans and a loose sweater, Tiffany headed downstairs to the kitchen. The airy room was bright with copper pots and pans suspended over the stove, plants arranged strategically on the gleaming tile counters, and oversized windows offering a view of the pasture near the broodmare barn.

The coffee was perking, muffins were baking in the oven and the previous night's dishes had been placed in the dishwasher before she heard Zane on the stairs. The inviting aromas of baking bread, coffee and cured ham wafted through the large kitchen.

"Efficient, aren't you?" he stated, offering her a lazy grin.

"I try to be." She glanced over her shoulder and felt her heart begin to pound irregularly as her eyes were caught in the silvery web of his gaze. Zane's black hair was still wet from his shower, his shadow of a beard had been shaved off to reveal the hard angle of his jaw and he was dressed casually in tan cords and a teal-blue sweater. Without his formal attire, he appeared more rakishly handsome than ever. Looking at him caused an uneasy fluttering in Tiffany's stomach.

He leaned against the counter, seemingly content to watch her work. Turning back to the coffee, she poured a cup and tried to hide the fact that her hands were unsteady.

"Cream or sugar?"

"Black is fine." He took an experimental sip, all the while observing Tiffany over the rim of the stoneware mug. "What happened to your cook?"

"She doesn't come in every day—remember? Only

a couple of days a week to keep the house up, and on special occasions."

Zane observed her sure movements. God, she wasn't what he'd expected in Ellery Rhodes's wife. "You're a bit of a mystery," he thought aloud as his eyes wandered from her braid, past her slim waist to the inviting swell of her jean-clad hips.

"Ha. And what about you? Appearing on my doorstep with an offer on the farm and a wild tale about Devil's Gambit being kidnapped by Ellery…." She let her voice trail off. She couldn't think that Ellery was alive, couldn't deal with it now. Ellery wouldn't have left. He couldn't have. Not when he knew that she would think he was dead! Though their marriage had been less than ideal, certainly Ellery cared for her in his own, distant way. He wouldn't have put her through the pain of the funeral, the adjustment to widowhood, the problems of running the farm alone….

"Not to mention dead husbands," he offered, as if reading her thoughts.

Tiffany's shoulders flexed, and she held back the hot retort forming on her tongue. It wouldn't be wise to anger him, not yet. She had to find out what he wanted, what kind of game he was playing with her. With an effort, she turned her attention to the boiling water on the stove. Carefully she cracked and added the eggs.

"My husband isn't alive," Tiffany whispered, as if to convince herself.

"You're sure?"

She didn't answer him right away. She removed the muffins from the oven, and, when they were cooked, spooned the poached eggs from the pan. Only then did she say, "Ellery wouldn't let me think he was dead—

he wouldn't put me through that kind of pain," she insisted, her quiet dignity steadfastly in place.

"Ellery Rhodes was a bastard." Zane's words were soft, but they seemed to thunder in the small kitchen.

"Your opinion."

"Granted, but correct nonetheless."

"And one I think you should keep to yourself!"

His bitter smile grew slowly from one side of his arrogant face to the other. He took a long swig of his coffee and noticed that Tiffany had paled. "Did you love him so much?"

"I don't understand," she began, but under his direct gaze, she changed the course of her thoughts. "Of course I loved him."

"Enough to cover up for him?"

Her simmering anger ignited, and pride took control of her tongue. "Wait a minute, Sheridan. You're way out of line."

He studied the honesty in her deep blue eyes and frowned into his mug. "My apologies," he muttered, before downing the rest of his coffee.

"If I had any brains at all, I'd throw you and your outlandish stories out of this place—"

"But you can't."

"Why not?"

He settled into the cane-backed chair he had occupied at the table the night before and flashed her a devastating smile that seemed to touch the darkest corners of her soul. "Because you believe me—" She raised her hands as if to protest and he silenced her with a knowing glare. "At least you believe a little."

Tiffany's chest was incredibly tight. She found it difficult to breathe. "I think, Mr. Sheridan, the only reasons I haven't asked you to leave are, one, because we didn't finish our discussion last night—a discussion that I have to admit piqued my curiosity about you— and two, because you helped out here last night when I was desperate." *And because I find you the most incredibly interesting man I've ever met,* she added silently to herself as she put the muffins in a basket and set them on the table next to the platter of ham and eggs. The attraction she felt to him was as crazy as the stories he spun about Devil's Gambit, and yet she couldn't fight it.

They ate in silence, neither breaking the unspoken truce while they consumed the hearty breakfast Tiffany had prepared.

After the table had been cleared, Tiffany heard Mac's footsteps on the back porch. Automatically she reached for the pot of coffee and poured a large mug of the dark liquid before adding both sugar and cream to the cup.

"Mornin'," Mac grumbled as he accepted the mug Tiffany offered. He took off his hat and placed it on top of the refrigerator. His eyes swept the interior of the kitchen and rested on Zane. The frown that began on Mac's crowlike features was quickly disguised as he took a long swallow of coffee.

So Sheridan had spent the night, Mac thought. He didn't much like the idea, didn't trust the Irishman. But Tiffany did what suited her, and if Zane Sheridan suited her, then it was none of Mac's business what went on between them. Tiffany had been alone too long as it was, and if he was uncomfortable in the Irishman's presence, Mac silently told himself it was his own problem.

"It's late for you to be getting in," Tiffany teased the ex-jockey with a warm grin.

"Not after a night that ended at three this morning."

Winking fondly at Mac, Tiffany moved toward the stove. "How about some breakfast?"

"Thanks much, but no." Mac eyed the leftover blueberry muffins but shook his head. "The missus, she made me eat before I left." He patted his lean stomach. "Couldn't hold anything else." He propped an elbow against the pantry door, finished his coffee and fidgeted. "I checked Ebony Wine this morning."

"I was about to go out there myself."

"No need. She's fine." Mac stared out the window toward the foaling shed and scowled. "She wasn't much of a mother the last time she foaled, so I don't reckon she'll miss this one much...." He shifted his weight from one foot to the other and set his empty cup on the blue tiles. "She should go into foal heat soon— next week, maybe. You plan on breeding her when she does?"

"If Vance says she's all right," Tiffany replied.

"To Moon Shadow?" Mac asked, and at the look on Tiffany's face he knew he'd made a monumental mistake saying anything in front of Zane Sheridan. He could have kicked himself for his lack of tact, but then he'd supposed that Sheridan knew what was going on. Apparently Tiffany hadn't confided in Sheridan, and Mac had let the cat out of the bag. Damn it all to hell anyway. Moving his slim shoulders in a gesture of indifference, Mac tried to undo the damage he'd caused before it was too late. "No reason to worry about it now, we've got a few days."

"I...I think I'll look in on Ebony Wine," Tiffany

stated, wiping her hands on a towel hanging near the stove and steering the conversation toward safer ground. "She had a rough night."

"Didn't we all?" Mac frowned but a good-natured twinkle lighted his faded eyes. In his opinion, Tiffany Rhodes was as smart as she was pretty. "I've got to go into town—check with a guy about some alfalfa. Need anything else?"

"Just a few groceries, but I can get them later."

"Suit yourself." He nodded in Zane's direction, forced his rumpled fedora back onto his head and walked out the door.

Zane's silvery eyes rested on Tiffany's face. The near-perfect features were slightly disturbed. Obviously something the old man said bothered her. It was as if she was hiding something from him. Zane had experienced that same sensation yesterday morning when the reporter was at the house, and again last night while attending to the stillborn colt. Something was bothering Tiffany Rhodes, and Zane suspected that it was more than his remarks about Devil's Gambit.

"Are you coming with me?" Tiffany asked as she walked down the short hallway to the den, slipped on her boots and pulled a worn suede jacket from the wooden hook near the French doors.

"Nothing better to do," Zane admitted, striding with her.

"Good." She scooped some envelopes from the top drawer of the desk, stuffed them into her pocket and headed outside. "I just want to drop these in the mail and pick up the paper before I go back to the foaling shed." She unlocked the French doors and stepped outside into the brisk morning air.

The world smelled fresh and new from the morning rain. Birds twittered in the trees, and the fog had begun to lift. Though the drizzle had let up, raindrops still clung tenaciously to the branches of the maple trees lining the drive. Shallow pools of water rested on the uneven surface of the asphalt.

Despite the problems with the foals and Zane's outlandish remarks about Devil's Gambit, Tiffany felt refreshed, as if the gentle morning rain had washed away the fears of the night. She noticed the dewy, crystallike web of a spider in the rhododendrons, and the woodsy scent of the earth beginning to warm from the first rays of a partially hidden sun.

It seemed the most natural thing in the world when Zane's fingers linked with hers, warming her hand. When he pulled on her hand, forcing her to stop near a thicket of oaks close to the end of the drive, she turned to face him and offered a smile. "What?"

"You don't know that you're driving me crazy, do you?" he asked gently, his gray gaze probing the vibrant blue depths of her eyes.

"And all the while I thought your wild stories and insane ideas about Devil's Gambit were genetic. Now it's my fault." Her blue eyes sparkled in the morning sunlight.

"Be serious," he suggested, his voice low and raspy. "I've wanted you from the first moment I laid eyes on you."

Tiffany laughed softly. "Now it's time for you to be serious."

"I am."

"You don't even know me—"

"I know you well enough to realize that we're good together."

"In what way?"

"All ways."

"Just because you helped Ebony Wine and you...saw to it that I fell asleep last night, it isn't enough to—"

"Shh." He tugged on her arm, forcing her closer. As he looked down upon her she felt as if he were stripping her of the barriers she had so carefully placed around herself, around her heart. She smelled the clean, masculine scent of him, felt the warmth of his body, knew in a minute that he intended to kiss her and that she wouldn't do a damn thing about it.

When his lips touched hers, she closed her eyes and couldn't withhold the moan that came from her throat. Both of his hands reached upward to cup her face. Strong fingers held her cheeks while his lips moved slowly, provocatively over her mouth. He touched the underside of her jaw, gently stroking the delicate pulse in her neck. When he lifted his head, his eyes had grown dark with unspoken passion.

Tiffany swallowed with difficulty, and her blood began to throb wildly in her veins. Feminine urges, long dormant, began to heat and swirl within her, captivating her mind as well as her body.

"Tiffany," he whispered hoarsely against the shell of her ear as his hand slowly found and removed the band at the end of her braid of hair. His fingers worked the shimmery golden-brown strands until her hair tumbled free of its bond to frame her face in soft brown curls.

Her arms wound around his waist as his mouth dipped once again to the invitation of her parted lips.

This time the kiss deepened, and Tiffany felt the thrill of his tongue as it sought out and mated with hers.

Liquid fire seemed to engulf her as desire flooded her veins and throbbed in her ears. *I can't want this man,* she reasoned with herself, but logic seemed to slip away. *He's using me....* But she found that she didn't care.

Beneath the still-naked branches of the towering oaks, she returned his passionate kiss and sighed in contentment when he pressed up against her and the evidence of his desire strained against the fabric of his cords.

Dear God, I don't want to love you, she thought as his arms encircled her and held her tightly to him. *I can't let myself fall for you.... I don't even know who you are or what you want from me. Is this moment just a diversion, an intricate part of your plan, or are your feelings real?*

Logic began to cool her blood, and he felt her withdrawing from him. "Let me love you," he whispered, refusing to let her go, his powerful arms holding her a willing captive.

She shook her head and tried to deny the traitorous feelings burning in her breast. "I can't...I just...can't."

"Because you still love your husband." His voice was low and damning. Dark fire smoldered in his eyes.

Her clear eyes clouded and her teeth sunk into her lower lip. When she shook her head, sunlight caught in the honeyed strands of her hair. "Because I don't know you well enough," she countered.

"You never will, unless you take a chance."

"I am. Right here. Right now. With you. Please... try to understand."

His arms dropped. "Understand what? That you don't know me?" He stepped away from her, granting a small distance between their bodies. "Or is it that you're suspicious of my motives?" His dark eyes searched her face. "Or maybe it's because you think I might be just slightly off my rocker."

She laughed despite the tension in the crisp morning air. "That just about says it all," Tiffany admitted, tossing her tangled hair away from her face. "Except that I think things are moving a little too fast for me," she said, her breathing still irregular. "Yesterday we were strangers, earlier this morning, 'friends,' and now you're suggesting that we become lovers. I'm not ready for all of this—not yet."

"Don't play games with me."

"It takes two to play," she reminded him, holding her head high, her gaze steady.

"You're a mature woman, Tiffany, not some seventeen-year-old girl. You've been married—"

"And I don't have casual affairs."

"There's nothing casual about what I feel for you." His arms encircled her waist, his warm hands splaying naturally against the small of her back.

"Give it time, Zane," she pleaded in a raspy whisper. He was so near she could feel the warmth of his breath in her hair, sense the desire heating his veins, witness the burning passion in his eyes. Her expression clouded with the indecision tormenting her mind. *How easy it would be to lie naked with him in the morning sun....*

With a sound of frustration he released her and leaned against the scaly trunk of one of the larger oaks in the thicket. Lethargic raindrops fell from the branches of the tree and glistened in his dark hair. He cocked his head to the side and forced a ragged but devastating smile. "Okay—so why not give me a chance to prove myself?"

"I am. You're still here, aren't you?"

She turned on her heel, walked the short distance to the road, extracted the envelopes from her pocket and placed them in the mailbox. Then, almost as an afterthought, she retrieved the morning paper from the yellow cylinder nailed to the fence post.

Rather than consider the implications of her mixed emotions toward Zane, she opened the paper and stared down at the headlines. Her breath froze in her throat. "Oh, dear God," she whispered as her eyes scanned the front page.

The bold headline seemed to scream its message to her in powerful black and white:

LOCAL BREEDER PLAGUED BY MYSTERIOUS DEATHS.

CHAPTER SIX

Tiffany felt as if the wet earth were buckling beneath her feet. She stared at the two pictures on the front page of the *Clarion*. One photograph had been taken yesterday. It was a large print of Tiffany sitting at her desk. The other, slightly smaller picture was of Moon Shadow after his loss in the Kentucky Derby.

Tiffany read the scandalous article, which centered on the mysterious deaths of the foals. Not only did Rod Crawford imply that there was something genetically wrong with Moon Shadow, who had sired all of the colts, but he also suggested that Tiffany, in an effort to save her reputation as a horse breeder, had hidden the deaths from the public and the racing commission. Crawford went on to say that any horse bred to Moon Shadow was likely to produce foals with genetic heart defects.

The article reported that since Tiffany had assumed control of Rhodes Breeding Farm, she had encountered more problems than she could handle. From the time her husband and the legendary Devil's Gambit had died, and Tiffany had been in charge of the farm, she had experienced nothing but trouble. It appeared that either Tiffany Rhodes was the victim of fate or her own gross incompetence.

"No!" Tiffany whispered, forcing the hot tears of

indignation backward. She crumpled the damning newspaper in her fist. No mention had been made of Journey's End or any other of Moon Shadow's living, healthy progeny. Rod Crawford had twisted and butchered her words in a piece of cheap sensational journalism. Nausea began to roil in her stomach. "Damn it, nothing is wrong with him! Nothing!"

Her words sounded fragile into the late morning air, as if she were trying to convince herself.

Zane had watched as Tiffany read the article. She had paled slightly before anger settled on her elegant features. Now she was clenching the newspaper in her small fist and trembling with rage.

"What happened?" he demanded.

"Rod Crawford wrote his article," Tiffany explained.

"The reporter who was here just yesterday?"

Tiffany let out a furious sigh and looked upward to the interlaced branches of the oak and fir trees. Shafts of sunlight passed through the lacy barrier to dapple the wet ground. "I didn't think the article would be printed this soon," she replied, somehow stilling her seething rage, "but I guess in the case of a scandal, even the *Clarion* holds the presses."

She expelled an angry breath and coiled her fist. "Damn it all, anyway!" She had trusted Rod Crawford and the *Clarion*'s reputation, and her trust had backfired in her face. The slant of the article was vicious, a personal attack intended to maim Tiffany's reputation. It was the last thing she had expected from a paper with the reputation of the *Santa Rosa Clarion*.

Zane touched her lightly on the shoulder in an attempt to calm her. "What are you talking about?"

"This." Her breasts rose and fell with the effort as she handed him the newspaper.

As Zane quickly scanned the article, his dark brows drew together in a savage scowl and his skin tightened over his cheekbones. A small muscle worked furiously in the corner of his jaw, and his lips thinned dangerously.

After reading the story and looking over the photographs, he smoothed the rumpled paper and tucked it under his arm. Every muscle had tensed in his whiplean body. He was like a coiled snake, ready to strike. "Is there any truth in the article?"

"Enough to make it appear genuine."

"Great." He frowned and pinched the bridge of his nose with his thumb and forefinger, as if attempting to ward off a threatening headache. "Why didn't you tell me about this?"

Tiffany clenched her impotent fists. "I had enough to worry about with you and your crazy theories about Devil's Gambit. I didn't want to cloud the issue with the problem with Moon Shadow's foals."

"Even after last night, when I was with Ebony Wine?"

"There wasn't time." Even to her own ears, the excuse sounded feeble.

"And that's why you didn't want me near Rod Crawford. You were afraid I'd tell him what I knew about Devil's Gambit, he would report it and something like this—" he held up the newspaper and waved it in her face angrily "—might happen."

"Only it would be much worse."

He shook his head in disbelief. "I wouldn't have, you

know." He could read the doubts still lingering in her eyes and silently damned himself for caring about her.

As if physically restraining his anger at her lack of trust in him, he handed the paper back to Tiffany. "I guess I can't blame you—I did come storming in here yesterday." He managed a stiff smile and pushed his hands into the back pockets of his cords. After taking a few steps, as if to increase the distance between them, he turned and faced her. Thoughtful lines etched his brow, but the intense anger seemed to dissolve. "So tell me—the colt that was born last night—he was sired by Moon Shadow. Right?"

"Yes."

Zane raked frustrated fingers through his hair. "Then the death last night will only support the allegations in Crawford's newspaper column."

Tiffany felt as if everything she had worked for was slowly slipping through her fingers. "I suppose so," she admitted with a heavy sigh. Dear God, what was happening to her life? Suddenly everything seemed to be turning upside down. Zane Sheridan, a man whom she barely knew, whom she desired as a man but knew to be an enemy, was clouding her usually clear thinking at a time when she desperately needed all of her senses to prove true. He was voicing her worst fears, and she had trouble keeping the worried tears at bay.

"You should have told me."

"I couldn't."

"Because you didn't trust me and you thought that I might use the information on Moon Shadow against you," he said flatly, as if reading her thoughts.

So close to the truth! Was she so transparent to this man she had met only yesterday? Or was it because he knew more about her than he was willing to admit? "Something like that," she allowed, raising one suddenly heavy shoulder. "It really doesn't matter now."

"Look, woman," he said, barely able to contain his simmering anger. "You'd better start trusting me, because it looks like you're going to need all the friends you can get."

Her eyes took on a suspicious light. "But that's the problem, isn't it? I'm not quite sure whether you're on my side or not—friend or foe."

"Wait a minute—" He looked at her incredulously, as if she'd lost her mind. "Didn't I just tell you that I'm attracted to you? Wasn't I the man trying to make love to you just a few minutes ago?"

Tiffany elevated her chin fractionally. Now was the time to see exactly where Zane stood. Her dark brows arched suspiciously. "Sleeping with the enemy isn't something new, you know. It's been documented throughout history."

"Oh, give me a break!" he spit, his palms lifting upwards as if he were begging divine interference. "Did Ellery scar you so badly that you can't trust any man?"

"Ellery has nothing to do with this."

"The hell he hasn't!" Zane thundered, shaking his head in disbelief. His arms fell to his sides in useless defeat. "You're not an easy woman to like sometimes," he said softly as he approached her. He was close enough to touch. He was offering his strength, his comfort, if only she were brave enough to trust him.

"I haven't asked you to like me—"

He reached out and grabbed her arm. "Oh, yes, you have. Every time you look at me with those wide, soul-searching eyes, you beg me to like you. Every time you smile at me, you're inviting me to care about you. Every time you touch me, you're pleading with me to love you."

Tiffany listened in astonishment, her heart beginning to pound furiously at his suggestive words. She closed her eyes in embarrassment. How close to the truth he was! His fingers wrapped more tightly over her upper arms, leaving warm impressions on her flesh.

"Look at me, damn it," he insisted, giving her a shake. When she obeyed, Zane's flinty eyes drilled into hers. "Now, lady, it looks as if you've got one hell of a problem on your hands. There's a good chance that I won't be able to help you at all, but I don't think you're in much of a position to pick and choose your friends."

She tossed her hair away from her face and proudly returned his intense stare. "Maybe not."

"So let's try to figure out why those foals are dying, right now."

"How?"

"First I want to take a look at Moon Shadow."

Tiffany hesitated only slightly. Zane was right. She needed all the allies she could find. She checked her watch and discovered that it was nearly noon. No doubt the telephone was already ringing off the hook because of the article in the morning paper. There was no time to waste. Straightening her shoulders, Tiffany cocked her head in the direction of the stallion barns.

"Mac usually takes him outside about this time. He's probably getting some exercise right now."

MOON SHADOW WAS in a far corner of the field. His sleek black coat shimmered in the noonday sun and he tossed his arrogant ebony head upward, shaking his glossy mane and stamping one forefoot warily.

Zane studied the nervous stallion. As a three-year-old, Moon Shadow had been impressive. He boasted a short, strong back, powerful hindquarters and long legs that could propel him forward in an explosion of speed at the starting gate that had been unmatched by any of his peers. He'd won a good percentage of his starts including two jewels of the Triple Crown. His most poignant loss was the Kentucky Derby, in which he had been jostled and boxed in near the starting gate and hadn't been able to run "his race," which had always been to start in front, set the pace and stay in the lead.

Zane blamed Moon Shadow's Derby disaster on several factors, the most obvious being that of a bad jockey. Moon Shadow's regular rider had been injured the day of the race, and his replacement, Bill Wade, was a green, uncaring man who had later lost his license to ride.

Mac was leaning over the fence, a piece of straw tucked into a corner of his mouth. Suddenly the black horse snorted, flattened his ears to his head, lifted his tail and ran the length of the long paddock. His smooth strides made the short dash appear effortless.

"He knows he's got an audience," Mac said as Tiffany approached. Wolverine was resting at the trainer's feet. At the sight of Tiffany, he thumped his tail on the moist ground. She reached down and scratched the collie's ears before propping her foot on the lowest board of the fence and resting her arms over the top rail.

"He's going to have more," Tiffany said with a sigh.

Mac's eyes narrowed. "More what?"

"More of an audience."

"What d'ya mean?" Instantly Mac was concerned. He read the worry in Tiffany's eyes.

"I'm afraid Moon Shadow is going to get more than his share of attention in the next couple of weeks. Take a look at page one." Tiffany handed Mac the paper before shading her eyes with her hand.

"Son of a bitch," Mac cursed after reading the article. He pushed his hat back to the crown of his head. "A pack of lies—nothing but a goddamn pack of lies." His eyes flickered from Zane to Tiffany before returning to Moon Shadow. "Damn reporters never have learned to sort fact from fiction." After smoothing the thin red hair over his scalp, he forced the frumpy fedora back onto his head. "A good thing you and Vance already told the Jockey Club about the dead colts."

"Yeah, right," Tiffany agreed without much enthusiasm. "But wait until the owners who have broodmares pregnant with Moon Shadow's foals get wind of this."

Mac frowned and rubbed the toe of his boot in the mud. "You'll just have to set them straight, Missy. Moon Shadow's a good stud. He's got the colts to prove it. Why the hell didn't that bastard of a reporter write about Journey's End or Devil's Gambit?"

Tiffany's eyes moved from Mac to Zane and finally back to the stallion in question. "I don't know," she answered. "Probably because he needed a story to sell papers." And he'd get one, too, if Zane decided to publicize his conjectures about Ellery and Devil's Gambit.

"How many foals were affected?" Zane asked.

"Three—no, Ebony Wine's colt makes four," Tiffany replied softly. "Three colts and a filly. Two died shortly after birth, the colt last night was stillborn and

Charlatan...well, he lived longer, a couple of days, but..." Her voice faded on the soft afternoon breeze.

The silence of the afternoon was interrupted only by the wind rustling through the fir needles and the sound of Moon Shadow's impatient snorts.

"And they all died from heart failure?" Zane asked, staring at the proud stallion as if he hoped to see the reasons for the tragic deaths in the shining black horse.

Tiffany nodded, and Mac shifted the piece of straw from one corner of his mouth to the other.

"Seems that way," Mac muttered.

"Unless Vance discovers something different in the autopsy of the colt born last night," Tiffany added and then shook her head. "But I doubt that he'll find anything else."

"What about other horses bred to Moon Shadow?"

"Fortunately, none of the foals of mares from other owners have been affected—at least not yet. I've corresponded with all of the owners. So far, each mare has delivered a strong, healthy foal."

"Thank God for small favors," Mac mumbled ungraciously.

"Some owners even want to rebreed to Moon Shadow," Tiffany said, almost as an afterthought.

"But you're not breeding him?"

"Not until we find out what's going on."

"I don't blame you." Zane's gaze returned to the imperious stallion, who was tossing his head menacingly toward the spectators.

"He knows we're talkin' about him," Mac said fondly. "Always did like a show, that one." He rubbed the back of his weathered neck. "Should've won the

Triple Crown, ya know. My fault for letting that son of a bitch ride him."

"Mac's been blaming himself ever since."

"I should've known the boy was no good."

"Quit second-guessing yourself. Ellery thought Bill was a decent jockey. Moon Shadow didn't win and that's that."

Mac frowned as he stared at the horse. "The closest I've come to a Triple Crown. Moon Shadow and Devil's Gambit were the finest horses I've ever seen race."

Tiffany stiffened at the mention of Devil's Gambit. "Mac's prejudiced, of course. The owners of Secretariat, Seattle Slew and a few others would have different opinions. But Moon Shadow sure used to be a crowd-pleaser," Tiffany remarked thoughtfully as she stared at the fiery black stallion.

"Aye. That he was," the old trainer agreed sadly as he rubbed the stubble on his chin. "That he was."

Tiffany spent the rest of the day showing Zane the farm. As Mac had stated, Ebony Wine seemed none the worse from her trauma the night before, and if Vance Geddes gave his okay, Tiffany wanted to breed her as soon as the mare was in heat.

As much as it broke her heart, Tiffany decided that Moon Shadow couldn't be allowed to sire any more foals until it was proved beyond a doubt that the cause of his foals' deaths wasn't genetic.

By the time she and Zane headed back to the house, it was late afternoon. The March sun was warm against Tiffany's back. As they walked toward the back porch, she slung her jacket over her shoulder. Zane had been with her all day, and it seemed natural that he was on the farm, helping with the chores, offering her his keen advice and flashing his devastating smile.

"So you've already had him tested," Zane remarked as he held open the screen door to the broad back porch.

"Yes. And so far the semen samples have shown nothing out of the ordinary. I've asked for additional tests, but Vance Geddes seems to think that nothing will be discovered."

"What about the mares?"

She frowned and sighed. "Each horse has been examined by several vets. Blood samples, urine samples...every test available. The mares seem perfectly healthy."

"So all of the evidence points to Moon Shadow."

Tiffany nodded as she wedged the toe of one boot behind the heel of the other and kicked it off. She placed the scarred boots in the corner of the porch near the kitchen door. "It looks that way," she admitted.

"But you don't believe it."

"A good stud just doesn't go bad overnight." She pursed her lips together and ran weary fingers through her unruly hair. "Something has to have happened to him—I just don't know what."

"All the mares were bred to him around the same time?"

"Within a few weeks—I think. However, there are still mares who haven't dropped their foals."

"And you think they may have problems?"

Her blue eyes clouded with worry. "I hope to God they don't," she whispered as she started toward the door to the house. Zane's hand on her arm restrained her.

"I need to ask you something," he said quietly. The tone of his voice sent a prickle of fear down her spine.

"What?"

"Do you have any enemies, anyone who would want to hurt you?" His eyes had darkened as they searched her face.

"None that I can think of."

"What about this Crawford, the guy who wrote the article? Why would he want to distort the truth?"

"I couldn't begin to hazard a guess." She looked at the paper Zane was still carrying under his arm. "I guess the *Clarion* is into sensationalism these days."

"No personal reasons?"

"No."

His eyes drove into hers. "How about someone else who might want to see you exposed as incompetent?"

Tiffany stiffened, and cold dread settled between her shoulder blades. "Like whom?"

"I don't know—a competitor maybe?" When she shook her head in disbelief, her hair tumbled over her shoulders. He tightened his fingers around her arms. "A spurned lover?"

"Of course not!"

His grip relaxed a little. "You can't think of anyone who would want to hurt you? Someone with a big enough grudge against you or this farm to want to see your dirty laundry in black and white?" He was staring at her boldly, daring her to reply. "It would have to be someone with inside information."

Tiffany's eyes grew cold, and she felt a painful constricting of her heart. "The only person who remotely fits that description is you."

Zane stiffened. Tiffany saw the anger flash in his

eyes, but he didn't bother to refute her accusation. His lips thinned until they showed white near the corners. "You know there was no love lost between myself and your husband. If Ellery were alive today, I'd probably do what I could to ruin him." He looked away from her and for a moment, pain was evident in the rugged planes of his face. "I despised the man, Tiffany, but you have to believe that I would never intentionally hurt you."

"Even if Ellery is still alive?" she whispered.

He closed his eyes against the possibility. The craving for vengeance that had festered in his blood still poisoned him, but as he gazed down upon Tiffany's face, Zane knew that he was lost to her. His hatred for Ellery couldn't begin to match the intensity of his feelings for this proud, beautiful woman. "If Ellery Rhodes walked through the door tonight, I would still detest him. But—" he reached out and gently stroked her chin "—because of you, I would leave."

Tiffany swallowed the uncomfortable lump forming in her throat and ignored the hot sting of tears against her eyelids. How desperately she longed to believe him. "Even if I asked you to stay?"

"What are you saying, Tiffany?" he asked, his face close to hers. "If Ellery is alive, would you leave him for me?"

"I...I don't know," she admitted, confused at the emotions warring within her. She ached to say yes and fall into Zane's arms, never to look back. If only she could love him for now, this moment, and cast away any thought to the future, or the past.

Slowly he pulled her to him, and Tiffany felt his larger body press urgently against hers. She leaned on him, and he kissed her forehead. "I can't make things different between us," he said, gently smoothing her hair away from her face.

"Would you, if you could?"

"Yes," he replied quickly as he had a vision of her lying naked in Ellery Rhodes's bed. "I wish I'd known you long ago."

In the privacy of the screened porch, with the fragrance of cherry blossoms scenting the air, nothing seemed to matter. It was a private world filled with only this one strong, passionate man. Tears pooled in Tiffany's eyes and clung to her lashes. "I think that it's better not to dwell on the past...or wish for things that could never be."

He tilted her face upward with his hands, and his lips claimed hers in a kiss that was filled with the desperation of the moment, and the need to purge all thoughts of her husband from his mind.

Her lips parted willingly for him, and his tongue touched the edges of her teeth before slipping into her mouth and plundering the moist cavern she so willingly offered.

A raw groan of frustrated longing escaped from his lips as he molded his hungry body to hers. She wound her arms around him, held him close, clinging to him as if afraid he would leave her empty and bereft.

"Tiffany," he whispered into her hair and let out a ragged breath. "Oh, Tiffany, what am I going to do with you?"

Whatever you want, she thought, returning his kiss with a bursting passion that had no earthly bounds.

His hands found the hem of her sweater and slipped underneath the soft fabric to press against the silken texture of her skin. Her breath constricted in her throat, and when his fingers cupped the underside of her breast she felt as if she were melting into him. A soft moan came from her throat as his fingers softly traced the lacy edge of her bra. She felt the bud of her nipple blossom willingly to his touch as his fingers slid slowly upward.

Zane's breathing became labored, a sweet rush of air against her ear that caused tantalizing sparks of yearning to fire her blood. "Let me love you, sweet lady," he pleaded, fanning her hair with his breath.

If only I could! Her desire throbbed in her ears, burned in her soul, but the doubts of the night filtered into her passion-drugged mind, and before she lost all sense of reason, she pulled away from him, regret evidenced in her slumberous blue eyes. "I...I think it would be best if we went inside," she said raggedly, hoping to quell the raging storm of passion in her blood.

The tense lines along the edge of his mouth deepened. "You want me," he said, holding her close, pressing the muscles of her body to his. "Admit it."

Her heart was an imprisoned bird throwing itself mercilessly against her rib cage. She lost her sense of time and reason. "I want you more than I've ever wanted a man," she whispered, trying to pull free of his protective embrace. "But wanting isn't enough."

"What is?"

Love, her mind screamed, but the word wouldn't form on her lips. How often before had she felt love only to see it wither and die? The love of Tiffany's mother had been so fragile that Marie had left her only daughter in the care of a drunken father. Edward's love hadn't been strong enough to conquer the drink that eventually killed him, and Ellery... Ellery probably didn't know the meaning of the word.

"I...I'm not sure," she admitted, her voice quavering unexpectedly.

"Oh, hell," Zane swore in disgust, releasing her. "Neither am I." He looked thoroughly disgusted with himself, and he rammed his hands into his pockets, trying to quiet the fury of desire straining within him. The heat in his loins seemed to sear his mind. Never had he wanted a woman so painfully. He felt as if his every nerve were raw, charged with lust.

Tiffany stared at Zane until her breathing had silenced and her racing pulse had slowed to a more normal rate. She entered the house, and the smells of roast and cinnamon filled her nostrils. "Louise?" she called as she went into the kitchen. The plump woman with graying hair and a ready smile was extracting a deep-dish apple pie from one of the ovens. "I thought you were going out of town for the weekend."

"Not until tomorrow." Louise set the hot pie on the tile counter and turned to face Tiffany. "I thought maybe you could use a little help around here today."

"You read the article in the *Clarion*."

Louise's full mouth pursed into an angry pout. "Yep. I read it this morning and canceled my subscription before noon. That was the trashiest piece of journalism I've ever read. Rod Crawford should be strung up by his—" her eyes moved from Tiffany to Zane "—hamstrings."

Tiffany smiled at the angry housekeeper. "You shouldn't have canceled your subscription."

"Humph. What I should have done was write a letter to the editor, but I suppose that would only make the situation worse, what with the publicity and all."

At that moment the phone rang, and Tiffany reached to answer it.

"It's been ringing off the hook all afternoon." When Tiffany hesitated, Louise continued. "Reporters mostly. A couple of other breeders, too. The messages are on your desk."

"I'll take the call in the den," Tiffany decided, straightening her shoulders.

"Vultures," Louise muttered as she opened the oven and checked the roast.

Tiffany answered the phone in the den on the sixth ring.

"Tiffany, is that you?" an agitated male voice inquired.

"Yes."

"This is Hal Reece." Tiffany's heart sank. Reece had bred one of his mares to Moon Shadow. Was he calling to tell her that the foal was dead? Her palms began to sweat and her pulse jumped nervously.

"What can I do for you, Mr. Reece?"

The stuffy sixty-year-old paused before getting to the point. "I read an article about your farm in the *Clarion*. No one told me there was any genetic problem with Moon Shadow."

"There isn't."

"But the article stated—"

"What the article stated was only half the story." Tiffany's eyes clashed with Zane's as he entered the den.

"Then you're saying that those foals didn't die?" he questioned, relief audible in his voice.

"No," Tiffany replied, bracing herself by leaning on the desk. "It's true we've lost a few foals—"

"Moon Shadow's foals," he clarified.

"Yes. But there is no reason to think that the problem is genetic. I've had Moon Shadow tested by several veterinarians. You're familiar with Vance Geddes, aren't you?"

"Why, yes. Good man, Geddes."

"He's been involved with the problem from day one. He's concluded that there's no evidence that the deaths were genetically related."

"But certainly they were linked."

"It appears that way."

"And the natural assumption is that it was the sire, as all the foals were his."

Tiffany heard the hopeful note in Hal's voice. She hated to discourage him. Forcing herself to remain calmly professional, she held her voice steady as she clutched the receiver in a deathlike grip. "Moon Shadow has proved himself a good stud. Journey's End and Devil's Gambit are proof enough of that. Most of the foals that he sired this year had no problems."

"No other owner has complained?" Reece asked, sounding dubious.

"None, and I've been in contact with each of them. So far, Moon Shadow has sired twenty-three perfectly healthy foals—something Mr. Crawford neglected to print."

"But three have died."

There was no use in hiding the truth from Reece or any of the other owners who had bred their expensive mares to Moon Shadow. It would only look worse later.

Tiffany gritted her teeth and closed her eyes. "Four. We lost another colt last night."

"Oh, God!" His voice sounded weak.

Zane was standing near the fireplace, one shoeless stockinged foot propped against the stone hearth.

"When is your mare due to foal?" Tiffany asked.

"Any day now."

"I'm sure you'll find that you have a healthy Thoroughbred on your hands."

"I'd better, Tiffany," Hal said softly. "I'm not a rich man, I can't afford a loss like this. I'm sure the insurance company wouldn't cover the cost of my stud fee—"

"Mr. Reece, if you do happen to lose the colt and we discover that the problem stemmed from breeding your mare to Moon Shadow, I'll refund the stud fee."

"And then what? My mare's lost nearly a year of prime breeding time."

Tiffany's face became rigid. "I won't be able to do anything about that, Mr. Reece. It's the chance we take as breeders." She heard herself repeating Zane's advice of the night before. "When your mare does foal, I'd appreciate a call from you."

"You can count on it. Good day," he replied frostily, and Tiffany replaced the receiver. As soon as she set it down the phone rang again.

"Don't answer it," Zane advised, seeing the way she had paled during her lengthy conversation.

"I have to."

"The calls can wait."

"I don't think so. I have ten or twelve owners who are probably in a state of panic."

The phone rang again.

"It could be the press," Zane argued.

"Then I'll have to deal with them as well. I can't just hide my head in the sand. This was bound to happen sooner or later." She reached for the phone and answered it. A male voice demanded to speak to Tiffany Rhodes.

"This is she," Tiffany replied. The man identified himself as a reporter for a San Francisco paper. The telephone call was a short interview, and by the time it was over, Tiffany felt drained.

Zane sat on the edge of the desk, his worried gaze studying her as she turned around, clicked on a small computer in the bookcase and started typing onto the keyboard when luminous green letters appeared on the screen.

"What're you doing?"

"Getting a printout of all the owners who still have broodmares pregnant with Moon Shadow's foals. I think it would be best if I called them, rather than having them read a story like the one in the *Santa Rosa Clarion*."

"This can wait until morning."

Tiffany shook her head and refused to be deterred. "I'd just as soon get it over with. The sooner the better." The printer began rattling out the list of owners as Tiffany checked the phone messages Louise had stacked on her desk. "Great," she mumbled. She held up one of the messages and handed it to him. "A reporter for a television station in San Francisco wants an interview." She smiled grimly. "What do you bet that it's not to talk about Journey's End's career?"

Zane frowned. "No wager from me, lady. I learned a long time ago not to bet money unless it was a sure thing—and then only when the man you're betting against is honest." His voice was low, and edged in anger. From the look on Zane's face, she knew that he was somehow referring to Ellery.

The printer stopped spewing out information, and the silence in the small room seemed deafening.

At that moment, Louise appeared, balancing a tray in her plump hands. "I thought you two could use a cup of coffee," she explained. Noticing the tension in the room and the silent challenge in Tiffany's eyes, Louise pursed her lips together thoughtfully and amended her offer. "Or I could get you something stronger—"

"Coffee's fine," Zane replied, turning to watch her and sending a charming grin in her direction.

"Yes, thank you," Tiffany said, once Zane's gaze had released her.

"Dinner will be in about an hour."

Tiffany managed a frail smile. "Louise, you're a lifesaver."

The large woman chuckled. "I'm afraid you'll need more than a hot meal before the evening's done."

"Don't be so optimistic," Tiffany remarked cynically.

"Just my nature," Louise replied before leaving the room.

"What else have you got on that computer?" Zane asked, studying the list of owners.

"Everything."

"Like what?"

"Health records on the horses, the price of feed, the stud fees we charged, equipment. Everything."

"Including a profile of your Thoroughbreds?"

"Every horse that's been a part of the farm."

"Can you get me a printout on Moon Shadow?"

She managed a tight smile. "Sure."

"How about the mares he was bred to, especially the four that lost their foals?"

Tiffany sat down at the keyboard. "This has already been done, you know."

"Humor me. I need something to do while you're tied up with the phone. I may as well be doing something constructive since I canceled my flight."

"Can't argue with that." Tiffany requested the information from the computer, and when the printer started spewing out profiles of the horses in question, Tiffany started with the first of what promised to be several uncomfortable telephone calls to the owners of mares bred to Moon Shadow.

CHAPTER SEVEN

"HERE, DRINK SOME of this," Zane suggested. He handed Tiffany a glass of white wine. "Maybe it will improve your appetite."

"And my disposition?" She accepted the glass and took a sip of the white Burgundy. The cool liquid slid easily down her throat, and she eyed her plate of forgotten food with a sigh.

"They really got to you, didn't they?" Zane asked as he leaned back in his chair and frowned into his glass. He had finished Louise's dinner of roast beef, parslied potatoes and steamed broccoli before noticing Tiffany's neglected plate.

"Let's just say I'm glad it's over," she replied and then amended her statement, "or I hope to God it is."

What if any of the unborn foals were to die shortly after birth? What would happen to her and the farm? The telephone conversations with the owners who had mares bred to Moon Shadow hadn't gone well at all. By the time she had contacted or left messages with all the owners, Tiffany had felt as if every nerve in her body had been stretched as tightly as a piano wire. During two of the more difficult calls, she had been threatened with lawsuits, should the foals be born with life-threatening heart problems.

She couldn't begin to do justice to Louise's delicious

meal. With a weary shake of her head, she pushed her plate aside, leaned back in the chair and ran tense fingers through her hair.

Zane offered her a sad, understanding smile. "Come on, the dishes will wait. Let's finish this—" he held up the opened bottle of wine "—and relax in the study."

"I don't think that's possible."

"Come on, buck up." He got up from the table and placed a comforting hand on her shoulder. "Things are bound to get better."

"That's a strange statement, coming from you," she stated. He shrugged his broad shoulders and his smile faded. "But I guess you're right," she continued, slapping the table with new resolve. "Things can't get much worse." *Unless another foal dies.*

The den seemed warm and intimate. The glowing embers of the fire and the muted illumination from a single brass lamp with an emerald-colored shade softened the corners of the room and reflected on the finish of the cherry-wood walls. The thick Oriental carpet in hues of green and ivory, the etchings of sleek horses adorning the walls and the massive stone fireplace offered a sense of privacy to the room.

Zane stoked the smoldering coals in the fireplace. *As if he'd done it a hundred times. Here. In her home.* His actions seemed so natural, as if he were an integral part of the farm. As he knelt before the fire, he lifted a chunk of oak from the large basket sitting on the warm stones of the hearth. "This should do it," he mumbled to himself as he placed the mossy log on the scarlet embers. Eager flames began to lick the new fuel and reflect in golden shadows on Zane's angular face. His shirt was stretched over his back, and Tiffany watched his fluid movements as he worked. When the fire was to his satisfaction, he dusted his hands together and studied the ravenous flames.

As she sipped her wine and observed him, Tiffany felt the long dormant stirring of feminine desire. Urges that were better denied began to burn in her mind. *I won't let myself fall for him,* she promised but knew that her efforts would prove futile. He was already an integral part of her life. Ever since last night, when he had bent over the lifeless foal and tried to force air into the still lungs, Zane Sheridan had become a part of Rhodes Breeding Farm. Whether she liked it or not.

She dragged her eyes away from his strong physique and concentrated on the clear liquid in her wineglass. "Don't you have some place you have to be?" she asked.

The lean frame stiffened. He hesitated for just a moment before turning to face her. "Later."

"Tonight?" she asked in attempted nonchalance. Her tongue caught on the solitary word.

He nodded curtly. "I've got some early appointments in San Francisco tomorrow." He noticed the slight tensing in her shoulders. *Damn her, that strong will and pride will be her downfall...or mine.* "Things I can't put off any longer." He finished his wine and stared at her. "Is that a hint?"

"No...I mean, I just think it's strange that you've been here—" she made a big show of checking her watch "—over twenty-four hours and still haven't gotten down to the reason you came."

"The time of reckoning—right?" His eyes met her gaze boldly before glancing at the portrait of the horse.

She took a seat on the edge of the gray corduroy couch. "Close enough. But first I want to thank you for helping last night. I really appreciate everything you did...."

"You're sure about that?"

She remembered waking up and finding him sleeping in the uncomfortable chair with his feet propped on her bed. "Yes," she whispered. "For everything."

"And now you want to know about Devil's Gambit," Zane thought aloud as he stood and stretched his arms over his head. It was an unconscious and erotic gesture. His sweater rose, displaying all too clearly his lean abdomen. His belted cords were slung low over his hips and Tiffany glimpsed the rock-hard muscles near his navel. She imagined the ripple of the corded muscles of his chest, his muscular thighs and lean flanks.... She had to look away from him and force her mind from the sexual fantasy she was envisioning. What was wrong with her? She'd never reacted this way to a man, not even Ellery. Until Zane Sheridan had walked into her life, she had considered herself nearly uninterested in the opposite sex.

One look from Zane's steely gray eyes had drastically altered her entire perception of her own sexuality. Her new feelings were at once exciting and frightening. Zane was the one man she couldn't begin to trust...not with her body or her soul. He had already admitted that he was waging a vendetta of sorts, and she didn't doubt for a minute that he was the kind of man who would use and destroy her because of his hatred of Ellery.

Zane took a final sip of his wine and then set the empty goblet on the mantel. "I meant to tell you about Devil's Gambit last night," he explained, "but Ebony Wine had other things on her mind."

Tiffany nodded and clutched the stem of her crystal glass more tightly as she remembered the agonizing scene in the foaling shed and the innocent stillborn colt. Had it been only last night? So many things had changed, including her respect and feelings for Zane. "So what about now?"

Zane angled his head to the side and studied the wariness in her eyes. She was sitting on the edge of the gray cushions, waiting for him to explain his reasons for being there. "No time like the present, I suppose." He walked over to the bar and splashed three fingers of Scotch into an empty glass. "I think your horse—"

"You mean Devil's Gambit?"

"Right. I think he's in Ireland, using an alias."

"Now I know you're crazy." What did he mean about Devil's Gambit being in Ireland? His story was getting more far-fetched by the minute.

If she had any guts at all, she would tell him to get out of her house…her life, take his wild stories and shove them. Instead she twirled the stem of the wineglass in her fingers and stared up at him.

"Just hear me out. Have you ever heard of a horse named King's Ransom?"

"Yes," she admitted, recalling the Irish Thoroughbred. "But I really don't keep up on the European horses, not as much as I should, I suppose. There just isn't enough time. Dustin handles that end of the business."

"I'm not surprised," Zane replied with obvious distaste.

"What does that mean?"

"Only that sometimes it's hard to tell Ellery and Dustin apart." He paced across the room before sitting on the warm stones of the hearth.

"So you know Dustin?" That knowledge came as a shock to her and she felt a new wariness steal over her heart. *Hadn't Dustin mentioned King's Ransom to her—something about the horse's fame as a stud?* Tiffany couldn't recall the conversation....

"We've met." Zane leaned his elbows on his knees and cradled his drink with both of his hands.

"And you don't like him any more than you liked Ellery."

"As I said, they're too much alike to suit my taste."

Tiffany was stunned. Dustin had his faults, of course, but she'd come to rely on her brother-in-law and his savvy for horses. It seemed as if Zane were determined to destroy anything and anyone who was solid in her life.

"Not much does, does it?" she countered.

"What?"

"Suit your taste."

He hesitated. His eyes darkened and for a moment she imagined that he might suggest that she suited him. Instead he lifted an appreciative dark brow. "You're right—not much."

Tiffany's throat constricted, and she sipped her wine to clear the tight lump that made it difficult to breathe.

If he noticed her discomfort, Zane chose to ignore it and get to the point. "Anyway, this horse, King's Ransom, was a disappointment when he raced. He had all the qualities to perform on the track—great bloodlines, perfect conformation and a long, easy stride. He had the look of a winner about him, but he just didn't seem to have the grit...or heart to be a champion. He never finished better than fifth, and consequently he was retired about seven years ago and put out to stud.

"The first of his offspring began running about four years ago, and even though they inherited all his physical characteristics, none of the colts and fillies were anything to write home about. It seemed as if they all ended up with his lack of drive."

"So what does this have to do with Devil's Gambit?" Tiffany asked. Her blue eyes mirrored her worry. Despite her arguments to the contrary, she was beginning to understand what Zane was hinting at.

"I'm getting to that. All of a sudden, less than two years ago, when that year's two-year-olds and three-year-olds hit the track, look out! Overnight, King's Ransom was producing some of the fastest horses in Europe."

"That's not impossible," Tiffany said uneasily. She felt a sudden chill and shivered before getting up and walking closer to the fire...to Zane.

"But highly improbable. It's the same principle as what's happening here with Moon Shadow, in reverse. Just as a good stud won't go bad overnight, the reverse is true. A mediocre stallion doesn't become the greatest stud in Ireland by a fluke." Zane was looking up at her with his magnetic gray eyes. He knew that he had Tiffany's full attention. Her glass of wine was nearly untouched, her troubled blue eyes reached into the blackest corners of his soul. *God, she was beautiful.* He swirled his drink and stared into the amber liquor, trying to still the male urges overcoming him.

"I own a mare that I bred about five years ago to King's Ransom," Zane continued. "The colt that was born from that union was just what I expected—a solid horse, a plodder, but nothing that would compare to his recent foals. I rebred that same mare to King's Ransom three years ago, and the resulting filly has already won two races and come in second in another. This horse is a full sister to the first."

Tiffany's dark honey-colored brows drew together pensively as she tried to remember what it was about King's Ransom… Vaguely she recalled a conversation with Dustin. Dustin had been going on and on about King's Ransom and his ability as a sire. At the time, it hadn't seemed all that important. Dustin was always raving about one horse or another—comparing his current favorite to the horses he and Tiffany owned.

"It might be worth it to breed one of the mares, say Felicity, to King's Ransom," Dustin had insisted.

"But the cost of shipping her would be prohibitive," Tiffany had replied. "The insurance alone—"

"I tell you, that stud's got what it takes!" Dustin had been adamant. "He could sire the next Devil's Gambit!"

Now, as Dustin's words came back to her, Tiffany paled. If what Zane was suggesting was true, then Dustin must have been involved! "I…I don't believe it," Tiffany said, taking a sip of her wine and trying to ignore the chilling implications running through her mind.

This was absurd. Ludicrous. Her relationship with Dustin had always been solid, and after Ellery's accident it had been Dustin who had helped her over the rough spots, given her his ear, offered a strong shoulder to cry on.

"Believe it. Devil's Gambit is siring foals and King's Ransom is getting all the credit. Your horse is being used, Tiffany!"

She squared her shoulders and trained disbelieving eyes on Zane. "I don't know why you came here," she said. "If it was to trick me into selling the farm, then you may as well leave now. All of this—" she moved both arms in a sweeping gesture meant to encompass everything that had transpired between them "—has been a very entertaining show, but I don't believe any of it. You're wasting your breath."

Zane pursed his lips together in frustration. With a frown he got up, crossed the room and picked up his briefcase.

"God, Tiffany, you don't make it easy," he muttered as he set the leather case on the wooden desk and silently wondered why it bothered him so much that he had to prove himself to this woman. He could hardly expect that she would believe his story without proof. After snapping the case open and extracting a white envelope, he handed the slim packet to her.

With trembling fingers Tiffany opened the envelope and extracted a faded photograph of a black stallion.

"This," he said angrily while pointing at the horse in the photo, "is a picture of King's Ransom. He looks a lot like Devil's Gambit, don't you think?"

The resemblance was eerie. Tiffany couldn't deny what was patently obvious. Even though the photograph was old and faded it was glaringly evident that the stallion's size and conformation were incredibly like that of the dead horse.

Zane reached inside his briefcase again. This time he took out the manila envelope he had given her the night before. It still contained the photographs he had insisted were those of Devil's Gambit. Tiffany might have believed him last night except for the fact that the white stocking on the horse's foreleg was missing.

"Are those two horses the same?" he demanded.

His jaw was rigid, his gaze blistering as he searched her face.

She studied the photographs closely. A cold chill of dread skittered down her spine. The horses were nearly identical, but definitely not one and the same. Only by placing the photographs side by side was Tiffany able to discern the subtle differences between the two horses. The slope of the withers was different, as was the shape of the forehead. Only a professional would notice the small dissimilarities.

Tiffany closed her eyes against Zane's damning truth.

"Are they the same horse?" he repeated, his voice low.

Slowly, she shook her head.

Zane set the pictures on the desk and expelled a heavy sigh. Finally, he had gotten through to her! He poked a long finger at the more recent photograph. "This," he said, "is the stallion that's supposed to be King's Ransom. I say he's Devil's Gambit."

Tiffany swallowed against the dryness settling in her throat. Here was the proof that her husband had lied to her, that her proud stallion was still alive, that everything she had believed for four years was nothing more than an illusion created by her husband. *Devil's Gambit and Ellery were alive!* "How did you know?" she finally asked in a forced whisper.

He rubbed his hand over his chin and closed his eyes. "I didn't really know, not for a long time. I guess I became suspicious when the second foal, the filly, exhibited such a different temperament from her brother.

"When she started racing as a two-year-old, I was certain she was the fastest horse on the farm, though her bloodlines weren't nearly as good as several other horses."

He walked over to the fire and looked into the golden flames, as if searching for easy answers to his life. "I didn't think too much about it until I got to talking to several other owners who had noticed the same phenomenon on their farms: all of King's Ransom's latest offspring were markedly different from his first foals." Zane smiled to himself, amused by a private irony. "No one was really asking questions—all the owners were thrilled with their luck, and of course, King's Ransom's stud fees have become astronomical since the latest colts and fillies have begun racing."

Tiffany lifted her hands and shook her head in silent protest. "It still could be a coincidence," she whispered. Her suggestion was a desperate attempt to right her crazily spinning world, to hold on to what she had believed to be true for four long years, and both she and Zane knew it.

"Look at the pictures, Tiffany," Zane quietly insisted. "You're knowledgeable enough to realize those two stallions are different. Something isn't right at Emerald Enterprises."

"Pardon?"

"Emerald Enterprises owns the farm."

"And therefore King's Ransom."

"If that's what you want to call him."

Still the connection to her horse wasn't completely clear. "And you think Devil's Gambit is somehow involved?"

"I know he is."

"Because...someone switched horses, planned the accident, thereby killing the replacement horse and Ellery? Then what about Dustin? How did he manage to escape with his life?"

"Maybe he planned it."

The words settled like lead in the room. Only the occasional crackle and hiss of the fire disturbed the thick, condemning silence. "Dustin wouldn't..." she said, violently shaking her head. "He couldn't kill Ellery...they were brothers...very close...."

"Maybe it wasn't intentional. I told you I think Ellery was in on the swindle."

Her frigid blue eyes held Zane's gaze. "That doesn't make a hell of a lot of sense, you know," she rasped, her body beginning to shake from the ordeal of the past two days. "Ellery owned the horse. Devil's Gambit was worth a lot more alive than he was dead!" She raised a trembling hand in the air to add emphasis to her words, but Zane reached for her wrist and clutched it in a deathlike grip.

"Just hear me out. Then you can draw your own conclusions."

"I already—"

He broke off her protests by tightening his fingers over her arm. "Please listen." His grip relaxed but his stormy eyes continued to hold her prisoner.

"All right, Zane. I'll listen. But in the end, if I don't believe you, you'll have to accept that."

"Fair enough." He released her and took a seat on the corner of the desk. His stormy eyes never left the tense contours of her elegant face. "When I requested a third breeding to King's Ransom, at the high stud fee, I was granted it. But because of the stallion's 'temperamental state' I wasn't allowed to witness my horse being bred."

"And you didn't buy that excuse?" Tiffany guessed.

"It sounded like bull to me. It just didn't make a lot of sense. I'd witnessed the first breeding but was out of the country when the second foal was conceived."

"So what happened?"

"I began asking a lot of questions. Too many to suit the manager of the farm. All of a sudden I was told that King's Ransom's services were, after all, unavailable. He was booked to cover far too many mares as it was, and I was asked to pick up my mare and leave."

"Before she was bred?"

"Right."

Tiffany began to get a glimmer of the truth, and it was as cold as a winter midnight.

Zane walked over to the hearth. As he sat on the warm stones he studied the amber liquor in his glass. "I picked up the mare, and the manager didn't bother to hide his relief to be rid of me. As I was leaving I saw a horse I recognized as King's Ransom running in a distant field. I thought it odd, since the manager had told me not five minutes before that King's Ransom was supposedly in the breeding shed."

"So you took these pictures!" she said breathlessly, the scenario becoming vivid in her confused mind.

"I'm a camera buff and happened to have my camera and telephoto lens with me. I grabbed what I needed from the glove box and photographed the horse. I took several shots and noticed that the stallion was running with a slight misstep. I hadn't heard about any injury to King's Ransom, and that's when I began to suspect that there might be two horses using the same name."

Tiffany's eyes were wide and questioning. "And from that you just deduced that one of the horses was Devil's Gambit?"

"It wasn't that difficult, really," Zane stated, his silvery eyes delving into hers. "Black Thoroughbreds are fairly uncommon, much rarer than bay or chestnut."

Tiffany nodded, her heart freezing with the fear that he was telling the truth. Dear God, what had Ellery done?

"Because of King's Ransom's age and coloring, it was relatively easy to discover what horse was being used in place of him to cover his mares. I did some research, and once I saw the pictures of Devil's Gambit again, I knew that he was the sire responsible for the faster offspring in the past few years."

"This is all still conjecture, you know," she said, trying to find any way possible to refute what he was saying. Even as she did so, she knew that she was grasping at straws.

"You're right. Except for one fact."

Tiffany steeled herself. "Which is?"

"That six years ago the ownership of the breeding farm where King's Ransom is standing at stud changed hands. A corporation now owns the farm. It took a lot of digging, but I finally found out that the primary stockholder in Emerald Enterprises is none other than your brother-in-law."

"Dustin?" Tiffany gasped, hoping with all her heart that Zane would come up with another name, any other name.

"One and the same."

Tiffany felt weak but outraged. Her knees buckled and she leaned against the desk for support. Even if everything Zane told her was the truth, she had to settle it herself with Dustin and Ellery...*if* Ellery was alive. *If* she could. Two very big "ifs." For a moment her voice failed her. When at last she could speak, all she could manage was a hoarse whisper. "I think, Mr. Sheridan," she suggested, "that you'd better leave."

"Are you so afraid of the truth?"

Tiffany closed her eyes, and her finely arched brows drew together. *Yes, Zane,* she thought, *I am afraid. I'm afraid that what you're telling me is reality. I'm afraid the man I trusted as a brother-in-law lied to me, I'm afraid that my husband has betrayed me and I'm afraid, so afraid of you—and what you do to me!*

She reached for her wineglass with shaking fingers. Her voice was husky. "You seem to have done your homework," she admitted. "But just because Dustin owns part of the farm in Ireland—"

"Did you know about it?" he demanded.

She managed to shake her head, and the golden light from the fire caught in the soft brown silk of her hair. Zane fought against the sudden tightness in his chest.

"Don't you think that's odd—since you're still business partners here in the States?"

Odd as hell, she thought to herself as she pushed the hair from her face and stared at the ceiling. Her brother-in-law had been the one solid thing in her life when her world had shattered in pain and desperation on the night that Ellery and Devil's Gambit were killed. Becoming a widow had been a new and frightening experience, and the scandal about Ellery and his tragic horse had only made facing widowhood worse. Reporters hadn't left her alone for over two weeks. If it hadn't been for Dustin and his strength… "I don't know everything about Dustin's business. He's just my brother-in-law, not my…"

"Husband?"

Her throat was parched, and the words forming in her mind were difficult to say. "Have you...did you...see any evidence to indicate that Ellery might still be alive?" she asked, her fingers tightening over the edge of the desk fiercely enough that her knuckles showed white.

"No."

A lump formed in her throat. "But you can't be sure?" she insisted in a breathless whisper.

Zane frowned darkly. "Oh, lady, I wish I could answer that one for you," he said fervently.

She felt the sting of tears and forced them back. "If Ellery was alive, he wouldn't have let me believe that he was dead," she said as much to convince herself as Zane. Her small hands balled into fists, and she pounded them against the varnished surface of the desk she had used for four years...Ellery's desk. "You know that you're destroying everything I've worked for, don't you? In two days, everything I've believed in is slowly being torn apart...and I don't understand why."

"Don't you want to know if your husband is alive?"

"Yes!"

"And if he is?"

"Oh, God." She clasped her hand over her mouth before she managed to steady herself. "I...I don't know."

"Would you divorce him?"

She shook her head and pressed back the tears threatening her eyes. "No. Not until I heard his side of the story."

"And when you did?" Zane asked, his features becoming harsh.

Tiffany let out a ragged breath. "I don't know. It's all so unbelievable—I don't have all the answers."

Zane's eyes bored into her as if searching for her
soul. *Damn Ellery Rhodes and what he had done to
his beautiful wife!* Despite the desire for revenge seep-
ing through his blood, Zane knew as he watched Tiffany battle against tears that he could never hurt her. It
would be easy to make love to Rhodes's wife, but Zane
knew instinctively that she would never forgive him if
he took advantage of her vulnerable state and she later
found out that her husband was alive.

She managed to slowly get hold of herself. "Why
does all this matter to you, and why on earth would
you want to buy this farm?" she questioned, her voice
a whisper. "You have your choice of every breeding
farm on the market—so why this one?"

"I'm not interested in just any farm. I already have
one in Ireland."

"And that's what you do—breed horses, when you're
not bothering widows?"

His lips thinned in disgust. Against his better judgment, Zane crossed the room and stood near the desk,
near the attractive woman leaning against the polished
surface. Her head was thrown back, her white throat
exposed, her silken hair falling in a reckless tumble of
honey-brown that touched the desk.

"Have I bothered you so much?"

"More than you'll ever guess," she admitted,
straightening. She rubbed her arms, hoping to warm
the inner chill of dread settling between her shoulders.
After glancing up at the portrait of Devil's Gambit, she
turned cold, suspicious eyes on Zane.

"You really believe everything you've told me, don't
you?"

"It's the truth."

"And is that why you want the farm? Do you want to buy me out, and then blow this whole thing wide open about Devil's Gambit? That way there would be an investigation and you would have a chance, as owner of Rhodes Breeding Farm, of recovering him?"

"I don't think it would work that way," Zane said stiffly. "You would still own the horse. That's not the reason I want this farm."

"Then what is, Zane? Why did you come here in the first place?" He was much too close, but she didn't give in an inch. Proudly she faced him, her soft lips pressed into a frown, her skin stretched tightly over the gentle curve of her cheek.

Zane's dark eyes drove into her very soul. "Ellery Rhodes stole from me."

"What are you talking about?"

Deciding to distance himself from her, Zane walked over to the bar and splashed another drink into his glass. *How much could he confide to Ellery Rhodes's widow without blowing everything?* "It's not a subject I like to discuss," Zane admitted after taking a long swallow of the warm Scotch. "But about six years ago Ellery won a large amount of cash from me."

"And you hate him for that?" Tiffany was incredulous. What kind of a man was Zane?

"Not until I found out that the game was rigged. Oh, by the way, your brother-in-law, Dustin, was in on it, too."

"I don't believe it."

"Believe it. Your husband was little more than a thief."

Tiffany was numb from the tattered state of her emotions. "And you've waited all this time, just to get even with him," she guessed, her voice without inflection. "It didn't matter that he was dead—you just had to do something, *anything* to get even."

Zane saw the disbelief and silent accusations in Tiffany's eyes. He wanted to purge himself, tell all of the story, but couldn't. Stasia's betrayal had been long ago, but it was still an open wound that continued to bleed. He'd accused himself of still loving his ex-wife, even after she'd run off with Ellery Rhodes. But Zane knew better. He doubted if he had ever loved Stasia, but his battered pride was still raw from her deceit.

"I want this farm," he said as thoughts about Stasia gave him renewed conviction. The look on his face was intense, slightly threatening.

"I'm sorry, Zane. I told you yesterday that if I ever decided to sell, the first option would be Dustin's."

"Even when you know that he deliberately lied to you?"

"If he did, you mean. I can't believe—"

Zane cut her off by slicing the air with his hand. He strode over to the desk, reached inside his briefcase and handed her a thick packet of legal documents.

"What are these?" she asked, slowly scanning the complicated pages.

"Corporate documents, ownership papers."

"How did you get them?"

"It doesn't matter. Just read." He hated to put the damning evidence in front of her, but she'd been so bullheaded about Ellery and Dustin, he'd had no choice. Tiffany didn't strike him as the kind of woman who would live in a fantasy world, but maybe when a woman loved a man as passionately as Tiffany loved Rhodes... He frowned darkly and finished his drink in one swallow. His inner vision of Tiffany entwined in Ellery Rhodes's arms turned his thoughts back, and a senseless anger took hold of his mind.

Tiffany sifted through the documents, and as she did her heart contracted painfully. Dustin's signature was scrawled all over the legal papers concerning Emerald Enterprises and the purchase of the farm in question. Without a doubt, some of Zane's story was true. Just how much, she would have to determine on her own, when issues such as the dead foals and her feelings for Zane didn't clutter her mind. Pursing her lips together she handed the papers back to Zane.

"They're yours," he said.

"I don't want them."

"I have extra copies, and I think you might want to go over these more carefully while I'm gone."

"You're leaving?" *Oh, God, not now. Not when I need your arms to protect me...*

"Have to," he admitted with obvious reluctance.

"I see," she replied, stunned. How long did she expect him to stay? He'd already mentioned that he had business back in San Francisco. It was only a matter of time until they went their separate ways.

She stared sightlessly down at the documents she still held in her hands. Since Zane had been with her, she had avoided thinking about the time he would leave. *This is crazy, let him go, before you do something you'll regret later....*

His hands molded over her upper arms. The warmth of his touch made her knees weaken, and she had to fight the urge to fall against him for support.

"While I'm gone, I want you to consider selling the

farm to me," he said sharply, his gentle fingers in stark contrast to his harsh words.

He was a man of contradictions, ruthless one moment, kind the next; sensitive to her desires as a woman, yet insensitive to her needs as a person. She told herself she couldn't possibly fall in love with him and yet she knew that fate had already cast the die. She was falling desperately and hopelessly in love with the stranger from Ireland.

"It's just not that easy, Zane. Dustin still owns twenty-five percent—I can't make a decision without him."

"Then consider selling out your portion. I'll deal with Dustin later." The tone of his voice was harsh, his jaw hard.

"It's just not possible."

"Anything's possible, Tiffany. Don't you know that?"

As possible as falling in love with you? Dear Lord, what has happened to my common sense?

As if reading her unspoken question, Zane smiled gently. The tense line of his jaw relaxed as slumberous eyes embraced hers. One long finger traced the elegant curve of her neck. "I'll be back in a few days," he promised.

Her lips trembled beguilingly. "There's no need. You know my position on selling the farm—"

"And what about Devil's Gambit?"

She frowned and pushed an errant lock of golden hair over her shoulder. "I...I don't know," she admitted, eyeing the portrait of the proud stallion. She needed time alone, time to think and sort out everything Zane had stated. How much of his story was fact and how much was pure fiction?

"You'll need a contact in Ireland."

The thought that Zane might be leaving the country shocked her. For this short time she'd had with him, she felt as if they'd grown incredibly close.

"I'll have to think about that—"

"Tiffany?"

"Yes?" She looked up and found him staring at her. For most of the evening he had forced himself to stay away from her physically. But standing next to her with the warmth of the fire against his back, smelling the scent of her perfume, seeing the honest regret in her blue eyes, was too much to bear. The restraint he had placed upon himself began to dissolve into the shadowy room.

He touched the seductive contour of her jaw, and she closed her eyes. His hands were gentle as they lingered near her throat. "Come with me to San Francisco," he suggested impulsively as his blood began to heat and he forgot his earlier promise to himself. He wanted Tiffany Rhodes as he'd never wanted a woman.

"Oh, Zane, I can't."

"Why not?" His fingers had wrapped around her nape, under the curtain of her hair. She had trouble thinking clearly as his hands drew her near to him, and his lips touched her eyelids.

"I have…too many things to do…too much to think about…."

"Think about me—"

"That, I can assure you, I will," she promised fervently, her words the barest of whispers.

When his lips touched hers, he tasted more than

the flavor of rich Burgundy. His tongue skimmed the soft surface of her mouth, gently prying her lips apart. Tiffany had no desire to stop him. She felt reckless, daring. Her raw emotions had pushed rational thought aside. Though she barely knew him, her body trembled at his touch, thrilled at his gentle caress.

His fingers slid down her arms to wrap securely over her waist, pulling her willing body to his. He moaned when he felt her hands, which had been gently touching his shoulders, grip the corded muscles more tightly. She was warm, pliable, yielding....

Silently cursing the doubts in his mind, he crushed her body to his. He felt the heat in her blood, tasted her need when her mouth opened willingly to him, smelled the heady scent of perfume mingling with burning pitch. The ache in his loins began to pound with the need of this woman—Ellery Rhodes's wife.

Tiffany let her arms hold him close. She knew he would be leaving soon, and she had to savor each sweet second she had with him. When she felt the weight of his body gently push her to the floor, she didn't resist. Her hands linked behind his head, and she let herself fall until the soft cushion of the carpet broke her fall and was pressed against her back.

"I want you," he whispered, his face taut with desire. "God forgive me, but I want you."

Her blue eyes reflected the golden flames of the fire, and her hair was splayed in tangled curls on the deep, green carpet. Passion darkened her gaze and lingered in her eyes. "There's no need for forgiveness," she murmured, her fingers stroking the back of his neck, his tensed shoulder muscles.

Her blood was pulsing violently through her veins,

heating the most intimate parts of her. Her heart felt as if it would burst with need, want. It continued to beat an irregular rhythm in her ears, making her oblivious to anything but the desire of this man…this stranger. As she gazed into his silvery eyes, she wondered if what she was feeling was love or lust and found she didn't care.

"Tiffany," he whispered against her hair. He was lying over her, his chest crushing her breasts as if he were afraid she would escape, his long legs entangled with hers. "I didn't want this to happen." His ragged breathing was filled with reluctance.

"I know," she whispered.

He kissed the curve of her neck and tingling sensations raced wildly down her body. Dear Lord, she couldn't think when he was touching her, couldn't reason…. Before she could try to explain her feelings, his rugged face loomed over hers. He gazed down upon her and passion darkened his eyes. *Think of Ellery,* she told herself, *there is a slim chance that he might be alive. Though he betrayed you, he is still your husband.*

Zane's lips captured hers, and despite the arguments in her mind she wrapped her arms around his neck and let her fingers wander in his thick, obsidian hair. His touch was electric, and all the nerves in her body screamed to be soothed by him.

I can't do this, she thought wildly, when his hands rimmed the boat neck of the sweater and teased the delicate skin near her collarbone. He lowered his head and pressed his moist tongue to the hollow of her throat, extracting a sweet torment that forced her pulse to quiver.

He kissed her again, more savagely this time, and she responded with a throaty moan. When he lifted his head, he gazed into her eyes, then pulled the sweater over her head, baring her breasts to the intimate room. A primitive groan slid past his lips as he looked down at her. The lacy bra, the sheerest of barriers to him, displayed the ripeness of her breasts and their pink tips. Already the nipples were rigid, thrusting proudly against the silky fabric and offering the comfort to soothe him if he would only suckle from them. "God, you're beautiful," he said, running first his eyes and then his tongue over the delicious mounds of white and feeling the silken texture of her skin beneath the sheer lace. She trembled with the want of him.

The wet impression of his tongue left a dewy path from one rose-tipped peak to the next. Tiffany struggled beneath him, arching up from the carpet and pulling him to her with anxious fingers digging into the thick muscles of his shoulders.

In a swift movement he removed his sweater and tossed it beside Tiffany's on the floor. She stared at him with love-drugged eyes. His chest was lean and firm; dark skin was covered when she lifted a hand to stroke him, and his nipples grew taut as she stared at him.

He lowered himself over her and covered her mouth with his. His tongue tasted of her, dipping seductively into her mouth only to withdraw again. The heat within her began to ache for all of him. She wanted him to touch her, fill her, make long, passionate love to her until the first shafts of morning light filtered through the windows.

When his mouth moved slowly down her neck to pause at the shadowy valley between her breasts, she cried out his name. "Zane, please," she whispered, begging for his touch. Thoughts of a distant past with Ellery infiltrated her mind. *I couldn't feel this way with Zane if Ellery were still alive.... I couldn't!*

In response to her plea, he unclasped the bra and removed it from her, staring at the blushing beauty of her breasts.

"What do you want, sweet Tiffany?" he asked, his slumberous gray eyes searching hers.

Her throat tightened and she closed her eyes. Her dark lashes swept invitingly downward. "I want you— all of you."

He dipped his head and ran his tongue over one proud nipple. "Do you want me to love you?"

"Please...Zane...yes!" *Didn't he know? Couldn't he see the love in her eyes as she opened them to search his face?*

"All of you?" He kissed the other nipple, but his eyes locked with hers for an electrifying instant. His teeth gently teased the dark point, and she quivered from the deepest reaches of her soul.

"All of me," she replied and groaned when he began to suckle hungrily at one delicious peak. His large hands held her close, pressing against her naked back and warming her exposed skin. Tiffany felt waves of heat move over her as he kissed her, caressed her, stroked her with his tongue. She cradled his head, holding him close, afraid he would leave her bereft and longing. As his mouth and tongue tasted her, drew out the love she felt, the hot void within her began to throb with desire.

"Make love to me, Zane," she whispered when the exquisite torment was more than she could bear. "Make love to me and never let me go...."

It was the desperate cry of a woman in the throes of

passion. Zane knew that Tiffany had unwittingly let her control slip. He positioned himself above her and his fingers toyed with the waistband of her jeans, slipping deliciously on her warm abdomen. She contracted her muscles, offering more of herself, wanting his touch. Her body arched upward eagerly, her physical desire overcoming rational thought.

Her fingers strayed to the button on his cords and he felt it slide easily through the buttonhole. Her hands did delightful things to him as she slid the zipper lower. He squeezed his eyes shut against his rising passion. His need of her was all-consuming, his desire throbbing wildly against his cords. His fingers dipped lower to feel the smooth skin over her buttocks, and he had to grit his teeth when she began to touch him.

"Tiffany," he whispered raggedly, forcing himself to think straight. He remembered all too vividly that Ellery Rhodes could very well be alive. If Zane took her now, and Ellery was alive, Tiffany would never forgive him. "Wait." His voice was hoarse. With gentle hands he restrained her fingers. She stared up at him with hungry, disappointed blue eyes.

God...what he wouldn't give to forget all his earlier vows to himself. If he made love to her now, before the mystery surrounding Devil's Gambit was resolved, before he had purchased the farm, she would end up hating him.

"I...had no intention..." *Of what? Making love to Ellery Rhodes's woman? As just revenge for what he did to you?* "...of letting things get so out of hand."

She read the doubts on his face and closed her eyes. "Forgive me if I don't believe you," she murmured, trying to roll away from him. "But I seem to recall a man who, this very morning, matter-of-factly insisted that we become lovers." Tears of embarrassment flooded her eyes.

"It's not for lack of any wanting on my part," he replied.

That much she didn't doubt. She'd felt the intensity of his desire, witnessed the passion in his eyes, felt the doubts that had tormented him. "Then what?" she asked, reaching for her sweater. "Are you teasing me, trying to find a way to convince me to sell the farm to you?" she accused.

He flinched as if she had physically struck him, and his entire body tensed. "You know better than that."

"I don't think I know you at all. I think I let my feelings get in the way of my thinking."

His fist balled impotently at his side and his face hardened. "Would you feel better about it, if we resumed what we started and I took you right here... even though Ellery might still be alive?"

"Of course not," she gasped. Her blood had cooled and reason returned.

He reached out and tenderly pushed her hair from her eyes. "Then wait for me," he asked, his voice low. "I just want to make sure that you won't regret anything that might happen."

"Are you sure you're concerned for my feelings, or your own?"

"Oh, lady," he whispered, forcing a sad smile. His fingers trembled slightly when he brushed a solitary tear from her eye. "Maybe a little of both." He reached for her and his fingers wrapped possessively around her neck. Closing his eyes against the passion lingering in his blood, he kissed her sensuously on the lips. "I'll be back...."

CHAPTER EIGHT

"THIS ISN'T THE smartest thing you've ever done, Missy," Mac warned as he finished his coffee and pushed his hat onto his head. He scraped his chair back from the table and placed the empty cup on the tile counter, not far from the area where Louise was rolling dough.

"The least you could do is show a little support," Tiffany teased. She smoothed the hem of her cream-colored linen suit and smiled at Mac's obvious concern.

"After that newspaper article in the *Clarion,* I'd think you'd have more sense than agree to another interview."

"Can't argue with that," Louise chimed in as she placed a batch of cinnamon rolls in the oven.

"Okay, so the interview with Rod Crawford was a mistake. This one will be different." Tiffany leaned against the counter and attempted to look confident.

"How's that?" Mac's reddish brows rose skeptically on his weathered face.

"The reporter from the *Times* is Nancy Emerson, a roommate of mine from college."

"Humph." Louise was busily making the second batch of rolls and didn't look up as she spread the cinnamon and sugar over the dough. "How do you know she won't do the same thing that Crawford did? In my book a reporter's a reporter. Period."

"Nancy's a professional."

"So was Crawford."

"I talked about the interview. I told her I would only do it if it didn't turn out to be a hatchet job."

"I bet she liked that," Louise remarked sarcastically as she began furiously rolling the dough into a long cylinder. "It's none of my business, mind you, but didn't you bank on the reputation of the *Clarion?*"

"Yes," Tiffany said with a sigh.

Mac noted Tiffany's distress. "Well, if you think you can trust her—"

"I just know that she won't print lies," Tiffany insisted. "She's been with the *Times* for over six years and written dozens of articles on horse racing in America and abroad. She's extremely knowledgeable and I figured she'd give an unbiased, honest report." Tiffany lifted her palms in her own defense. "Look, I had to grant an interview with someone. I've had over a dozen calls from reporters in the past three days."

"I can vouch for that," Louise agreed as she sliced the rolls and arranged them in a pan.

Louise had insisted on working at the farm every day since Zane had left and Tiffany was grateful for the housekeeper's support. Life on the farm had been hectic in the past few—had it only been four?—days. It seemed like a lifetime since she'd been with Zane.

"Well, I guess you had no choice," Mac allowed.

"None. The longer I stall, the more it seems as if we're hiding something here."

"Aye. I suppose it does," Mac mumbled as he sauntered to the back door. "I'll be in the broodmare barn if you need me." He paused as his fingers gripped the doorknob, glanced back at Tiffany and shifted uncomfortably from one foot to the other. "It looks like Alexander's Lady's time has come."

Tiffany felt her heart fall to the floor. Alexander's Lady was pregnant with Moon Shadow's foal. Tiffany closed her eyes and gripped the edge of the table. Louise stopped working at the counter.

"Oh, Lord," the large cook muttered, quickly making a sign of the cross over her ample bosom. Then, with a knowing eye in Tiffany's direction, she smiled kindly. "This one will be all right, honey...I feel it in my bones."

"I hope to God you're right," Tiffany whispered.

"It's in His hands now, you know. Not much you can do 'bout it," Mac advised with a scowl. "Worryin' ain't gonna help."

Tiffany studied Mac's wrinkled brow. "Then maybe you should take your own advice."

"Naw—I'm too old and set in my ways to stop now. Anyway, worryin's what I do best." The trainer raised his hand in the air as a salute of goodbye and opened the door to the back porch, just as the doorbell chimed. Mac's frown deepened. "Looks like your friend is here."

Tiffany managed a thin smile. "Good. We may as well get this over with."

"Good luck," Louise muttered, once again hastily making the sign of the cross with her flour-dusted hands as Tiffany walked out of the kitchen.

"Tiffany! You look great," Nancy said with heartfelt enthusiasm as Tiffany opened the door.

The slim, dark-haired woman with the bright hazel eyes appeared no different than she had six years ago. Dressed in navy-blue slacks and a crisp red blouse and white jacket, Nancy looked the picture of efficiency. Short dark-brown curls framed a pixielike face filled with freckles and smiles.

"It's good to see you, Nance. Come in." Tiffany's grin was genuine as she hugged her friend. It had been years since she'd seen Nancy. Too many years. The two women had parted ways right after college. Tiffany's father had died, and Nancy had moved to Oregon to marry her high school boyfriend.

"And what a beautiful house," Nancy continued, her expressive hazel eyes roving over the sweeping green hills surrounding the white-clapboard and brick home. "This is something right out of *Gone with the Wind!*"

"Not quite, I don't think."

"All you need is a couple of mint juleps, a porch swing and—"

"Rhett Butler."

Nancy laughed. "I suppose you're right. But, God, Tiff, this is *fabulous!*"

"The house was Ellery's idea," Tiffany admitted as Nancy's eager eyes traveled up the polished oak banister and marble stairs to linger on the crystal chandelier. "He thought the farm would appear more genuine if it had a Southern atmosphere."

"This is beyond atmosphere, Tiffany, this is flair!"

Tiffany blushed a little under Nancy's heartfelt praise. She'd forgotten what it was like to be around the exuberant woman. Though Nancy had to be thirty, she didn't look a day over twenty-five, and part of her youthful appearance was due to her enthusiasm for life.

Tiffany showed Nancy the house and grounds of the farm. "This is heaven," Nancy insisted as she leaned against a redwood tree and watched the foals romp in the late-morning sun.

"I like it."

"Who wouldn't? Let me tell you, I'd give an arm and a leg to live in a place like this."

Tiffany laughed. "And what would you do? You're a city girl by nature, Nance."

Nancy nodded in agreement. "I suppose you're right."

"You'd miss San Francisco within the week."

"Maybe so, but sometimes sharing a two-bedroom apartment with two kids and a cat can drive me up the wall. The girls are five and four, and you wouldn't believe how much energy they have."

"They probably get it from their mother. Genetics, you know."

"Right. Genetics. The reason I'm here."

Tiffany ignored the comment for now. "So why don't you bring the kids out here for a weekend sometime?"

Nancy's bright eyes softened. "You mean it?"

"Of course."

"They're a handful," the sprightly reporter warned.

"But they'd love it here, and I adore kids."

Nancy was thoughtful as she stared at the horses frolicking in the lush grass of the paddock. "So why didn't you have any?"

Tiffany shrugged. "Too busy, I guess. Ellery wasn't all that keen on being a father."

"And you?"

"It takes two."

Nancy sighed and lit a cigarette. A small puff of blue smoke filtered toward the cloudless sky. "Boy, does it. Raising the kids alone is no picnic. Ralph has them every other weekend, of course, but sometimes… Oh, well. Look, I'm here for an interview, right? Tell me what you've been doing since you took over the farm."

Nancy took a tape recorder from her purse and switched it on. For the next hour and a half Tiffany answered Nancy's questions about the farm—the problems and the joys.

"So what's all this ruckus over Moon Shadow?" Nancy asked, her hazel eyes questioning.

"Hype."

"What's that supposed to mean?"

"Come on, I'll show you." Tiffany led Nancy to the stallion barn and Moon Shadow's stall. Moon Shadow poked his ebony head out of the stall, held it regally high and flattened his ears backward at the sight of the stranger. "Here he is, in the flesh, the stallion who's been getting a lot of bad press."

"What you referred to as 'hype'?"

"Yes. He's fathered over a hundred Thoroughbreds in the past eight years, several who have become champions."

"Like Devil's Gambit?"

Tiffany's heart seemed to miss a beat. She didn't want to discuss Devil's Gambit with anyone, including Nancy. "Yes, as well as Journey's End."

"Rhodes Breeding Farm's latest contender. He promises to be the next Devil's Gambit," Nancy observed.

"We hope so."

Moon Shadow's large brown eyes wandered from Tiffany to the reporter and back again. Tiffany reached into the pocket of her skirt and withdrew a piece of

LISA JACKSON 457

carrot. The proud stallion nickered softly and took the carrot from Tiffany's hand.

"He's been a good stud," Tiffany emphasized while rubbing the velvet-soft black muzzle.

Tiffany continued to talk about Moon Shadow's qualities and the unfortunate incidents with the dead foals. Whenever Nancy posed a particularly pointed question, Tiffany was able to defend herself and her stallion by pointing to his winning sons and daughters.

Nancy had snapped off her tape recorder and stayed through lunch. Tiffany felt more relaxed than she had in days when she and Nancy reminisced about college.

"So what happened between you and Ralph?" Tiffany asked, as they drank a cup of coffee after the meal.

Nancy shrugged. "I don't really know—it just seemed that we grew in different directions. I thought that the kids would make a difference, but I was wrong." When she saw the horrified look in Tiffany's eyes, she held up her hand. "Oh, don't get me wrong, Tiff. It wasn't that Ralph wasn't a good father—" she shrugged her shoulders slightly "—he just wasn't comfortable in the role of breadwinner. Too much responsibility, I suppose. Anyway, it's worked out for the best. He's remarried, and I'm dating a wonderful man."

"And the girls?"

Nancy sighed and lit a cigarette. "It was rough on them at first, but they seem to be handling it okay now."

"I'm glad to hear it."

"It's hard to explain," Nancy said softly. "It just seemed that the longer we lived together, the less we knew each other or cared...."

"That happens," Tiffany said. Hadn't she felt the

same doubts when Ellery was alive? Hadn't there always been a distance she was unable to bridge?

"Yeah, well…" Nancy stubbed out her cigarette. "As I said, I think it's for the best. Oh, God, look at the time! I've got to get out of here."

Tiffany watched as Nancy gathered her things, and then she walked her friend to the car. "I was serious when I told you to bring the kids out for a weekend. Just give me a call."

"You don't know what you're asking for."

Tiffany laughed. "Sure I do. It'll be fun. Come on, Nance, those girls could use a little fresh country air, and they'd love being around the horses."

Nancy eyed the rolling hills of the farm wistfully. "Be careful, Tiff, or I just might take you up on your offer."

"I'm counting on it."

Nancy's car was parked in the shade of a tall maple tree near the back of the house. When they reached the car, Nancy turned and faced Tiffany. "This has been great," she said. "The best interview I've done in years."

"Do you do many stories about Thoroughbreds?" Tiffany asked.

"Some—mainly from the woman's angle," Nancy replied. "Most of the time I write human interest stories—again, from the woman's perspective. The reason I got this assignment is that I read the article in the *Clarion* and stormed into my editor's office, insisting that since I knew you, I would be the logical person to write a more in-depth article for the *Times*. He really couldn't argue too much, since I used to cover all the local and national races." Her hazel eyes saddened a little. "I think you, and not your horse, were the victim of bad press, my friend."

Tiffany shrugged, but smiled. "Maybe." A question formed in her mind, and she had to ask. "When you were working on the races, did you ever hear of a stallion named King's Ransom?"

"Sure. But he wasn't much of a champion, not until recently. From what I understand his services as a stud are the most sought-after in Ireland."

"Who owns him?"

Nancy smiled. "That's the interesting part. It's kind of a mystery. He's syndicated of course, but the largest percentage of the stallion is owned by Emerald Enterprises." Tiffany's heart felt as if it had turned to stone. *Zane had been telling the truth!*

"Which is?"

"A holding company of sorts," Nancy replied.

"I see," Tiffany said, her heartbeat quickening. "What about a man by the name of Zane Sheridan?" she asked.

Nancy was about to get into the car but paused. "Now there's an interesting man."

"Oh?" Tiffany cocked her head to the side and the smile on her lips slowly faded. "Do you think he's somehow involved with Emerald Enterprises?"

"I don't really know, but I doubt it. He owns a farm near the one owned by Emerald Enterprises. Why are you so interested?"

"I'm not…not really." Tiffany lied in ineffectual nonchalance. "He was here a couple of days ago, looking at some horses."

"He's a bit of a mystery," Nancy said. She leaned against the car door and stared up at the blue sky as she tried to remember everything she could about the breeder from Ireland. "He's a tough guy, from what I hear. Ruthless in business. He grew up on the streets of Dublin. Had several scrapes with the law and ended up working as a stable boy at an Irish Thoroughbred farm in the country. The owner of that particular farm took a liking to him, sent him to school, and once educated, Sheridan made a small fortune breeding horses." She sighed as she tried to remember the fuzzy details of a scandal that had occurred in the past.

"And then, well, it's kind of foggy, but from what I remember, he was in some sort of trouble again. A scandal, and he lost his fortune and his wife. I can't remember all the details right now."

The news hit Tiffany like a bolt of lightning. Though stunned, she managed somehow to ask, "His wife is dead?"

"No—she ran off with this guy named...God, what was it? Rivers, I think. Ethan Rivers, an American.... Like I said, it's kind of a mystery. No one really knows what happened to this Rivers character or Sheridan's wife."

The thought of Zane being married did strange things to Tiffany. "How long ago was this?" she asked.

"Geez, what was it? Five years, maybe more like seven, I'm really not sure." She pursed her lips as she thought and then, when she checked her watch, nearly jumped out of her skin. "Look, I've got to go. Deadlines, you know. I'll call you soon."

"Good. I'd like that."

Nancy got into her car and settled behind the wheel. The engine started, and Nancy rolled down the window. "The article on the farm should be in the paper no later than Thursday. I'll send you a copy." With a brilliant smile, she fingered a wave at Tiffany and forced the little car into gear.

Tiffany watched the car disappear down the tree-lined drive, but her mind was miles away. Nancy's visit had only increased her restlessness. Where was Zane and why hadn't he called?

HOURS LATER, TIFFANY was walking back from the half-mile track near the old barn when she heard a familiar voice.

"Tiffany!"

A tall man wearing a Stetson was running toward her. Tiffany shielded her eyes from the ever-lowering sun and smiled when she recognized her brother-in-law.

"Dustin!" She hadn't expected him back for another week.

"Hello, stranger," he said as he reached her and gathered her into his arms to twirl her off the ground. How had she ever doubted him? "What's this I hear about you getting some bad press, little lady?"

"Some?" Tiffany repeated with a shake of her head. "How about truckloads of it."

"You can't be serious." He flashed her a brilliant smile.

"Four of Moon Shadow's foals have died—all from heart failure."

Dustin lifted his hat, pushed a lock of brown hair out of his eyes and squinted into the setting sun toward the exercise track, where Mac was still working with a yearling. "So I read."

"You and the rest of the world." Tiffany pushed her hands into the pockets of her jeans. Her conversation with Zane came hauntingly back to her, and she wondered just how much she could confide in Dustin. He did own twenty-five percent of the farm and was entitled to know everything that was going on...well, almost everything. "I have owners who are threatening me with lawsuits if the mares they bred to Moon Shadow drop foals that die."

"How many mares are involved?" Dustin's hand reached out and took hold of her arm. They had been walking toward the old barn where Tiffany had been headed. Near the building, Dustin stopped her.

"About twelve," she said. "Some of them took the news fairly well. The others, well...they weren't so understanding."

"In other words they're ready to rip your throat out."

"Close enough."

"Damn!" Dustin let out an angry blast. "This is the last thing we need right now. Okay, so what about the mares that have already foaled?"

"The foals that eventually died were from our mares. So far, every mare bred to Moon Shadow from another farm has dropped a healthy colt or filly."

"So much for small favors."

"I guess we should consider ourselves lucky that this isn't a contagious virus," she said.

"You're sure?" Dustin didn't sound convinced.

"Um-hm. Vance checked everything carefully. At first he thought it might be sleepy foal disease, but fortunately it wasn't."

"Yeah, fortunately," Dustin muttered sarcastically.

Tiffany pushed open the door to the old barn and checked the supply of grain stacked in sacks in the bins. The interior was musty and dark, the only light filtering through the small window on the south side of the building and the open door. Dustin leaned against a post supporting the hayloft and watched her make notes in a small notebook.

Once she had finished counting and was satisfied that the inventory of feed was about what it should be, she started back toward the door.

Dustin's hand on her arm stopped her. His topaz-colored eyes pierced into hers. "So what happened to those foals?"

Tiffany shook her head and her honey-brown tresses glowed in the shadowy light from the windows. "Your guess is as good as mine."

"What does Vance say?"

"Nothing good, at least not yet."

He leaned against the post, shoved the hat back on his head so he could see her more clearly and drew Tiffany into the circle of his arms. His voice was low with concern, his gold eyes trained on her lips. The intimate embrace made Tiffany uncomfortable. All Zane's accusations concerning Dustin began to haunt her. Maybe she should ask him flat out about the circumstances surrounding Devil's Gambit's death, but she hesitated. There was just enough of the truth woven into Zane's story to give her pause.

Dustin read the worry on her features. "Do you think there's a possibility that Moon Shadow's to blame for the deaths?"

Tiffany frowned and tried to pull away from him. "No."

"But all the evidence—"

"Is circumstantial."

"I see." Dustin released her reluctantly and cleared his throat. "So what are you doing with him?"

"Nothing. I can't breed him. Not until I know for certain that the problem isn't genetic."

"Then you do have reservations?"

Tiffany bristled slightly. "None, but what I don't have is proof. Unfortunately, Moon Shadow has already been tried and convicted by the press. He's as good as guilty until proved innocent."

"Bitter words..."

"You haven't been here trying to talk some sense into the reporters, the owners, the television people."

"No," he conceded with obvious regret. "But I bet you handled them."

Tiffany lifted a shoulder. "As well as I could. I had an interview with Nancy Emerson from the *Times* this morning."

Dustin smiled. "Your old roommate?"

"Uh-huh."

He breathed deeply. "Good. It never hurts to know someone in the press."

Tiffany decided to set her brother-in-law straight. "I didn't buy her off, you know."

"I know, I know, but at least she's on our side. She should be objective. Thank God for small favors."

Something in Dustin's attitude made Tiffany uneasy. *You're overreacting,* she told herself, all because of Zane Sheridan and his wild accusations.

Dustin smoothed back his wavy hair. "I've got to hand it to you, Tiff. You've come a long way," he said appreciatively. "There was a time when I didn't think you would be able to pull yourself together."

"I have you to thank for getting me back on my

feet," she replied, uncomfortable with the personal tone of the conversation. She was reminded of Zane and the accusations he had made about Dustin. Today, in the fading sunlight, those allegations seemed positively absurd. Dustin was her brother-in-law, her friend, her partner. The man who had pulled her out of the depths of despair when Ellery and Devil's Gambit had been killed.

Then what about the farm in Ireland, the one owned by Emerald Enterprises? What about Dustin's signature on the ownership papers? What about King's Ransom?

She decided to broach the difficult subjects later, once she had learned the reason for Dustin's unexpected visit. Was it possible that he knew Zane had been here? Had someone tipped Dustin off, possibly Zane himself?

Tiffany felt a growing resentment and anger at Zane. Single-handedly he had destroyed her trust in the only family she had ever known.

"Come on," she suggested, pushing her worrisome thoughts aside as she walked through the open door of the barn. "I'm starved. Louise made some cinnamon rolls this morning, and I bet we can con her out of a couple."

Dustin looked as if he had something he wanted to say but held his tongue. Instead he walked with Tiffany to the house and waited patiently while she kicked off her boots and placed them on the back porch.

"Are you staying long?" she asked, once they were in the kitchen and seated at the table.

Dustin hedged slightly. "Just a couple of days."

"And then?"

"Back to Florida."

"To check on Journey's End?"

"Right." He took a long swallow of his coffee, and his golden eyes impaled her. "You think you could spare the time to come with me?" he asked, his voice uncommonly low.

Tiffany ignored the hidden innuendoes in his tone. They'd covered this territory before, and Dustin obviously hadn't taken the hint. The scene in the old barn emphasized the fact. Dustin had never hidden the fact that he would like to pursue a more intimate relationship with her, but Tiffany just wasn't interested. Dustin seemed to assume that her lack of interest was due in part to loyalty to Ellery, and Tiffany didn't argue the point. He just couldn't seem to get it through his thick skull that she wasn't interested in a relationship with a man—any man.

Except Zane Sheridan, her mind taunted. Would she ever be able to get him out of her mind? In four days, he hadn't phoned or stopped by the farm. All of his concern for her while he was here must have been an act, a very convincing act. Still, she couldn't forget him.

"Tiff!"

"Pardon?"

Dustin was frowning at her. He'd finished his coffee, and the cup was sitting on the table. His empty plate showed only a few crumbs and a pool of melted butter where his cinnamon rolls had sat. "You haven't heard a word I said," he accused.

"You're right."

"So where were you?"

"What?"

"You looked as if you were a million miles away."

"Oh, I guess I was thinking about Moon Shadow,"

she lied easily, too easily. "Mac thinks another one of his foals will be born tonight."

Dustin leaned back in his chair and let out a low whistle. "No wonder you're worried. If this one dies, the press will be crawling all over this farm again. Maybe I'd better stay a few extra days."

Waving off his offer, she shook her head. "No reason. You know you're welcome to stay as long as you like, but if you have things to do, go ahead and do them. I can handle everything here."

He walked around the table, stood behind her and placed his hands on her shoulders. "You're sure?"

Tiffany tensed. "Of course I am."

As if receiving her unspoken message, he dropped his hands to his sides. "You know that's one of the qualities I admire about you, Tiff, your strength."

"I guess I should be flattered."

Dustin stepped away from her and rested his hips against the counter. All the while his eyes rested on her worried face. "Is something else bothering you?" he asked.

"Isn't that enough?"

"I suppose so." He shrugged his broad shoulders and folded his arms over his chest. Silent reproach lingered in his eyes. The air in the kitchen became thick with tension.

Tiffany heard the screen door bang shut. Within minutes Mac was in the kitchen.

"Don't tell me, you smelled the coffee," Tiffany guessed, reaching for a cup and feeling relieved that the inquisition with Dustin was over for the moment.

"Aye, that I did."

"Well, pull up a chair, sit yourself down and help yourself to a roll, while I get you a mug."

Mac's faded eyes rested on Dustin. Not bothering to hide a frown, he cocked his head toward the younger man. "'Evenin', Dustin. Didn't expect you back for a while."

Tiffany handed Mac the cup.

Dustin managed a tight grin as he offered the older man his hand. "I read an article about the foals dying and thought I should come back—" his gold eyes moved to Tiffany "—since no one bothered to tell me what was going on."

"I thought I'd wait until Vance had something concrete to go on," Tiffany stated.

"And how long would you have waited?"

"Not much longer."

"It was a hell of a way to find out, you know," Dustin said, his anger surfacing, "by reading about it in the paper." He rammed his fingers through his hair in frustration. For a moment he appeared haunted.

"You're right. I should have called, but I didn't because there wasn't a damned thing you or I or anyone else could do."

"I suppose you're right about that," Dustin conceded with a frown and then turned his attention to Mac. "I was just trying to convince Tiffany here that she ought to come to Florida and see for herself how Journey's End is doing."

"Not a bad idea," Mac agreed, though there were reservations in his eyes. He removed his hat and took a chair at the table. "That way she could check up on Bob Prescott, see that he's doing a good job of training the colt."

Prescott was a young trainer who traveled with the horses while they were racing. He was a damned good man around a horse, but there was something shifty about him that Mac didn't like. The missus called it jealousy. Mac wasn't so sure, but he couldn't put his finger on the problem, and Bob Prescott had molded Journey's End into a fine racing machine.

Dustin's smile froze. "See, Tiffany, even Mac agrees that you could use a vacation. A little Florida sun might do you a world of good."

Tiffany managed a thin smile for both men and finished her coffee. "It'll have to wait until we're over this crisis." She leaned back in the chair and held up a finger. "However, you can bet I'll be at the Derby this year."

"You think Journey's End will make a good show of it?" Dustin asked as he placed his empty cup in the sink and wiped an accumulation of sweat from his brow.

"Not a show nor a place, but a win," the crusty old trainer predicted.

"High praise coming from you," Dustin observed.

"Journey's End is a fine colt. He's got the heart, the look of eagles if you will, but his temperament's got to be controlled…guided." He lifted his wise old eyes to Dustin's face. "I just hope that Bob Prescott knows what he's doing."

"He does."

"Then Journey's End should win the Derby," Mac stated without qualification. "He's the best horse I've seen since Devil's Gambit or Moon Shadow."

Dustin nearly choked on his final swallow of coffee and turned the subject away from Devil's Gambit.

"We all know why Moon Shadow lost the Derby, don't we?" Dustin asked pointedly.

Mac's faded eyes narrowed. "Aye, that we do. I haven't made any excuses about it, either. I should never have let that jockey ride him."

"He was Ellery's choice," Tiffany intervened, sensing an argument brewing between the two men.

"And I shouldn't have allowed it." Mac straightened his wiry frame from the chair, and his fedora dangled from his fingers as he turned to Tiffany. "I called Vance. I'm sure we'll have another foal before morning."

Tiffany took in a ragged breath. "Let me know when the time comes."

"Aye. That I will." With his final remarks, Mac walked out of the room and the screen door banged behind him.

Tiffany whirled on Dustin. "That was uncalled for, you know," she spit out.

"What?"

"Those remarks about Moon Shadow and the Derby."

"Serves the old man right. I never have figured why you keep that old relic around, anyway."

Tiffany was furious and shaking with rage. "Mac's not old, nor a relic, and he's the best damned horseman in this state, maybe the country. He knows more about Thoroughbreds than you or I could hope to know in a lifetime. Let's just hope, brother-in-law, that he doesn't take your remarks to heart and quit on us. We'll be in a world of hurt, then, let me tell you!"

Dustin had visibly paled but scoffed at Tiffany's remarks. "You're giving him too much credit," he said with a shrug as he stared out the window. "You're genuinely fond of the old goat, aren't you?"

"Mac's been good to me, good to this farm, good to Ellery and good to you. Why you continue to ridicule him is beyond me. Unless you'd secretly like to see him leave."

"It wouldn't affect me one way or the other."

"Like hell, Dustin. We had an agreement, remember?" she reminded him. "I run the operations of the farm, you handle the PR. Right now, because of all the adverse publicity with Moon Shadow's foals, it seems to me that you've got more than your share of work cut out for you!"

With her final remark Tiffany stormed out of the kitchen, tugged on her boots and went off to make amends with Mac. Why did Dustin have to provoke the trainer now when she needed Mac's expertise the most?

MAC WAS ALREADY at his pickup when Tiffany caught up with him. "I'm sorry," she apologized. She was out of breath from her sprint across the back lawn and parking lot.

"No need for that, Missy," Mac said with a kindly smile as he reached for the door handle on the old Dodge. "What Dustin said was the truth."

"No, it wasn't. Even with his regular jockey, there was no assurance that Moon Shadow would win."

"He was the odds-on favorite."

"And we all know how many long shots have won when it counted. Besides, it's all water under the bridge now," she assured him. "We'll just pin our hopes on Journey's End. And maybe this time, we'll win the Derby."

"I hope so," Mac said, pursing his lips together thoughtfully as he studied the lush Northern California countryside that made up the pastures of Rhodes Breeding Farm. "It's time you got a break." He opened the door to the truck. "I'll be back after dinner to check on Alexander's Lady. My guess is she'll foal around midnight."

"See you then." Tiffany stepped away from the old truck and Mac started the engine before shoving it into gear. Tiffany felt her teeth sink into her lower lip as she watched the battered old pickup rumble down the long driveway.

THREE HOURS LATER Tiffany was in the foaling shed, watching, praying while the glistening chestnut mare labored. The air was heavy with the smell of sweat mingled with ammonia and antiseptic.

Vance and Mac were inside the stall with the horse while Tiffany and Dustin stood on the other side of the gate. Alexander's Lady was lying on her side in the thick mat of straw, her swollen sides heaving with her efforts.

"Here we go," Vance said as the mare's abdomen contracted and the foal's head and shoulders emerged. A few minutes later, the rest of the tiny body was lying beside the mare.

Vance worked quickly over the newborn, clearing the foal's nose. As Tiffany watched she noticed the small ribs begin to move.

Tiffany reached for the switch that turned on the white heat lamps to keep the precious animal from catching cold.

"Let's leave the lamps on for two or three days,"

Vance suggested, his round face filled with relief as the filly tested her new legs and attempted to stand. "I don't want to take any chances."

"Neither do I," Tiffany agreed, her heart warming at the sight of the struggling filly. She was a perfect dark bay, with only the hint of a white star on her forehead.

Tiffany slipped into the stall and began to rub the wet filly with a thick towel, to promote the filly's circulation. At that moment, the mare snorted.

"I think it's time for Mom to take over," Vance suggested, as he carefully moved the foal to the mare's head. Alexander's Lady, while still lying on the straw, began to nuzzle and lick her new offspring.

"Atta girl," Mac said with the hint of a smile. "'Bout time you showed some interest in the young-un." He stepped out of the stall to let mother and daughter get acquainted.

Vance stayed in the stall, watching the foal with concerned eyes. He leaned against the wall, removed his glasses and began cleaning them with the tail of his coat, but his thoughtful gaze remained on the horses, and deep furrows lined his brow.

"Is she all right?" Tiffany asked, her heart beating irregularly. Such a beautiful filly. She couldn't die!

"So far so good." But his lips remained pressed together in an uneasy scowl as he attended to the mare. Alexander's Lady groaned and stood up. She nickered softly to the filly.

As if on cue, the little newborn horse opened her eyes and tried futilely to stand.

"Come on, girl. You can do it," Tiffany whispered in encouragement. The filly managed to stand on her spindly, unsteady legs before she fell back into the straw. "Come on..."

"Good lookin' filly," Mac decided as the little horse finally forced herself upright and managed the few steps to the mare's side. "Nice straight front legs... good bone, like her dad." Mac rubbed his hand over the stubble on his chin.

Tiffany's heart swelled with pride.

"She looks fine," Vance agreed as he watched the filly nuzzle the mare's flanks and search for her first meal.

"So did Charlatan," Tiffany reminded him, trying her best not to get her hopes up. The filly looked strong, but so had Felicity's colt. And he had died. A lump formed in Tiffany's throat. She couldn't imagine that the beautiful little filly might not live through the night.

"Keep watch on her," Vance stated, his lips thinning.

"Round the clock," Tiffany agreed. "We're not going to lose this one," she vowed, oblivious to the worried glances being exchanged between the veterinarian and the trainer.

"What have you decided to name her?" Dustin asked, seemingly entranced by the healthy young horse.

"How about Survivor?" Tiffany replied. "Better yet, how about Shadow's Survivor?"

"As in Moon Shadow?" Dustin inquired.

"Yes." Tiffany glanced at the suckling baby horse. The fluffy stub of a tail twitched happily. "I like it."

"Isn't it a little premature for a name like that?"

"I hope not," Tiffany whispered. "I hope to God, it's not."

"Missy," Mac said gently, touching her sleeve.

"Don't say it, Mac," Tiffany said, holding up her

hand. "This little filly is going to make it. She's got to!" Tiffany's lips pressed together in determination, as if she could will her strength into the little horse.

"I just don't want you to be too disappointed."

"I won't be." Tiffany's jaw tensed, and her blue eyes took on the hue of newly forged steel. "This horse is going to live."

"I'll stay overnight in the sitting-up room, watching the monitor. If anything goes wrong, I'll call," Mac volunteered.

"Good." Vance washed his hands and removed his bloodied white jacket. "I want this filly babied. I want her to stay inside for a full three days, under the lamps. We're not out of the woods yet, not by a long shot. And as for the mare, make sure she gets bran mash for three days."

"You got it," Mac agreed, casting one last worried glance at the filly. "Now, Missy, why don't you go up to the house and get some sleep? You can take over in the morning."

Tiffany glanced at the two horses. "Gladly," she whispered.

As she walked out of the foaling shed and into the windy night, Tiffany felt the sting of grateful tears in her eyes. Large crystalline drops began to run down her cheeks and catch the moon glow. *Everything would be perfect,* she thought to herself as she shoved her hands into the pockets of her jacket and started walking on the path to the house, *if only Zane were here to see for himself the strong little daughter of Moon Shadow.*

CHAPTER NINE

ZANE CRADLED HIS drink in his hands as he stared at the two other men in the office. His attorney, John Morris, sat behind the oiled teak desk. The other fellow, a great bear of a man, had been introduced by John as Walt Griffith. He was staring out the window at the black San Francisco night.

Walt Griffith wasn't what Zane had expected. When Zane had asked John to hire the best private investigator in California, he'd expected to meet a slick L.A. detective, a man who was street smart as well as college educated. Instead, John had come up with Griffith, a semiretired investigator nearly seventy years old, with thick, gray hair, rotund waistline, clean-shaven jowls and an eye-catching diamond ring on his right hand.

Griffith made Zane slightly uneasy, but he managed to hide his restlessness by quietly sipping his bourbon and water.

"So you want to locate your ex-wife," Griffith said at last while frowning at the city lights illuminating that particular section of Jackson Square.

"That's right." Zane shifted uncomfortably in his chair, and his lips tightened at the corners.

"Maybe she doesn't want you to know where she is."

"She probably doesn't." Zane cocked his head and studied the large man. What was he getting at?

Griffith clasped his hands behind his back. "I wouldn't do this for anyone, you know, but John and I—" he looked at the worried attorney "—we go way back. He says you're straight."

"Straight?" Zane repeated, turning his eyes to the attorney. John took off his reading glasses and frowned.

"I assume that John knows you well enough," Griffith continued. "He told me you weren't a wife-beater or some other kind of psycho."

Zane cocked a dubious dark brow at his friend. "Thanks," he said with a trace of sarcasm.

Griffith turned and leaned against a bookcase filled with leather-bound law books. He withdrew an imported cigar from the inside pocket of his suit coat and studied the tip. "Let me tell you, boy," he said, pointing the cigar in Zane's direction. "I've seen it all, and I'm not about to do anything that smacks of brutality." His small, brown eyes glittered from deep in their sockets, and Zane had the distinct impression that Griffith had gotten himself into trouble more than once from something "smacking of brutality." "If I didn't owe John a favor, I wouldn't have bothered to take your case at all. You seem to have somewhat of a checkered past yourself."

Zane forced a severe smile and his gray eyes met Griffith's intense stare. "I wouldn't physically abuse a woman, any woman. Including Stasia."

"Abuse doesn't have to be physical."

Zane's anger got the better of him, and his fingers tightened around his drink. "There's no love lost between Stasia and me," he admitted, his eyes sparking furiously. "But I have no intention of hurting her. Actually, the less I have to do with her, the better. The only reason I want to locate her is because I think she'll be able to help me with some answers I need." Zane smiled at the irony of it all. "Believe me, Griffith, if there was another way to deal with this problem, I'd be glad to hear it. I don't relish the thought of confronting my ex-wife any more than you want this assignment."

Griffith struck a match and lit his cigar. As he puffed, a thick cloud of pungent smoke rose to the ceiling. "Answers?" he asked, rolling Zane's words over in his mind. "About the other woman?"

Zane nodded.

Griffith's thick gray brows rose questioningly as he became interested in the Irishman's case. "Does she know you're checking up on her?"

Zane was cautious. He had to be with this man. "Tiffany?"

"Right."

Zane shook his head and scowled into his drink. "No."

"Humph." Griffith drew in on the cigar until the tip glowed red. "This other woman—this Rhodes lady, what's she to you?" he demanded.

"A friend."

Griffith shook his great head, and his eyes moved from Zane to John. "I thought you said he'd put all his cards on the table."

"He will." John glared severely at Zane. "You wanted the man." He motioned to indicate the investigator. "So help him."

At that moment, Zane realized he'd run out of options. He hesitated only slightly, and the smile that curved his lips appeared more dangerous than friendly. "All right, counselor, I'll level with Griffith, *if* he promises that everything I tell him will be kept in the strictest confidence."

"Goes without saying," Griffith grumbled, lowering himself into the chair next to Zane and folding his hands over his round abdomen. "Now, Mr. Sheridan, kindly explain why you're so interested in these two women, your wife and your...'friend.'"

As SHE CAME downstairs the morning after Alexander's Lady had foaled, Tiffany felt as if a great weight had been lifted from her shoulders. She had slept soundly, and only once, at about four, had she woken up. After turning on the monitor in the den and assuring herself that both the mare and the filly were alive and resting as well as could be expected, she trudged back up the stairs and fell into her bed. She had gone to sleep again instantly and had awakened refreshed.

"Good morning," Tiffany said with a cheery smile as Louise entered the kitchen and placed her purse on the table.

Louise's eyes sparkled. "It must be, from the looks of you," she decided. "Don't tell me—that Sheridan fella is back again."

"No," Tiffany quickly replied. She avoided the housekeeper's stare by pulling a thermos out of the cupboard near the pantry, and managed to hide the disappointment she felt whenever she thought about Zane. "Alexander's Lady is now the mother of a healthy filly," Tiffany stated, forcing a smile.

"Thank God!" Louise removed her coat and hung it in the closet. "This calls for a celebration!"

"Champagne brunch maybe?" Tiffany suggested.

Louise thought for a moment and then nodded.

"Why not? It's about time we had some good news around here." She pulled her favorite apron out of the closet, tied it loosely around her waist and began rummaging through the drawers looking for the utensils she needed. After grabbing a wooden spoon, she tapped it thoughtfully against her chin and said, "I can fix something for when? Say around noon?"

"That would be perfect," Tiffany agreed. "Vance should be back by then and maybe we can persuade him to stay."

At that moment the telephone rang, and without thinking Tiffany reached for the receiver and settled it against her ear. "Hello?" she said into the phone, hoping for a fleeting second that the caller would be Zane.

"Tiffany? Hal Reece, here."

Tiffany's heart fell to the floor, and her stomach tightened painfully. Obviously his mare had foaled. Her fingers tightened around the receiver. "Yes?"

"I just wanted to report that Mile High delivered."

Tiffany braced herself for the worst. She was already imagining how she would deal with the press, the lawsuit, the other owners.... "When?"

"Three nights ago."

"And?" Tiffany's heart was thudding so loudly she was sure Hal could hear it.

Louise stopped rattling in the cupboards; the serious tone of Tiffany's voice warned her of impending doom. Usually she wouldn't eavesdrop, but this time, under the circumstances, the kindly housekeeper couldn't hide her interest in the strained conversation.

"And, I'm glad to say, we have three-day-old colts— healthy ones," Hal announced.

"Colts? Plural?"

"That's right, Tiffany," Hal said, his voice nearly bursting with pride. "Can you believe it? After everything we worried about, I end up with twins—and beauties at that."

"Wonderful," Tiffany replied as she sagged against the pantry doors and tried desperately to keep her voice professional. Louise's worried face broke into a wide grin.

"I knew it all along, you know," the proud owner went on, "but we did have a few tense moments during the labor. From the look on the trainer's face while Mile High was delivering, I thought the colt was still-born, but that wasn't his concern at all! He just hadn't expected number two." Hal went on to describe in minute detail all the physical characteristics of each of his new horses and ended by saying, "Look, Tiffany, I would have called you a couple of days ago, but, well, I wanted to be sure that…you know, we didn't have any problems."

"I understand," Tiffany replied, remembering Charlatan's short life. "I'm just pleased that it turned out so well."

"Yes, yes. And, uh, look, I'm sorry about the things I said the other night. I was…well, there's just no excuse for my behavior."

"It's okay," Tiffany said with a sigh.

"Have you heard from any of the other owners?" Hal asked.

"You're the first."

"Well, good luck. And mind you, if anyone tries to give you any trouble, let me know. Maybe I'll be able to help."

"Thank you."

He was about to ring off, but changed his mind. "One other thing, Tiffany."

"Yes?"

"As soon as all this...ballyhoo over Moon Shadow passes, I'd like to breed a couple of mares to him again."

Tiffany smiled. Hal Reece's words were the final olive branch offered to bridge the rift between them. "Thank you," she said gratefully, "I'll be in touch."

Tiffany hung up the phone and grinned at Louise.

"Good news?" Louise guessed with a knowing smile.

"The best. Hal Reece's mare gave birth to twins. *Healthy* twin colts. Three nights ago. They've been examined by a vet, given a clean bill of health and even insured by the insurance company."

"That does it," Louise said with a toss of her head. "We'll have that celebration brunch after all."

"Hal is only one owner," Tiffany murmured as if to herself, "but at least it's a start." After pouring herself a hot cup of coffee, she filled the thermos, pushed open the door with her shoulder and started down the steps of the back porch. Wolverine, who had been lying beneath a favorite juniper bush near the brick stairs, trotted over to greet her.

"How's it going, boy?" Tiffany asked, checking to see that he had food and fresh water in the appropriate dishes. The collie tilted his head to the side, and his tail wagged slowly as she spoke. Tiffany set the thermos on the top step, took a sip from her coffee and scratched the old dog behind the ears. "Haven't you been getting enough attention lately?" she asked in an understanding voice. "All those horses are kind of stealing the show right now, aren't they?"

Wolverine whined and placed a furry paw on her bent knee.

Tiffany laughed and shook her head. "You're still the boss, though, aren't you?" As she picked up her things and turned toward the foaling shed, Wolverine trotted behind her, content with the little bit of attention he'd received.

The hinges on the door creaked as Tiffany entered the whitewashed building. Mac was standing at Alexander's Lady's stall and writing on a white card that Tiffany recognized as the foaling record.

"Good morning, Missy," the trainer said, without bothering to look up. When his job was finished, he placed the foaling record back on the post near the stall. Once the card was complete, Tiffany would enter the appropriate information into the farm's computer.

"That it is," she said, mimicking Mac's speech pattern.

Mac's brown eyes twinkled. "What's got you in such good spirits?" Forcing a tired smile, he leaned over the railing of the foaling box. "Could it be this little lady, here?"

"She's got a lot to do with it," Tiffany admitted. The little filly hid behind the protection of her mother's flank. At the filly's skittish behavior, Alexander's Lady's ears flattened to her reddish head, and she positioned herself between the intruders and her foal.

"Mama's takin' her job seriously," Mac decided.

"Good."

The newborn poked her inquisitive nose around the

mare's body and stared at the strangers through intelligent brown eyes.

"I told you she'd make it," Tiffany said. The precocious little bay looked so healthy. *The filly couldn't die. Not now.*

Mac's knowing eyes traveled over the mare and foal, but he didn't offer his thoughts to Tiffany. She read the hesitation in his gaze. It's still too early to tell, he was saying without uttering a word.

As Tiffany watched the two horses, she realized that the stall had already been cleaned. The smell of fresh straw and warm horses filled the small rooms attached to the broodmare barn which were used for the express purpose of foaling.

"You didn't have to stay in the sitting-up room," Tiffany remarked, knowing that she was wasting her breath. Mac was from the old school of horse training. "There's a monitor in the den."

"Aye, and what good does it do ya?"

"I used it last night."

Mac laughed. "As if you don't trust me." She was about to protest, but he stilled her with a wave of his arm. "I like to be close, especially since we've had so much trouble. If anything goes wrong, I'm right next door." He cocked his head in the direction of the sitting-up room positioned between the two foaling boxes. "It's what I'm used to."

Tiffany didn't argue. Mac had been around horses long before the introduction of video cameras and closed-circuit television. "There's fresh coffee up at the house, and Louise is in the process of whipping up a special brunch, if you can stick around."

"The missus—"

"Is invited, too."

Mac rubbed a hand over the stubble on his chin and cracked a wide smile. "She might like that, ya know. She's always grumblin' 'bout cookin' for me," he teased.

"I'll bet." Tiffany laughed in reply. Emma McDougal positively doted on her husband of over forty years, but Mac was none the worse for his wife's spoiling. "Why don't you grab a cup of coffee, or take this thermos and then go home for a while? Bring Emma back with you around eleven."

"And what about you?"

"I'll stay here until Vance arrives." Tiffany checked her watch. "And then, if Vance approves, we'll let John watch the horses."

"If you think you can trust him—"

Tiffany waved Mac off. "John's only nineteen, I grant you, but he's been around horses all his life, and he's the best stable boy since—"

"You?" Mac asked, his eyes saddening.

Tiffany pushed aside the unpleasant memories. When she had been a stable boy to her father, Mac had been with the horses on the racing circuit, but he had learned of her duties through Ellery. "Maybe," she acknowledged. "Now, go on, get out of here."

Mac took his cue and left Tiffany to watch over the new mother and filly. The little bay foal scampered around her mother on legs that had grown stronger with the passing of the night. "You're going to make it, aren't you?" Tiffany asked, before glancing at the foaling record and noting that everything had been recorded perfectly. The time that the mare's water broke, when the foal was born, when it stood, and when it first suckled were duly noted along with the foal's sex and color. Everything looked normal.

Tiffany looked at the impish bay horse and let out a long sigh. "Let her live," she prayed in a soft whisper that seemed to echo through the rafters in the high ceiling.

She was just straightening up the sitting-up room when she heard the door to the foaling shed creak open.

"Tiffany?" Dustin called softly.

"In here." She peeked around the corner and was surprised to find Dustin dressed in a business suit. "What's going on?" she asked, pointing a moving finger at his neatly pressed clothes.

"I'm going back to Florida."

"Today?" She stepped back into the corridor to meet him. His face was set in hard determination, and a small frown pulled at the corners of his mouth.

"Have to."

Tiffany held her palms up in the air. "Wait a minute! You just got here yesterday."

Dustin's gold eyes held hers. "Do you want me to stay?" he asked, his voice much too familiar in the well-lit building. The only other sound was the whisper of hay being moved by the horses' feet.

"Yes...no..." She shook her head in bewilderment. "If you want to. What's the rush?"

He looked genuinely disappointed and refused to smile. "I only came back to make sure that you were all right," he admitted, his frown deepening. "And from the looks of it, you're fine." His eyes slid down her slim form. She was clad only in worn jeans and a pink pullover, but with her hair wound over her head and the sparkle back in her intense blue eyes, she appeared both elegant and dignified, a no-nonsense lady who had her act together.

"Did you expect to find me in a crumpled heap—falling apart at the seams?"

Dustin shook his head but didn't smile at her attempt to lighten the mood. "I guess not. But it happened once before," he reminded her.

"That was different. Ellery was killed." She watched the smooth skin over Dustin's even features but saw no trace of any emotion that would betray his inner thoughts. Dustin acted as if he believed his brother dead.

"Right," he agreed.

"As well as Devil's Gambit."

Dustin looked up sharply, and in that split second Tiffany knew that he was lying to her. For the past four years, Dustin had been lying through his even white teeth. Without considering the consequences of her actions, she turned toward the stall and forced herself to appear calm, though her heart was pounding irregularly in her chest. It was time to find out how much of Zane's story was fact and how much was fiction, and she had to do it now, before Dustin left.

"I was thinking," she remarked, sliding a furtive glance in Dustin's direction.

"About?"

"Well, I still don't want to use Moon Shadow as a stud. Not until I understand what happened to those four foals, and I hear from the other owners."

Dustin nodded. Tiffany saw the movement from the corner of her eye. She propped her elbows on the rail and continued to watch the filly.

"So I was hoping to send some of our mares to other stallions, if it's not too late to nominate them."

"Sounds good to me." Dustin checked his watch and shifted from one foot to the other.

"You have any ideas on whom I should call?" she asked, her throat dry with dread.

"What?"

She shrugged. "Well, you're always high on one horse or the other. You know, a few years ago you thought we should breed Felicity to King's Ransom."

Dustin stiffened. The movement was slight, nearly imperceptible, but Tiffany caught it. "He's a good sire. Proof enough of that on the European tracks recently."

"Do you still think it's a good idea to send Felicity to him?"

"An impossible one, I'd say. King's Ransom's got to be booked solid."

Tiffany lifted one shoulder. "I just thought that maybe you knew the owner—could pull a few strings."

Dustin's eyes narrowed in suspicion. He came over to the stall and stood next to her. "You want favors? That's not like you, Tiff. You're the one who always plays by the rules."

"This is an unusual case—"

Dustin's arms reached for her, drew her close. "What is it with you?" he whispered against her hair. "What's going on here?" His finger traced the line of her jaw before lingering on the pout of her lips.

Her mind racing fast, Tiffany slid out of the circle of his arms and clasped her arms behind her back. She cocked her head upward to meet his gaze. "I just feel pushed against a wall sometimes," she said, knowing she was treading on thin ice with the turn in the conversation. She forced her hands into the pockets of her jeans and hoped to God that she wasn't betraying her inner feelings.

"And how would breeding one of our horses to King's Ransom change that?"

"It wouldn't, I suppose. There are plenty of good studs, here in the States." Lord, she hoped that she was a better actress than she had ever given herself credit for. "But we need a winner—a real winner."

"We've got Journey's End," he volunteered, intrigued with the change in her. His brother's widow was a mystifying creature; wild one minute, sedate the next. Intelligent, proud and sexy as hell. Dustin decided then and there that he would gladly give half his fortune for the chance to tame her fiery spirit.

"I know," Tiffany replied. "But what we really need is another horse like Devil's Gambit."

Dustin paled slightly, his hands dropped to his sides, but for the most part, he managed to keep his composure intact. "He's gone, Tiff. So is Ellery. You've got to face it. You're never going to have another horse just like Devil's Gambit, and you've got to forget this unreasonable loyalty to a dead man."

He captured her arm with his fingers and tugged her gently to him. "You need to live again, Tiffany. Without the ghosts of the past surrounding you. Ellery is gone.... Think about letting another man into your life." He paused dramatically, and his gilded eyes darkened with passion.

Tiffany wanted to recoil from him and shout that another man was already in her life, that she had committed her heart to a man she barely knew, and she was dying inside without him. Instead, she pulled away before the embrace became more heated.

"Think about me," he suggested, his eyes raking over her in lusty appraisal.

"I...I have too much on my mind to think about starting new relationships," she said, knowing the excuse was as feeble as it sounded. If she wasn't careful, Dustin would see through her act. "The foals—" she angled her head in the direction of the newborn filly "—Journey's End's career...a lot of things."

Dustin tugged at his stiff collar, but his golden eyes never left her face. "You said you felt pushed against the wall."

"I do." She lifted her shoulders in a nonchalant gesture and gambled with what she hoped was her trump card. "Someone's offered to buy me out."

Dustin froze. "What?"

It was too late to back down now. "A man was here last week."

"*What* man?"

"An Irishman. Zane Sheridan."

Dustin looked as if he would sink right through the floor. All of his well-practiced composure seemed to slide through the concrete.

"Ever heard of him?"

"Yeah. I know him." Dustin shook his head. "What does he want with this farm? He already breeds horses in Europe."

"Maybe he wants to break into the American market," Tiffany suggested, her fingers tightening over the railing of the stall. God, she was a terrible liar.

Dustin began to pace the length of the short corridor. "Maybe," he said as if he didn't believe a word of it. His mouth tightened and he ran a hand over his brow to catch the droplets of cold sweat that had begun to bead on his forehead. "I suppose he told you all sorts of wild stories."

"Like?" Tiffany coaxed.

"Like—hell, I don't know." He held up a hand in exasperation and looked up at the cross beams of the shed. "I may as well be honest with you, Tiff."

Here it comes. Dustin is about to confess, Tiffany thought, suddenly cold with dread.

"There wasn't much love lost between Sheridan and Ellery," Dustin announced. His topaz eyes softened, as if he wished he could save her some of the pain he was about to inflict. For the first time Tiffany realized that Dustin did, in his own way, truly love her. "They were involved in a poker game—for high stakes. Sheridan lost. I don't think the man likes to lose, and he took it none too well, let me tell you. He even went so far as to claim that Ellery had been cheating. God, I was there. I don't know how Ellery could have cheated. From where I sat, Ellery won fair and square."

"How—how much money was involved?"

"Somewhere around two hundred thousand dollars, I think. Supposedly it wiped Sheridan out. But apparently he's back on his feet again."

Tiffany's mouth was dry with tension. "You haven't seen him since?"

"No, but I know he breeds horses in Ireland. I've seen a few of them race. He's got a two-year-old filly who's ripping up the tracks."

"The filly sired by King's Ransom?"

Dustin cast her a worried glance and nodded curtly. "I wouldn't trust that man, Tiffany. He's got a reputation in Europe for being ruthless." Dustin began stalking back and forth in front of the stall. "I don't understand why he wants to buy you out. What did you say to his offer?"

"That I wasn't interested, and if I ever did want to sell out my part of the operation, you had first option."

Some of the tension in his shoulders dissipated. "Good." He raked his fingers through his hair. "Did he say anything else?"

"Not much," Tiffany lied with a twinge of regret. "But I think he'll be back with a concrete offer."

"Great," Dustin muttered, his gold eyes impaling her. "Whatever you do, Tiff, don't sell out to that bastard."

"Are you still interested in owning all the farm?" she asked. Several years before, Dustin had offered to buy her out, but she had steadfastly refused.

"Of course I am. I just never thought you'd want to sell."

"I'm not sure that I do."

"Then you will give me first option?"

"When the time comes...."

Dustin appeared relieved, but there was something else that he was hiding from her; she could read it in the shadows of his eyes.

"Dustin." She touched his sleeve lightly. "Is there something you're not telling me?"

Dustin walked away from her and pushed his hands into the back pockets of his slacks. His shoulders slumped in defeat. "Well, maybe I shouldn't be telling you this," he grumbled, condemning himself. "It's all water under the bridge now."

Tiffany's heart nearly stopped. Was Dustin going

to admit that Devil's Gambit was alive and siring foals as part of an incredible charade that would rock the Thoroughbred racing world on two continents? She felt almost physically ill with dread.

"Ellery was involved with a woman back then."

"Oh, God," she whispered, rocked to the very core of her soul as she began to understand what Dustin was saying. She felt cold all over; her heart was heavy in her chest. "A woman that Zane was in love with?" she guessed, praying that she had misunderstood her brother-in-law.

Dustin's brows quirked at Tiffany's familiar use of Sheridan's name. He let out an angry oath. "More than that, I'm afraid. She was Zane Sheridan's *wife, Stasia.*"

Tiffany sucked in her breath and her throat began to ache painfully. Truth and fiction began to entangle in her confused thoughts. What was Dustin saying? "Wait a minute…" Dustin was giving her too much information and it made her head swim. She had thought he was going to confess about Devil's Gambit, but instead he had brought up Zane's ex-wife…and *Ellery.* Dear God, was that why Zane had come to the farm, his gray eyes filled with revenge? Had he pretended interest in her only to throw her off guard? "Nancy Emerson said something about Zane's wife running out on him, but not with Ellery. The man's name was—"

"Ethan Rivers."

Tiffany swallowed against the dread flowing in her blood. "No." She had to deny what Dustin was suggesting and her shoulders slumped.

"Tiffany, listen!"

She shook her head and fought against hot tears. "Are you trying to tell me that Ellery used an alias?"

She clamped her fingers over the top rail of the stall for support.

"Sometimes."

Pained blue eyes delved into Dustin's murky gaze. "But why?" Alexander's Lady sensed the tension and snorted.

Dustin waved off Tiffany's question as if it were insignificant. "Sometimes it was just easier...if people didn't know we, Ellery and I, were brothers."

"I don't understand." *And I don't think I want to. It would be easier not to think that Ellery used me in the past and that Zane is using me still....*

"You don't have to," Dustin said harshly and then softened a little when he saw her stricken face. "Tiffany, it really doesn't matter, not now. When Ellery and I were first getting started, we had to do a lot of... maneuvering to get established. Sometimes, when we were in Europe trying to sell some of our stock, it was just easier for Ellery to pose as a rival bidder to drive up the price of one of our own horses. Once in a while it backfired and no one bought the horse in question, but other times, well, we came out of it a few dollars richer. We didn't really hurt anyone by it."

Tiffany's eyes grew round with horror. "Oh, no?" she rasped as anger replaced despair. She leaned against a post for support, but her blue eyes blazed with rage. "You can justify it any way you want, even give it such fancy terms as 'maneuvering to get established,' Dustin, but I think what you and Ellery did was manipulate people and the system to pad your wallet." Tiffany felt sick inside, empty. "That's illegal—"

"Probably not," Dustin denied. "Immoral, maybe, and probably unethical—"

"And crooked." She saw the fury spark in his eyes and she forced control on her own anger. "Oh, Dustin. Why didn't Ellery tell me?" she asked in a broken whisper. Her knees threatened to give way. She had been married to Ellery, loved him in her own way, and he had betrayed her trust.

"Hey, don't get down on Ellery," Dustin said as if reading her thoughts. "This all happened before he knew you, and he did a hell of a lot for you and your bum of a father. Where would you have been if Ellery hadn't supported you, paid your way through college and then married you?"

"I don't know," she admitted. "But the lies—"

He touched her chin and lifted it, forcing her to look into his eyes. He felt her tremble with rage. "Look, it's over and done with," Dustin said, his eyes searching hers. "Ellery's dead...." He lowered his head and would have kissed her if it hadn't been for the question she had to ask.

"Is he, Dustin?" she demanded, pulling away from him and wrapping her arms protectively over her breasts.

Dustin was visibly stunned. "What kind of a question is that?"

"A legitimate worry, wouldn't you say?"

"Tiffany, listen to what you're saying!"

"How do I know that he isn't alive and using that alias...Ethan Rivers...or another one for that matter, in Europe somewhere?" Her hands were shaking at her sides. "For all I know, he could be living in France or England or Ireland, racing horses, married to someone else." She was rambling and she knew it, and she had to get hold of herself before she tipped her hand and gave her act away.

"I was there, Tiffany, at the accident. I saw Ellery...." His face went ashen and in that single moment of honesty, Tiffany believed her brother-in-law. "As hard as it is for you to accept, Ellery's gone."

Tiffany managed to square her shoulders, but tears pooled in her eyes before trickling down her face in a broken silvery path. "I didn't really doubt it," she admitted, brushing the unwanted tears aside. "But you've just told me some things that are a little hard to accept."

Dustin glanced at his watch again and cursed. "Damn! I've got to go if I'm going to catch that plane." He looked at her longingly once again, silently offering himself.

Tiffany shook her head and lifted it with renewed determination. Her eyes, when they met Dustin's direct gaze, were cold.

"If you need me—"

"No. Journey's End needs you," she said. "The Florida Derby is next week."

"You could come down," he suggested without much hope.

"Not until I make sure that this little one—" Tiffany cocked her head in the direction of the inquisitive filly "—and her brothers and sisters are okay."

With a reluctant sigh, he turned away. "I'll call," Dustin promised, wondering why the hell he cared. He had lots of women who would do anything he wanted, so why was he hung up on his brother's wife?

"Good."

With only a moment's indecision, Dustin walked crisply out of the foaling shed, and Tiffany slumped against the wall in relief. *Ellery* was Ethan Rivers? *Ellery* had run off with Zane's wife, Stasia? The woman who had been Ellery's mistress when Tiffany was in college?

Tiffany's head was throbbing with unanswered questions. "Oh, Zane," she whispered brokenly. "What are you involved in?"

She was still going over the conversation with Dustin in her mind when Vance Geddes arrived to check the mare and foal. His brow knitted with worry as he started the examination, but the furrows slowly eased as he studied the frisky filly.

"It looks like she's going to make it," he said, relief audible in his voice. "By the time Charlatan was this old, there were already signs of distress."

"Thank God," Tiffany murmured, her mind only half on the conversation. Where was Zane? Why did he want the farm? Why hadn't he explained about Stasia and Ellery?

"Tiffany?" Vance asked for the second time.

"Oh, what?"

Vance shook his head and offered a small smile. "I said it looks as if we can take her out in a few days. I think you've got yourself a racehorse here."

"Wonderful." Tiffany eyed the little filly fondly. "Now we really do have a reason to celebrate."

"Pardon?"

"I was hoping that you could join the rest of us for lunch…brunch—" she lifted her shoulders "—whatever you want to call it."

"I'd be glad to. Just let me get cleaned up."

"I'll meet you at the house," she said, leaving the foaling shed and instructing the stable boy to look after the mare and filly. She headed toward the house and didn't notice the warm spring sunshine, the gentle breeze lifting the branches of the fir trees near the drive or the crocuses sprouting purple, gold, and white near the back porch.

All of her thoughts were centered on Zane and what, if anything, he wanted from her.

By the time Tiffany got back to the house, Louise was working furiously. The smell of honey-glazed ham, homemade apple muffins, black coffee and steamed vegetables filled the room. Louise was humming as she carefully arranged a rainbow of fresh fruit in a crystal bowl.

"It smells great in here," Tiffany said as she walked into the kitchen and tried to shake off the feeling of impending dread that had settled on her shoulders during her discussion with Dustin. "What can I do to help?"

Louise smiled. "Nothing. All the work's about done. Just go change your clothes. We're eating on the sun porch."

"Ummm. Fancy."

"It's a celebration, isn't it?"

"That it is. Let me set the table—"

"Already done."

"You are efficient, aren't you?"

"I don't get much of a chance to show off anymore. It feels good," Louise admitted, holding up the clear bowl of fruit for Tiffany's inspection. The cut crystal sparkled in the late morning light.

"Beautiful," she murmured, and the housekeeper beamed. "If you're sure there's nothing I can do…"

"Scat! Will ya?" Louise instructed with a severe frown that broke down completely as she laughed.

Tiffany chuckled. "All right. I'll be down in about twenty minutes."

She walked toward the stairs and remembered the times she and Ellery had entertained. It had been often and grand. Louise had always enjoyed "putting out a spread" as she had called it. Ellery had insisted that entertaining potential buyers was all part of the business, and he had been at his best when dressed in a black tuxedo and contrasting burgundy cummerbund while balancing a glass of champagne between his long, well-manicured fingers.

It seemed like aeons ago. And all that time, while Tiffany was married to Ellery, he was probably leading a double life as a stranger named Ethan Rivers, and having an affair with Zane Sheridan's ex-wife, Stasia.

Tiffany's heart twisted painfully and she balled small fists in frustration. How could she have been so blind?

It would be easy to blame it on youth or naiveté, but the truth of the matter was that she had been so anxious to love someone and have him love her in return, she had closed her eyes to the possibility that her husband had been anything but what she had wanted to see.

Stop punishing yourself, she warned, as she slipped out of her clothes, rewound her hair onto her head and stepped into the shower. *It's over and done!*

Or was it? Was Dustin telling the truth when he said that Ellery was dead, or was it just part of a complex cover-up to hide the fact that Devil's Gambit was alive and that another horse and *another man* died in the fire? Oh, dear God, would Ellery have been involved in anything so vile as murder? The thought turned her blood to ice water and she had to steady herself against the wet tiles. A cold wave of nausea flooded over her, and Tiffany felt for a minute as if she were going to vomit.

"Oh, God," she cried softly, forcing herself to stand.

No matter what else, she couldn't—wouldn't—believe that Ellery would take part in the death of another human being.

She turned off the shower and wrapped herself in a bath sheet without really thinking about what she was doing. With trembling fingers, while her head was still pounding with the cold truth of the past, she dressed in a bright dress of indigo polished silk, and pinned her hair in a tousled chignon. After touching up her makeup and forcing her morbid thoughts to a dark corner of her mind where she could examine them later, she started down the stairs. As she did, the doorbell chimed loudly.

"I'll get it," she called to Louise and hurred down the remaining three steps to the foyer and walked to the door, her heels echoing sharply against the imported tile.

Squaring her shoulders, she opened the door, expecting to find Mac's wife, Emma McDougal. Instead, her eyes met the silvery gaze of the only man who had ever touched her soul.

"Zane," Tiffany whispered, and felt the need to lean against the door for support. It had been more than a week since she had seen him, and in that time so many truths had been uncovered.

Now, as she looked at the man she loved, Tiffany felt as if she were staring into the eyes of a total stranger.

CHAPTER TEN

ZANE LEANED AGAINST one of the white columns supporting the roof of the porch and stared at Tiffany. His hands were thrust into the pockets of his jeans, and his slumped posture was meant to be casual, but his shoulder muscles were tight, so tense they ached.

God, she was beautiful, more beautiful than he remembered. Dressed in shimmering blue silk, with her golden brown hair pinned loosely to her crown, Tiffany looked almost regal. A single strand of gold encircled her throat, and thin layers of silk brushed against her knees.

After what seemed like a lifetime, Zane finally spoke. "Are you going out?" he asked, his gray eyes delving into hers. One look at Ellery Rhodes's widow had destroyed all of Zane's earlier promises to himself. After the meeting with Griffith just three days ago, he had silently vowed that he would stay away from Ellery Rhodes's widow. Now, as he gazed into her intriguing blue eyes, he knew that keeping away from her would be impossible. Despite all the excuses he'd made to himself to the contrary, seeing Tiffany again was the single reason he had returned to Rhodes Breeding Farm.

Tiffany, recovering from the shock of seeing him again, managed to square her shoulders and proudly hold his gaze. Though her heartbeat had quickened at the sight of him, she forced herself to remember Dustin's condemning words. *Sheridan's got a reputation for being ruthless.... Ellery was involved with Zane Sheridan's wife.*

"No," she finally replied, "I'm not going out.... We're having a special lunch, sort of a celebration."

Zane detected new doubts in her exotic blue eyes, doubts that hadn't clouded her gaze when he had last seen her. The small hairs on the back of his neck prickled in warning. Something was wrong here, and he intended to find out what it was. Silently he cursed himself for staying away so long. In the course of the past week, someone had destroyed all the trust Tiffany had previously felt for him. It didn't take long to figure out who was to blame, and his fists balled at the thought of Dustin Rhodes.

Zane straightened and walked closer to her. "Tiffany, what's wrong?" he asked, gently placing his fingers on her shoulders and pulling her close.

"Don't," she whispered, knowing that her battle was already lost. She wanted to melt into him. Just seeing him again had been enough to make her heartbeat race in anticipation. Maybe Dustin had been wrong about Zane, maybe he had lied.

She leaned heavily on Zane, letting his strong arms wrap around her. Her face was pressed to his chest, and she could feel the warmth of his breath on her hair, hear the even rhythm of his pounding heart.

Don't fall under his spell again, a small voice inside her cautioned. *Remember what Dustin said about Ellery and Zane's wife. He's probably here just to get information about Stasia. He's been using you all along.*

"Tiffany?" Zane urged, his voice low, husky. She closed her eyes and let his earthy scent fill her nostrils. It felt so right to have his arms around her. Without examining her motives, she clung to him as if she expected him to vanish as quickly as he had appeared.

"I...I didn't think you were coming back," she whispered, ignoring the doubts filling her mind. He was here, now, with her. Nothing else mattered.

"I said I would."

"But it's been—"

"Too long." The corded arms tightened around her, and his warm hands splayed against the small of her back, pressing her body to his and heating her skin through the thin material of her dress. "I should have called," he admitted, feeling his body beginning to respond to the soft, yielding contour of hers, "but I've been in and out of airports for the better part of a week."

She lifted her head and studied the weariness in his face. Wherever he'd been, the trip had taken its toll on him. The brackets near the corners of his mouth had deepened, and there was a general look of fatigue in his eyes. His clothes, a pair of jeans and a plaid shirt, were clean but slightly rumpled, and his chin was just beginning to darken from the day's growth of beard.

"Have you been out of the country?" she asked.

"Part of the time."

Because of Devil's Gambit, or your wife?

Tiffany knew that she should pull away from him, now, before she was lost to him forever. She shouldn't let him into her house or her life. Not again. Too many events in his past were entangled with Ellery's life and left unexplained. There were too many questions that demanded answers....

For a passing moment she considered confronting him with what she had learned from Dustin, just to gauge his reaction, but she couldn't. The sight of his drawn face, windblown black hair and slightly wrinkled clothing did strange things to her heart. Despite all of Dustin's accusations, despite the lies, she still loved this rugged man from Ireland with every fiber of her soul.

"Come inside," she invited, managing, despite her doubts, the trace of a smile. "Louise is making a special brunch."

"Why?" Zane's dark brows cocked expressively. He was getting mixed signals from Tiffany; one moment she seemed to have a wonderful secret she wanted to share with him, and her indigo eyes sparkled; the next second her smile would fade and her lips would compress into a determined line of defiance.

"Alexander's Lady had a filly—a healthy filly," Tiffany said, pushing her dark thoughts aside.

Zane relaxed a little, and he gently touched her cheek. She had to concentrate to keep her mind on the conversation. "I assume from your expression that she had been bred to Moon Shadow."

"Yes." Tiffany attempted to extract herself from his embrace, to put some mind-clearing distance between his body and hers, but his strong arms refused to release her.

"When was the filly born?"

"Just last night."

"Isn't the celebration a little premature?" he asked softly, remembering the other colt, the one that had lived a day or so before collapsing from heart failure and dying.

"Maybe, but I doubt it. Vance thinks the filly will live," Tiffany said with conviction. She recognized the unspoken question in Zane's eyes and knew that he was thinking about Charlatan's short life. "Vance wasn't so sure last night," she admitted, "but this morning the filly's been scampering around her stall like a champion. Even Vance has taken her off the critical list."

Zane hazarded a charming half-smile that touched Tiffany's heart. "That is good news." He kissed her lightly on the forehead, and Tiffany's heart seemed to miss a beat. *How could she react this way, love this man, when he had lied to her?*

"And there's more," she managed to say. "Hal Reece called and told me that his mare, Mile High, gave birth to twin colts—healthy colts, about three days ago. He's even been able to insure them."

Zane's grin spread slowly over his rugged features. He squeezed her for a minute and laughed. God, when was the last time he'd laughed? It had to have been years ago…. It was so easy with Tiffany, so natural. "You're right, you should celebrate."

Tiffany's eyes warmed. "Louise would love it if you joined us."

"Us?"

"Mac and his wife, Emma, Vance, Louise and myself." She read the hesitation in his gaze and realized that he felt like an outsider. Her elegant features sobered. "It's not a private party, Zane," she said softly with a seductive smile, "and you're very much a part of it. After all, you were here the night Ebony Wine delivered. Besides, Louise would skin me alive if she knew you were here and wouldn't have brunch with us after all the work she's gone to."

"Then how can I refuse?"

"You can't."

She pulled away from him, but his fingers caught her wrist. "Tiffany?"

"What?"

When she turned to face him, he tugged on her arm again and pulled her close against his body. "Just one more thing."

"Which is?" she asked breathlessly.

In answer, he lowered his head and his lips brushed seductively over hers. His breath was warm and inviting, his silvery eyes dark with sudden passion. "I missed you," he whispered against her mouth, then his lips claimed hers in a kiss that was as savage as it was gentle. The warmth of his lips coupled with the feel of his slightly beard-roughened face made her warm with desire.

Tiffany moaned and leaned against him, letting her body feel the hard texture of his. His tongue gently parted her lips and flickered erotically against hers. Heat began to coil within her before he pulled his head away and gazed at her through stormy gray eyes.

"God, I missed you," he repeated, shaking his head as if in wonder at the conflicting emotions warring within his soul.

Tiffany had to clear her throat. "Come on. Louise will have my head if her meal gets cold." Still holding his hand, she led him toward the back of the house and tried to forget that Zane had once been married to Ellery's mistress.

"I HAVEN'T EATEN like this since the last time I was here," Zane remarked to Louise, who colored slightly under the compliment. Everyone was seated at the oval table in the sun room, which was really an extension of the back porch. The corner of the porch nearest the kitchen had been glassed in, affording a view of the broodmare barn and the pasture surrounding the foaling shed. Green plants, suspended from the ceiling in wicker baskets or sitting on the floor in large brass pots, surrounded the oak table, and a slow-moving paddle fan circulated the warm air.

"We should do this more often," Tiffany decided as she finished her meal and took a sip of the champagne.

"Used to be," Mac mused while buttering a hot muffin, "that we'd have parties all the time. But that was a long time ago, when Ellery was still alive."

Tiffany felt her back stiffen slightly at the mention of Ellery's name. When she looked away from Mac she found Zane's gray eyes boring into hers. An uncomfortable silence followed.

"Hasn't been any reason to celebrate until now," Louise said, as much to diffuse the tension settling in the room as to make conversation. Her worried eyes moved from Tiffany to Zane and back again.

"What about Journey's End's career?" Vance volunteered, while declining champagne. He shook his head at Mac, who was tipping a bottle over his glass. "I've got two more farms to visit today." When Mac poured the remainder of the champagne into his own glass, Vance continued with his line of thinking. "If you ask me, Journey's End is reason enough to celebrate."

"Maybe we'd better wait on that," Tiffany thought aloud. "Let's see how he does in the Florida Derby."

"That race shouldn't be too much of a problem if Prescott handles him right," Mac said.

"What then?" Zane asked the trainer.

"Up to Kentucky for the Lexington Stakes."

"And then the Kentucky Derby?"

"That's the game plan," Mac said, finishing his drink and placing his napkin on the table. He rubbed one thumb over his forefinger nervously before extending his lower lip and shrugging. "I just hope Prescott can pull it off."

"He's a good trainer," Emma McDougal stated. She was a petite woman of sixty with beautiful gray hair and a warm smile. She patted her husband affectionately on the knee in an effort to smooth what she saw as Mac's ruffled feathers. She knew that as much as he might argue the point, Mac missed the excitement of the racetrack.

"When he keeps his mind on his horses," Mac grumbled.

"Don't you think he will?" Zane asked.

Mac's faded eyes narrowed thoughtfully. "He'd better," he said with a frown. "We've come too close to the Derby before to let this one slip through our fingers."

Tiffany pushed her plate aside. "Delicious," she said to Louise before turning her attention back to the trainer. "Would you like to work with Journey's End in Lexington? You could help Bob Prescott get him ready."

"Oh, there's no doubt I'd like to, Missy," Mac replied, ignoring the reproachful look from his wife. "But it wouldn't do a lick of good. Journey's End, he's used to Prescott. We can't be throwin' him any loops, not now. Me going to Kentucky would probably do more harm than good."

"So the die is cast?" Tiffany asked, feeling a cold premonition of doom as she looked through the windows and noticed the thick bank of clouds rolling over the mountains from the west.

"Aye, Missy. That it is…that it is."

TIFFANY SPENT THE rest of the afternoon with Zane, and for the first time in more than a week she began to relax. She had planned to drive into town in the afternoon but decided that she'd rather spend the time on the farm.

In the early evening, she took Zane into the foaling shed and proudly displayed Shadow's Survivor. Within the confines of the large stall, the inquisitive filly cavorted beneath the warm heat lamps.

"Vance says she'd be able to go outside in a couple of days," Tiffany said.

"I'll bet you're relieved." Zane's eyes moved from the mare and foal to Tiffany.

"I'll be more relieved when I hear from the rest of the owners," she responded as she led Zane out of the foaling shed. "Until I know that no more foals will die, I can't really relax."

Dusk was just beginning to settle on the hills surrounding the farm. Lavender shadows lengthened as the hazy sun settled behind the ridge of sloping mountains to the west. Clouds began to fill the darkened sky. "This is my favorite time of day," she admitted, watching as the stable boys rounded up the horses for the evening. The soft nickering of mares to their foals was interspersed with the distant whistle of a lonely stallion. Tiffany chuckled. "That's Moon Shadow," she explained. "He always objects to being locked up for the night."

"Do you blame him?" Zane asked.

"Oh, no. That's what makes him a winner, I suppose."

"His defiance?"

She frowned into the gathering darkness and linked her arm through his. A cool breeze pushed her dress against her legs as they walked. "I prefer to think of it as his fire, his lack of docility. He's always had to have his way, even as a foal. He was the boss, had to be in the lead."

"The heart of a champion."

Tiffany pursed her lips thoughtfully and her elegant brows drew together. "That's why I hate what's been happening to him—all this conjecture that there's something wrong with him."

"Have you found an answer to what happened to the dead foals?"

After expelling a ragged sigh, Tiffany shook her head. "Nothing so far. Vance has gone to independent laboratories, asked for help from the Jockey Club and the racing commission, and still can't get any answers."

"Not even enough information to clear Moon Shadow's name?"

"No." She placed a restraining hand on her hair as the wind began to loosen her chignon. "The new foals—the healthy ones—should prove that the problem isn't genetic."

"Unless another one dies."

She shuddered inside at the thought.

Zane noticed the pain in her eyes and placed a comforting arm over her shoulders. "You really love it here, don't you?"

"What?"

He rotated the palm of his free hand and moved his arm in a sweeping gesture meant to include the cluster of buildings near the center of the farm, the sweeping green pastures enclosed by painted white fences, the horses grazing in the field and the gentle green hills guarding the valley. "All of it."

She couldn't deny the attachment she felt for this farm. It was the only home she'd known. She felt as much a part of it as if it had been in her family for generations. It was, and would always be, the only thing she could call her heritage. "Yes," she answered. "I love it. I love the horses, the land, the excitement, the boredom, *everything*."

"And is that what I felt when I came back here this morning?"

"What do you mean?"

"When I arrived here, you looked at me as if I were a thief trying to steal it all away from you."

"Did I?"

He didn't answer, but she saw the determination in the angle of his jaw. He wouldn't let up until he found out what was bothering her. She had no recourse but to lie or to confront him with what she'd learned from Dustin.

The day with Zane had been so wonderful, and she knew that it was about to end. "It had nothing to do with selling the farm to you, Zane. You, or anyone else, can't force me to sell."

The arm around her tightened. She felt the unleashed tension coiling his body. "Then what?"

"While you were gone, a few things happened," she admitted. They had been walking down a wide, well-worn path, past the old barn and through a thicket of maple trees surrounding a small pond. The water in the small lake had taken on an inky hue, reflecting the turbulent purple of the sky.

"What things?"

"Dustin came home."

All of the muscles in Zane's body tightened. The thought of Dustin Rhodes, here, alone with Tiffany, made his stomach knot with dread. It was insane to feel this...jealousy. Dustin owned part of the farm; he could come and go as he pleased. Zane's jaw hardened, and his back teeth ground together in frustration.

"You weren't expecting him?"

"No."

"Then why did he return?"

"He said it was because of all the bad press surrounding Moon Shadow. He wanted to make sure that I was all right."

"He could have called."

"I suppose," she admitted, taking a seat on a boulder near the pond. "But I think he wanted to see me face to face."

"Why?" Zane demanded, his eyes glittering in the dark night.

"Dustin helped me pick up the pieces when Ellery was killed," she whispered. "I was pretty shook up."

"Because you loved your husband so much?" he asked, reaching for a flat stone and thrusting it toward the water. He watched as it skipped across the pond creating ever-widening ripples on the water's smooth surface.

"Because my whole world was turned upside down."
The wind picked up and clouds shadowed the moon.

"And if he walked back into your life right now?"
Zane asked, bracing himself against the truth.

"It would be upside down all over again."

"And who would you lean on?"

Tiffany breathed deeply. "I hope that I'm strong
enough to stand by myself—no matter what happens,"
she said softly.

The air was thick was the promise of rain, and the
clouds covering the moon became more dense. High
above, the branches of the fir trees danced with the
naked maples.

Zane turned to face her and his broad shoulders
slumped in resignation. Gray eyes drove into hers.
"You know that I'm falling in love with you, don't
you?"

Tiffany's heart nearly stopped. *If only I could believe you, Zane. If only you hadn't lied to me. If only I
could tell what was true and what was false.*

She wrapped her arms around her knees and shook
her head. "I don't think love can enter into our relationship," she said, staring at the dark water and refusing to face him.

"It's nothing I wanted," he admitted and pushed his
hands into his back pockets. "But it happened."

"Zane—" her protest was cut short when he strode
purposely over to the rock and scooped her into his
arms. "Please don't…" she breathed, but it was the
cry of a woman lost. When his lips crushed against
hers, she responded willingly, eagerly to him, mindless of the wind billowing her dress or the heavy scent
of rain in the air.

He gently laid her on the grass near a stand of firs, and his fingers caught in the golden strands of her hair. Slowly he withdrew the pins and twined his fingers in the silken braid as he pulled it loose. The golden hair fell to her shoulders, framing her face in tangled honey-brown curls.

"I've wanted to make love to you from the first moment I saw you," he whispered. His body was levered over hers, and his silvery eyes caught the reflection of the shadowy moon. She trembled when his hands lingered on her exposed throat to gently stroke the sensitive skin near her shoulders.

"That's not the same as loving someone," she replied, her voice breathless as his hand slowly, enticingly, slid down the silky fabric of her dress and softly caressed her breast.

A spasm of desire shot through her. "Oh, my God," she whispered while he looked at her, touching her with only one hand. Her breathing became rapid and shallow as slowly he caressed the silk-encased peak, rubbing the sheer fabric against her. Tiffany began to ache for the feel of his hands against her skin.

The fingers slid lower, down her thigh, to the hem of her dress. She felt the warm impression of his fingertips as they stroked her leg through her sheer stocking.

I shouldn't be doing this, she thought wildly. *I don't even really understand what he wants of me....*

"Tell me you want me to make love to you," he rasped against her hair. His tongue traced the gentle shell of her ear, and his breath fanned seductively against her skin.

"Oh, Zane...I..." Her blood was pounding in her temples. She trembled with desire.

"Tell me!"

"Oh, God, yes." She closed her eyes against the truth and felt the hot tears moisten her lashes. *I don't want to love you,* she thought for a fleeting moment. *Dear Lord, I don't want to love you.* He lowered his head and kissed her eyelids, first one and then the other, tasting the salt of her tears and knowing that he couldn't deny himself any longer.

"I love you, Tiffany," he whispered, while his fingers strayed to the pearl buttons holding the bodice of her dress together, and his lips touched her neck, moving over the smooth skin and the rope of gold. His tongue pressed against the flickering pulse in the hollow of her throat.

"No." *If only she could trust him.*

"I've loved every minute I've spent with you…."

Each solitary button was slowly unbound, and the shimmery blue fabric of her dress parted in the night. Her straining breasts, covered only by a lacy, cream-colored camisole and the golden curtain of her hair, pressed upward. The dark points seductively invited him to conquer her, and Zane felt hot desire swelling uncomfortably in his loins at the dark impressions on the silky fabric.

He groaned at the sight of her. He slowly lowered his head to taste one of the ripe buds encased in silk. His tongue toyed with the favored nipple until Tiffany's heart was pounding so loudly it seemed to echo in the darkness. His hands caressed her, fired her blood, promised that their joining would be one of souls as well as flesh.

Somewhere in the distance, over the sound of Zane's labored breathing, she heard the sound of lapping water and the cry of a night bird, but everything she felt was because of Zane. Liquid fire ignited from deep within her and swirled upward through her pulsing veins.

His warm tongue moistened the lace and left it wet, to dry in the chill breeze. She shuddered, more from the want of him than the cold. When his hands lifted the dress over her head, she didn't protest.

Tenderly at first, and then more wildly, he stroked her breasts until she writhed beneath him, trying to get closer to the source of her exquisite torment. He removed the camisole slowly and then let his lips and teeth toy with one sweet, aching breast. Tiffany moaned throatily, from somewhere deep in her soul.

His tongue moistened the dark nipple until it hardened beautifully, and then he began to suckle ravenously, all the while touching the other breast softly, making it ready. Just when Tiffany thought she could stand no more of the sweet torment, he turned to the neglected breast and he feasted again.

"Oh, Zane," Tiffany cried, her fever for his love making demands upon her. She was empty, void, and only he could make her whole again.

His hands continued to stroke her while he slowly removed the remaining scanty pieces of her clothing. She felt her lace panties slide over her hips. Warm fingers traced the ridge of her spine and lingered at the swell of her hips.

He touched all of her, making her ready, while she slowly undressed him and ran her fingers hungrily over his naked chest. His muscles rippled beneath her touch, and she was in awe at the power her touch commanded.

He kicked off his jeans almost angrily and was only satisfied when he was finally lying atop her; hard male muscles pressed heatedly against their softer feminine counterparts.

The need in him was evident; his eyes were dark with desire, his breathing labored, his heartbeat thudding savaging against her flattened breasts. A thin sheen of sweat glistened over his supple muscles. His lips pressed hungrily, eagerly over hers.

"Let me love you, sweet lady," he coaxed, rubbing against her seductively, setting her skin aflame with his touch.

Her blood pulsed wildly in her veins. All thoughts of denial had fled long ago. The ache within her, burning with the need for fulfillment, throbbed with the want of him.

"Please," she whispered, closing her eyes against the glorious torment of his fingers kneading her buttocks.

Her fingers stroked him, and he cried out her name. He could withhold himself no longer.

With only a fleeting thought that this woman was the widow of Ellery Rhodes, he gently parted her legs and delved into the warmth of the woman he loved. His body joined with hers and he became one with the wife of the man he had vowed to destroy. He whispered her name, over and over again, as if his secret incantation could purge her from his soul.

He watched in fascination as she threw back her head and exposed the white column of her throat. Her fingernails dug into the muscles of his back before she shuddered in complete surrender. His explosion within her sent a series of shock waves through his body until he collapsed over her.

"I love you, Tiffany," he whispered, his breathing as raspy as the furious wind. He twined his fingers in her hair and let his head fall to the inviting hollow between her breasts. *Oh, but to die with this beautiful woman.*

Tiffany's entire body began to relax. The warmth within her seemed to spread into the night. Zane touched her chin with one long finger and kissed her lips.

Lying naked in the dark grass, with only the sounds of the night and the gentle whisper of Zane's breath, she felt whole. Large drops of rain began to fall from the black sky, but Tiffany didn't notice. She was only aware of Zane and his incredible touch. His fingers traced the curve of her cheek. "I meant it, you know," he whispered, smiling down at her.

"What?"

"That I love you."

Tiffany released a tormented sigh and pulled herself into a sitting position. "You don't have to say—"

His fingers wrapped possessively around her wrist and his eyes bored into hers. "I only say what I mean."

"Do you, Zane?" she asked, her face contorted in pain as the doubts of the morning and her conversation with Dustin invaded her mind. God, how desperately she wanted to believe him.

"What is it, Tiffany?" he asked, suddenly releasing her. "Ever since I arrived, I've gotten the feeling that something isn't right. What happened?"

Tiffany decided there was no better time for the truth than now. Before she became more hopelessly in love with him, she had to settle the past. She reached for her dress, but Zane restrained her. "I want answers, Tiffany."

"Not nearly as badly as I do." She pulled away from him and grabbed her clothes. As she quickly dressed, she began to talk. "I told Dustin that you had been here and expressed interest in buying the farm." The rain began in earnest, running down her face and neck in cold rivulets.

Zane's expression grew grim. "He wasn't too pleased about it, I'd guess."

"That's putting it mildly. He nearly fell through the floor."

"And what did he suggest?"

"That I shouldn't even consider selling to you. In fact, he seemed to think that I shouldn't have anything to do with you."

"He's afraid, Tiffany."

She began working on the buttons of her dress while Zane slipped on his jeans. "That's what I thought, too. At one point I was certain that Dustin was going to confess about switching horses and admit that Devil's Gambit is alive."

Zane was reaching for his shirt but stopped. "Did he?"

"No."

He slipped his arms through the sleeves but didn't bother with the buttons. His shirttails fluttered in the wind. "Then what, Tiffany? Just what the hell did he tell you that upset you so?"

Tiffany wrapped her arms around her breasts and stared at Zane. The wind caught her hair and lifted it off her face which was glistening with raindrops. "Dustin said that not only did you lose most of your money to Ellery in an honest poker game—"

"Honest my ass!"

"—but that Ellery also ran off with your wife."

Zane gritted his teeth together and rose. "Damn!" he

spit out as he stood and stared at the pond, legs spread apart, hands planted on his hips.

Tiffany's heart ached as she watched him. *Deny it, Zane,* she thought. *Tell me Dustin lied...anything...tell me again that you love me.*

"He told you only part of the story," Zane said. He walked over to the boulder and propped one foot on it as he stared across the small lake. "It's true, Stasia ran off with Ellery, and at the time I felt like killing them both."

He still loves her, Tiffany realized, and fresh tears slid down her cheek to mingle with the drops of rain.

"So did you come here looking for her?" she asked, her voice thick and raw.

"No."

"Then why?"

"I can't lie to you, Tiffany."

"You already have."

"No—"

"I asked you if you were married," she whispered.

"And I'm not."

"You just conveniently forgot that you had been?" She looked up at the cloudy sky. "You never even mentioned her."

"She's not something I like to think about," he confessed.

"But your feelings were strong enough to bring you here. You can't expect me to believe that you're not looking for her."

He walked over to the grassy knoll on which she was sitting, knelt down and placed his fingers over her shoulders. She quivered betrayingly at his familiar touch. "I knew she wouldn't be here, but yes, I need to find her."

Tiffany closed her eyes against the truth. "Why?"

"Because she's the only one who can clear up what happened to Devil's Gambit...and Ellery."

"Ellery is dead," Tiffany murmured, hugging her knees to her and setting her chin on them.

"How do you know?"

"I asked Dustin."

"He wouldn't tell you the truth—"

"Dustin cares about me, Zane. He admitted some pretty horrible things, such as conning other owners at the yearling sales in Europe. He said that Ellery would pose as another person, someone named Ethan Rivers."

"Did he explain about Devil's Gambit?"

"No."

"But?" he coaxed.

"From his reaction, I'd have to guess that your assumption about Devil's Gambit is correct. He wouldn't admit that Devil's Gambit was alive, but it was fairly obvious when I mentioned King's Ransom and Devil's Gambit in the same breath that something wasn't right."

"You should be more careful around him," Zane warned. "He's dangerous, and he has a lot to lose if he's uncovered."

"I'm not sure that he's the man in charge."

"What do you mean?"

"I don't know, just a feeling I got that there was someone else pulling his strings."

"I don't know who it would be."

"Neither do I."

"That's why I have to find Stasia," Zane said. "She might be able to help us."

"I doubt it."

Zane lifted his head and his sharp eyes bored into Tiffany. "You knew her?" he guessed incredulously.

Tiffany nodded, remembering Stasia's long, dark hair, even features and seductive dark eyes. Stasia's sultry beauty was enough to capture any man, including Zane. "She was here on the farm with Ellery when I was in college. Later, once I had returned, my father died and Ellery asked me to marry him."

"What happened to Stasia?"

"I don't know. Ellery wouldn't talk about it. The day after he asked me to marry him, she moved out. I never saw her again, but I'm sure that she despises me."

"Probably," he said with a snort. "Stasia knows how to carry a grudge." He saw the unasked questions in Tiffany's wide eyes and began to explain about a time in his life he would rather have forgotten.

"When I met Stasia, she was barely eighteen. She was beautiful and anxious to get out of a bad home situation. I thought at the time that I was in love with her, and we got married. I was just starting then, trying to set up a successful farm of my own. Fortunately, I had a few decent breaks. I was lucky and after a few years, I...we, Stasia and I, owned a small farm about thirty miles from Dublin. It was a beautiful place," he said, smiling slightly at the fond memories, "thick green grass, stone fences twined with bracken, the rolling Irish countryside...a perfect place for breeding Thoroughbreds. That's when I started breeding successfully. And how I met Ethan Rivers."

"Ellery," Tiffany whispered.

Zane's smile had left his face and his rugged features pulled into a dark scowl. "One and the same. It happened about six years ago. Ethan was looking for some yearlings and came out to the farm. Later that night we began drinking and playing poker with another man from America who was supposedly interested in some of my horses."

"Dustin," Tiffany guessed, not daring to breathe.

"Right again. Anyway, on that night, Dustin folded early, claimed the stakes were too high for him. But I kept on drinking and playing, urged on by my lovely wife."

"Oh, no—"

"That's right. Stasia was already involved with Ethan Rivers, and when I lost it cost me two hundred thousand dollars. I had to sell the farm to pay Rivers off."

"But if you thought the game was crooked—"

"I didn't. Not then. Only much later, when I went back to that pub and got to talking to one of the regulars, I learned that the old man, who was named O'Brien, had watched the game and thought it might be rigged. A few days later, he'd overheard Dustin and his brother talking—about the game and Stasia."

"Why didn't he talk to you sooner?" she asked. "There must have been plenty of time before you sold the farm."

"O'Brien was caught eavesdropping by Ellery. Ellery was furious that he might be found out, and he threatened the old man with his life. O'Brien didn't doubt for a minute that Ellery would make good his threats to kill both him and his wife. By the time his conscience got the better of him and he found me, I'd managed to sell the farm."

"Who would buy it so quickly?"

Zane's jaw became rigid and his eyes turned deadly. "A corporation."

Tiffany finally understood, and her throat went dry with dread. "Emerald Enterprises."

"That's right. The farm I used to own now belongs to Dustin and Ellery, if he's still alive."

"Oh, God, Zane," she murmured, covering her face with her hands. *Had she been so young and foolish that she had never seen Ellery for what he really was?* She lifted her eyes and felt her hands curl into fists of frustration. "I don't understand. Knowing how you must feel about him, why would Dustin allow you to breed any of your mares to King's Ransom?"

"First of all, I didn't know that Emerald Enterprises was Dustin Rhodes. The original sale of the farm was handled through a broker, and neither Dustin's name nor Ellery's ever appeared on any of the documents. As for Dustin, either he's just gotten cocky and doesn't think he'll be discovered, or maybe he thinks I've buried the hatchet. After all, I have been able to put myself back on my feet. It took several years, mind you, but I was able to start again. I didn't lose everything when I sold the farm, and I managed to keep two good mares and a stallion."

"And from those three horses, you started again?"

"Yes. Fortunately I'd already established myself as a breeder. The three good horses and my reputation gave me a decent start."

"And...and your wife?"

"She left me immediately. I suspected that she'd followed Ethan—who I later found out was Ellery—to America. When Stasia filed for divorce, I didn't fight her.

"I spent the next several years working to reestablish myself."

"And you never forgot taking your revenge on Ellery," Tiffany whispered as thunder rumbled in the distant hills.

"No. That's the reason I came here. When I heard that Ellery had married, I assumed that it was to Stasia." Zane walked back to the lake and stared across the black water, watching as the raindrops beat a staccato rhythm on the clear surface. "Of course later I learned that he had married a woman by the name of Tiffany Chappel."

"And you wondered what had become of your ex-wife." Tiffany felt a sudden chill as she finally understood Zane's motives. He had come looking for Stasia....

"Yeah, I wondered, but I found that I really didn't give a damn." He shrugged his broad shoulders. "The next thing I heard about Ellery Rhodes was that he, along with his famous horse, had been killed. My fever for revenge had cooled, and I decided to put the past behind me."

"Until you found the horse you think is Devil's Gambit."

"The horse I *know* is Devil's Gambit."

Zane hazarded a glance at the threatening sky before looking back at Tiffany and noticing that she was shivering.

"Come on," he suggested softly. "We'd better get inside before we're both soaked to the skin."

Tiffany refused to be deterred when she was so close to the truth. Her emotions were as raw as the wind blowing over the mountains. Everything Zane was suggesting was too far-fetched, and yet parts of his story were true. Even Dustin had backed him up. She ran shaky fingers through her hair and watched his silhouetted form as he advanced on her and stared down at her with bold gray eyes.

"When I figured out the scam that Ellery and his brother had pulled, I knew he had to be stopped. Using one stud in place of another, and falsifying the death of Devil's Gambit is a scandal of international proportions."

"Then you think that Ellery is still alive?" she murmured, feeling lost and alone.

"That, I'm not sure of."

"Dear God," she whispered, sagging against him. Had she just made love to a man while still married to another? Guilt and fear darkened her heart. "I don't think he's alive," she murmured.

"Because Dustin says so?" he asked cynically.

"Yes. And because I don't believe that Dustin or Ellery would have let another man die in that trailer." The image of the truck carrying Devil's Gambit, as well as Ellery, charred and twisted beyond recognition, filled her mind and she shuddered.

Zane placed comforting arms over her shoulders and kissed her rain-sodden hair before urging her forward, toward the path that led to the house. "You have to face the fact that your husband might still be alive," he whispered.

"I...I don't—"

"Shh!" Zane whispered, cutting off her thought. He cocked his head to one side and listened.

"What?" Tiffany heard the faint sound rumbling in the distance, barely audible over the rising wind. With a sickening feeling, she recognized the noise. "Oh, no!" The sound became louder and more clear. Thundering hooves pounded the wet earth, charging through the pastures with lightning speed. "One of the horses is loose," she said, turning toward the direction of the sound and trying to break free of Zane's arms.

"Wait." Zane restrained her just as the black horse broke through the trees and bolted toward the lake. He raced to the edge of the pond with his ebony tail hoisted and his long legs stretching with boundless energy.

"Moon Shadow," Tiffany whispered, her heart pounding with dread as she watched the magnificent creature rear and whirl on his hind legs when he reached the water's edge.

Tiffany started toward him, all her thoughts centered on the horse and how he could injure himself by slipping on the wet grass. Zane's fingers tightened over her arm. "I'll go after the horse, you call the police."

"The police?" Tiffany's mind was racing with the stallion.

"If he gets out and onto the road, it could get dangerous. Not only for him, but for motorists as well."

"Oh, God. I don't think he can get out," she said, trying to convince herself. Shielding her eyes against the rain, she squinted into the darkness, searching the black night, trying to recall the boundaries of the farm. The horse splashed in the water and started off at a dead run to the opposite side of the pond.

"What's on the other side of the lake?" Zane pointed in the direction in which Moon Shadow disappeared.

"Nothing…some trees, it's all fenced."

"No gate?" He started to follow the stallion, his long legs accelerating with each of his strides.

"Yes, but it should be closed."

"Good. With any luck, I'll be able to catch him." Zane chased after the horse while Tiffany turned toward the buildings near the house.

Her heart was pounding as she ran through the open field, stumbling twice when her heels caught in the mud. Once, when she fell, she heard her dress rip, but didn't bother to see how bad the damage was. All her thoughts centered on Moon Shadow. *Who had let him out? Was it carelessness on the part of the stable boy or...what?* At the sinister turn of her thoughts, she raced more quickly. *No one would let the prized stallion out on purpose!*

Once she made it to the stallion barn, her heart hammering, her lungs burning for air, she noticed that the door to Moon Shadow's stall was swinging outward. It caught in the wind and banged loudly against the building. Other stallions within the building stamped nervously and snorted at the strange sounds.

Tiffany hurried inside and with numb fingers, flipped on the lights, flooding the building with illumination. The horses moved restlessly in their stalls.

As quickly as her trembling fingers could punch out the number, she called Mac. Rain peppered the roof of the barn as she counted the rings…three, four, five… "Come on," she urged. Finally the trainer answered.

"'Lo," Mac called into the phone.

"Moon Shadow's out," Tiffany explained breathlessly to the trainer. "His stall was unlatched and he bolted."

Mac swore loudly. "Where is he?"

"I don't know," she replied, trying to remain calm. Her chest was heaving, her words broken, her heart thudding with fear. "He took off past the old barn and the pond."

"God in heaven," Mac whispered. "We've been workin' on that fence on the other edge of the lake."

Tiffany swallowed hard against the dread creeping up her throat. "Is it down?" she whispered, her fingers clenched around the receiver.

"I don't think so...." He didn't sound too sure.

"What about the gate?"

"It should be closed."

"But you're not certain?"

Mac swore roundly and then sighed. "I'll be right over. Is anyone else around?"

"Just Zane. Everyone went home for the night."

"I'll call John and a few of the other stable hands that live close. We'll be at the house in ten minutes."

"I'll meet you there."

She hung up and then dialed the number of the local police. Within minutes she was explaining her situation to the officer on the other end of the line.

When she had finished with the phone call, Tiffany hurried outside and listened to the sounds of the night. The rain was beginning to sheet and run on the pavement. It gurgled in the gutters and downspouts. In the distance, faint to her ears, she heard the sound of running hoofbeats...on asphalt.

"Oh God," she swore in desperation. *Moon Shadow was on the road!*

Tiffany began running down the long driveway toward the county road that bordered the farm. She heard the truck before she saw it, the loud engine reverberating through the night.

"No," she cried, spurred even faster. Her legs were

numb, her lungs burning. Headlights flashed between the trees bordering the farm, and the roar of the truck's engine filled the night.

She heard the squeal of locked brakes, and the sound of the truck's dull horn as it slid out of control on the wet pavement.

"Moon Shadow!" Tiffany shrieked over the deafening noise.

A stallion squealed, the truck tore through the trees, crashing against the solid wood until finally there was nothing but silence and the sound of the pouring rain.

"Oh, God, no," Tiffany whispered as she raced to the end of the drive. Tears blurred her vision and her voice seemed distant when she screamed. *"Zane..."*

CHAPTER ELEVEN

TIFFANY RACED DOWN the slick pavement of the county road, mindless of the rain running down her back. The smell of burning rubber filled the night and the truck's headlights angled awkwardly up through the broken branches of the giant oaks, like a pair of macabre searchlights, announcing the place of the accident.

As she approached, all she could hear was her own ragged breath and running footsteps. "Zane, dear God, where are you?" she screamed, listening for a sound, any sound indicating there was life in the wreckage. Her mind filled with a dozen bloody scenarios involving Zane and Moon Shadow, but she pushed her horrible thoughts aside and dashed toward the jackknifed truck.

"Goddam it, man, what the hell was that horse doing loose?" a gravelly voice demanded. The truck driver was crawling out of the cab and swearing profusely. Rain poured down upon him, and the broken branches of the trees snapped as he stepped onto the road.

Zane must be alive! Who else would be absorbing the angry trucker's wrath?

Tiffany made it to the wrecked truck. Her heart was thudding wildly in her chest, and she had to gasp for air. The truck was lying on its side, the cab at an awkward angle. It looked like some great downed beast

with a broken neck. In her mind's eye Tiffany saw another truck, the rig that had taken Ellery and Devil's
Gambit from Florida to Kentucky, the one that had
rolled over and burst into flame, killing both horse and
driver. Her stomach turned over at the painful memory.

From inside the cab the sound of a CB's static
pierced the darkness and brought her thoughts crashing to the present.

"Zane?" she cried, looking into the darkness,
searching for any sign of the man and the horse.

"Hey, lady! Over here!" The large truck driver commanded her attention by calling out in his gravelly
voice. "What're you doin' out here? Jesus, God, you're
soaked to the skin!"

"Zane... My horse—"

"That black son of a bitch? He's your goddamn
horse?" His agitated swearing continued. "Christ,
woman, can't you see what that horse of yours did?
He ran right up the road here—" the trucker pointed
a burly arm toward the bend in the road "—like some
demon. Scared the hell out of me, let me tell you."

"He got out.... I'm sorry...." She looked around
frantically, dread still taking a stranglehold of her
throat. "Where is he...? Where is Zane?"

"Who the hell is Zane? The horse?"

"No!"

"Tiffany," Zane shouted from somewhere in the
thick stand of oak and fir trees near the road. Tiffany's
head snapped in the direction of the familiar sound,
her heart nearly skipped a beat and relief washed over
her in soothing rivulets.

Without another glance at the truck driver, who was
busy clearing debris from the road and placing warn-

ing flares near his truck, Tiffany hurried toward the familiar welcome of Zane's voice.

Then she saw him. Wet, bedraggled, mud-streaked and walking toward her. He was leading a lathered Moon Shadow, who skittered and danced at all the commotion he had inadvertently caused. "Oh, God, Zane," she cried, "you're alive."

Without further thought, she ran to him and threw her arms around his neck. "I thought… Oh, God, I heard the horse and the truck. I was sure that…" Tears began running freely down her face, and she sobbed brokenly, clinging to him.

"Shh." He wrapped one strong arm around her and kissed her forehead, smearing mud on her face. "I'm all right, and I think Moon Shadow will be, too. But you'd better have the vet look at him. He's limping a little."

"What happened?" she asked, refusing to let go of the man she loved, letting her body feel his, confirming that he was here, alive and unhurt. Rain glistened in his ebony hair, sweat trickled down his jutted chin and a scarlet streak of dried blood cut across his hollowed cheek. Still he was the most ruggedly handsome man she had ever known.

"The fence was down. I followed Moon Shadow through it and called to him, but he wouldn't listen."

"Of course," Tiffany replied, patting the horse's sweaty neck fondly. "He never does."

"He just took off down the road. Bolted as if he were jumping out of the starting gate. I heard the truck coming and tried to stop him by cutting across a field. That's when I got this." He pointed to the ugly slash on his face. "When I realized I didn't have a prayer of catching him in time, I called to the horse and yelled at the truck driver, waving my arms, hoping to catch his eye. Even though I was farther down the road, I thought the driver might see my shirt before the black horse. Anyway, Moon Shadow jumped over the ditch and ran into the trees just as the truck hit the brakes."

"Hey, you think I could get some help over here?" the furious trucker shouted.

Zane went to help the driver just as Mac's old Dodge rumbled down the road. After parking the pickup some distance from the mangled truck and trailer, Mac scrambled out of the Dodge. "Holy Mother of God," he whispered as he eyed the wrecked truck. He expelled a long whistle and grabbed the lead rope from the front seat of his pickup. "What the devil happened?"

Then he saw Moon Shadow. Knowing that Zane and the trucker were doing everything that could be done with the truck, Mac walked over to Tiffany and snapped a lead rope onto Moon Shadow's wet halter. "Well, Missy," he said, eyeing the wrecked truck. "It looks as if you've had yourself quite a night." His eyes narrowed as he surveyed the anxious stallion.

"One I wouldn't want to repeat," she admitted. "Zane says Moon Shadow's walking with a misstep," she said. "Left hind leg."

"Let's take a look at him." Mack talked to the horse while he ran his fingers down his back and along each leg. "Yep, it's a little tender," Mac decided. "But I don't think anything's broken, probably bruised himself, maybe a pulled tendon. I'll take him back to the barn, cool him down and check for any other injuries." He tugged on the rope, and Moon Shadow tossed his great black head. "I always said *you* should have been the one named Devil's something or other," Mac grumbled affectionately to the nervous stallion.

The sound of a siren pierced the night and increased in volume. Bright, flashing lights announced the arrival of the state police. A young officer parked his car, leaving the lights flashing in warning, and walked stiffly toward the crumpled truck. "What happened here?" he demanded.

"One of the horses got out," Zane replied, tossing a broken branch off the road.

"And I damned near hit him," the trucker added with a shake of his head. "Just lucky that I didn't."

The officer's suspicious eyes moved from Zane to Tiffany. "Are you the lady who called?"

"Yes."

"*Before* the accident?"

"That's right. I was afraid something like this might happen."

The officer studied the wreckage and whistled. "Where's the horse?"

"Over here." Mac led Moon Shadow to the officer. The black stallion shied away from the flashing lights of the police car, and reared on his back legs. The lead rope tightened in Mac's hands, but he began to talk to the horse and gently led him away from the crowd.

"Blends in with the night," Officer Sparks remarked, watching the nervous black stallion shy away from the crumpled vehicle. The policeman turned his hard eyes back on Tiffany. "How'd he get out?"

"Someone left the stall door unlatched, and he found a hole in a fence we're repairing."

"Wait a minute, let's start at the beginning." He

walked back to his car, reached for a notepad on the dash and began writing quickly.

"Why don't we do this inside," Zane suggested, "where it's warmer and drier?"

The young officer pursed his lips together and nodded. "Fine. Just let me take a few measurements and report what happened on the radio. Then we'll call a tow company and see if we can get this rig moved."

Three hours later the ordeal was nearly over. After two cups of coffee and what seemed to be a thousand questions, the police officer was satisfied that he could accurately report what had happened. The trucker had taken the name of Tiffany's insurance company and had left with the towtruck driver, who had driven up with a truck similar in size to the wrecked rig. Moon Shadow was back in his stall and Mac had attended to his injury, which turned out to be a strained tendon. With Zane's help, Mac had applied a pressure bandage and called Vance, who had promised to stop by in the morning and examine the horse.

"You're sure Moon Shadow's all right?" Tiffany asked the trainer. She was just coming back into the kitchen. After the police officer and the trucker had left, she had gone upstairs, showered and changed into her bathrobe. Her hair was still wet, but at least she was clean and warm.

"He'll be fine," Mac assured her. He was sitting at the table and finishing his last cup of coffee.

"Where's Zane?"

Mac scowled at the mention of the Irishman. "He went to clean up. Same as you." He looked as if he were about to say something and changed his mind. "He knows horses, that one."

"Who? Zane?"

"Aye."

"I think he's worked with them all his life." Tiffany poured herself a cup of the strong coffee and took a sip as she leaned against the counter. "Mac, is something bothering you?" Tiffany asked, her brows drawing together in concern. "Is Moon Shadow all right?"

Mac was quick to put her fears to rest. "Oh, I imagine he'll have a few stiff muscles tomorrow, and it won't hurt to have Vance take a look at him. But I think he'll be fine."

"Great," Tiffany said with a relieved sigh.

Just then, Zane strode into the kitchen, wearing only a clean pair of jeans and a T-shirt that stretched across his chest and didn't hide the ripple of his muscles as he moved. He had washed his face and the scratch there was only minor.

"Another cup?" Tiffany asked, handing Zane a mug filled with the steaming brew.

"Thanks."

Mac rotated his mug between both of his hands and stared into the murky liquid. He pressed his thin lips together and then lifted his head, eyeing both Tiffany and Zane.

"Now, Missy," he said, "who do ya suppose let Moon Shadow out?"

Tiffany was surprised by the question. She lifted her shoulders slightly. "I don't know. I think it was probably just an oversight by one of the stable hands."

"Do ya, now?"

"Why? You think someone let him out on purpose?" Tiffany's smile faded and a deep weariness stole over her. So much had happened in one day and she was bone tired.

Mac reached for his hat and placed the slightly damp fedora on his head. "I checked the stallion barn myself earlier. Moon Shadow was locked in his stall."

Tiffany dropped her head into her hand. "I don't want to think about this," she whispered quietly, "not now."

"I think you have to, Missy," Mac said. "Someone deliberately let the stallion out."

"Buy why?"

"That one I can't answer." His gaze moved to Zane. "You wouldn't know anything about it, would you?"

Zane's gray eyes turned to steel. "Of course not."

"Just askin'," Mac explained. "You were here when it happened." He rubbed his hand over his chin. "And the way I understand it, you had a grudge against Ellery Rhodes."

"That was a long time ago," Zane replied.

"Aye. And now you're here. Pokin' around hopin' to buy the place." He shot a warning glance to Tiffany.

"Mac," she said, horrified that he would consider Zane a suspect. "Zane caught Moon Shadow tonight. If it hadn't been for him, the horse might be dead."

Mac rubbed the tired muscles in the back of his neck and frowned. "I know you're a fine horse breeder," he said to Zane. "You have the reputation to back you up, but sometimes, when revenge or a woman's involved, well…a man's head can get all turned around."

"I would never do anything to jeopardize a horse," Zane stated calmly. "And I care too much for Tiffany to do anything that might harm her." His voice was low and deadly. His indignant eyes impaled the old trainer.

Mac managed to crack a smile. "All right, Sheridan. I believe you. Now, can you tell me what you think is going on around here? It seems to me that someone is trying to sabotage the operation. Who would do that? Maybe a man interested in buying a farm and gathering a little revenge to boot?" With his final remark, Mac pushed his chair away from the table. The legs scraped against the wooden floor. After straightening his tired muscles, he turned toward the back porch. He paused at the door, his hand poised on the knob, and glanced over his shoulder at Tiffany. "And just for the record I'll be sleeping in the stallion barn tonight. Wouldn't want to have another 'accident,' would we?"

"You don't have to—"

"I'm sleeping in the barn, Missy," Mac insisted. "That's all right with you, isn't it?"

"Of course, but really, there's no need…."

Mac tugged on the brim of the fedora over his eyes before stepping outside. Tiffany heard his footsteps fade as he walked down the back steps.

"Mac's grasping at straws," Tiffany said, feeling the need to explain and apologize to Zane. She lifted her palms and managed a frail smile. "He…he's just trying to find an explanation."

"And I'm the logical choice."

"Everyone else has been with the farm for years, and, well, Mac's a little suspicious when it comes to strangers."

Zane set his empty cup on the counter and rammed his hands into his pockets. His eyes narrowed, and his lower jaw jutted forward. "And what do you think, Tiffany?"

She lifted trusting eyes to his. "I *know* you didn't let Moon Shadow out."

"So who did?"

"God, I don't know. I'm not really sure I want to. I'm just so damned tired..." She felt her shoulders slump and forced her back to stiffen. "If I had to guess I'd say that it was probably just some kids who broke into the place and thought they'd get their kicks by letting the horse out."

"Not just any horse," he reminded her. "Moon Shadow."

"He's been getting a lot of attention lately."

"How would the kids know where to find Moon Shadow?"

"His picture's been in the paper."

"And at night, to an untrained eye, Moon Shadow looks like any other black horse."

"But—"

"What about your security system?" Zane demanded.

"You said yourself that the fence was down."

"Wouldn't that dog of yours bark his head off if a stranger started poking around the place?" he demanded, daring her to ignore the logic of his thinking.

"I...I guess so."

"You see," he surmised, "there are too many unanswered questions. I don't blame Mac for thinking I was involved." He raked his fingers through his hair and let out an exasperated sigh.

"He's just worried...about me."

"So am I." Zane's arms circled her waist and he leaned his forehead against hers. "Someone's trying to ruin you and I think I know who."

Tiffany squeezed her eyes shut and shook her head, denying his suggestion before he had a chance to speak. "Dustin," she thought aloud, "you think he's behind all this?"

"No question about it."

"But he's in Florida—"

"Is he?"

Tiffany hesitated. She hadn't actually seen Dustin get on a plane. "Journey's End races the day after tomorrow."

"And Dustin was here this morning." His strong, protective arms drew her close. "If you do have a saboteur, sweet lady, I'm willing to bet on your brother-in-law."

"Just because one horse got out—"

"And four foals died."

"No!" Tiffany tried to jerk away but couldn't. His powerful arms flexed and imprisoned her to him.

"And the story was leaked to the press."

"It wasn't leaked—we never tried to hide what was happening with the foals." She sprang instantly to Dustin's defense. No matter what else had happened, Dustin was the man who had helped her when Ellery had died. "Dustin himself was concerned about the story in the papers. That's why he came back."

"So he claimed."

"You're just trying to find someone, anyone, to blame all this on!"

"No, Tiffany, no," he whispered, his breath fanning her damp hair. "I'm trying to make you understand the only logical explanation. If you think Dustin's so innocent, what about Devil's Gambit and King's Ransom?"

"I...I can't explain that."

"What about the fact that Ellery may still be alive?"

"But he's not—"

"We're not sure about that," Zane said slowly, making no attempt to release her. She sagged wearily against him. "But we both know that Dustin posed as a rival bidder, interested in Ethan Rivers's horses, when in fact Ethan was Ellery and Dustin was his brother. Dustin admitted to bidding on his own horses, just to drive the prices up."

Tiffany's throat went dry. "But I just can't believe that Dustin would try and ruin our operation. It doesn't make any sense. He owns part of the farm."

Zane's voice was firm. "Has it ever occurred to you that Dustin might want to own it all? Hasn't he already offered to buy you out?"

"Only because he thought it was too much for me," she whispered, but the seeds of distrust had been planted, and she hated the new feelings of doubt that were growing in her mind. Three weeks ago she would have trusted Dustin with her life. Now, because of Zane's accusations, she was beginning to doubt the only person she could call family. She shuddered, and Zane gathered her still closer, pressing her face against his chest.

"I'm not saying that Dustin doesn't care for you," he said, gently stroking her hair.

"Just that he's using me."

"He's the kind of man who would do just about anything to get what he wants."

She shook her head and stared out the window. Raindrops ran down the paned glass. "Funny, that's just what he said about you."

Gently Zane lifted her chin with his finger, silently

forcing her to look into his eyes. "I've done a few things in my life that I'm not proud of," he admitted. "But I've never cheated or lied to anyone."

"Except me?" Tears began to scald her eyes.

"I didn't lie about Stasia."

"You omitted the facts, Zane. In order to deceive me. Call it what you will. In my book, it's lying."

A small muscle worked in the corner of his jaw, and he had to fight the urge to shake her, make her see what was so blindingly clear to him. He couldn't. He'd wounded her enough as it was. Tiffany seemed to stare right through him. "I've never wanted anyone the way I want you, Tiffany," he whispered. "I wouldn't do anything that would ever make you doubt me."

Her throat tightened painfully, and she squeezed her eyes against the hot tears forming behind her eyelids. "I want to trust you, Zane. God, I want to trust you," she admitted. "It's just that you've come here when everything seems to be falling apart…"

"And you blame me?"

"No!"

"Then look at me, damn it!" he insisted. Her eyes opened and caught in his silvery stare. "I love you, Tiffany Rhodes, and I'll do everything in my power to prove it."

She held up a protesting palm before he could say anything else. She felt so open and raw. Though he was saying the words she longed to hear, she couldn't believe him.

He took her trembling hand and covered it with his. "You're going to listen to me, lady," he swore. "Ever since I met you that first morning when Rod Crawford was here, you've doubted me. I can't say that I blame you because I came here with the express purpose of taking your farm from you…by any means possible."

Her eyes widened at his admission.

"But all that changed," he conceded, "when I met you and began to fall in love with you."

"I…I wish I could believe you," Tiffany whispered. "More than *anything* I want to believe you." Her voice was raspy and thick with emotion. She felt as if her heart were bursting, and she knew that she was admitting far more than she should.

His fingers tightened over her shoulders. *"Believe."*

"Oh, Zane…"

"Tiffany, please. Listen. I want you to marry me."

The words settled in the kitchen and echoed in Tiffany's mind. Her knees gave way and she fell against him. "I want you to be my wife, bear my children, stand at my side…." He kissed the top of her head. "I want you to be with me forever."

She felt the tears stream down her face, and she wondered if they were from joy or sadness. "I can't," she choked. "I can't until I know for certain that Ellery is dead."

Zane's back stiffened. "I thought you were convinced."

"I am." Her voice trembled. "But what if there's a chance that he's *alive*?"

His arms wrapped around her in desperation, and he buried his head into the hollow of her shoulder. "I'll find out," he swore, one fist clenching in determination. "Once and for all, I'll find out just what happened to your husband."

"And if he's alive?" she whispered.

"He'll wish he were dead for the hell he's put you through."

She shook her head and pushed herself out of his possessive embrace. "No, Zane. If Ellery's alive, he's still my husband."

"A husband who used and betrayed you." Anger stormed in his eyes, and his muscles tensed at the thought of Ellery Rhodes claiming Tiffany as his wife after all these years. *The man couldn't possibly be alive!*

"But my husband nonetheless."

"You're still in love with him," he charged.

"No," she admitted, closing her eyes against the traitorous truth. "The only man I've ever loved is you."

Zane relaxed a bit and gently kissed her eyelids. "Trust me, Tiffany. Trust me to take care of you, no matter what happens in the future." He reached for her and savagely pressed her body to his, lowering his head and letting his lips capture hers.

Willingly, her arms encircled his neck, and she let her body fit against his. The warmth of him seemed to seep through her clothes and generate a new heat in her blood.

When his tongue rimmed her lips, she shuddered. "I love you, Zane," she murmured as her breath mingled and caught with his. "And I want to be with you."

He leaned over and placed an arm under the crook of her knees before lifting her off the floor and carrying her out of the kitchen. She let her head rest against his shoulder and wondered at the sanity of loving such a passionate man. Zane's emotions, whether love or hate, ran deep.

Carefully he mounted the stairs and carried her to

her bedroom. Rain slid down the windows and the room was illuminated only by the shadowy light from the security lamps near the barns. "I never wanted to fall in love with you," he admitted as he stood her near the bed and his fingers found the knot to the belt of her robe. Slowly the ties loosened, and he pushed the robe over her shoulders to expose the satiny texture of her skin.

She was naked except for a silky pair of panties. Zane kissed her lips, the hollow of her throat, the dark stiffening tips of each gorgeous breast as he lowered himself to his knees.

She wanted to fall to the floor with him, but his hands held her upright as slowly he removed the one scanty piece of cloth keeping her from him. His fingers lingered on her skin and rubbed her calves and thighs as he kissed her abdomen, moistening the soft skin with his tongue. His eyes closed, and Tiffany felt his eyelashes brush her navel. Tingling sensations climbed upward through her body, heating her blood as it raced through her veins.

The heat within her began to turn liquid as his tongue circled her navel. Tiffany's knees felt weak, and if it hadn't been for the strong arms supporting her, she would have slid to the floor and entwined herself with him.

Zane's hands reached upward and touched the pointed tip of one swollen breast. It hardened expectantly against the soft pressure of his fingers and Tiffany closed her eyes against the urge to lie with him. Zane groaned against her abdomen, and his hot breath warmed her skin.

"Zane," she pleaded, the sound coming from deep

in her throat as her fingers caught in his black hair. "Love me."

"I do, sweet lady," he murmured against her skin, his warm hands pressing against the small of her back, pushing her closer to him.

As if in slow motion, he forced her backward, and she fell onto the bed. Her hair splayed against the comforter in tangled disarray. Her cheeks were flushed, as were her proud breasts with their alluring dark peaks.

As she watched him, Zane quickly removed and discarded his clothes. When completely naked, he came to her. Lying beside her elegant nude body, he caught his fingers in the silken tresses of her hair and rolled atop her. Corded male muscles strained against hers as he captured one blossoming nipple in his mouth. His tongue slid enticingly over the soft mound, and she cradled his head against her, moaning in contentment as he suckled. Her breasts, swollen with desire, ached for his soothing touch, yearned for the tenderness of his lips and tongue.

"Tiffany, I love you," he vowed as his hands roved over her skin, exploring the exquisite feel of her. His lips murmured words of love against her ear, forcing the heat within her to expand until she could stand the torment no longer.

"Please," she whispered into his ear, her fingers running over the smooth skin of his upper arms and back, feeling the ripple of solid muscles as he positioned himself above her. "Now!"

The ache in his loins throbbed for release, and he took her eagerly, becoming one with her in the heated splendor of his love. His lovemaking was violent, explosive, as he claimed her for his own and purged from her body forever any thoughts of the one man who had betrayed them both.

Tiffany soared to the heavens, her soul melding with Zane's as the clouds of passion burst open and showered her in hot bursts of satiation. She shuddered against his hard male frame; her love for him was complete and infinite. Tiffany knew that no matter what the future held, she would never stop loving him.

"I love you," she heard him vow again and again. Listening to the wonderful sound, she smiled and curled her body close to his to fall into a deep, exhausted sleep.

It was barely dawn when Tiffany awakened. She reached for Zane, but he was gone. The bed sheets were cold. Thoughts of the night before began swimming in her sleepy mind; then she heard him walk back into the room.

"Zane?" she murmured, groggily trying to focus her eyes.

He came to the bed and sat on the edge near her. "I didn't mean to wake you."

He was completely dressed, as if he were leaving. "What's going on?" she asked, glancing at the clock. It was only five-thirty. Even Mac didn't start work until after six.

"I have to go."

"Where?"

"Back to San Francisco."

She looked into his eyes and saw the sadness lingering in the gray depths. "Why?" she asked, forcing herself into a sitting position. She tugged at the comforter to cover her naked breasts and then leaned forward so that her face was near his. Something was wrong. She could feel it. In the course of a few short hours, Zane's feelings toward her had changed. Her heart, filled with love of the last few hours, twisted painfully.

"I have things I have to do," he said. "You'll just have to trust me."

"Does this have anything to do with Dustin?" she asked, shivering from the cold morning air.

"I don't know." He placed a warm hand on her shoulder. "Just trust me, okay?"

She nodded and forced a frail smile. "You'll be back?"

He laughed and broke the tension in the room. "As soon as I can. If I'm not back in a couple of days, I'll call."

"Promises, promises," she quipped, trying to sound lighthearted. He was leaving. Her heart seemed to wither inside her.

"I left the phone number of my hotel on the notepad in the kitchen. If you get lonely—"

"I already am." Lovingly she touched the red scratch on his face. "My hero," she whispered with a seductive smile.

"Hardly."

She curled her hand around his neck and pulled his face next to hers.

"Look, lady, if you don't cut this out, I'll never get out of here," he growled, but a pleased grin stole over his angular features to charmingly display the hint of straight white teeth against his dark skin.

"That's the idea."

Zane let out an exasperated sigh. "Oh, Tiffany, what am I going to do with you?"

"I don't know," she murmured against his ear as her fingers began working at the buttons of his shirt. "Use your imagination."

An hour later he was gone, and Tiffany felt more alone than she ever had in her life. She was more alone than she had been on the morning her mother had abandoned her, for then she had still had Edward, and when her father had died, she had married Ellery. When Ellery was suddenly killed, Tiffany had relied on Dustin.

Now, as she cinched the belt of her robe more tightly around her waist and stared out the window at the rain-washed countryside, Tiffany was completely alone. She had no one to rely upon but herself. She shivered more from dread than from the morning air, and she watched as Zane's car roared to life and disappeared through the trees.

CHAPTER TWELVE

AFTER ZANE HAD gone, Tiffany found it impossible to return to bed. Instead she dressed and walked outside, stopping only to scratch Wolverine behind the ears. The dog responded by wagging his tail enthusiastically.

"Some hero you are," Tiffany reprimanded fondly. "Where were you last night when I needed you?"

She refilled Wolverine's bowls and walked to the stallion barn. The rain had become no more than a drizzle, but the ground was still wet, and when she ventured off the pavement, her boots sank into the soaked earth.

Mac was already up and checking on Moon Shadow's injury.

"So how is he?" Tiffany asked, patting the black stallion's neck and forcing a smile at the grizzled old trainer. Mac had slept in his clothes and it was obvious from the way he was walking that his arthritis was bothering him.

"Moon Shadow?" He pointed a thumb in the direction of the horse's head. "He's fine."

"And you?"

"Getting too old for all this excitement."

"Why don't you take a day off?" Tiffany asked. "You deserve it."

"Not now, Missy," he said, shaking his head. "What

would I do while the missus knits and watches those soap operas? Nope. I'm better off here. 'Sides, I want to see what Vance has to say after he looks this old boy over." Mac gently slapped Moon Shadow's rump, and the stallion snorted and tossed his head in the air.

"I thought I'd check on Shadow's Survivor next," Tiffany said.

"Good idea."

Mac walked with her and Wolverine trotted along behind. The rain had stopped and the clouds were beginning to break apart, promising a warm spring day. Tiffany realized for the first time that the flowering trees were beginning to bloom. Pink and white blossoms colored the leafless trees with the promise of spring.

"Say, Missy," Mac said as they approached the foaling shed.

"Yes?"

"I noticed that Sheridan's car is gone."

"He left early this morning."

"Because of what I said last night?"

"No." Tiffany shook her head and smiled sadly.

"I was out of line."

"You were concerned. We all were...are." She ran her fingers through her hair and squared her shoulders. "Something's got to give, doesn't it? We can't go on this way much longer."

Mac frowned and reached for the handle of the door. "You're right—it's time our luck changed, for the better."

They walked inside the foaling shed and heard the soft nickering of Alexander's Lady. A tiny nose attempted to push through the rails of the stall. "Here's our good news," Tiffany said with a smile as she tried to reach out and touch the skittish filly. "Maybe I should change her name to that. How does Good News strike you?"

"Better'n Shadow's Survivor or whatever the hell you came up with before," the old man chuckled.

"I don't know...."

"She's your horse, Missy. You name her whatever you like." Mac grinned at the sprightly little filly. "Just wait, little one," he said to the inquisitive young horse. "As soon as we get the okay from the vet, you'll get your first look at the world."

THE REST OF the day was filled with more good news. Two owners called to say that their mares had delivered healthy foals sired by Moon Shadow, and Vance Geddes checked Moon Shadow's leg injury and gave the stallion a clean bill of health.

"As soon as that tendon heals, he'll be good as new," Vance predicted after examining the stallion.

"He sure knows how to get into trouble," Tiffany complained with a fond look at the horse in question.

"Maybe it's not the horse," Vance suggested.

"What do you mean?"

"Seems to me, he had a little help getting out of the stall last night."

"I suppose."

"Got any ideas who unlatched his stall door?" Vance asked, placing all his veterinary supplies back in his case and walking out of the stallion barn.

"No. I thought it might be vandals, but Zane seems to think it was an inside job, so to speak."

"Somebody with a grudge?"

Tiffany lifted her shoulders. "I couldn't guess who."

"You got any trouble with employees?"

"Not that I know of."

"Haven't fired anyone, a stable boy...or maybe done business with someone else, made a competitor angry?"

"No." She sighed wearily and spotted Louise's car rumbling down the long drive. "I've thought and thought about it. I'm sure I've made a few enemies, but no one that would want to hurt me or my horses.... At least I don't think so."

Vance put his bag into the truck and grimaced. He turned his kindly bespectacled eyes on Tiffany. "Just be careful, okay? Anyone who would let Moon Shadow out would do just about anything to get what he wants."

"If only I knew what that was," she said anxiously. "Any news on the foals' deaths?"

"Not yet," Vance said, sliding into his pickup, "but I've got a couple of new ideas. They're long shots... probably end up in dead ends, but maybe..."

"Keep me posted."

"Will do." Vance had just pushed his key into the lock and was about to start the engine, but Louise shouted at him. "Hey, wait!" the housekeeper called as she bustled up to Vance's truck. She was waving a newspaper in the air. "Look, here, on page one." She proudly handed Tiffany the sports section from the *Times*. In the lower left-hand corner was a picture of Journey's End along with the article written by Nancy Emerson.

Tiffany's eyes skimmed the columns of fine print and her face broke into a smile. Then, slowly, she re-read Nancy's report, which did bring up the subject of the dead colts but also concentrated on Moon Shadow's career as well as his two strongest progeny, Devil's Gambit and Journey's End. The article ended on an upbeat note, suggesting that Moon Shadow's victories on the racetrack and as a proved sire overshadowed the unfortunate deaths of the four foals.

"Wonderful," Tiffany said, feeling a little relief. "At least we got a chance for rebuttal."

"Now," Vance stated, "if we can just come up with the reason those foals died."

"You think you're on to something?"

"I'm not sure," Vance replied. "I'll let you know in a couple of days. Like I said—it could be another dead end."

"Let's hope not," Tiffany prayed fervently.

"Come on, you two," Louise reprimanded. "Things are turning around, just you wait and see."

"I don't know about that," Tiffany replied.

"Why? What happened?"

"Moon Shadow got out last night. It looks as if someone did it deliberately."

"What!" Louise was more than shocked.

As the two women walked toward the back porch, Tiffany explained the events of the evening before and Louise clucked her tongue in disbelief.

"But who would do such a thing?" Louise wondered once they were in the kitchen.

"That's the mystery."

"You got any ideas?"

"No...but Zane seems to."

Louise's eyes sparkled. "That one, he'll figure it out. Just you wait and see."

When the telephone rang, Tiffany expected the caller to be Zane, but she was disappointed.

"Hello, Tiff?" Dustin asked through the fuzzy long-distance connection.

"Dustin? Where are you?"

"In Florida and, well, brace yourself for some bad news."

Tiffany slumped against the pantry, the receiver pressed against her ear. Her fingers curled over the handle until her knuckles showed white. "What happened?" she asked, dread steadily mounting up her spine.

"It's Journey's End," Dustin said.

Tiffany's heart pounded erratically, and she felt as if her whole world were falling apart, piece by piece. "What about him?"

"He was injured. Just yesterday, while working out. From everything we can tell, he's got a bone chip in his knee."

"Oh, God," Tiffany said, letting out her breath in a long sigh. When would it end? She ran shaking fingers through her hair and wished that Zane were with her now.

"It looks bad, Tiff. I think his career is over—"

"Before it really began."

"We can retire him to stud."

"I guess that's about the only thing we can do," she reluctantly agreed, her shoulders slumping. "Other than the knee, how is he?"

"The vet says he'll be okay, but we'd better not count on him racing anymore. It wouldn't hurt to have Vance look at him when he gets home."

"How is Bob Prescott taking the news?"

There was a long silence on the other end of the line. "That's a little bit of a sore point, Tiff. I think Prescott ran him knowing that something was wrong."

"No!"

"I can't prove it."

Tiffany felt sick inside. "Let me talk to him," Tiffany demanded, rage thundering through her blood. The last thing she would stand for was anyone on her staff mistreating a horse.

"Too late."

"What?"

"I fired him."

"On suspicion?" Tiffany was incredulous.

"He's been involved in a couple of shady things," Dustin said. "I just didn't want to take any more chances."

"But who will replace him?"

"I'm talking to a couple of guys now. Big-name trainers…I'll call you after I meet with them."

"I don't know—"

"Look, I've got to go. I'll make all the arrangements to send Journey's End home."

"Wait. Before you hang up."

"What?" Dustin demanded impatiently.

"Last night someone let Moon Shadow out of his stall."

There was silence on the other end of the line. "What do you mean 'someone let him out'?" Dustin asked, his voice cold.

Tiffany gave a brief account of the events of the evening and Dustin's voice shook with rage. "Zane Sheridan was there again? What does he want this time?

Don't tell me he's still pressuring you into selling to him."

"No, Dustin, he's not," Tiffany replied.

"Then why the hell is he hanging around?"

"Maybe he enjoys my company—"

"I'll bet. If you ask me, he's the culprit who let Moon Shadow out. He's probably trying to make it tough on you so you'll sell him the farm." Dustin swore descriptively.

"I don't think so."

"That's the problem, isn't it—sometimes you just don't think. Period."

With his final words, Dustin slammed down the phone, and Tiffany knew in her heart that everything Zane had said about her brother-in-law was true. A deep sadness stole over her, and she spent the rest of the day locked in the den, going over the books, hoping to block out the bitter truth about Dustin and what he had done.

Dustin would be back on the farm with Journey's End by the end of the week. When he arrived, Tiffany planned to confront him with the truth.

FOUR DAYS LATER, she still hadn't heard from Zane. Things had settled into the usual routine on the farm, and she had spent her time working with Mac and the yearlings.

The fence had been repaired, and there had been no other disturbances on the farm. Moon Shadow was healing well, and Mac had prepared a neighboring stall in the stallion barn for Journey's End. "A shame about that one," the old trainer had remarked when he learned about the accident. "Sometimes fate seems to deal out all the bad cards at once."

Later that night, Tiffany was seated in the den going over the books. The house was dark except for the single desk lamp and the shifting flames of the fire burning noisily against dry oak. Tiffany felt cold and alone. The portrait of Devil's Gambit seemed to stare down from its position over the mantel and mock her. Where was Zane? Why hadn't he called?

She tried to force her attention back to the books and the red ink that was beginning to flow in the pages of the general ledger. The farm was losing money. Without Moon Shadow's stud fees or any income from Journey's End's racing career, Tiffany had little alternative but to sell several of the best yearlings.

The rap on the French doors surprised her, but she knew in an instant that it had to be Zane. She saw his haggard face through the glass, she opened the doors with trembling fingers and flung herself into his arms.

He stepped in with a rush of cold air that chilled the room and fanned the glowing embers of the fire and billowed the sheer draperies. "Thank God you're here," she whispered against his neck before lifting her head and studying the intensity of his gaze.

The look on his face was murderous. Dark shadows circled his gray eyes, and a weariness stole over his features making the angular planes seem more rugged and foreboding. He looked as if he hadn't slept in weeks.

"Zane?" she whispered as his dark eyes devoured her.

"It's just about over," he said as he closed the door and walked over to the fire to warm himself.

"What is?"

"Everything you've been going through." He reached for her and drew her close to him. "I wish I could make it easier for you—"

"Easier?"

"Shh." He brushed his lips over hers, and his hands locked behind her back, gently urging her body forward until her supple curves pressed against him and he groaned, as if in despair. She felt her body respond to his and heard the uneven beat of her own heart when he kissed her hungrily and his tongue touched hers. Her fingers lingered at his neck, and she felt the coiled tension within him, saw the strain on his face.

"What happened?" she asked, when at last he drew his head back.

"It's a long story."

"I've got the rest of my life to listen," she murmured.

Zane managed a wan smile. "Oh, lady, I've been waiting for four days to hear you say just those words," he whispered, his arms tightening around her. "God, I've missed you." He kissed the curve of her neck, his lips lingering near her earlobe, before he gently released her.

"So tell me."

He rammed his fingers through his black, wind-blown hair and poured them each a drink. "I found Stasia," he admitted roughly, Tiffany's heart nearly missed a beat. "It wasn't all that easy, and if she'd had her way, I never would have located her."

He walked over to Tiffany and handed her a snifter of brandy, before taking a long swallow of the warm liquor and sitting on the hearth, hoping that the golden flames would warm his back.

"How did you find her?"

"A private investigator by the name of Walt Griffith."

His gray eyes searched hers. "I had him do some checking on you, too—"

"What!"

He smiled devilishly and his eyes twinkled. "I didn't figure you'd like it any more than Stasia did. But it was necessary. To find Ellery."

Tiffany nearly dropped her drink. Her hands began to shake as she lifted the glass to her lips.

"I'm getting ahead of myself," Zane said. "Walt found Stasia living with some artist-type in Carmel. When I approached her she was shocked, but managed to fall right back into character—she agreed to tell her side of the Ellery Rhodes story for a substantial fee."

"You paid her?" Tiffany was outraged.

Zane's eyes rested on her flushed face and he smiled. "Believe me, it was worth it."

Tiffany wasn't so sure. "What did you find out?"

"About the accident that supposedly killed Devil's Gambit."

Tiffany's heart was pounding so loudly it seemed to echo against the cherry-wood walls. "Wait a minute," she insisted as the cold truth swept over her in a tidal wave of awareness. "What you're saying is that—"

"Stasia was Ellery's mistress. Even when he was married to you, he was having an affair with my ex-wife. Seems that they were hooked on the excitement of carrying on when there was the danger of being discovered."

"I…" Tiffany was about to say that she didn't want to believe it, but she knew it was the truth. She'd come to the same conclusion herself once she had talked to

Dustin. The affair explained so much about Ellery that she had never understood.

"So Ellery?" she asked breathlessly.

"Was killed in the accident," Zane assured her.

"I...never wished him dead," Tiffany whispered, walking across the room and sitting next to Zane on the hearth.

"I know. You just had to know the truth." Zane looked into her eyes and smiled. "It's going to be all right, you know."

"God, I hope so."

"We'll be together."

Tiffany's eyes filled with tears of happiness. "Then you're right—everything will work out."

"Stasia admitted that the horses were switched," he said, continuing with his story. "Ellery had thought that the insurance forms had already been processed—"

"The ones that were waiting for his signature?"

"Yes. No one but Ellery, Dustin and Bob Prescott knew that Devil's Gambit had pulled a ligament after his last race."

"Not even Mac?"

"No."

"When?"

"While exercising a few days after his last race. It looked as if Devil's Gambit, the favored horse, wouldn't be able to race in any of the Triple Crown races. If Ellery could make it look as if Devil's Gambit had died in an accident, when in fact it was really another, considerably less valuable horse who was killed, he could breed Devil's Gambit under an alias in another country, collect stud fees and get the insurance money to boot. It was better odds than just putting him out for stud before he'd really proved himself."

"Oh, God," Tiffany said with a long sigh. Nervously she ran her fingers through her hair.

"It wasn't a foolproof plan by any means and it was extremely risky. But Ellery enjoyed taking risks—remember the stunts he and Dustin would pull in Europe when he posed as Ethan Rivers?"

Tiffany nodded, her stomach turning over convulsively. What kind of a man had she married? How had she been so blind?

"There was always the chance that Devil's Gambit would be recognized because of the Jockey Club identification number tattooed on the inside of his lip. And of course there was the remote possibility of something going wrong with Ellery's plans."

Tiffany had broken out in a cold sweat. She wrapped her arms around herself as she relived the horrible night when she was told that Ellery and Devil's Gambit were killed.

"Everything backfired when Ellery was trapped in the truck and killed along with the switched horse, which, by the way, Bob Prescott supplied. It seems that the trainer was involved in the scam with Ellery and Dustin."

"And all this time I've let him work with our horses…. God, how could I have been so stupid?"

"There's no shame in trusting your husband, Tiffany," Zane said softly and kissed the top of her head before smiling. "In fact, your next one will insist upon it."

She felt his warm arm slide around her waist. "And Dustin—what about him?" she asked.

"He decided to gamble and carry out Ellery's plan."

"With Bob Prescott?"

"Right. Stasia claims he was absolutely furious that the insurance forms hadn't been signed, and that you, not he, as the new forms indicated, would get the settlement." Zane shrugged and finished his drink in one swallow. "But by that time it was too late."

"So what are we going to do?"

His arm tightened possessively around her, and his fingers toyed with the lapels of her robe. "For now, go to bed. Tomorrow we'll deal with Dustin."

"How?"

"I have it on good authority that he'll be here with Journey's End. Come on." He pulled her gently to her feet and walked her to the stairs. "I haven't slept in days—" he slid an appreciative glance down her body "—and somehow I get the feeling that I'll have trouble again tonight."

They mounted the stairs entwined in an embrace. Once in her bedroom, he let his hand slip inside her bathrobe and felt the shimmery fabric of her nightgown. "I've been waiting for so long to be with you again," he whispered into her ear as he untied the belt of the robe, pushed it gently over her shoulders and let it drop unheeded to the floor.

TRUE TO ZANE's prediction, Dustin arrived around nine. He marched into the kitchen and stopped abruptly. The last person he had expected to see was Zane Sheridan. Dustin's composure slipped slightly and his broad shoulders stiffened. His jeans and shirt were rumpled from the long, cross-country drive, and three days' growth of beard darkened his chin. In contrast, Zane was clean-shaven and dressed in fresh corduroy pants and a crisp shirt. His hair was neatly combed, and the satisfied smile on his face made Dustin's hair stand on end.

The differences in the two men were striking.

Dustin cast a worried glance in Tiffany's direction before placing his Stetson on a hook near the door.

"'Morning, Dustin," Zane drawled. He was leaning against the counter sipping coffee while Tiffany made breakfast.

Dustin managed a thin smile. "What're you doing here?"

"Visiting." Zane took another long drink.

The meaning of Zane's words settled like lead on Dustin's shoulders. "Oh, no, Tiffany," he said. "You're not getting involved with this bastard, are you?" He hooked a thumb in Zane's direction.

Zane just smiled wickedly, but Tiffany stiffened. "I don't see that it's any of your business, Dustin. Is Journey's End in the stallion barn?"

"Yes."

"With Mac?"

"He was there and that veterinarian, Geddes."

"Good."

Dustin became uneasy. "What's going on?"

Zane propped a booted foot on a chair near the table. "That's what we'd like to know." Zane's gray eyes glittered ominously, and Dustin was reminded of a great cat about to spring on unsuspecting quarry. His throat went dry.

"Tiffany?" Dustin asked.

She turned to face her brother-in-law and he saw the disappointment in her eyes. *She knows. She knows ev-*

erything! Dustin's palms began to sweat, and he tugged at the collar of his shirt.

"I think you need to answer a few questions, Dustin. Did you let Moon Shadow out the other night?" she charged.

Dustin's gold eyes narrowed treacherously, but he refused to fall into any of Sheridan's traps. "Of course not. I...I was in Florida."

"It's over, Rhodes," Zane cut in. "I checked the flights. You were booked on a red-eye."

"No—I mean, I had business in town...."

Tiffany's shoulders slumped, but she forced her gaze to bore into Dustin's. "Zane says that Devil's Gambit is alive in Ireland, that he's siring foals while King's Ransom is taking all the credit." Dustin whitened. "Is it true?" Tiffany demanded, her entire body shaking with rage and disappointment.

"I don't know anything about—"

"Knock it off," Zane warned, straightening to his full height. "You're the primary owner of Emerald Enterprises, which happens to own a farm where King's Ransom stands. I saw Devil's Gambit and I've got the pictures to prove it." His face grew deadly. "And if that isn't enough proof to lock you up for the rest of your life, Stasia is willing to talk, for the right price."

"None of this is happening." Dustin turned his gold eyes on her. "Tiff, you can't believe all this. Sheridan's just out for revenge, like I told you.... Oh, my God," he said as he recognized the truth. "You're in love with the bastard, aren't you? What's he promised to do, marry you?" He saw the silent confirmation in her eyes. "Damn it, Tiffany, don't be a fool. Of course he proposed to you. He'd do anything to steal this farm from you."

"The only time I was a fool, Dustin," Tiffany stated, her voice trembling with rage, "was when I trusted you."

"I helped you—when your world was falling to pieces, I helped you, damn it."

"And you lied. About Devil's Gambit and about Moon Shadow." Her eyes blazed a furious shade of blue. "You let me think that Moon Shadow was the cause of the dead foals and you leaked the story to Rod Crawford."

"What are you saying?" Dustin demanded.

"That the jig is up. Vance Geddes has discovered that the only unhealthy foals sired by Moon Shadow were all conceived during one week—a week you were on the farm," Zane said, barely able to control his temper. "He hasn't discovered what you injected the mares with yet, but it's only a matter of time before he knows just what happened."

"That doesn't mean—"

"Give it up, Rhodes!"

Dustin turned furious eyes on Tiffany. "You've got it all figured out, haven't you? You and your lover! Well, I'm not going to bother to explain myself. It looks as if I'm going to need an attorney—"

"I'd say so," Zane stated. "The police are on their way. They've already rounded up Bob Prescott, and I'm willing to bet that he sold you out."

Dustin visibly paled. He lunged for Tiffany; his only chance of escape was to take Tiffany hostage.

Zane anticipated the move and as Dustin grabbed

for Tiffany, Zane landed a right cross to Dustin's cheek that set him on his heels.

"Don't even think about it," Zane warned as Dustin attempted to get up. In the distance, the sounds of a police siren became audible. "I'd be thinking very seriously about an attorney myself, if I were you," he said.

When the police arrived, they read Dustin his rights and took him in for questioning. As he left he was still rubbing his jaw and glaring angrily at Zane.

"I've waited a long time for that," Zane admitted. He stepped onto the back porch and watched while the police cars raced out the drive with Dustin in custody.

"I just can't believe it's over," Tiffany murmured, her eyes looking over the rolling hills that she'd grown to love. "And to think that Dustin was behind it all...."

Zane tilted her chin upward and looked into her worried eyes. "Like you said, it's over." He kissed her tenderly on the eyelids and tasted the salt of her tears, before leading her back to the den. "I came here intending to ruin you," he admitted roughly. "I wanted to buy this farm no matter what the cost." He took out the legal documents that John Morris had prepared. After showing her the contract of sale, he tossed it into the fireplace, and the coals from the previous night burst into flame against the crisp, white paper. "It was all so damned pointless," he said. "All I want is for you to be my wife."

"And I will be," she vowed.

"Even if it means living part of your life in Ireland? We have to bring Devil's Gambit home, you know."

"It doesn't really matter where," she said. "As long as I'm with you."

Zane folded her into the protection of his arms. "I'm not a patient man," he said.

"Don't I know."

"And I'm not about to wait."

"For what?"

"To get married. The sooner the better."

"Anything you want," she said, her blue eyes lingering on his handsome face.

"Anything?" With a wicked smile, he urged her slowly to the floor with the weight of his body. "You may live to regret those words."

"Never," Tiffany whispered as Zane's lips covered hers and she entwined her arms around the neck of the man she loved.

* * * * *

New York Times and USA TODAY Bestselling Author

KRISTAN HIGGINS

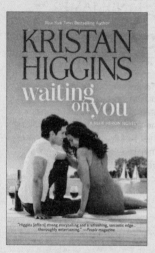

Does being nobody's fool mean that you're nobody's love?

Colleen O'Rourke is in love with love…just not when it comes to herself. Most nights, she can be found behind the bar at the Manningsport, New York, tavern she owns with her twin brother, doling out romantic advice to the lovelorn, mixing martinis and staying more or less happily single. See, ten years ago, Lucas Campbell, her first love, broke her heart…an experience Colleen doesn't want to have again, thanks. Since then, she's been happy with a fling here and there, some elite-level flirting and playing matchmaker to her friends.

But a family emergency has brought Lucas back to town, handsome as ever and still the only man who's ever been able to crack her defenses. Seems like maybe they've got some unfinished business waiting for them—but to find out, Colleen has to let her guard down, or risk losing a second chance with the only man she's ever loved.

Available wherever books are sold!

Be sure to connect with us at:
Harlequin.com/Newsletters
Facebook.com/HarlequinBooks
Twitter.com/HarlequinBooks

HARLEQUIN® HQN™
www.Harlequin.com

PHKH858

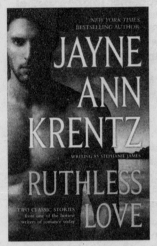

REQUEST YOUR
FREE BOOKS!

2 FREE NOVELS
FROM THE SUSPENSE COLLECTION
PLUS 2 FREE GIFTS!

YES! Please send me 2 FREE novels from the Suspense Collection and my 2 FREE gifts (gifts are worth about $10). After receiving them, if I don't wish to receive any more books, I can return the shipping statement marked "cancel." If I don't cancel, I will receive 4 brand-new novels every month and be billed just $6.24 per book in the U.S. or $6.74 per book in Canada. That's a savings of at least 22% off the cover price. It's quite a bargain! Shipping and handling is just 50¢ per book in the U.S. and 75¢ per book in Canada.* I understand that accepting the 2 free books and gifts places me under no obligation to buy anything. I can always return a shipment and cancel at any time. Even if I never buy another book, the two free books and gifts are mine to keep forever.

191/391 MDN F4XN

Name _____ (PLEASE PRINT) _____

Address _____ Apt. # _____

City _____ State/Prov. _____ Zip/Postal Code _____

Signature (if under 18, a parent or guardian must sign)

Mail to the Harlequin® Reader Service:
IN U.S.A.: P.O. Box 1867, Buffalo, NY 14240-1867
IN CANADA: P.O. Box 609, Fort Erie, Ontario L2A 5X3

Want to try two free books from another line?
Call 1-800-873-8635 or visit www.ReaderService.com.

* Terms and prices subject to change without notice. Prices do not include applicable taxes. Sales tax applicable in N.Y. Canadian residents will be charged applicable taxes. Offer not valid in Quebec. This offer is limited to one order per household. Not valid for current subscribers to the Suspense Collection or the Romance/Suspense Collection. All orders subject to credit approval. Credit or debit balances in a customer's account(s) may be offset by any other outstanding balance owed by or to the customer. Please allow 4 to 6 weeks for delivery. Offer available while quantities last.

Your Privacy—The Harlequin® Reader Service is committed to protecting your privacy. Our Privacy Policy is available online at www.ReaderService.com or upon request from the Harlequin Reader Service.

We make a portion of our mailing list available to reputable third parties that offer products we believe may interest you. If you prefer that we not exchange your name with third parties, or if you wish to clarify or modify your communication preferences, please visit us at www.ReaderService.com/consumerchoice or write to us at Harlequin Reader Service Preference Service, P.O. Box 9062, Buffalo, NY 14269. Include your complete name and address.

SUS13R

LISA JACKSON

77876	MEMORIES	___ $7.99 U.S.	___ $8.99 CAN.
77728	CONFESSIONS	___ $7.99 U.S.	___ $9.99 CAN.
77578	STRANGERS	___ $7.99 U.S.	___ $9.99 CAN.

(limited quantities available)

TOTAL AMOUNT	$ _____
POSTAGE & HANDLING	$ _____
($1.00 FOR 1 BOOK, 50¢ for each additional)	
APPLICABLE TAXES*	$ _____
TOTAL PAYABLE	$ _____

(check or money order—please do not send cash)

To order, complete this form and send it, along with a check or money order for the total above, payable to Harlequin HQN, to: **In the U.S.:** 3010 Walden Avenue, P.O. Box 9077, Buffalo, NY 14269-9077; **In Canada:** P.O. Box 636, Fort Erie, Ontario, L2A 5X3.

Name: _____
Address: _____ City: _____
State/Prov.: _____ Zip/Postal Code: _____
Account Number (if applicable): _____
075 CSAS

*New York residents remit applicable sales taxes.
*Canadian residents remit applicable GST and provincial taxes.

HARLEQUIN® HQN™
www.Harlequin.com

PHLJ0413BL